DOG DAY KNIGHTS

JASON DOLL

SPRING

1

Shadows lay dying across the warped road. Frozen ruts of mud tormented feet and threatened ankles. Zarius kept his head low, skin raw and aching under a shoddy wool tunic and scarf. He raked a hand through his thick black coils of hair, trying to frizz them up to fend off frostbite. He couldn't feel his ears.

So many hovels all around him. Some small enough to fit in a wagon, others built out over time. Brown daub walls and low, bushy thatched roofs. Zarius stopped when he saw the one he'd been told of, slouched to the left, like it had an ache in the back. The straw on the roof poked all about like fraying hair. The lone door seemed to function as both the eye and the mouth, but even that was a crooked set of teeth. Warm colors splashed through the slats. A harsh wind sucked away a thin black trickle of smoke through a violet sky. The Sun was gone, the sky abandoned to glittering impostors.

Where the fuck am I?

Zarius raised a shaking hand and winced as he knocked. He stamped his feet and shuffled his arms under his tunic. Wind lashed down the street and howled in his ears. What if the door just didn't open? What if he came all this way only for every signpost, every guiding finger to be wrong? What if it wasn't him? He'd built it all up so high in his mind, the first glimpse of purpose he ever really attached himself to.

A clunk. The door cracked and revealed only a shadow silhouetted by flickering firelight. The acrid smell of smoke wrinkled Zarius's nose and drew him in to the promise of warmth.

"Who are you?" a thick voice asked.

"My name is Z-Z-Zarius," he said. He cursed his chattering teeth. The cold was black and wicked, wrapped around his thoughts, laying siege to his body. Much longer outside, and he might cease to move at all.

"I don't know you."

"It's a . . . It's a long story."

The figure just hovered there. The door closed an inch. "So what? I'm supposed to let you in?"

A spark of anger. "I guess either that or I go back to look for w-w-where my nuts froze off."

The shadow inside leaned forward. "Who the hell are you? Why are you *here*?"

"I came to find the Day Knight."

A strange silence descended. The breeze slowed down, and even the fire beyond the door ceased to crackle.

The man snorted, maybe scoffed. "What about him?"

Shadows melted into the night. Zarius gritted his teeth. Here he was being interrogated at a house fit for a beggar. He'd foreseen these questions, but they never seemed so derisive in his head. Never made him feel so stupid. But still. He came all this way.

"I want him to train me."

The man shook his head as if he had twenty pounds dangling from his neck. "I don't know what anyone told you, but there is no Day Knight here. Not anymore."

Zarius's hands shook harder, and not from the cold. His eyes stung as a quiet roar began to build in his ears. "You quit?"

"I almost *died.*"

Resisting the urge to punch a hole in the wall, Zarius lowered his head. The collapse of all his fragile, misguided dreams carried him down into an abyss. "Then give me ten minutes to sit by the f-f-*fucking* fire and I'll be on my way."

For a moment, nothing happened, but when the door swung open, Zarius rushed in like a starving dog, desperate for heat.

The hovel was barren and impoverished, and Zarius's hair brushed the low ceiling. A hunk of frozen bread sat on a rickety wooden table. Meager vegetables and a thin cut of salted meat in a wicker basket below. A scatter of hay and moth-eaten blankets made up a bed against one wall. Only one chair, but there *was* a fire.

Zarius crouched down next to the flames and held out dark, quivering hands. For a moment, he closed his eyes and relished the sweet heat. He didn't even look back at the man, supposedly the origin of all the legends he'd been told. This was, after all, the Day Knight himself. It had to be. But their brief interaction had struck Zarius like a stone to the head. Maybe he *used* to be the Day Knight. That self-ordained protector of this tiny farming village. But in his own words, not anymore. That left Zarius a vagrant on the verge of death, and he adjusted to his new reality as to an ill-fitting shoe. It was all he could do to keep from bursting into pieces.

The has-been pulled the lone chair over next to the fire and sat down. It croaked under his weight as he tippped forward to gaze into the flames. Fire illuminated his surprisingly youthful face, but his blue eyes were old and troubled, deep and cerulean. His nose was crooked. Valleys of forehead forged into the line of his long, thin brown hair. A thick, unkempt beard curled off his chin.

"You *were* the Day Knight?" Zarius asked. His voice was flat, stupefied. The moaning wind battered the walls, the protest of unfulfilled suffering. Zarius inched closer to the warmth.

"I was," said the man.

"And you're not anymore."

The man sat back and turned to the wall, even though Zarius's gaze remained on the fire. "That's right."

"Well that fucking sucks."

The stranger cocked an eyebrow and finally looked back. "Why is that? Who sent you here?"

"Nobody sent me." Zarius tossed a stray piece of straw and watched it curl up and blacken in the flames. The fire digested its meager meal with pops and crackles, and the room smelled cold and smoky. It seemed more an outpost than a home.

"Then what?" asked the stranger.

"I heard about you in Endlin."

"In *Endlin*?" The stranger's eyes widened, tinged orange. "They talked about me in . . . You came here all the way from Endlin?"

"Yep."

The man pursed his lips and rubbed a finger and thumb together. He did that for a long time. "What did you hear? What convinced you to come all this way?"

"I heard that he was a bitch and an idiot."

After a thunderclap of silence, the supposed Day Knight burst into laughter, and the quiet tension broke. Even Zarius started to smile, but only for a moment. The man, though, kept chuckling for a long time.

"You wanted to be trained by a bitch and an idiot?" he asked.

Zarius turned to him. He had a sharp look—big, dark eyes in a narrow skull. And he tried to bring the full weight of it all to bear, using it like a weapon. "I wanna do good. I want to protect people. The knights of Endlin are thugs and rapists, so anyone worthy of their scorn sounded pretty good to me. And besides, they still called you a Knight."

The man shuffled his feet in the cold dirt, levity draining from his face. He pulled his arms in from the sleeves of his wool over-shirt and hugged himself. "I'm sorry you came so far."

Frustration lit through Zarius. His stare faltered. "Why'd you quit?"

"There's far worse evil than men in this world," he said. He locked eyes with Zarius. His face morphed and shifted, orange and red. "I went looking for it. Out of hubris, some might say. I think I was just naïve. I wanted to impress people. I didn't think anything would actually be there, but I looked, and I found plenty."

Goosebumps crawled down Zarius's spine.

The man rose from his chair and stretched. A few pops sounded from his back, and he slunk the couple steps to his meager bed. "Stay the night. I'd hate to have to scrape you off my doorstep in the morning."

Zarius's heart clenched. He wracked his brain for something to say, some words to make a spark, but the man lay down and faced the wall. The moment passed. When the fire began to burn down, Zarius fed in another log and basked in the feeble warmth. All the while, he tried to think. What could he say? What might strike a chord and make this guy see that he was worth something? The thought of returning to Endlin made him feel ill—no, it enraged him. He sat there fuming and churning until he slumped over on the cold dirt and fell into an exhausted slumber.

2

Christian clutched his wooden pint as if it might stop the table from wobbling. When he lifted it to take a good swig, half of the ale went down the front of his shirt, and the rest of the guys at the table burst into hoots and laughter.

"Woah, woah." Carmichael Blaine wrapped Christian's shirt in a fat, hairy fist and steadied him. "What if a barbarian horde bears down on us, Christian? The Day Knight can't be drunk!"

The other guys at the table guffawed through red, bloated faces. Christian wore an uneven smile and only gave a loose shrug. His vision was grainy, and it went black altogether when an unseen hand caught him hard across the face. The slap echoed off the stone walls of the tavern, loud enough that the din of conversation quieted as on the precipice of violence. But when prying eyes saw Christian holding the side of his face, leaning down against the table, a wave of laughter crashed over the room, and the chatter went on.

Meanwhile, Christian's table was in a frenzy, clunking their glasses together and snorting as they watched Christian rub the bright red handprint on his face. Tears welled in his eyes, so he kept his head down until they subsided.

"Oh come on Christian." Carmichael patted him roughly on the back. "I was just trying to perk you up. Keep you sharp, eh?"

Christian lowered his hand and straightened up, but he didn't say anything or look at anyone.

"Maybe I'm just frustrated," Carmichael went on. Beads of sweat shone on his forehead, glistening over a round, chubby face. His beady brown eyes were hateful. "Petty thieves and criminals are one thing, but I'm wondering why people keep getting beat down. Keep getting killed. I thought you were gonna straighten things out around here?"

Carmichael's friends snickered, and Christian just sat there and took it.

"I think the problem's deeper," said Carmichael. "All this time, and you haven't once gone after the bog witch. Maybe that's the answer. I think it's your duty, as the Day Knight and all, to *find the answer*. Root it out at the source, you know?"

"She's not real," Christian mumbled.

"Not real?" Carmichael feigned shock to his friends and slung a heavy arm around Christian's shoulders. "Well hell, you already been there done that have ya? You shoulda told us."

Christian didn't say anything. The red handprint glowed on his face, and he let his ale fester before him. In thick, stumbling thoughts, he wondered who was watching. Hopefully not Catherine.

"Nahh," Carmichael said, squeezing his arm to pull Christian in toward him, the smell of body odor rising. "You ain't been out there. We know it, you know it. A little scared, sure. Who ain't scared of a witch? But I would've thought the Day Knight might try to do us some actual good for once, instead of chasing crimes that wouldn't even make the stockades in Endlin. Huh?"

When Christian tried to lean away, Carmichael squeezed him,

but Christian threw his arm off and glared. "There's nothing out there, you fucking asshole."

One of the other guys at the table stood up, but Carmichael put up a big hand. "Woah woah, settle down Andrew." He fixed Christian with hooks for eyes. "Now if I was a simpler man, I might think you just insulted me, and I might take you outside and beat you half to death. But I don't think you meant to do that, did you?"

Somber, Christian sat still for a moment before he slowly shook his head.

"No no, course you didn't." Carmichael tousled his hair. "Of course, I'll be expecting a bog flower from you tomorrow. Just to show you're doin your due diligence and all that goodness. Seein as you're our protector and all. I want you to go to the bog and find a flower, alright? Simple enough. There's nothin out there, right?"

"A bog flower?" Christian smacked a dry mouth. The lurking threat hung over him.

"Bog flower," Carmichael repeated. "And if I don't see that next time you show up here, well, I might just have a little anger toward you. And you know how I get when I'm angry."

Carmichael shoved him out of his chair, and Christian landed hard on the stone floor. His shoulder sang as he struggled to pick himself up and dust himself off, and the guys at the table chortled like ogres. He stood there for a moment next to the table, like he was about to say something, and Carmichael leaned toward him, scowling. In the end, Christian said nothing, and he turned and went away.

3

When Zarius jolted awake, infested by a deep, bone-rattling chill, he pulled himself upright and huddled closer to what was now just a pile of red embers. He grabbed a log off the adjacent pile.

"Don't."

A hooded figure sat in bed, swaddled in blankets.

"It's freezing," Zarius said.

"Look how much I've got."

Zarius looked at the few logs next to the fire. Not much. He clenched his teeth and scooted up until he was practically sitting on the fire's remains. The legs of his wool pants began to smoke before he pulled them away.

"What's your name again?" asked the man.

"Zarius."

"Zarius?"

"And yours?"

"Christian," said the man.

Zarius just stared into the embers, holding out his hands, trying to eke out the last warmth and drive it into the core of his spirit. Christian got up and shuffled over to sit in his chair again, blankets hanging off him. He dislodged a thick sheepskin pelt and passed it to Zarius. Zarius took it and draped it over his head, around his shoulders. Together, they sat there in silence. Zarius wanted to ask for food, but he saw well enough that, like the wood, Christian possessed very little of it. Maybe half a pound of salted meat. Some sad looking vegetables. Relics of a harvest long past.

"You're hungry," said Christian.

"Starving," Zarius said.

"I haven't eaten for two days."

"What is it, a contest?"

Christian smirked. He got up and retrieved the little basket, balancing it on his knees as he sat down again. He picked up the hunk of meat and a crooked carrot and stuck them out toward Zarius.

Zarius only glanced at him, then back to the fire. "I'm not stealing from the poor."

Now Christian laughed, and he jostled the items in his hands. "Take them. At least a few bites. I'll get more."

"That shit looks as frozen as my nuts."

"Yeah. You're gonna have to gnaw on them to soften them up."

"Jesus Christ," Zarius said, but he took them, stomach howling. He immediately started gnawing and slobbering on the beef, trying to get it loose enough to bite off.

"Lord's name in vain," said Christian unaffectedly. "Not a believer?"

"Believer in what?"

Christian stared at him. "You're not a Christian?"

"What have they ever done for me?"

Christian shrugged. After a moment, Zarius went on.

"I don't pray. I get shit done. God helps those who help themselves, right?"

Christian gazed at him. "Does He? I'm not a Christian either."

Zarius stopped gnawing for a moment and gazed at him. That surprised him. He'd never met another nonbeliever. At least not someone honest about it. "Hell of a name you have then. They should've called you Atheist."

"I'm no atheist."

This gave Zarius an even longer pause. "What the hell does that mean?"

Christian's eyes were on the fire's corpse, and he didn't say anything. Occupied as he was getting a bite of meat, Zarius didn't press, but he did wonder. He came here without much expectation besides finding the so-called Day Knight. Zarius had imagined him bold and ostentatious, a beacon of strength—for some backcountry hicks, at least. Certainly not overgrown, decrepit, and living in a shithole with hardly a scrap of food or log of firewood to his name.

"I thought you'd be rich," Zarius said as he finally tore off a piece of meat and let it soften in his mouth.

Christian laughed, and there was a genuine joviality in it that made Zarius twitch. "So did I."

"You're not as old as you look, are you?" Zarius asked plainly.

"*Damn.*" Christian's grin faded. He ran a hand through his stringy hair. "Do I really look that bad? I'm only twenty-five."

Zarius's eyes widened. He held back a snort of disbelief. He would've guessed pushing forty at the youngest.

More silence followed. Zarius worked slowly on his breakfast, because truthfully, he was afraid of the moment he would be sent away. He wasn't afraid of the open country; he knew how to survive. He was afraid of going back to the purposeless void in his head. This Day Knight expedition had occupied his thoughts for three months or more. The initial plan, the weeks of scrounging for pennies in the slums. All the while, he dreamed what it would be like. A Knight, a purpose. A goal in his shapeless, passionless life. He dreaded to give that up, and he cringed at all the stock he'd put into it.

After finishing a couple bites of meat and the entirety of the frozen carrot, Zarius glanced warily toward Christian. The young man was sitting ramrod straight, eyes closed, face soft. His hands rested under the blankets in his lap, and he was taking deep breaths that steamed out of his nostrils to join the faint smoke of the fire.

"What are you doing?" Zarius asked.

A second passed before Christian opened his eyes and focused on Zarius without joy or ire. "Meditating."

"What's that?"

"You want to try it?"

Zarius looked around the hovel as if searching for something. "I guess I can put my other plans on hold."

Christian smiled and readjusted in his chair. "So you sit up straight and close your eyes. You breathe deeply, and . . ." He frowned. "Well . . . Hm. So you know, like, your thoughts, right?"

Zarius just raised his eyebrows.

"Okay," Christian went on. "So you have your thoughts. Imagine . . . Like you're on a river. And there's trees and maybe people and all sorts of stuff on the banks of the river. Those are your thoughts. But you're trying not to focus on them. You're trying to focus on the river. It helps to use your breath. Try to focus on your breath and not any of your thoughts."

A few slow blinks didn't help him find any logic in those words. Zarius scrunched up his face and gazed into the fire. "Uh . . . I don't think that made any fucking sense."

"It *does* make sense." Christian huffed. "Look, just try it. Or don't. Hell, I don't give a shit. But I'm going to meditate for a while. You can sit there, or you can get up and leave. Whatever."

Chagrined, Zarius made no move to get up. When he snuck a glance at Christian, he saw his eyes closed again, his chest and shoulders rising and falling in huge, long breaths. But over a few minutes, Christian didn't look like just a guy with his eyes closed. It was hard to decipher, but his face looked somehow more peaceful and yet more concentrated. Intriguing.

Zarius settled into his warm patch of dirt and sat upright. He let his eyes close, and his first task was to tame his breath, which he realized was pretty quick and shallow. He worked on extending each breath from inhale to exhale, and that alone preoccupied him for a minute. After that, he turned his attention to his mind.

Even as he did so, it didn't make sense to him. He felt like he was thinking about thinking, so he started thinking about not thinking, but that didn't feel any less like thinking. Lips twitching, he remembered what Christian said, and he tried to turn that focus onto his breath.

Long, cold streams of air down into his lungs where they warmed before he expelled them. The smell of smoke. The taste of meat still on his tongue. Weak heat leaking off the embers before him, battling the thick fog of cold in the room. Soon enough, he'd be back out there. Hitching rides on carriages, supply wagons, whoever would take him. The implied threat of violence if he was forced to employ it. The journey to get here stretched behind him like a grand vista, mountains and valleys. It wasn't even *that* far to Endlin, but he had stumbled a lot along the way.

Zarius opened his eyes, frowning. Nope. Bullshit. There was no way. He didn't even understand the concept, but when he looked at Christian, that placid tranquility struck him again, this time with frustration. This guy was putting on some kind of clown show, and somehow, Zarius had gotten roped into it. He wasn't even the Day Knight anymore, so what was Zarius still doing here?

Sudden tears stung Zarius's eyes in the cold, and he furiously scrubbed them away. What kind of fucking idiot was he? He traveled all this way, far from everything he'd ever known, for nothing. For the shadow of a hope that he might find some purpose here. That he might find someone who could guide him. But it was all fucked. Just like always. It was all smoke, no fire. He clenched his fists so hard that they started to shake, and the anger rocked his soul like an earthquake.

Well maybe he'd just go and be a Knight anyway. Maybe he'd just figure it out on his own. He didn't need this old young man anyway, whatever the hell he was. Zarius burned with the desire to prove himself. He wanted to scream at Christian to open his eyes and listen, to somehow glance into Zarius's soul and see that he was ready, that he wanted this. He was willing to suffer for it; he already had. And how could Christian just *give up*?

Every fiber of his being screamed at him to leave and excoriated him for his mortal stupidity. But there was nowhere else *to* go. All his life, he left, and he ran. Endlin was a never-ending stream of new endeavors to fail at, new people to con or to use. Now, he was in a desolate farming village on the outskirts of nowhere where most of these destitute peasants had not two coins to rub together. Besides, it was cold out there. Frigid. And at least in here, the wind couldn't find him. And that look on Christian's face. That peaceful calm. It antagonized Zarius. How could someone in a place like this wear a face like that?

4

Heavy armor clung to Christian's back, but it was more a reassurance than a hindrance. A second skin he'd grown to know and count on. After all, it had saved his ass more than once.

Below him, Louelle—a sturdy, chestnut horse with a splash of white flecks—cantered steadily along a well-worn path. She wore her bit and bridle with authority, long head held high with royal grace that she must have been born with; she couldn't have learned it in Ten-Berry. A masked Sun gazed down out of a thinly overcast sky, offering little warmth. But Christian sweated beneath his armor and underclothes. Big puffs of steam shot from Louelle's nostrils. Tiny snowflakes drifted around them.

Christian's mind was turbulent. The memory of the previous night still lodged among his thoughts, rattling its saber. Carmichael. Christian's mouth twisted into a sneer at even the thought of his name. Fat, evil bastard. But he was more than that. He represented far more.

Of course Christian didn't give any credence to the words of an oaf like Carmichael Blaine. He'd never waste breath on such a man outside of drunken stupor, but Carmichael was as much a denizen of Ten-Berry as Christian himself. The distaste of the Day Knight's name was not unique to him alone. Plenty of others thought that way, and while Christian could stomach the rejection of one man, the larger sense of a town-wide dislike made his teeth clench.

When Christian set out to be a Knight, when he left home and traveled the many miles to study and train in Endlin, he always intended to be a Knight in Ten-Berry. To be *the* Knight *of* Ten-Berry. The village was his home, his family's home, and the thought seemed noble and righteous. Endlin provided few resources to a remote farming village, and security was far from guaranteed. He wanted to offer that. He wanted his fellow citizens to rest a little easier at night, to take strolls with fewer glances cast over their shoulders.

They didn't know what he went through to pursue that. He had no money, so he spent months waiting outside of a combat school every day, scrounging for a glance from the teacher. He begged for food and money to keep his post next to that school. Waiting and waiting and filled with so much doubt. When the teacher finally invited him in for one conversation, Christian groveled. When he got his shot, he outworked everyone. He ran himself ragged to best the sons of nobles and merchants, to prove that he belonged. He ground out a dedication that soared beyond any of his classmates', and he suffered their ire and beatings.

Over the time he spent away, though, his father passed away. His mother remarried—thanked God time and time again for the miracle of not dying alone as an old woman—and her new husband moved her to Endlin. She found Christian there, but the nature of the city revolted him. After his father's death, he clung even harder to the ideals he set out with, and his mother made no effort to convince him otherwise. After all, he was a man, and a man had to make his own decisions.

When Christian returned to Ten-Berry, he did so with his father in his heart and achievement on his mind. Ezekiel Clent—the sole blacksmith of Ten-Berry and an old family friend—provided bits and pieces of armor until Christian could stand proudly in a near-full set. Ezekiel provided a sword. Ezekiel offered him guidance, and Christian saw it all as heaven-sent, Ezekiel most of all. He thanked the Sun, and he set out to accomplish his goal.

Patrols. Swordfights. Bounties. Christian hunted bandits and murderers with information from the tavern and the town hall alike. Cornelius Flember, Ten-Berry's magistrate, began to inform Christian directly. Christian began to call himself the Day Knight out of a lifelong affinity for and newfound faith in the Sun.

The Day Knight achieved success, but not admiration. As soon as he began, he found detractors in the likes of Carmichael Blaine and a startling number of others. Once the notion of a local Knight began to take hold, the Day Knight was never enough. Didn't work hard enough. Didn't know enough. Every nearby robbery, murder, and rape was dropped at his feet like evidence of his inadequacy. A few friends cheered him on, but the voices opposed were always far louder and jeered far longer. Most people simply didn't care or didn't notice, and that upset the young Day Knight. He thought himself worthy and deserving of admiration, so the taste of odium was all the more bitter.

At some point, the notion of a grand, farcical clash between the fabled "bog witch" and the Day Knight began to circulate, and that really took hold for his critics. The bog was a half day's ride away, but it was barren and desolate. Stories of a witch had circulated for generations, though no firsthand accounts ever seemed to surface. Still, the bog witch became a frequent theme for the denigration of the Day Knight.

They said he was too scared. They all knew it was bullshit, but they said it anyway. Too scared of the bog, too scared of a ghost. How could he protect them if he was just so *scared*? Christian gritted his teeth and clenched Louelle's reins as she continued along the path.

Something broke in him when Carmichael's hand struck his face. The humiliation, the degradation, it was too much. He would prove to them that he had no fear. He knew they'd move onto something else; he knew a simple bog flower would never put him in their good graces, but he would show them that the Day Knight didn't back down. The Day Knight rose to all challenges. Let them find a new banner to hang for his disgrace, but it wouldn't be the bog witch, not anymore.

All of these thoughts swirled in Christian's head as Louelle forged along the patchy wagon trail. Only a couple of other meager villages lay out in this direction. Besides that, nothing. Untamed prairie. Towering siltstone bluffs sawed against the sky. Ancient cottonwood trees presided over any patch of fertile soil, branches naked for the winter.

At a certain point, Christian steered Louelle off the path and into the dormant grasslands. Low hills pockmarked the ground, and the horse trotted over them peacefully. No fear leaked into Christian's heart, but his face burned with shame. He knew this was stupid. He knew it meant nothing, but something in him commanded him onward. He was already this far, anyway. Another hour or so to the bog. He'd find the flower and go home and throw it in Carmichael's face.

The prairie was desolate. A thin layer of snow gave it the appearance of a tundra. The bleak sky whitened until it was difficult to tell where the horizon stopped and the sky began. Louelle plodded along, and DK idly reached down to pat her neck or stroke her mane, muttering his appreciation to her. She was a good horse, and he liked her very much.

After some time, something disrupted the horizon. At first, Christian thought it was a flock of black birds on the snow, but as he rode on, he realized it was farther away. It was the tips of tree branches reaching out from a shallow valley. The many fingers of bog spruce, alder, red maple, all clustered together in their little wetland. He was almost there.

Closer to the bog, the ground rose in a steady incline until it abruptly fell away. Thus, the bog was rimmed by high ground, leaving it in a bowl in the earth. Christian didn't think much as he approached, and those black fingers began to rise higher into the air. When he made it to the lip of the valley, the trees were still a good distance away. He guided Louelle toward a break in the hillside through which he could ride down to the valley floor, but as he drew nearer, Louelle slowed to a walk and then stopped.

Christian blinked. It took him a moment to react, but he looked down as if Louelle would look back up at him. But she just stood and breathed. Those little puffs of steam joined the white void all around them. All he could hear was their breathing and the soft pattering of snowflakes hitting the ground.

Christian nudged Louelle with his heels, but she didn't budge. Her temper was as even as her stride, so he felt no animosity toward her, only confusion.

"What's wrong girl? We're not there yet." He pressed his heels another couple times, but Louelle actually backpedaled a couple of steps.

Now thoroughly perplexed, Christian slid off the saddle and landed hard in his armor. He grunted and began to stretch, his muscles tight and sore after a long ride. After getting some blood flowing, he turned his attention back to Louelle.

Louelle gazed at him with big brown marbles, her pupils fixed on his. Christian removed his helmet and stepped up to pat her head.

She nuzzled him, her breath hot against his cheeks, and when they separated, she bobbed her head a couple times. Christian watched through narrowed eyes, as if he might discern some ethereal message from her movements alone. Maybe one to be feared.

"You don't want to go in there."

Even as Christian spoke the words, he could not accept them into his heart. They were laced and dripping with fear. He turned around and gazed at the treetops, just visible over the rise. Lines deepened on his face as he turned and looked around. He saw the stunted, ossified trunk of a tree that had been struck by lightning, and he took Louelle's reins in his hands and walked her over to it. She complied without protest, and he tied her reins to the trunk, though the knot was only an inch or two below the blunted end of the trunk. It could easily slip off. Christian grimaced and looked at her again. He knew she was smart. He also knew he wouldn't turn back now.

5

Zarius stared as Christian's eyes finally came open. Christian blinked a couple times, and his eyes shifted away, as if he were embarrassed.

"You just did that for like an hour," said Zarius.

Christian shrugged. "An hour ain't shit."

Zarius widened his eyes, then slowly shook his head. "Whatever you say man."

Fiddling with the edge of one blanket, Christian finally rose from his chair and stretched again. He gathered the mass of blankets off his body and tossed them onto his bed.

"I'm going for a run," he said.

"*Now?*" Zarius asked. "It's freezing."

Christian smiled. "All the better."

After a swig from a tan leather skin filled with water, Christian stepped to the door. No change of clothes, no bite of food, nothing. He seemed to hover for a moment, and Zarius flew up to his feet.

"Wait," he said. "Can I come with you?"

"It'll be a hard run."

Zarius took a step toward him. "Try me."

After a moment, Christian shrugged. He opened the door and stepped out into a razor-toothed breeze. The cold snapped Zarius's skin taut, and he fought to keep his teeth from chattering. All traces of warmth evaporated in a second, replaced by dread and regret. But he clenched his jaw and followed. Zarius sensed something hanging in the balance, a test of sorts, and he always stepped to challenges, even imagined ones.

When Christian took off at a jog, Zarius pursued him, though not without an air of disbelief. This guy didn't even change clothes, didn't take a moment to think. He surfaced out of that hour-plus-long trance bullshit and decided to *run*? That was abnormal, but it meant something to Zarius. He couldn't decide what.

Down the street they went, hugging one side next to the hovels to avoid all those deep ruts and ice puddles. Errant snowflakes drifted out of a slate-gray sky. Zarius's nose hairs began to freeze within the first minute, and his estimation of Christian's sanity waned in turn.

They ran down the road to the meager stone wall of Ten-Berry. Just a stack of rocks sealed together with mud. The eastern gate was nothing but a gap in the wall. Loose stones lay next to the wall where they'd been dislodged with no one to replace them. Through the gate they went, and as soon as they left Ten-Berry behind, Christian hit another gear. Zarius sped to keep up, and he was forced to measure his breath.

Pounding along a wagon trail, Zarius began to shed the questions and uncertainties. This was where he thrived: action. Progress. No time to think, no benefit to it. All he had to do was focus on Christian and manage his exertion. So he did. No words passed between them, but Zarius came abreast of Christian and would have outpaced him if he knew their destination. Instead, he matched steps, and they ran side-by-side against the steely wind.

The Sun was lost behind layers of dirty cotton clouds. Everything looked gray. The silhouettes of naked trees scratched at the sky. In no time, Zarius had a sweat worked up, but each breath still stung his throat and lungs. Christian made no indication that he was the slightest bit uncomfortable. At a certain point, absent any landmarks Zarius could see, Christian pushed the pace again.

As Christian pulled out ahead, Zarius took the first really good look at him in daylight. His height was average, a few inches shorter than Zarius. While he sported a rather narrow frame, Zarius could see even under his billowing clothes that he wasn't scrawny. Maybe even kind of jacked, in fact, though Zarius couldn't understand how on his starvation diet. Maybe it was a ruse. That was a Knight if he ever saw one, not the body of some catatonic hermit.

Zarius's feet began to ache fiercely, supported by nothing but a thick pair of cloth shoes, but Christian's were even poorer than Zarius's. Real work began. Zarius had to disassociate from that pain and from the stitch beginning to throb in his side. Christian was slowly gaining ground, so Zarius goaded his legs up another notch. He wouldn't be left behind.

Up ahead, a line of trees appeared. Elms, black walnut trees, the odd towering cottonwood, all clustered together in a long line across the horizon, naked save for their bark. Christian seemed to be heading for them, but Zarius was too afraid to hope. When the trees came into view, though, Christian accelerated again.

"*Shit,*" Zarius gasped. He poured it on.

They were just short of an all-out sprint now. Never once did Christian look back to check on him, but Zarius was certain he was trying to lose him. He sucked in panting breaths and ran on.

Sweat soaked into Zarius's clothes, then froze in the wind. Wet, cold snot dripped out of his nose. His mouth was somehow dry *and* frozen. These thoughts came in surging waves, but each time they broke over him, he refocused on Christian's back and resolved not to lose it.

They were a stone's throw apart. The trees came up fast, standing black and austere against the faceless sky. Christian blasted through the tree line without hesitation, but Zarius stuttered, afraid of hidden obstacles. He thought of those wagon ruts in the road in Ten-Berry, saw his ankle bending over a root, tendons snapping.

Christian disappeared. The trunks enfolded him as one of their own, a ghost, like maybe he was never there at all. Zarius found the ground relatively clear, and he sped up again, but a strange panic began to rise in his throat. That was it. He lost. Not just the race, but some vague chance to prove himself.

Losing focus, Zarius turned his shoulders to avoid a tree trunk but clipped it instead. Pain zipped down his arm as he twirled around and went sprawling into frozen grass. A little cloud of snow stirred up around him, and he scrambled back to his feet to keep running. He was lost, but he ran on anyway. His whole face stung.

The trees broke for a stretch, a little clearing between Zarius and more trees ahead. In his frenzy, Zarius didn't see or hear the creek hidden in a depression before him until it was too late. As soon as he started to skid, a rough pair of arms locked around him and dragged him to the ground. He and Christian went sliding right up to the edge of the creek, and Zarius fought up to his feet as if he were under attack. There he stood, panting, looking down at Christian, whose chest rose and fell only a little faster than when Zarius was watching him at the fire.

Zarius, meanwhile, collapsed to his knees as the adrenaline drained out of him. He began to shiver viciously.

"The creek is clean," said Christian.

Without hesitation, Zarius tipped forward onto his chest and stuck his hands down. He cupped the gelid water and drank, wincing and gasping after each swallow. But it was so good, so pure. After a few mouthfuls, he turned over on his back, even shaking as he was. The tree branches made black veins across the taut gray sky.

Christian squatted down next to him, staring hard into his face. "Why are you here?"

Zarius sat up and met his eyes, still gasping. Frozen globes clung to his eyelashes. His face was slick and wet. "I wanna be a Knight."

"What does that mean to you?"

Mouth open, Zarius hesitated. "It means I can protect people."

"Who?"

He stared. "Whoever needs protecting."

"You're no student," said Christian. He stood up. "You're a drifter. What do you want from me?"

"I don't know," Zarius said through gritted teeth. "I came here to learn. I didn't come with all the answers."

Christian snorted and turned his back, walking to the edge of the river. He stared into the opaque water, babbling as it rushed through its channel, sucking tiny bits of snow from the banks as it went.

"I gave it up," Christian said, shaking his head.

Zarius barely heard him, but he rose to his feet, challenging. "Why?" He wanted *that* answer. Everything he went through to get here, everything he went through before that, demanded he know. "*Why?*" So much suffering couldn't be for nothing.

When he turned around, Christian wore a tombstone for a face. "Because I found true evil, and that evil told me if I ever pursued it again, it would kill me."

A shudder passed through Zarius, masked by the cold. A hard breeze threw invisible gravel against his face. "And you decided to just take it?"

No reproach tinged Christian's face, but there was anger. A grand, penetrating anger, anger that it seemed he could turn on the world, and it would yield below his feet. "It won't be easy."

"Nothing ever is."

"You could die."

"I could die of frostbite."

The anger evaporated from Christian's face, replaced by a withdrawn stoicism even more frightening. "I've spent a lot of time feeling sorry for myself, but something . . . When I saw you . . . I think that's over. If you want to be a real Knight, I feel obligated to train you. Something is telling me to do it." He turned his eyes up to the sky and seemed to focus on the faintest lantern of the Sun, suspended high beyond the clouds. "I think I almost faded away."

6

Christian stooped under a heavy cloud of foreboding. He picked his way slowly through the trees, careful to avoid the many half-buried roots that might roll his ankle and strand him in here. His own idiocy was never so apparent.

Why the fuck was he out here? Toiling through the hostile landscape of the bog, searching in vain for a flower that appeared never to have existed at all. Every minute or less, he stopped to look around, maintain his bearings. He was making notches in every few tree trunks to track his path, and even that seemed beyond foolish. His safety depended on nothing but his own instinct. One wrong turn could have him wandering out here for hours.

Besides that, the bog besieged him with its inconsequence. He saw nothing interesting; he found no stimulation. The air smelled faintly dank and very cold. His underclothes froze and thawed, froze and thawed under his armor. His mouth tasted rank no matter how much water he drank or how many handfuls of snow he ate.

He didn't know how much time had passed. Above him, the sky was obscured by the many reaching trees. The layer of overcast had grown thicker, and the Sun was lost. No way to keep time.

Despite the blandness of the landscape, something deep and indescribable nettled Christian, like a thorn in his spirit. He found himself looking over his shoulder, stopping to listen, always seeing nothing, hearing nothing. But he *sensed* something.

After examining the base of another tree to find no bog flowers, not so much as one striped, violet petal, Christian straightened up and stared. In the distance, about as far as he could see, a fog shrouded the trees. A fog that wasn't there before. Of course, he told himself it must have been. It was a fog of cold, the curtain of winter draped on the landscape. He just didn't notice it earlier.

Still, Christian stood there for a while and gazed at it. Goosebumps began to roll across his arms and legs under his armor, and he took a tentative step back. Was it getting closer? His heart began to thump harder, sending extra blood to his brain and extremities. He took a deep, slow breath, but his heart reared like a spooked horse.

The fog was rolling toward him, thick and viscous. Some strange natural phenomenon. Bog fog. Yeah. That sounded normal, sounded logical. Even if he could grasp that as the truth, the sight of it frightened him. It was a gray wall marching toward him, swallowing trees like oats drowning in a bowl of milk. Inch by inch, the wall came toward him, and Christian decided enough was enough. That fog, besides being unsettling, would further discombobulate him.

When he set off back the way he came, it was difficult not to run. It took serious mental effort, and that alone threw Christian off. He wasn't used to fear, not like this, not of the unknown. He never feared what he could see, but this was something else.

As he picked his way quickly through the trees, plotting by way of the gouged trunks, he glanced over his shoulder and saw the fog was closer. Gaining on him, even though he was certain that earlier, it was moving at a crawl. His heart leaped, but he caught it and stuffed it back down. No. Don't panic. Not here. That's how you die.

Sweat gathered on Christian's head, sliding down his face under his helmet. His breath puffed out of his faceplate in clouds of steam, and he rushed from one tree to the next, examining the marks, then hurrying on. Except when he stopped at one, he happened to glance at another.

Under his hand, he felt the gouge he'd made, but with his eyes, he saw the same mark on another tree across from him. He ran over to it, felt the mark under his hands, then looked around. His blood went cold, and he froze where he stood.

All of the trees around him were scored. No order to them. No direction. He ran a dozen steps and found all the trees here the same. All bore the marks of his progress. And that meant someone else was out here. Something else was marking the trees.

When Christian turned around, he knew the fog would be there, and it was. Almost within spitting distance, thicker and darker than ever. It stretched all the way to the tops of the trees, and within moments, it rolled over him. A cold, slimy sensation washed through the cracks in his armor, like he could really *feel* it.

In that moment, he knew something was wrong, but worse than that, he knew there was nothing he could do about it. He could run, but what good would it do? He didn't know what direction he was going in, didn't know if he'd followed the right path back or if it was a mistake the whole time.

It was a trick. Something tricked him. Something knew he was there. And now the fog. He couldn't see ten feet in front of him. Tension pulled his thoughts taut like vielle strings, ready to snap at the lightest touch. His body vibrated on the edge of a full-blown fight-or-flight reflex. He tried to breathe, breathe, breathe. Where was the Sun? Where was the Sun? He closed his eyes and focused on his breath. Reel it in. Get a grip *now*.

Christian set off. He just picked a direction. Standing still might have served the same end, but at least moving helped him not to go insane. Moving let him pretend that he was getting out of there, escaping whatever was conjuring up this nightmare.

That was when the notion really hit him, with none of the obfuscation of legend or myth: the bog witch. Stark reality drove spears of ice between the chinks of his armor, skewered him with cold terror. A witch. In the bog. He sped up, breaking into a run, but his foot caught a root and spilled him to the ground. He landed hard in his armor, almost lost his breath.

Jagged, shuddering laughter hit his ears and almost broke his mind. Christian came up from his knees, bringing his sword in a full arc at the source of the laughter: a tree. His blade stopped dead. A huge brown hand, leathery and streaked with veins, caught his sword mid-swing, and a great black shape leaned down toward him out of the mist.

Christian screamed, shut his eyes, yanked with all his might, but the terror of closed eyes was worse. They flew open again, and he found his sword lodged in the side of a tree. No hand. No laughter. He tore his helmet off as if that might dispel any more illusions, but he felt naked without it. Like disembodied fingers might wiggle out of the fog down the back of his armor.

A breath hitched through him. Christian dislodged his sword with some effort and sheathed it to don his helmet. He slid his faceplate up and tried to wipe his sweat- and tear-slicked face. His gloved hand only smeared the wetness around, and he took out his sword again.

He knew something was coming. The same way that earlier, he sensed a presence, now he knew it had taken form, and it was out in the fog, looking for him. He was on the verge of a complete mental breakdown, but he grasped his sanity with both clammy hands. If he lost it, he would die. He could break down at home, not here, not now. He had to get the fuck out of this godforsaken place.

Centered by desperation, he set off again. Didn't matter which way. Nothing mattered except getting out. He didn't run so that he wouldn't fall. He didn't bother looking around. The fog swam on all sides of him like a living cloud, and he hated it. It was his enemy, as were the trees. It was as if the whole bog came to life to oppose him.

"Christian. Hey Christian."

A harsh whisper stabbed through his ears and brought fresh goosebumps to his skin. His scalp shrank against his skull so tightly that his ears began to ring. He didn't look for the voice, didn't even slow down. Like a child with his eyes squeezed shut and a blanket pulled over his head against the monsters of the night, he pretended he didn't hear it at all.

Laughter rang out of the trees from a distance behind him. His knees wobbled with every step, but he forced them to keep him upright. Keep going. His thoughts latched onto the Sun, and he began a stream of prayer that immediately became as essential as breathing.

Please get me out of here. Please help me. I'm sorry. I'm sorry I was stupid. Please don't let her get me. Please get me out. Protect me. Please.

A humanoid shadow materialized in the fog beside him. It stomped and stumbled along next to him for a few steps before it collapsed and fell, and the fog swallowed up its memory. Christian never looked at it, but he saw it. And still, he knew the presence he sensed wasn't upon him, not yet. But the whole bog swelled with putrid, living breath.

All at once, that evil presence collected into a single point in front of him. At the same time, the fog began to dissipate. A hole in the ground, a wound through the side of the earth. Surrounded by rocks and chunks of stone. The entrance was blacker than night. And Christian knew he was at the witch's lair. His traitorous feet had brought him right to her.

So much evil washing out of that hole. It overwhelmed him. He collapsed to his knees, bombarded by vicious, abstract thoughts. Blood, death. His stomach leaped once, twice, and he tipped forward onto all fours and vomited. Panting, he looked up. Two bowed legs were right next to his head. He made a break for it anyway.

7

Zarius orbited DK like an unruly planet. A month into training, Zarius had decided DK, for the Day Knight, was a cooler name than the oxymoronic Christian. Now, spring was in full swing. A real vein of warmth pulsed in the air, even as the Sun slid toward its bed. Zarius turned a dirt clod into a dust cloud with his foot while DK plodded along in his usual quiet.

"Training won't start any later tomorrow, you know," said DK.

"You already said that." Zarius rolled his eyes, but really, he was concealing his jubilation.

"I *will* drag your ass out of bed if I have to."

Zarius groaned. "You're just saying it again."

"Don't say I didn't warn you."

Grinning, Zarius let his body wobble from side to side as he walked, swaggering down the street. They made it to the town square. A gaggle of women in dresses, aprons, and bonnets clustered around the stone well, fetching water, and little clusters of people were scattered here and there, chattering along. A group of dirty children tried to land pebbles in little circles they'd made in the dirt while some mangy dogs bounded around them. Everyone was relieved to escape the iron fist of winter, a particularly harsh one, they all said. They took every opportunity they could to bask in spring's promise.

A couple people nodded to DK, and DK nodded back. On the other hand, Zarius received only confused stares and raised eyebrows. He was still a stranger, a rarity for Ten-Berry. Nobody paid much attention to anything during the winter, so Zarius considered this his coming-out party. Coming out to a bunch of dumb hicks, but still.

They passed under the Beggar—a single cottonwood that grew a few feet from the well. A century old at least, and now the central mascot for all of Ten-Berry. A long, vertical trunk exploded into a dozen thick limbs high in the air. Across the square, mirth rolled out of the tavern in staccato as the door opened and shut. It was a long, squat building with stone walls and a thick thatch roof. When DK and Zarius went in, the room heaved with activity. Everyone and their mothers were out for a drink. Next week, planting would hit full swing, so they were relaxing while they could.

The tavern was one of the largest buildings in Ten-Berry. Zarius, coming from Endlin, was surprised that he could see every wall from where he stood. It was just one big room, crammed with shoddy wooden chairs and tables, and it was absolutely overflowing with bodies. People were jammed in three deep at the bar, calling for drinks. Husbands and wives sat cheek-by-cheek on single chairs, crushed up against tables.

Like a hunting dog, Zarius spotted a couple of red-faced fellows who looked like they were exchanging the pleasantries of a near departure. Zarius wandered over to the table and began to hover, but a couple of other guys were doing the same thing. He scowled at them dead-on, eyes promising violence, until they drifted away, grumbling. As soon as the men at the table stood up, Zarius was there, so close that they had to squeeze past him, accompanied by some disdainful glares. But the table was his, and Zarius sat himself down and waved at DK.

DK slid into the opposite chair shaking his head, but he couldn't conceal a half-smile. "That was . . . tactful."

"Who gives a shit?" Zarius asked, pleased with himself. "Got us a table didn't I? I think that means *you* have to get the drinks."

They were nearly shouting over the remarkable commotion vibrating around them. The scent of ale hung heavy on the air, masking the ever-present body odor. Zarius looked right at home, tipping back on his chair and grinning, while DK looked uncomfortable. He glanced around, fixed his eyes on the table, glanced around again.

"What's wrong?" Zarius asked, furrowing his brow.

DK shook his head. His greasy hair slapped against his shoulders. "It's just . . . been a while. I don't know. It feels weird."

"How long's it been?"

Tapping a finger on the table, DK looked up at him. "Since before I went to the bog."

Zarius's jaw dropped. "Two *years*?"

A sheepish grin crossed DK's face as he nodded.

"Holy hell. Well." Zarius pointed at the bar. "Might as well let em know."

DK followed his finger, shrugged, and got up. He forged into the crowd, and Zarius watched him go. Damn. Two years without a drink, no wonder he was so somber. As Zarius watched, though, he saw the looks flashing toward DK. Most people paid him no mind, but of the ones who did, none of them reached out or said anything to him. Zarius almost couldn't believe it.

In the month he'd spent getting his ass kicked in training day in and day out, Zarius came to know DK as a wise, thoughtful guy who wouldn't hurt a fly outside of a swordfight. Zarius thought he was *cool*. But to see so many people ignoring him and then whispering in his wake made Zarius shift in his chair. What about DK could have them acting like *that*? Zarius didn't like it.

As the whispers unfolded, and the typical questions were asked, Zarius found that some eyes were turning on *him*. He sat a little straighter, faced forward across the table without really looking at anything. In his periphery, though, he saw people talking, and he sensed that it was about him. It was a strange sensation for he from the teeming streets of Endlin where you might never see the same face twice. DK shows up to the tavern after two years, and nearly every damn person starts talking about it. Zarius squirmed under their gazes.

When DK returned with two wooden mugs of ale, he didn't look any worse for wear. In fact, he looked almost emboldened. He sat taller, didn't hide his face toward the wall. Zarius glanced around and still found plenty of people watching them. He furrowed his brow as he accepted a mug from DK.

"Did you kill these people's families or something?" Zarius asked.

DK blinked, holding his ale. "Uhh. What?"

"I'm watching all these motherfuckers watching *us*." Now Zarius dragged a firm glare in a line across the room, and all the prying eyes flittered away.

DK shrugged. He held up his mug to Zarius, and Zarius knocked his own against it. They drank.

"Ten-Berry's boring," DK said as he set the mug down and wiped a forearm across his mouth. "What else do they have to talk about?"

"So you're like a fucking celebrity here or what?"

He snorted. "Hardly. Most of them don't care for me. Or at least they didn't, back in the day. It's been a long time."

"Don't start acting like you're all *old* and shit. You're twenty-five, not seventy."

Another long sip delayed DK's response. "That's pretty much seventy in Ten-Berry years."

Zarius rolled his eyes. "Did anybody say anything to you?"

"Nope."

"*No?* Did you see anybody you know?"

"A couple."

Zarius squinted his eyes and swirled his ale in his mug. "I feel like there's something you're not telling me."

"We-he-he-he-hellll looky here. Look who it is." A fat figure appeared next to their table, blocking some of the firelight from the roaring hearth on the far wall. He looked down with a strange smirk. Three of his buddies crowded up behind him, but they couldn't posture much with all the full chairs and loitering bodies. His face was bloated and red; he had to balance himself with one hand on the table.

"Carmichael," said DK. He returned the gaze and gave a slow nod.

"*Everyone everyone look!*" Carmichael's voice reverberated off the walls as he bellowed. So loud and so commanding that it cut through even the ongoing uproar. The drop in volume that followed was eerie, and the attention that turned toward the little table in the back of the room oppressive.

"The Day Knight has returned!" Carmichael shouted. "We're all saved!"

Carmichael's buddies all burst into breathless laughter, but the rest of the tavern produced only a smatter of uneasy chuckles. The conversation slowly picked up, and Zarius saw DK's face blooming pink. He saw his master struggling in his seat.

Carmichael's own laughter subsided. "I thought I—"

Zarius stood up, took a step forward, and twisted his hips in one fluid motion. He caught Carmichael with a closed fist across the jaw as if he'd swung a stone in a sock. *Shcock*.

That stone fist dropped Carmichael like a sack of grain. Before his head so much as slammed against the table on the way down, Zarius took a step past him and delivered at his closest crony. *Thunsh*.

Zarius landed a straight jab dead center in a man's face and broke his nose. Blood burst forth as the man clutched himself and went reeling into a full table of people. Jaw clenched, Zarius wheeled to continue the onslaught, but Carmichael's other two buddies dragged him down in a heap.

Chaos erupted in the tavern. People were trying to get up and scramble away only to trip and fall all over each other. Zarius was under a pile of bodies, clawing, trying to punch whatever flesh he could get at, and a couple errant fists found his torso in the melee. Flashes of red and yellow firelight crossed his vision through the shadows of so many people, and soon a pair of sturdy hands hooked him under the shoulders and began dragging him out from a mess of humanity.

When Zarius's legs got clear, he tore free, ready to turn around and attack, but it was DK's staunch, angry face he found. Without a word, DK turned around and hurried toward the door, and Zarius chased after him. They melded into a jam of people, and after twenty seconds or so, they squeezed through the door onto the street.

Heads down, they hurried through the gathering crowd, everyone babbling in confusion, and escaped into the town square.

Darkness had fallen, so they didn't go far before they slowed down and stopped. DK wheeled on Zarius, eyes hard, frown deep, but no tirade came. Eventually, he just blustered out a huge sigh and hung his shaking head.

"Goddamnit Zarius."

"He started it." Zarius used his shirt to wipe some blood off his knuckles. His torso throbbed in a couple of spots, but that was negligible. He gave far better than he got, and he grinned to remember it. "Who was that guy anyway?"

DK made a sound that was half-scoff half-grunt-of-indignation. "*See?* You can't just—you just knocked that guy out. You don't even know who he *is*."

"I know he's an asshole."

They were walking back toward the hovel. Zarius mourned the loss of his first beer in Ten-Berry, but he got his first country fist fight in exchange. A push, he decided.

"That may be," said DK. "But you can't just go around *punching* people."

"I hammered his ass. Did you see how fast he went out? *Bam*."

"*Yes* I . . ." DK snickered once, again, then let out a stream of laughter. He stopped for a moment to indulge it, but as soon as Zarius started laughing, DK stopped and gave him a shove.

"Alright," DK said. "He was an asshole, and he deserved that. But you didn't *know* he deserved it. You can't just be doing that every time we go out in public. And it was still wrong."

"Wrong by whose account?" Zarius asked. "*His*? No shit. I wouldn't wanna eat a mouthful of table either."

"You're not listening to me." They made it back to their hovel and went inside. DK took the chair, and Zarius sat down in his little bedroll he'd made up opposite DK's.

"All joking aside," said DK. "You can't be—"

"I know I know," Zarius cut in. He dropped his grin and just stared at DK. "I can't just go around punching people. I need to have restraint, especially in the field. A real Knight does this, a real Knight does that. DK, I know. I saw the look on your face when that guy came up, and he fucking pissed me off.

"*You* gotta stand up for yourself, man. Don't be taking bullshit from some sheep-fucking hick. There's a line between restraint and . . . I don't know, being a bitch. If you let people like that get at you before, that's your shit. But *we*, and I mean you and me, ain't playing that shit. Somebody spits on my shoe, whatever. But he spits in my face? I'm hitting that motherfucker. Sometimes you gotta hit em."

To Zarius's surprise, DK didn't brush him off. He actually sat back for a moment before he knelt down to stoke the embers of the fire. Zarius just watched him, starting to worry that he'd struck a nerve. But when DK next looked up, he was nodding.

Their eyes met. "I think you might be right, to a degree," said DK. "I essentially let that guy bully me back in the day. I cared a lot about what they all thought of me, and as abrasive as he might seem, Carmichael has a finger on the pulse of Ten-Berry in some way. Like you said, there is a line. Just . . . maybe not such a quick trigger next time, please?"

Zarius smirked. "I can agree to that."

A heavy knock on the door made them both jump. Zarius dug his dummy sword out of his bedroll and stood up, brandishing it. DK put an open palm toward him, settling him, and did not retrieve his own, *real* weapon before he went to the door. When he opened it, it wasn't Carmichael Blaine with an angry mob but the pinched, pudgy face of Cornelius Flember. As soon as Zarius saw it wasn't retribution at the door, he threw his sword down and went to stand just behind DK.

"Christian," said Cornelius in his high, stringy voice. "A word?"

DK was stoic as he stepped back and gestured Cornelius in. Cornelius wore the clothing of a nobleman—a fur-lined overcoat, clean linen pants, thick leather shoes. He lumbered right over to the chair and sat down only to find Zarius and DK standing, looking down at him. He glanced around, as if noticing he was in the *only* chair, and stood back up. They were all clustered in the center of the small room.

"Well," said Cornelius. "Might I say first that it's good to see you. It's been some time, hasn't it?"

"Some time," DK agreed. "Good to see you too, Cornelius."

Cornelius stepped toward them, and a short arm shot out toward Zarius. "Hello young man. I don't think we've met. I'm Cornelius Flember, magistrate of Ten-Berry."

Hesitant, Zarius shook his hand. "Zarius."

Cornelius nodded and returned his gaze to DK. "Of course, you know I didn't come to exchange pleasantries."

DK scratched his head, and a stray piece of hair sprung loose. "I wouldn't think so."

"I was roused from my reading by a rather indignant Carmichael Blaine. Drunk and indignant. He, and a sizable assortment of other tavern-goers on this fine evening, claim that your young friend Zarius here assaulted him without provocation. Might I emphasize, *indignant*. He nearly blew what hair I have left right off the top of my head."

DK sighed and cleared his throat. "Well. All I can really say is that I would disagree that it was unprovoked. What does he want to do about it?"

"Mr. Blaine desires very strongly that Mr. Zarius here would be strung up by the neck until death. Of course I have no intention of delivering such a sentence over a bar squall. And certainly not at the advisement of Mr. Blaine, who we all know enjoys his drink."

"Okay . . ." DK glanced at Zarius, but Zarius tried to remain silent and invisible. "So what then?"

"Well I suppose I just came to give you a word of caution." Now Cornelius fixed his eyes firmly on Zarius, and Zarius did not look away. "Ten-Berry is already wary of outsiders, let alone transient ruffians. You wouldn't have to work hard to convince me that Carmichael Blaine deserved whatever you gave him, but in the same turn, believe me when I tell you that repeated instances of such behavior will not turn out well. Even if they *didn't* come to me, some people around here maintain their own sense of justice."

DK stepped aside and let Zarius take the floor. Zarius realized the line he was standing on even without the intense stare DK was giving him.

"I understand, Mr. Flember," said Zarius. "I have the fullest intent of honoring your laws and customs. Christian here has already given me a thorough tongue-lashing for my foolish indiscretion. You see, I'm from the streets of Endlin, where, like you said, we have our own sense of justice. But I know now that Ten-Berry isn't Endlin, and I assure you I'll adjust my behavior accordingly."

"Well that's just wonderful to hear." Cornelius sprouted a smile and nodded. "Thank you both for your understanding. I know Christian as a fine young man, and this little hiccup won't stop me from finding the same in you, Zarius. But the streets of Endlin, eh? I should tell Carmichael he's lucky you didn't put a dagger through his neck."

Zarius's smile tightened.

"What are you doing here, if I might ask?" Cornelius went on. "It's not usual that we get visitors, let alone from Endlin." He glanced around the hovel again and saw the two bedrolls. "Are you here to stay?"

"I came to have him train me," said Zarius, gesturing at DK. "I'm going to be a Knight."

Cornelius turned slowly back toward DK, eyes widening. "A Knight? Christian, as far as I knew, you'd given that up."

DK managed a grin and shrugged. "I guess I've had something of a change of heart."

"Heavens above!" Cornelius clapped his little hands together one time in front of his sizable paunch. "That's wonderful news. You know, I just haven't had the same peace of mind since you stopped. Every carriage loaded with gold or valuables has me sweating into the night. You know how they get after me when things happen, as if bandits are my fault! Oh that's great. You'll be resuming your old routines? Bounties, patrols, all of it?"

"Well spring only just hit its stride." DK spoke slowly, meting out the words. "But, I suppose, in time . . . yes. I'm resuming my post as the Day Knight."

"Excellent. Excellent." Cornleius shook both their hands and went to the door. "Well I expect I'll be seeing you shortly then. Don't worry about Carmichael, but please do try to keep things civil. I would greatly appreciate it."

With that, Cornelius left, and Zarius waited a few seconds before he snorted.

"Good Lord," said Zarius. "How can somebody out in the sticks have a stick so far up his ass? Christ."

DK grinned and just shook his head. "I didn't know you could turn it on like that. A tongue-lashing for your foolish indiscretion? It's like something possessed you."

Zarius laughed. "You don't know how many constables I ran into in Endlin. I learned pretty quick that I could speak my mind and go in the stockades for two weeks, or shine their shoes and be out in ten minutes."

"That was impressive." DK yawned and stretched, and he went to warm his hands by the fire. The smell of smoke hung about the room. "I think I'm gonna go to bed. Guess I don't have to worry about you being hungover."

As DK went over to his bed and started undressing, Zarius picked at some dirt under his fingernails. "Did you really mean what you said?" Zarius asked.

"What?"

"That you're gonna be the Day Knight again?"

DK stood half-naked and gazed at the crackling flames. "I can't very well train you otherwise, can I?"

8

DK. He came to like the nickname, and it grew dear to him. So, DK walked with his head held high, shoulders square, and he felt strong.

The last couple of months had been a hard lesson in strength and conditioning for Zarius, and a welcome refresher for DK. He'd always kept up a fitness regimen, even in the dark depths of his depression, but nothing like when he was in the full swing of Knight activities. He loved waking up sore and falling into bed exhausted. It almost embarrassed him how much he loved it, because he'd given it up by his own free will.

"Where are we going?" Zarius asked, dragging his feet behind DK.

"You'll see."

"I'm too tired to see."

"Not too tired to complain."

"Never."

DK smiled but didn't turn back. He knew by now that for all his bitching and moaning, Zarius would keep moving. All DK had to do was start ribbing him, and no matter how tired Zarius was, he'd perk up and start running, fighting, yelling, whatever. Even the vaguest insinuation of weakness or inadequacy fired him right up.

A spring breeze carried a chill that made them both shiver. The sky above was a brilliant azure, streaked by the smoke from dozens of hovels where breakfasts cooked and warmth gathered. DK and Zarius hurried down the street through the wind, hugging the edge of the road as a wagon passed through, horse hooves clopping and big wheels creaking. The aroma of cooking sausage made DK a little dizzy, but he pushed away his appetite and continued into the town square.

A quiet hubbub pervaded the square as merchants began to set up their stalls. Not many of them in the springtime, but still some. Salted meats, pickled vegetables, some dried grain brought out from the granary. One or two stands with meager clothing and ratty furs. DK glanced through them nonchalantly as they went on. A few industrious buds glistened on the Beggar's high branches.

Some commercial buildings resided here, shadows of what you could find in other, larger villages and cities, but critical to Ten-Berry's ecosystem, nonetheless. A tannery, a cooperage, a smokehouse. Crouched wooden buildings without fanfare. No grandiose architecture, very little stone. One building, though, was made mostly of gray bricks, a luxury in Ten-Berry. It was a squat, L-shaped structure with a wooden overhang above a large, thick wooden door, bolted with strips of iron. As they got closer, methodical clanks echoed through the door and into the street, and DK steered toward it.

"The forge?" Zarius asked.

Silent, DK approached the door and knocked hard. Without waiting for an answer, he pushed it open and poked his head in. After the harsh Sunlight of the spring morning, the interior of the forge was gloomy and dark. DK squinted until he could make out

Ezekiel's back at the forge, his thick forearm rising and falling in hypnotic rhythm.

Clank. Clank. Clank.

DK let himself in, Zarius following behind, and shut the door. They stood there for a minute as Ezekiel hammered a piece of red-hot steel in perfect, mesmeric time. The thick, square-headed hammer landed with remarkable accuracy and consistency. As always, DK watched with more than a tinge of awe.

Finally, Ezekiel paused and thrust the piece of steel into a big barrel of water. Steam hissed out as if by a magic spell and clouded the blacksmith's shape for a minute. An alchemist of metal. When Ezekiel removed the piece and held it up in the red, glowing light of the forge to inspect, DK cleared his throat.

Ezekiel turned around without startling, and his wizened eyes crinkled, a smile furrowing through the deep wrinkles of his face. A halo of wiry, white hair gathered around the crest of his bald head. He dropped the nascent metalwork on a nearby workbench and picked up a rag so blackened with soot that it appeared to do nothing but smear along his equally blackened hands.

"I'll be," said Ezekiel. "I wasn't expecting you."

"Is it alright if we drop in?" DK asked.

"Of course of course." Ezekiel waved his hand toward a table and a few chairs gathered into the corner. A few pieces of parchment were cluttered about it, and as Zarius took a seat, he pored over them.

"Looks like magic," he said.

DK chuckled and nodded as Ezekiel came over and slowly collapsed into a chair with a grunt.

"How are you boys?" Ezekiel asked. "How's the training coming?"

DK looked at Zarius.

"I feel like I got chewed up and tossed around by a giant dog," said Zarius. "So it's good I guess."

Ezekiel laughed hard enough that both DK and Zarius chuckled along with him. "Well that's something. A giant dog, eh? I could use one of those."

"I don't think you could," said Zarius.

Grinning, Ezekiel nodded with his eyebrows up. "Maybe you're right. But I suppose you didn't stop by to hear about what *I* need. Whaddya got?"

"A proposition," DK said. "If you have time."

"I don't have much," said Ezekiel. "But I certainly use what I've got. What can I do for you?"

"Zarius needs a sword. And armor."

Zarius sat bolt upright. His eyes got huge, and his lips parted. "*What?* Seriously?"

"Hm," Ezekiel grunted. His eyes went vacant and shifted to the air above their heads. "A sword and armor." He got up and went over to another corner of the room where a few big wooden trunks resided.

Zarius half stood up but settled back down when DK didn't move.

"Are you serious?" he asked. "I don't have any money."

DK snorted. "You think I do?"

Face clouding, Zarius just sat there and stared at him. The rattle of steel filled the room as Ezekiel bent over into one trunk, muttered, and moved to another. More shuffling, and he came out with a chainmail vest, eyeballing it.

"Come over here," he said.

Zarius hopped up and hurried over, and Ezekiel tossed the vest at him. Zarius caught it with a grunt and staggered back a step. "Damn you're strong."

Ezekiel grinned and went back to rooting around in the trunk. "Try it on."

With some difficulty, Zarius got the vest over his head. It fit alright. Didn't quite reach his waistline, but it wasn't too tight.

"Hauberk would take quite some time," said Ezekiel. He came out of the trunk with a few plates of curved iron and began holding them up against Zarius's shoulders and torso. "Probably have better luck trading for one. You're a lanky one, you know that?"

Zarius just stood in silence as Ezekiel walked around him, tossing some pieces, holding onto others.

"Yeah," said Ezekiel. "I'd get the sword done first. Not much use for armor without a weapon. But you've got mail enough for now and I could fasten up some of these plates."

Ezekiel looked at DK, still sitting across the room. "Two months, give or take. I can fasten up this vest in no time and at least get him started. I've already got some odds and ends for the next trader who comes through, so it depends on the timeline. Sword I could get done in a couple weeks with what I've got on my board already. Endlin delivered a huge order for plates. Like nothing I've ever seen."

"You make armor for *Endlin*?" Zarius asked. "Don't they have, like, a million blacksmiths up there?"

"And not one of them forms steel like I do." Ezekiel winked.

Zarius turned to DK with a face asking, *Is this guy for real?* And DK laughed out loud as he stood up.

"You know we'll gratefully take whatever time you have to spare," said DK.

Zarius screwed his face up and looked back at Ezekiel. "But how am I supposed to pay you?"

A stout, solid hand came down on Zarius's shoulder, as black as his hair, and Ezekiel just grinned at him. "Does a father charge his son for bread?"

"*My* father sure as hell would have."

Ezekiel gave a wry smile and patted Zarius's chainmail-laden shoulder. "Well never mind then. Christian is like a son to me, and I have to say, I'm beyond relived to see him out and about again."

As he spoke, Ezekiel shifted his eyes over Zarius's shoulder and met DK's.

"Truly a relief. To know he's training, working, it's just . . ." Ezekiel's tongue wet his thin lips, and his eyes shimmered. When he continued, his voice was a little softer. "It makes me glad, that's all. I gave him all the steel he's got, and if he thinks you're worth it, well then I'll give some to you too. I'm an old man. What use have I for money?"

Without a word, DK walked over and pulled Ezekiel into a hug, squeezing him hard, and Ezekiel returned it. All those kind words laved his spirit with warm water. DK loved Ezekiel, and he himself felt as though he was emerging from a long and uncertain hibernation. One that almost took his life.

After a few seconds, DK stepped away and clapped Zarius on the back. "Well, we've got some training to get after. What do you say?"

"Take all that off," said Ezekiel, reaching to help Zarius. "I'll get those plates fastened on in a few days, and it'll be ready for ya. It's a start at least."

As he removed the chainmail, Zarius kept shaking his head. "I just . . . I don't know what to say." He stuck a hand out. "Thank you."

Ezekiel gripped it and shook it, smiling all the while. "No trouble at all. I wouldn't mind seein you boys whenever you have time for an old man. You know how I like the stories I can't write for myself anymore."

"Of course." DK shook Ezekiel's hand in turn, and he and Zarius left.

On the walk back to the hovel, Zarius continued to drag behind, but his head was turned to the ground, eyes wandering.

"What's up?" DK asked.

Zarius didn't speak for a while. "It's just hard to believe," he said, finally. "I don't feel like I deserve this."

DK let those thoughts hang as they walked. The walk passed quickly, and as soon as they got back, DK set to work building up the fire to make a little stew to tide them over for training. As he worked, Zarius sat in the chair, still blank-faced, but he finally stood up and tapped DK on the shoulder.

DK straightened and faced him. Zarius's face was sharp and angular. His close-set eyes beamed out like chips of gleaming obsidian. "Thanks, DK," he said. "For everything you've done so far."

DK smiled and nodded. "Of course. You asked for it, after all."

"Yeah." Zarius laughed. "I guess I did. I just . . . didn't expect all this. I don't know what I expected."

"I don't know what I expected either, when I saw you standing out there. But I sure am glad you found me."

9

Zarius hissed through his teeth. DK cocked an eye at him as he settled onto a bald patch of earth. They were nestled at the base of a little hill, surrounded by buffalograss and big patches of tallgrass beginning to shoot up all over. But the hillside was relatively tame, and it lay exposed to the vastness of the sky above. A few pillars of white fluff occupied the blue plain, but the Sun beamed down unencumbered.

"What's wrong?" DK asked.

"You already know."

"Well you have to keep trying. It's an order."

"I can't *fucking* do it," Zarius spat. "It doesn't work for me."

"You aren't trying hard enough."

"Man I've *been* trying," Zarius cried. "I try every time, but it doesn't get any better."

DK sighed and scratched his head. A gentle wind stirred the hair off his shoulders. "You have to give it time."

"It's already *been* two months. I tried that very first night, and I've tried every time since then, and it's always the same."

"You can't force it. You just have to let go. This isn't a run. It's a totally different kind of exercise."

"An exercise that doesn't fucking work," Zarius grumbled.

"How would you know if you can't even do it?"

Zarius threw his arms up and collapsed backward onto the grass. The sky was so bright and the Sun so brilliant that he had to squeeze his eyelids as hard as he could. Idle birdsong reached them from far away, then quieted. Wind whispered through the grass.

"Alright alright *fuck*," Zarius said. "You just do your thing, and I'll get there."

"You better not just—"

"I'll *try*. I *will* try. Okay? Jesus. Let me get my shit together. You're gonna sit out here for an hour anyway, so I've got more than enough time."

"I could make it two."

"Then *do it*. See if I care. I'll be right here, like always."

With that, silence fell. Zarius propped himself up and watched DK's eyes close and his posture solidify. The rise and fall of his chest began to grow longer and larger until Zarius really had to watch to see it happen at all. For his part, Zarius didn't let loose the tirade of curses dancing on his tongue, didn't even throw out an angry grunt. He sat there, a few paces from DK, wondering why he wasn't good enough.

Well. Might as well get the futility out of the way now before he was left to twitch for an hour. He settled into the grass. DK's spot was worn to the bare earth from so much sustained usage, so Zarius had to deal with hundreds of grass blades tickling his calves and bare feet. The Sun beat down like a hammer, and it was a warm spring day. Sweat began to form on Zarius's head and the top of his bare back.

Trying to ignore all these sensations, Zarius straightened his back and started dragging out each breath. He didn't worry about his thoughts at first; he just relaxed his breath and enjoyed that experience. His thoughts riffled through his head like a book reading itself. Scraps of images from training, running, eating. Things DK said, expressions he made when he thought Zarius wasn't trying hard, expressions he made when he *did* think Zarius was trying hard. Sword moves. Strategy. Doctrine.

After several minutes of this, Zarius picked a moment and, on his next exhale, he tried to blow all of these thoughts through his nose like one giant snot rocket. For one precious moment, it worked, but then they all came rushing back in. It was like a bubble bursting underwater. Poof. All that empty space filled back up in an instant.

Zarius tried again. Several times. He went through the same process. His thoughts dominated his mind, then he began to painstakingly collect them. When he thought he had them lassoed, he slapped the horse and watched them all be dragged away only for the cavalry to arrive moments later and slaughter him.

Never in his life had Zarius thought about thoughts. His mind just went and went and went. Sometimes he listened to it, sometimes he didn't, but it was always there, chattering away, presenting a lot of useless shit. Sometimes there were nuggets of gold in all the debris, but they didn't receive any more conscious attention than anything else.

That is to say, when Zarius knew what to do, he did it. When he knew what to say, he said it. The analysis of his own mind frightened and confused him, and when he heard DK talk, he felt certain that theirs were not constructed the same way. DK sounded like a sergeant naming off his privates, sending them away until he was ready for them again. Zarius was more like a beekeeper. He couldn't tell a bunch of fucking bees what to do.

Frustration mounted, and after about ten minutes and maybe five good attempts, Zarius gave up. The worst part was that he did see some kind of purpose in it all. When he grasped those few seconds of quiet and clarity after he thrust all his thoughts away, they were startling in their tranquility. And that made it all the more aggravating when they died so quickly. It was like peering into another world, seeing things through different eyes.

Zarius lay back, careful not to disturb DK, and started pulling out strands of grass with his fingers. Blisters throbbed on his hands from the training sword he'd been using. His body was sore and achy. But he didn't mind any of that. He actually liked it. He just couldn't figure out this meditation business. This whole Sun thing.

It just didn't seem fair. He got his wish—to train for Knighthood, but suddenly DK pulls out some ethereal bullshit that Zarius can't get a grip on and says it's as important, if not more so, than whatever he can do with a sword. Of course it would be that way. It only made sense that even after everything it took to get here, some bizarre shit would push all his goals a little farther than he could reach.

A breeze danced across Zarius's skin. Little bugs crawled over his flesh, and he idly brushed them away. He thought about Endlin and the friends he left behind. Sometimes the quiet out here disturbed him, the vastness of the land. You could die out here. Get lost enough, and you might not find your way back. For the first nineteen years of his life, he never left the walls of Endlin, and here they had no walls to protect them.

He thought of all the fights, all the blood spilled over nothing. All the other street urchins like himself, eking out a living by con, craft, or cruelty. Whatever it took to survive. And how it seemed that the world couldn't care less about his existence, that he didn't matter, dead or alive.

Out here, everyone was someone. These people had families and friends who they saw every day. They returned to the same work day in and day out, and they didn't all kill themselves over it. Some of them even seemed happy. There were no nobles here. A few merchants lived in stone houses in the northwest corner of Ten-Berry, but that was it. Everyone else was on the same level, just peasants. And again, some of them were happy. Zarius saw very little joy in those alleys where he slept in Endlin.

"What are you thinking about?"

Zarius's eyes fluttered. He sat up to see DK's dazzling blue eyes gazing at him. "Has it already been an hour?"

"How should I know?" DK asked.

Zarius scoffed and let himself fall back. "I'm thinking about everything."

DK laughed. "Wow. Well, oh wise one, have you figured it out?"

"What? Everything?"

"Yeah."

"Nope."

"Guess you'll have to keep at it." DK stretched and leaned back to rest against the side of the hill. Endless Sunlight poured over them.

"I don't want you to think I'm not trying," said Zarius. "I know we've been over it, but seriously. I don't know what it is. My thoughts don't just *go away*."

Zarius expected another immediate rebuke, but this time DK was quiet for a while.

"Well, look. It's not like I can look inside your head and tell you what you're doing wrong. Maybe what's in your head doesn't even look like what's in mine. I've never tried to teach this to somebody. But it gives you, like, a presence, you know?"

DK sat up again and gazed over at Zarius. "It puts me in the moment, because that's where we need to be. That's what really matters. If this doesn't work for you, okay, but you're gonna have to figure out what does."

It made little sense to Zarius, but he heard the desperation in DK's voice, and he *wanted* to understand. "Okay."

"It's the Sun, you know? It's all in the Sun."

"Not this again," Zarius moaned.

"I'm serious." DK stood up to look down at his apprentice. "That's what we're after. The Sun doesn't know what time it is; it doesn't even know what time *is*. It's always there, always doing the exact same thing in the exact same way. It moves across the sky, but it can only be where it is right now.

"I know it sounds crazy, but believing in the Sun is such a huge reason for who I am and what I can do. There's no *God*. If there was, then where the hell is He? Right?"

"True," Zarius agreed.

"No. There is no God, not like they say. But I know there's something. After . . . Well, after what happened, I know it. It's kind of like I knew it before, but I didn't really *believe* it. That's why I called myself the Day Knight, because I thought something was special about the Sun. After the bog, I knew it in my soul. But I wasn't willing to act anymore. Now it's all so . . ." DK sat back down heavily, eyes going distant. "Now it's all different."

"What do you mean?" Zarius finally sat up, intrigued. The mention of the bog always made him eager to hear more.

"I never paired strong belief with being the Day Knight. I called myself the Day Knight, but I didn't really believe. In the years since the bog witch, I learned true belief, but I wasn't calling myself the

Day Knight anymore. Now that it feels like they're coming together, it just . . . it's crazy. It feels great, honestly. I made it through a lot of shit to get here."

Zarius nodded. "I'm glad you did."

DK met his gaze. "Thanks. Me too. And I'm glad you're here. I wouldn't be doing this if you weren't here, so I can only look at the Sun again and think it's all part of some grand design. At least that it was meant to be, we're both meant to be here, and I know that means I'm meant to try to teach you what I know. I *know* meditation works, and I *know* the Sun is guiding me. So I'm sorry if I get after you too hard or start to annoy you, but I've gotta answer the call, you know?"

Zarius rubbed some loose grass between his fingers. "Fair enough. I came to you for training, and you're training me. I believe that you believe what you're saying, and I'm trying to understand, but I don't think it's something you can just *tell me.*"

"I think you're right." DK shrugged. "We're figuring it out together. Just don't get down on yourself, alright? And tell me to fuck off if you feel like you need to. But I'm trying to train you hard, because I feel like that's what you want. And I feel like it's right."

"Don't let up," Zarius growled. "Whatever it is, I can handle it. Even some religion ass bullshit."

DK burst into laughter, but when he settled down, he had a serious glint in his eyes. "Hey, it's not bullshit, alright? If not for the Sun, I'd be dead."

"Yet you still haven't explained how. You haven't even told me the story."

DK's face remained drawn as his eyes fell to the ground. "It's not an easy place for me to go."

10

"*Row,*" DK screamed. "*Row. Faster.*"

Zarius's muscles rippled as he thrust the oars forward and back again. Tendons bulged out of his neck, and he wore a blindfold around his eyes.

DK glanced up at the approaching shore. "*Come on,*" he yelled. "You're not even fucking close. They're gaining on us. *Row, Z. Row.*"

"Aghhh fuck you," Zarius seethed. But he rowed faster, gasping, drenched in sweat. The Sun was like an aggravated eyeball with a hot gaze on them. No cloud cover.

The bottom of the rowboat dragged against the sand of the shore. DK leaped out of it as Zarius tore off his blindfold and fumbled for his sword on the wooden deck.

"*Come on,*" DK shouted. "*They're coming at you.*"

As he yelled it, he charged from the edge of the sandy beach back toward the water. Zarius just managed to get his feet in the sand when DK was on him. He threw up a guard and absorbed a huge shot from DK's sword.

Whanngggg.

DK reared back and delivered again, and Zarius pulled his blade back in time to meet it.

Whannggg.

Zarius staggered back. The impacts were overwhelming, and DK pushed him.

Shkank. Skank. Whanngg.

In a flurry, DK performed a combination of moves that put Zarius on his heels and then knocked him backward. He collapsed into the water, gasping. His hands dug into the sand, but his shaking arms couldn't push his body up. Water dripped from his face and hair as DK stood over him, the edges of his toes in the surf.

"*Get up,*" DK screamed, leaning down. "*Get the fuck up, Z.*"

"I . . . can't," Zarius gasped. His whole body heaved as he tried to catch his breath.

"You can't?" DK asked. "You *can't? You won't.* Everyone is right there. Everyone you ever knew or loved is ten steps away being raped and murdered, and you won't get up? *You won't save them?* Then you're *shit.* You're *nothing.* You're a coward who won't—"

"*Aaaghhhh.*" Zarius found the hilt of his blade under the water and came up like a lake monster. His eyes glinted with vengeance, and he pressed DK on an attack.

Shclank. Shkank. Tchang. Tchang. Whannggg.

Zarius drove DK backward onto the beach. As the last powerful swing took Zarius's arm to one side, though, DK swept a leg through and took his feet out. Zarius went horizontal and landed hard in the sand. He couldn't even choke out a breath for a couple moments, and then he curled up, gasping.

DK, too, was breathing hard, and he stepped back to let Zarius recover. "Good," he said. "Good job."

"Fuh, fuh, fuck you," Zarius said.

DK grinned and went to drag the boat a little higher onto the beach. He fetched their waterskins from inside and dropped one on Zarius's chest as he walked over and sat down.

Zarius uncorked it and began gulping down water between gasps before his head fell back. DK watched him, and he couldn't deny a swell of pride. Zarius was trying as hard as DK could ask him to. He showed up every day and put in the work. There was a Knight in him yet.

"God *damn*," Zarius said.

"Twenty pushups," DK replied. "You lost."

Still panting, Zarius flipped over and started cranking out push-ups. He got to about twelve before he started to struggle, but he fought through the rest as DK watched. When he finished, he just lay there on his face in the sand, and DK laughed.

"It's hot as balls," Zarius said, his voice muffled by the beach.

"Not even," DK said.

Zarius lifted his head to glare at him. Sand stuck to his wet face and hair. "Not for the guy getting his ass rowed all over the lake."

DK tipped his head to one side and nodded. "Really pleasant, actually."

Still regaining his breath, Zarius managed to get to a sitting position. "God I hate that drill. When am I ever gonna be in a fucking beach invasion?"

"Never, I'm sure."

After a couple seconds, Zarius flattened his face. "Asshole."

"Rowing is good for you."

"Yeah so is eating. And sleeping."

"You do plenty of *all* of that."

Zarius turned and whipped a handful of sand into Quail Lake. Little geysers appeared where the grains struck. A decent breeze rattled through the fledgling leaves of the towering cottonwoods clustered around the beach. The Sun occupied the free patch of sky and scattered Light across the water.

DK let himself fall back on the sand, taking deep breaths, absorbing the Sun through every pore he could open. The lake water dried on his skin. Sand stuck to him all over his back, but it didn't bother him. He let his awareness loosen as the Sunlight washed over him.

Zarius's voice cut through DK's reverie. "What the fuck is that *smell?*"

A split second later, goosebumps flushed down DK's flesh from the top of his head to his toes. His scalp pulled taut like a drawn bow, and water began to well in his eyes. In the same moment, he scrambled to his feet just before a boulder of fear landed in the waters of his soul. Whatever Zarius smelled, DK sensed.

"*Something's here,*" he hissed.

DK took a fighting stance, and Zarius flew up to stand behind him, clutching his blunted dummy sword. DK hardened himself to his emotions, casting them off like lepers. He zoned in. The Sun on his back gave him strength. A strange chuffing sound came through the trees somewhere nearby. DK took a couple unwilling steps back before he stopped.

"Oh *God.*" Zarius blew a bunch of air through his nose and plugged it.

Now DK smelled it. Rot. But he didn't react to it, didn't take his hands off his sword. He scanned the tree line until he focused on a silhouette coming toward them.

"Z get out of here." DK was hardly thinking. Barbarous evils banged on the doors of his mind. "Run."

"*What?*" Zarius cried. "Where? What is it?" The words tumbled out all together.

The shape emerged from the shadows of the trees into

undeniable fact. DK's face twisted. It was a whitetail deer, a big doe, but half of her skin was gone. Bits of black sludge dripped from a gaping slash through her flank. Instead of whites and soft browns, though, her skin was mottled with yellow and green, sporting large, oozing sores. She pulled her intestines along the ground behind her as she staggered onto the beach on three legs, only a stump where the fourth should have been. But even her insides looked wrong. It looked almost . . . fake.

The deer collapsed onto her front knees and went still. Her flayed neck swung until she fixed her lifeless, insane black eyes on them. She let out a resounding bleat so unnerving that it pushed them back a couple steps. DK couldn't take his eyes away, and the sensations washing over him were putrid and vile.

"What the *fuck* is that?" Zarius hissed.

The deer tipped over onto its side and began kicking its legs, throwing up curtains of sand as it writhed. The bleats turned to agonized wails that so grated DK's ears it made him want to scream. Without thought, he sprinted forward, wielding his sword, and slashed down into the deer's yellowed neck flesh.

Black blood sprayed out of the wound and coated DK's legs up to his thighs. He let out a strangled grunt as he ripped his sword free and jumped back. The blood was ice cold. The geyser faltered almost immediately, and the deer ceased to struggle. Trying not to vomit, DK looked from the deer to the iridescent coating of fluid on his shins and back again.

The flesh was lumpy and uneven, but beyond that, it wasn't all connected. Through various parts of the deer's torso, DK could see gaps in the skin with the stark white of bone showing through. Small holes appeared up and down her entire body, as if she had been inexpertly woven together. The eyes looked more like painted rocks jammed into a misshapen skull. And something about it made him sick. The fear did not dissipate, and DK began to back up.

A stone rose in his throat as he turned around and saw Zarius standing there, frozen, eyes locked on the deer. "What was that?" Zarius asked breathlessly. "What's wrong with it?"

"I don't know," DK croaked. "We need to get the fuck out of here."

11

They trekked the few miles back to Ten-Berry in silence. At times, DK broke into a run, and Zarius had to chase him on dead, wobbly legs. Rather than determination, though, now Zarius ran with the fear of being left behind. As if DK knew something he didn't, and that by falling back, Zarius would make himself easy prey for some unholy monster.

By the time they made it to the hovel, Zarius collapsed onto his bed, panting. He watched DK's glassy eyes as his master stripped off all his armor and practically bolted through the door. After a bit, Zarius heard sounds outside the hovel, the sloshing of water. Then silence again. A few minutes, then more water. This pattern repeated almost ten times before Zarius dragged his haggard body up and went outside.

He found DK scrubbing his legs with well water from a bucket. Zarius looked closer and couldn't see so much as a fleck of blood or grime anywhere on him, but DK scrubbed like he was fighting off a deadly infection. The skin on his shins was bright red from where he scraped it with his fingernails. Even when Zarius appeared, DK didn't stop, didn't even look up.

As Zarius watched, a strange fear took hold of him. The way DK just scrubbed and scrubbed and scrubbed. DK dumped more water over his legs and continued to wash himself, and Zarius's stomach turned.

When DK got up and started heading back down the street toward the village center, Zarius stepped up and grabbed his arm. DK tried to shake him off, but Zarius held fast until DK turned a piercing, raging eye on him.

"*Let me go*," he snarled.

"Dude, you're okay," Zarius said, pleading. "Your legs are clean man. You're okay."

DK thrashed like a vicious toddler, and Zarius held on until he was sure he would tear DK's arm out of the socket. When he finally let go, DK hurried down the road as Zarius watched helplessly. This time, DK didn't come back, but Zarius was sure he was off in some other corner, scouring his legs.

After standing dazed for a minute, Zarius headed for the town square himself, but he didn't look for DK. Instead, he jogged straight to Ezekiel's forge, banged on the door, and let himself in.

The room was dark, the forge only a dim red glow. Zarius waited for his eyes to adjust before he went to the interior door on a side wall and knocked. He heard a grunt and some faint rustling, and he knocked again, driven by anxiety.

When Ezekiel appeared, his eyes were scrunched up, his wiry hair all astray. "What is it?" he asked, his voice thick. "Sorry, Zarius? I was having a nap."

"Something happened to DK." Zarius's voice came out embarrassingly strangled, but Ezekiel's face went pale as his eyes snapped to clarity.

"What? Where? Is he okay?"

"I don't know. He keeps scrubbing his legs."

"What?"

"We saw something. Some kind of, I don't know. Some messed up looking deer. It scared the hell out of him. He won't stop scrubbing his legs."

Ezekiel stood there for a few moments. Zarius knew it all sounded crazy, but the intensity in Ezekiel's face at least reassured him.

"You don't know where he is?" Ezekiel asked.

"No. He ran off."

"Okay. Okay." Ezekiel put a hand on Zarius's shoulder and gave him a light squeeze. "It's alright, Zarius. We can go look for him, but I'm sure he'll turn up. This is . . ." Ezekiel's face was hard and full of pain.

"What's wrong with him?" Zarius asked.

"I don't know, son. But there was . . . there was a time, long before you came . . . Well, I don't know how much Christian has told you."

"He went to the bog."

"Yes. He went to the bog. And when he came back . . . He wasn't himself. Not for a long time. For a while, well, he hardly seemed like *anything*. I worried we might never get him back, but we did. It took time. Whatever you saw might have triggered something in him, reminded him of what he saw . . . back then."

"So what?" Zarius cried. "He'll just be different now? But what about . . . How am I going to . . ." He reached up and grabbed two fistfuls of his hair.

Now Ezekiel grabbed both of Zarius's shoulders and shook him gently. "Don't worry. Don't worry. It's going to be alright. He'll pull through it. He's done it before."

"But how long will it take?"

"I don't know. All we can do is pray for him, and be there for him."

A light went on in Zarius's mind. Hope crossed his face like a cloud in front of the Sun. "We have to get him to his meditation spot."

As Zarius turned to run out of the forge, Ezekiel caught him. His grip was astonishing. "Hold on, Zarius. Just slow down. We need to let him recover, okay? I know you want to help him, but he might not respond well right now. Trust me, I was with him in the early days after the bog. He could get violent. We just need to let him come back from whatever place he's gone to, in his head. I doubt it will take him long. He knows the land, and he's stronger now. He'll come back."

"I don't understand." Zarius wanted to tear Ezekiel's hand off his arm.

"I know. Just trust me, okay? Trust Christian. We can help him, and we will, but I think right now we need to let him sort things out and at least come back on his own. He needs that."

"Are you sure?" Zarius gazed hard at the old man.

Ezekiel sighed and paused for a few moments. "About as sure as I can be. Here, since I'm up, why don't you help me get the forge going? I'm almost done with your sword."

Disturbed, Zarius dragged his feet after Ezekiel. He helped the old blacksmith get an even layer of charcoal on the bottom of the forge. They got it lit, and Zarius worked the bellows while Ezekiel pushed the fuel around until the charcoal stones were all glowing hot. He did just enough to get himself out without any more harassment.

Throughout it all, Zarius was lost in his thoughts. The apprehension gnawing at his gut both dismayed and surprised him. He never cared that much for many people in his life, never had a close friend he trusted entirely. And to find out how he felt about DK now, through this agonizing anxiety, seemed unfair. He was really worried about his friend. What if Ezekiel was wrong? What if DK never came back?

12

Darkness slobbered all over the land, and the air was cold with no Sun. DK crouched next to a tree, rubbing handfuls of grass and soil over his legs. Long streaks of dried blood flaked away, replaced by a shining ooze from the shallow wounds he'd given himself. His stomach cramped so hard that he gasped and went down to one knee, so hungry he was. He didn't know where he was, only that it wasn't Ten-Berry.

By the light of a silver half-moon, DK scraped out a little clearing next to this big cottonwood tree, preparing a nest. But when he lay down in the cold dirt, his eyes didn't so much as flutter. They refused to close, lest some unspeakable horror creep up on him. Deep down, he was waiting. Waiting to hear that unearthly bleat, the staggering steps of dead legs.

Instead, he began to hear the smacks of chewing. His stomach moiled in response. Something nearby was eating. The chewing turned to tearing, the ripping of flesh. DK listened as strips of meaty skin were torn away from each other, like wet fabric being pulled apart. His eyes were glued open, but he couldn't move.

The chewing got clearer and louder until it was all he could hear. He wasn't seeing, wasn't feeling, only hearing. That sound was all that existed in the world; the world was the sound. Something demonic tearing up flesh and eating it, right on the other side of this tree.

Finally, something broke in him. DK let out a little whimper, unable to stand the sound anymore. He stood up and walked around the tree. Surely it would vanish. There was nothing there. Except there was.

A humanoid crouched over a shadowy pile on the ground. In the darkness, DK could only make out the vaguest shape of it, but it was there. He watched its arms move, heard that ripping of meat, and saw its hands moving to its mouth. The awful smacking and grinding of bone on flesh, the spurting and gushing of ample fluids.

DK gagged and let out a short dry heave, and the figure in front of him froze. Ice filled DK's veins. His hands reached feebly for the hilt of a sword that wasn't there. No sword. No Sun. No protection.

It looked at him over its shoulder, but he couldn't see its face. He did hear the high-pitched, chattering laughter that came out of it, though, and he took a step back. The thing resumed its meal, all those godawful sounds.

"Stop," DK groaned.

Now it stood up. It reached DK's height, and it turned around, facing him in the darkness. DK could make out nothing but the faintest glint of eyes reflecting the weak moonlight.

"Stop," the figure repeated. It mimicked DK's voice.

DK didn't say anything. His mind was in pieces.

"Stop," it repeated. It laughed again. "Stop."

When DK took a step back, it stepped forward. Another, another, matching his movement. The fear intensified. When DK turned around to run, he heard it come crashing toward him through the bushes.

DK let out a scream that doubled, reproduced from just a dozen paces behind him. He went flying out of the stand of trees and onto open ground. Tallgrass crowded his legs, reaching up to his waist, and when he snuck the quickest glance over his shoulder, something was chasing him. Over the wind in his ears, he heard it babbling nonsense, laughing, shrieking. He ran as fast as he could, but he couldn't gain any distance on it.

Finally, it was all too much. DK broke down. Fear made his legs clumsy until he hitched, missed a step, and went down in a heap in the grass. He heard the thunder of footsteps, and his whole body clenched like one muscle. Teeth so tight it was a wonder they didn't shatter, all his tendons bulging.

Silence. Deadly silence. But DK didn't relax. He didn't open his eyes. He remained curled in a ball on the ground, straining with effort, because he knew that it was standing over him. Leaning down, holding its breath. Waiting for him to look.

13

Zarius paced around the town square in darkness. The Sun had only just collected the last threads of its purple robe, and a million stars studded the sky like a diamond shattered into black wool. He pinched each finger against his thumb in turn—a sort of nervous tic—as he paced around, thinking. DK hadn't come back, and it took all of Ezekiel's insistence for Zarius not to go looking for him. He didn't know where to look anyway. Ten-Berry was only so big, but the wilderness was endless.

The same devious questions tortured him. Wondering if DK would return at all, if he would be himself. Zarius worried that he'd lost his friend, his master, and his only shot at real purpose in one fell swoop. Nascent anger bubbled under his thoughts like a volcano considering eruption. He couldn't stand the emptiness of the hovel, so here he was, walking around in the dark. He hovered near the Beggar as if it were a silent guardian.

Every time the tavern door opened, the brief blast of mirth and gaiety would pull him out of his hypnosis for a few moments. His legs carried him nearer to it like a desert wanderer toward the sound of running water. When he noticed it—really focused on it—he went inside without a second thought.

The presence of other people grounded him, and the buzz of laughter and conversation dulled his thoughts. The smell of ale wafting through the room danced through his head, and he made his way right toward the bar. The tavern wasn't as busy tonight, so he got up to the wooden bar top without difficulty.

A woman came down behind the bar, stopped a few people away to fill up a drink for someone else. Zarius focused on her. She wore her fine blond hair in a long braid hanging over one shoulder. Her overtunic was a steady brown with a white, linen apron draped over top of it. When she came down and stopped in front of him, Zarius just stared at her for a moment. Her face was round, eyes big and hazel, and she gave off no air of servility or even conviviality.

"Uh, can I help you?" she asked.

Zarius's eyes fell to the bar. "I just realized I don't have any money. Never mind."

She laughed, and the sound surprised him. "Say." She narrowed her eyes at him. "Aren't you the guy who was here with Christian the other night? Started the fight?"

Heat flushed through Zarius's face. "Oh. Yeah."

"Gotta hand it to you. Carmichael has needed a good punch in the face for, oh, I don't know, the four and a half years I've been working here. Probably longer than that."

Zarius managed to smile, and he met her eyes again. Her gaze was strong and unfaltering.

"Happy to," he said.

"What's your name?"

"Zarius. You?"

"Catherine." Catherine stood on her tiptoes and looked over Zarius's head. "Christian not with you?"

The light died in Zarius's eyes. "No."

Catherine paused for a moment. "Is he okay?"

Zarius's head lowered again. He didn't know what to say. Was this just a question designed for later ridicule? Just another shovelful of shit to dump on DK?

"Yeah," he said eventually.

Catherine raised her eyebrows. "Are *you* okay?"

Zarius snorted. "I just wish I wasn't fucking *broke*."

Quick as a flash, Catherine poured an ale for him and handed it out. Zarius's eyes lit up as he reached for it, and he was about to thank her when she jerked it back. Confused anger streaked his thoughts, and if this turned out to be some joke at his expense, he would lean across the bar and clock her. Damn the consequences.

"Where's Christian?" she asked again. "And *is he okay*?"

"Who the fuck are you?" Zarius asked. "Why do you give a shit?"

Catherine's face twitched as she slowly placed the ale on the bar and let it go. "I guess I just care a little bit." She eyed him with reproach. "That's all."

"Never heard him say your name." Zarius picked up the ale, scowling. "You sure must care a whole lot."

Zarius left it at that as he took his ale and sat at the first empty table he found. It was a four-top, but he took it anyway and hung his head over his ale, taking idle sips while his thoughts turned his brain into a nuthouse. When he heard the clunk of the chairs moving around him, he knew he'd made a mistake.

"Hey," said Carmichael Blaine when Zarius looked up. His shock of brown hair was crazy over his fat face, and his eyes oozed hatred.

Zarius just stared at him and waited. Waited for the first fist to fall. He'd told that magistrate he would behave, and to Zarius, that meant not throwing the first punch. If it came to self-defense, he'd kill them all.

"I think you might owe me an apology," said Carmichael.

Silence. Carmichael's buddies leaned in across the table, staring at Zarius, but Zarius was locked onto Carmichael. He stared deep into those beady brown eyes and saw a coward. A bully insulated by the size and remoteness of a village like Ten-Berry, emboldened by brainless companions. Any self-respecting villain in Endlin would have bled him like a pig.

"You wanna shit your own teeth, fatass?" Zarius growled.

Carmichael reached for him, but a sweet voice stopped him.

"Heyyy." It was Catherine. Every last head at the table turned to look up at her.

"Carmichael, weren't you gonna come up and see me for a drink?"

What the fuck? Zarius asked. Was that the same voice he heard five minutes ago?

Carmichael cleared his throat and adjusted the collar of his sweat-stained linen shirt. "Well hi Catherine. Of course, of course I was. I just . . . There was a . . ." He turned toward Zarius, beginning to scowl again.

"There was a what?" She rested her hand lightly on his shoulder, and Carmichael jolted.

"Well this *guy* is the one who—"

"Oh you boys are so silly." Her little hand stayed on his shoulder. "Come on. Let's not have any more fights. My dad said if it happens again, he's gonna have to ban you all. You don't want that, do you? Then I couldn't see you anymore." Her lower lip jutted out, and Carmichael started muttering to himself before he sighed and stood up.

As he did so, his hand just so happened to slap Zarius's ale into his face and all over his chest and lap.

"Oh shit," Carmichael said as his buddies hid their mouths and snickered. "Oopsie daisies."

Zarius began to tremble as his vision went white-hot, but he didn't stand up. He let them filter away, guided by Catherine's hypnotic voice. After a minute, the trembling ceased, and through incremental breaths, he managed to get the smallest amount of control back. No first punches. No first punches. No first punches.

When something landed on the table with a *thunk*, he opened his eyes and saw Catherine looking down at him as she deposited a fresh ale on the table. Before she could so much as open her mouth, Zarius stood up out of his chair and left.

14

Nearly forty-eight hours after the encounter with the deer, DK came staggering through Ten-Berry's town square toward his hovel. When he made it inside, covered in mud and grass and filth, he collapsed onto his bed and passed out. Shapeless fragments of dreams tormented him until something roused his spirit to wakefulness. A smell that penetrated right to the core of his being and got his stomach in a riot.

Ezekiel and Zarius were there, feeding ingredients into the iron cauldron. As soon as DK sat up, they both looked at him, then turned their heads right back to the stew. They murmured quietly to each other, and DK couldn't quite make it out at first, like they were speaking a different language.

His head was in ruins, everything jumbled up. His neck and back ached terribly. He shifted so that his back was against the wall, and he stared between Ezekiel and Zarius at the flames lapping the underside of the cauldron. The firelight danced across the walls. They cast sheepish glances his way, and he was aware of them, but he focused on the smells and the snaps of the fire.

A few minutes passed. They didn't speak to him. But when

Ezekiel came over with a bowl of stew and a spoon, DK took it from him. He shoveled in one scoop and scalded his mouth so badly that he spit it all out on his bed. Zarius and Ezekiel looked at him, then away. DK sat frozen for a few minutes and then tipped the bowl up and drained the entire thing.

Zarius's eyes widened, and Ezekiel took the bowl from DK, refilled it, and gave it back again. DK repeated the process—letting it cool, swallowing it whole. Four times over before he was full to bursting. This time, he set the bowl beside him instead of passing it to Ezekiel, and the old man went over and let himself down into the chair. It was pushed up against the back wall so he only partially faced DK. Zarius sat on the dirt floor next to the fire, also at an angle, as if DK were welcome either to be present or not.

"I think she found me." DK's voice came out high-pitched and rattling. Even he thought it didn't sound like him, and he bent his head between his knees.

Only the fire spoke for a few moments.

"Would you like to talk about it?" asked Ezekiel.

"Talk about it?" DK asked. He flipped his head up. "Talk about *what*?"

Ezekiel hesitated. "About what happened."

DK jabbed a finger toward Zarius. "Ask *him*. He saw it. Go tell them all. They think that shit wasn't real?" DK clutched his hair. Spittle flew from his lips as he forced the words through clenched teeth. "They wanted to tell me it wasn't *real*? Those fucking cunt *fucks*."

Ezekiel winced, and Zarius just sat staring, lips slightly parted. After a beat, the old man got up and walked over. He made some effort to help himself down to the floor, and he sat next to DK and put an arm around his shoulder. Tears welled in DK's eyes and began to leak out against his will. They dripped from his downturned face, and his body bounced as he stifled sobs.

"It's alright, Christian," said Ezekiel. "You're safe."

"None of us is *safe*." DK's voice was thick. He picked up his head again. "I saw her out there. I saw what she did to me."

"And you're still here."

"I'm still here because she wouldn't let me die."

"I don't believe that."

"Well you *should*." The words got weaker. "What did I do?" He started jouncing again, tears sliding from his eyes as he huddled against Ezekiel. "Why did I deserve that?"

When Ezekiel spoke again, his voice was strained and aching as he hugged DK to him. "You didn't, Christian. You didn't deserve it."

The pain of that night surfaced, driving into him like sheets of hail. Skeletons rose from the dead and besieged the hovel. He could hear their bones beating on the walls, the dirt tumbling from their mouths. He sobbed until the energy drained out of him, and then he sat, still and silent, bombarded by abstract images and emotions. Traces of thoughts he once had, pain he once endured.

After a while of this, he shuffled Ezekiel's arm off his shoulder. "I'll go to sleep now."

When the old man started struggling to get up, Zarius hurried over and gave him a hand. DK took one final glance at them both, painted in shimmering warmth by the fire, and turned to the wall.

15

Over the next week, Zarius got a sense of what DK must have been like before he arrived. DK never left the hovel except to shit and "borrow" food from Ezekiel. The rest of the time, he either slept or sat in his bed, staring at the fire, if there was one, or right at the wall. At Ezekiel's recommendation, Zarius didn't bother him. At first, he was too scared to anyway. After a few days, though, he filled up with so much despair that he thought he might drown in his sleep.

Without any other recourse, Zarius took up his own training. He resumed the rigorous schedule DK had laid out for them, and now he did it without having to be dragged out of bed every morning. He got himself up and ran for miles. He went to the dilapidated, little-used sparring pits nestled in one corner of Ten-Berry and set up a wooden dummy he and DK had made, against which he practiced all the moves DK had shown him. He even went to the little bald patch of grass in the hills outside the village where he tried and failed to meditate. But he kept trying. Over and over and over again.

Activity helped abate his anxiety, but only some. Every time Zarius returned to the hovel and found DK in the same spot, he shuddered. It was unnatural. He realized how much DK had changed since those first few days in the dead of winter, and now it seemed he had regressed past even that point. DK barely spoke, no matter what approach Zarius tried. Even when Zarius prodded to get some advice out of him for a sword move or a piece of footwork that was troubling him, DK just sat there, mute.

One night, Zarius lost precious control of his emotions. He couldn't help it. The sight of DK sitting there, gazing at a fire he would only build when Zarius wasn't around, so unnerved him that he finally snapped.

"Is this what you are now?" Zarius asked, rising up from his bed on exhausted legs. "Is this all you're gonna do? You won't even *talk* to me? Come on, DK. The shit is over. You can't just . . . you can't just *leave me here*, man. I *need* you. I need your help. I can't do all this on my own. *Please*."

DK's eyes smoked as he fastened such a hard gaze on Zarius that it stole the next words out of his throat. "Are you done?" DK asked him.

"You're just gonna let her win?" Zarius asked. "One punch and you're down?"

"You're a child. You don't know anything."

Zarius slumped into his bed, stinging. He rolled over to face the wall and ground his teeth in a raging anguish, long into the night.

The next morning, he attacked his training, but a looming cloud of hopelessness gathered over him. He could run to all the ends of the earth. He could practice what he knew. But he couldn't teach himself new moves. He couldn't show himself how to go on patrol. Or could he?

Another agonizing week passed, but finally, one evening, Zarius hurried over to Ezekiel's forge. He knocked eagerly and entered, and he found the old man hard at work. When the door clunked shut, though, Ezekiel turned around and beamed when he saw Zarius.

"Hey hold on," said Ezekiel. He grabbed a black sooty rag and smeared it across his charcoal hands.

Ezekiel walked over to a wooden rack and pulled a sword off it. A real sword. There was nothing fanciful about it. No ornate engravings or ostentatious caps on the quillons. But it was real. It existed, and Ezekiel passed it into Zarius's hands.

In awe, Zarius held the leather grip and turned the sword over, examining the blade. He gave it a twirl, weighing it in his hand. No, it wasn't fancy. But it was strong, sound, and balanced. Even Zarius, the uninitiated, knew it was a fine piece of work, and he looked up at Ezekiel with a proud and gracious grin.

"Ezekiel. Thank you."

Smiling, Ezekiel clapped a hand against one shoulder. "I know you'll use it well. Here, I've got some more for you. Sorry it's taking longer than I thought."

Ezekiel produced a piece of armor—the chainmail shirt with all those plates fastened onto it. A new sheath with a belt that he measured against Zarius's waist along with a leather skirt in place of a hauberk. Hand guards. Shin guards. And to top it all off, a helmet.

"Holy shit," Zarius breathed.

Ezekiel took the sword from him and set it down, exchanging it for the helmet. "Here, try it on."

It was a tall, cylindrical helmet with a flat top and a big faceplate. Zarius tried it on and was surprised to find it slid snugly over his head. He flipped the faceplate up and grinned at Ezekiel.

"This is so cool."

Ezekiel smiled back. "It's not really the style anymore, but the trader had one, and I thought it looked about right for you. None of it's polished much, not what I made anyway. Hard to do it all yourself. But it's strong. You're gonna have to wear that chainmail a couple times and tell me how it fits, where the gaps are. I'm sure it'll need some adjustments, but that's a start."

Zarius removed the helmet and held it before him like an icon, gazing into its rectangular eyeholes. "I don't know what to say. Thank you."

"Nonsense. It was my pleasure." He picked up Zarius's sword and admired it. "I used to get quite a kick out of making things for Christian. Not sure why I liked it so much. I guess it just doesn't feel as much like work when you get to see where it's going and what it's being used for."

"I'll try to make you proud."

"Not at all Zarius." Ezekiel patted his shoulder again. "I'm proud already."

The smile slowly faded from Zarius's face as he gazed into the eyeholes of the helmet, and Ezekiel watched him.

"He'll come around," said Ezekiel. That damn wise old man. "It might not seem like it now, but all we can do is believe in him."

"I don't even know when I'll get to use this." Zarius resisted the urge to drop the helmet to the floor. "I don't know when he'll show me." He meant more than just how to wear a helmet.

"Do what you can on your own. If you stick to it, I think he'll follow suit. As much as you feel like you need him, he needs you right now. He needs you to keep being you."

Somber, Zarius nodded. He ferried all the precious items home in multiple trips because of the weight, and DK said not a word as Zarius slowly collected the makings of a Knight at the foot of his bed. Part of him hoped there'd be something. Some glimmer of recognition, some words of encouragement, but the room stayed barren. Still, Zarius was proud. Beyond happy. To have so many possessions he could call his own was as foreign as it was inspiring.

And he decided right then to follow Ezekiel's advice. He would keep being himself, even if that meant leaving DK behind.

The next morning, Zarius rose early and began sorting through all the pieces of armor. In a long, awkward process, he began to don his partial steel suit. Several times, he realized one piece was supposed to go under another, so he'd take it all off and start over. After almost an hour, though, he stood at the foot of his bed, gunmetal gray, weighed down by almost thirty extra pounds. The sensation was strange, and Zarius stepped back and forth from foot to foot, adjusting to it.

Finally, Zarius took a deep breath and shrugged. He picked up the waterskin he'd filled the night before and slung it around his back. He took a moment to admire his sword before slipping it into the sheath. His armor clanked and creaked as he went over and fetched up a piece of bread and some salted meat, which he set after immediately. After a few minutes, he stifled a belch and went to the door.

"Where are you going?"

Zarius jumped. He didn't even notice DK was awake. When he turned back, moving his shoulders and head together, he was surprised and a little startled to see anger boiling on DK's face.

"Uhh. I'm going on a patrol."

"You don't know how to do that."

Zarius shrugged with an air of defiance. "Guess I'll have to figure it out then, won't I?"

"You *can't* go on a fucking patrol."

"Why not?"

DK rose to his feet. "Because you won't find shit. And if you do, you'll get yourself *killed*. You barely know how to fight."

"I told you I came here to learn to be a Knight." He turned back to the door. "If you won't teach me, I'll do it myself."

As soon as Zarius opened the door, DK was there, slamming it shut and squeezing between it and Zarius.

"What the fuck," Zarius said as he lurched back a step. "Get the fuck out of the way."

"You can't go on a fucking patrol," DK snarled.

"Watch me, bitch," Zarius growled.

Fury lit up DK's eyes, but Zarius was wearing a full suit of armor. Maybe that emboldened him. Maybe it was despair emitted as anger. But he knew right then that he would not be stopped from leaving. Zarius stepped up and shoved DK out of the way with both arms. DK stumbled off to the side, and Zarius yanked the door open. Morning Sunlight poured in through the opening, shining off of Zarius's armor.

"Zarius *wait*," DK barked.

Something made Zarius pause. Barring himself in the doorway, he turned one last time and looked at DK.

"Hold on," DK said, softer. "Wait for me."

Hope soared in Zarius's chest, as delicate as a robin egg. He betrayed none of it, only raising an eyebrow under his faceplate. "What?"

"I said wait for me," DK grumbled. He opened the rotting, split trunk in the corner of the room by his bed and started dumping out old armor. Zarius watched in silence, still in disbelief. As if it were all just a trick.

"Come on," DK waved a hand at him. "You've gotta take all that shit off."

Zarius gripped the doorway and sneered. "Why?"

"Cause you fucking did it all wrong. You've got straps and shit sticking out all over the place. Take it off. I'll help you."

16

Little more than fear occupied DK's mind as he opened the door and stepped into the Sunlight. All he had otherwise was a desperate certainty that he could *not* let Zarius go out there alone. First time in armor, first time with a real sword. No. If something happened to him, it would be blood on DK's hands. Worse than seeing an apprentice get injured, though, DK would be letting something bad happen to a friend. A real, honest friend. And that much, even in his terror, he could not stomach.

Apprehension squeezed his gut as he led a jubilant Zarius down the street, toward the edge of the village. As they approached the low stone wall with a haphazard gash through it, DK saw Patrick Killington leaning on it with a shoddy spear in hand. His curly red hair glowed like fire in the Sunlight, and even with his eyes closed, his face threatened a wide, toothy grin, like his mouth could only be shaped otherwise by force.

The heaviness of their steps roused Patrick. His eyes fluttered open, and when he saw Zarius and DK, his jaw dropped. He made a show of rubbing his eyes, pinching his arm, and then came scampering toward them.

"Now there ain't no way, that's a blizzard in hell. No way. *Christian*? That you under there?"

DK slid back his faceplate. His helmet was a stout, rounded one, his armor completer and more refined than Zarius's. Over time, Ezekiel had either forged or traded for what resembled a whole set, and even DK felt like he struck an imposing figure in it. He managed a grin, though his stomach was in knots and his mind on fire.

"*Hell*," Patrick said, stopping in front of them. "Heaven almighty. I'll say. *Christian*. It's been, well I haven't seen you in all that getup in . . ."

"Years," DK finished.

"Must be," said Patrick. He had a hand on his hip, lips never quite closing all the way. "And this must be Zarius back here?"

Zarius flipped his own faceplate up. "Hey Patrick."

"*Damn*. Now ain't I the odd one out. You got an extra set somewhere?"

DK chuckled, but it was strained. "Somebody's gotta watch Ten-Berry for us while we're gone."

Patrick snapped into a quick salute that made Zarius laugh. "Aye aye captain. First Lieutenant of the Ten-Berry Guards at your service."

Smirking, DK nodded. "Yeah. Something like that."

"I see you still got this old thing too." Patrick tugged at the faded blue tunic over DK's chest plate. It featured a cartoonish painting of the Sun that DK had done himself, also faded by time. The tunic sported a few holes, from moths or old sword slashes, and DK's cheeks burned a little as Patrick brought attention to it.

"Yeah," he said. "Superstition or something, I guess."

"Well hell, I like it," said Patrick. "Sun looks kinda *crazy* there. That crazy face you put on it. Damn. Well you're goin *out* out, then. Patrollin?"

"Patrollin," DK repeated. He almost choked on the word.

"That's somethin alright. They all said you was done for good. No hide nor hair of the Day Knight, that's what they said. Bunch of morons."

"We'll find out who the morons are."

Patrick burst into laughter, doubling over with one hand on his knee. He stood up chuckling, nodding, winking at them. "That's a good one. Damn good. Well hell, don't let me stand in your way."

Smiling uneasily, DK nodded. "Thanks Patrick. Keep an eye on things."

Patrick saluted again as they walked past him. "For God and country, captain."

They walked through the gate and out into the wide open world.

"I think he might be in love with you," said Zarius.

"Shut up," said DK. "He just gets excited."

"No shit. I thought he might piss himself."

"I used to see him all the time going in and out. I guess he missed me."

"He wasn't the only one."

DK didn't respond. It was strange, being greeted like that. Throw on a suit of armor, hold your chest high, and people reacted. It was like coming back as his own ghost, even hearing the words "Day Knight" so often again. A dead man's name, and DK was wearing his armor, carrying his sword.

Long strips of white, voluminous clouds streaked the pale blue sky above them. The Sun was on its way up, rung by rung, ascending toward the heavens. Warmth cascaded down, filtered by the clouds, and DK let his mind be drawn to it. In fact, he veered off the path and started working backwards at an angle.

"Ah man," said Zarius from behind him. "No. Come on."

"We'll meditate first," said DK.

Zarius groaned loud and long, tipping his whole head back.

"Stop being a baby."

"Fucking meditation. Great. I was worried you'd forget."

DK looked back at him. "Hey, you're lucky I'm here at all."

"I was literally about to go without you."

"You heard me." DK led the way through the rising hills until they reached the spot. He settled on his worn patch of dirt, setting his helmet next to him, letting the Sunlight blanket his face. Zarius had some difficulty in getting to the ground, but he managed it.

"Jesus," he said. "I'm already sweating like a pig."

"Better get used to that," said DK as he closed his eyes. "We've got a long road ahead of us."

"Where are we gonna go?"

"I don't know."

"Quail Lake?"

DK opened his eyes and fixed them on Zarius. "No."

Zarius held his gaze for a moment. "Will we ever go back?"

"Does that matter right now? Really?" DK shut his eyes again and didn't respond when Zarius grumbled something under his breath.

Silence took hold, but it was a silence full of life. Air moving within itself, filling DK's ears. A breeze tiptoed through the grass. The Sunlight caressed his face, warm and reassuring. It soaked through his pores, lining his veins, massaging his spirit. DK focused on his breath. Long, steady draws in, hold, smooth exhalation, hold. He repeated this several times, each time going deeper. The harder he focused, the more his mind ceased to exist at all. Thoughts were like birds in a distant sky. He could see them. Maybe they passed in front of the Sun. But they had no ownership over him.

An ugly face reared against the placid imagery, and that was her. DK's mind tensed up, but his body remained still. The blurred red face of a demon, unknowable yet unmistakable. The Sunlight brought it not into focus but perspective. It was a red face superimposed over a calm blue sky. Then it was a blue sky over a red face. Then the face was gone.

DK knew she was out there, and he knew that she knew *he* was out here. Quail Lake told him enough. The bog witch knew. She knew the Day Knight was back. Just as word spread through Ten-Berry, energy spread through the invisible planes. A vibration long dormant resumed again when the Day Knight spoke his own name, and the witch's eyes flew open.

That deer was nothing but a message. Born again to die again. The bog witch didn't spend these last two years in hiding as he did. No. She worked. The nebulous certainty of it brought goosebumps to DK's skin. She remembered him all too well, and she wanted him more than ever. Right then, DK knew in his soul—though he would later debate the matter with himself—he knew, in that moment, that the story he started long ago would not end until he killed her.

Those slow, deep breaths blunted each nagging thought in turn. All that terrible anxiety that gripped him for those days after Quail Lake began to subside. The armor on his back, the familiarity of it, encouraged him. His tunic heated up under the Sunlight, and he felt the Sun emblazoned not only on his chest but his spirit. He was the Day Knight. No matter what happened, no matter what unholy destruction gave him his end. From that moment, he would never relinquish or even question the title again. It was his. Eternal, the Day Knight.

An indiscriminate amount of time passed before DK rose to the surface and opened his eyes. His thoughts didn't swarm in, rather lined up for consideration. After a moment, he sniffed and stood up, and Zarius hopped right to his feet. Sweat ran down both of their faces, and DK donned his helmet.

"Alright," he said. "Let's go."

17

By the time they made it to the first rocky outcroppings of the badlands north of Ten-Berry, Zarius was panting and sweating. His underclothes were soaked all the way through. The armor weighed and chafed on him. Even with his faceplate up, he felt like he couldn't breathe. The Sun, once a tentative ally, was now his mortal enemy, and he cursed it. It was trying to cook him alive.

"Christ," Zarius gasped when DK finally stopped to take a breather.

"Eyes bigger than your legs?" DK asked.

"Fuck you."

DK didn't so much as smirk. He took off his helmet and leaned against a steep rock wall. Crumbles of siltstone rattled off his armor. His hair was slick and stringy, the deep tan on his face tinged with red.

"What's wrong?" Zarius asked, catching his breath.

"I don't know," said DK. "I have a bad feeling."

"We're gonna be *fine*."

"And how much would you be worth if we weren't? You're exhausted. If we got in a swordfight right now, could I count on you?"

This brought Zarius rearing up to full height and cut the gasps out of his throat. "Fight me then, bitch."

"I'm not the one you'd need to be worried about," DK shot back. "This isn't a fucking game."

"I know that."

"Do you? Here you basically fuckin made me come out here when I didn't want to. Now you're gasping like a dying fish and I'm just wondering what if the fucking bog witch sent worse than a rotting deer this time?"

Zarius stood there, gazing at him. A bright green grasshopper took flight between them. "You think that thing was from the bog witch?"

"Of course it was." DK shook his head, wearing a disgusted scowl. "I was stupid to think I could just . . . that nothing would happen. She sent it as a warning, and that won't be the last thing we see."

"Then why wait?" Zarius asked. "I say good. Let her come find us. Saves us the trouble."

DK laughed. "You have no idea what you're talking about."

"How should I? You've barely told me anything."

DK's face darkened. "You don't wanna know."

"Well I'll need to eventually, won't I? How else am I supposed to help you kill her?"

A long pause preceded DK's next words. "I would never take an apprentice in there."

Zarius balled his fists, then stormed past DK and into a wide, shallow ravine surrounded by rock faces. He took several steps, paused, and saw DK adjusting his helmet and following along. Zarius steeled himself and continued. The gravity in DK's words joined the weight of the armor on his back.

It wasn't just that DK believed there was danger; it was the nature of the danger. Zarius heard the fear in DK's voice when he spoke of the bog witch, as if her name alone carried some kind of supernatural invocation for violence, or worse. Despite his best efforts, Zarius felt a few cold worms of fear wriggling under his armor.

They navigated through the badlands. High walls of soft, earth-colored stone. Weeds and grass sprouted wherever the soil could cling on. The Sun was hot, but the air moved in cool, quick channels through the rock valleys. They saw a few diamond-backed snakes curled up on flat stones, and Zarius steered well clear of them. A couple of hawks wheeled around far above them, winged shadows unbound from their casters, lost to the infinite sky.

After another hour, they reached the top of the rise of badlands, where layers of limestone and sandstone stacked vigorously to create a large bluff. Climbing was out of the question, but they managed to scramble up one reasonable stone wall to the base.

As soon as Zarius crested this hill, he sat right down, gasping, but he couldn't tear his eyes away from the vista spreading before him. They had gained some good elevation over Ten-Berry, and the village lay nestled in the fields of tallgrass, as if some grand farmer had once lost a seed that sprouted a little outpost instead of crops. Hundreds of gentle hills gave texture to the sprawling acres of untamed grasses. Stands of cottonwoods wove through like veins. A gust of wind made the whole landscape wave like a flag.

Overhead, the Sun cast light in all directions like a porthole into heaven. Scattered clouds trotted across the sky in haste. Zarius took it all in, even he of short attention span. The view held him in a soft, insistent grip until he slipped free and turned to DK.

"Pretty cool," he said.

Silent, DK just nodded. He slicked his wet hair back over his head and pulled out his waterskin to take a long drink.

Zarius mimicked him, relishing even the hot flow of stale water over his tongue. He wanted to say *Fuck I'm tired* but thought better of it. His eyes drifted over the landscape. The badlands surrounded the bluff on all sides for a good distance. Movement caught his eye off to the right.

Zarius stood right up, looking hard.

"What is it?" DK jumped up next to him.

"See that?" Zarius pointed.

DK followed his finger, staring for several seconds. The movement disappeared behind a rocky hill. "Looked like people?"

"I think I saw a couple heads," Zarius said.

They watched for a moment but didn't see anything else. "Eh," said DK. "People hike around up here. It is a nice day." He settled back to the ground, but Zarius remained upright.

A few seconds later, he saw a flash from that same spot—the Sun reflecting off of steel.

"Holy shit," Zarius said. "I think there's people in armor too."

DK scrambled up even faster and looked again, but the culprit was gone. "You sure?" He looked hard at Zarius.

"Pretty sure. The Sun reflected off something, and now it's gone."

"Fuck. Alright, let's go check it out."

They slid down the hill back into the valleys of stone and made off in the general direction of the movement. Zarius was surprised when DK took off at a light jog. That meant he thought it might be serious. A flare of exhilaration lit up, but it was quickly dashed by exertion. Even a mild trot in this armor was no joke.

Minutes passed as they weaved through the corridors. Zarius was already wondering how DK would admonish him for wasting their time and energy as they came toward the sloping end of the badlands. At the same time, though, Zarius heard a muffled, high-pitched scream, and DK broke into a sprint. They flushed out of the rock halls and saw a flurry of movement to their left, behind a grassy knoll.

Three men had two girls pinned to the ground. One man was huge, the Sun shining off his bald head. He had several haphazard pieces of armor strapped to his body, and a sword sat sticking out of the grass beside him. A skinny man had his knee pressed to one girl's neck, brandishing a dagger. The big bald guy was in the middle of pulling the third man—short and stout—off one of the girls and setting upon her himself, hands going up under her skirts.

"*Hey,*" DK bellowed as they charged toward them.

The men all started scrambling to their feet as DK approached to within a stone's throw of them. Zarius, for all his effort, lagged behind, but the nascent sense of confrontation started pumping adrenaline into his veins, blunting his fatigue.

"Get the fuck off of them," DK growled, wielding his sword.

"Who the *fuck* are you guys?" asked the big guy, his voice gruff and hoarse. He looked pissed.

"Let them go," DK said.

The leader of the group looked back at the girls, who now huddled together at the bottom of the hill, crying and hiding their faces. His two cohorts gathered beside him.

"Christ they got *knights* out *here*?" the skinny man cried.

"These ain't no knights." The bald one sneered. "Look at his tunic. These are some local rich boys playing dress up."

"I don't know, Derrick. Look at how he's—"

Derrick smacked the skinny man hard upside the head, making him stagger. "Why the *fuck* would you say my name? You fucking dumbass. *Monty,*" he said loudly. "How bout you *Peter*? What do you think?"

Peter, the squat one, huddled close behind Derrick as if he were a wall. "You're the only one's got armor. And they got swords. Monty and I got daggers."

"You think they're legit?" Derrick asked, shaking his head.

DK and Zarius had advanced to within a few paces. Zarius's heart was pounding. He was surprised it didn't turn his armor into a steel drum for all of them to hear.

"Look at that one," said Derrick, pointing at Zarius, who stood a few steps behind DK. "He's chickenshit."

Peter's anguished face didn't change. "I don't think—"

"You faggots are going to fight," Derrick barked at them. "Or I'll kill you myself."

DK turned over his shoulder and spoke to Zarius through his helmet. "I'll take the big one and one of the others. You take the other. Z, you good?"

Zarius couldn't answer. Terror and adrenaline combined in a frantic concoction that stirred his brain like a butterchurn. In one moment, everything DK ever said about combat made sense. The immediacy and immensity of it. Death was now at hand. The ground was full of graves. One wrong move might be his last, and a minute ago, he was enjoying the view of a nice landscape without another thought in the world.

"Z," DK snapped. "*Are you good?*"

"See?" Derrick crowed, violence glowing in his eyes. "*Come on.*" He charged, but his cronies hesitated, hovering near the sniffling girls.

DK bolted forward to meet him. They each cranked back, and their swords met in the middle with a crash that echoed across the grass.

Whanggggg.

The impact pushed DK and Derrick both back a step, but they closed the gap and connected again.

Shkank. Shkinggg. Whanngggg.

The harsh melody of steel on steel, power on power. Each man delivered heavy shots that the other absorbed and returned. Zarius watched, stunned, as DK executed steps and moves with determined precision. Real combat, real swords, but he was as measured as during a training exercise.

Even Derrick's buddies looked shellshocked by the eruption of violence. Two men slashed and jabbed at each other, trying to draw blood, while the others just stood by and watched.

"*Come on,*" Derrick bellowed.

The rage in his voice sparked Monty and Peter into action. Peter charged toward Derrick like a scolded dog called to heel, and Monty jumped from foot to foot for a moment before he came around the unfolding duel and made for Zarius.

The moment came. At the last possible second, Zarius's hands snapped to action. His sword came to guard, he set his feet, and when Monty came slashing at him wildly with a long, gleaming dagger, Zarius tracked the blade and deflected it.

Shkank.

Monty swung again, but Zarius stepped back and let the blade pass by. When he went to step in to take a shot, though, Monty deftly flicked his wrist back. Zarius tried to lunge out of the way, but the dagger screeched over the steel of his helmet and glanced off. Adrenaline pumping, Zarius threw his sword up in desperation. His feet were sloppy, his hands erratic, but his long blade and the quick swing caught Monty too close to avoid it. Monty tried to angle his dagger to deflect the blow, but he didn't quite adjust in time. Two of his fingers caught the business end of the sword. Blood spurted from his hand as two digits tumbled to the grass.

Monty screamed like a banshee and went reeling away. His dropped his dagger as he clutched his wounded hand into his gut.

Blood began to soak his shirt as he hobbled off in no direction, howling. Stunned, Zarius just stood there for a moment, as if he expected another blow to materialize out of thin air. Then he managed to put his eyes on DK.

Derrick had Peter by the back of the shirt, holding him like a big meat shield while Peter slashed wildly with his dagger. *"Go,"* Derrick shouted. He shoved Peter forward. DK caught him across the torso with an arcing swing that drew a crimson line across his gut and sent him stumbling off to the side. Derrick tried to spring a trap against the momentum of DK's sword, but the Day Knight let his swing carry him out of harm's way to reset.

Again, DK and Derrick faced each other. Peter was on the ground, groaning, trying to drag himself to safety. Monty was on his way toward a distant thicket of trees, howls echoing back to them. The girls' eyes flew about for a couple moments before they got up and booked it. Derrick turned to watch them go, and he showed his teeth in a vicious sneer.

"You ruined my dinner."

Zarius approached behind DK, but when he got close, DK shoved a hand through the air. *"No.* Stay back, Z."

Heart still flying, Zarius took a moment to process what he said. "But there's two of us."

"He knows you ain't salty enough," Derrick spat, grinning. "This is a fight between men."

Rage dropped a brick on Zarius's brain, but the reverberating impact of steel on steel kept him rooted. DK and Derrick clashed again, stepping into each other. Every failed slash and missed strike further inflated the vein pulsing on Derrick's forehead. Rivulets of sweat shone on his face and head and dripped from his beard. But he was ferocious.

Shkaannggg. Whannggggg. Shunk.

Derrick hammered DK's guard two times, the second shot more powerful than the first, and then he delivered a straight jab that bypassed DK's defense and jammed straight into one side of his chest plate. DK gasped and staggered back a couple steps, and Zarius almost screamed as Derrick bore down on him.

In an instant, DK reset his feet and parried Derrick's next swing. He followed with a riposte of his own that Derrick narrowly avoided, and the cascade of violence ceased as quickly as it started. They were two asteroids on a collision course. Even Zarius knew only one of them was leaving the field alive.

"Who are you anyway?" Derrick asked, panting. "Where'd a pissant like you learn to fight?"

DK didn't respond. He remained in a fighting stance, forcing Derrick to stay alert, but Zarius could see a slight hunch in DK's posture. He was in pain from that shot Derrick landed, but Zarius didn't see any blood leaking down his pants. The armor did its job, but DK still looked injured. Sweat and body odor fouled the air.

"Got you pretty good, eh?" Derrick asked. He threw his head toward Zarius. "Don't trust your *bitch* to get the job done?"

The rage surged back like a thunderclap, booming through Zarius's skull. Bitch? *Bitch?* He'd show this fat fuck a bitch. DK needed help. Zarius was here. He ran forward, cocking his sword way back over his shoulder.

"*No*," DK yelled.

They all moved at the same time.

With Zarius's sword out of reach, his body was exposed. Derrick let him take one extra step forward before he flicked his lighter, smaller weapon forward. The tip of Derrick's blade made right for Zarius's unarmored groin, but DK sprawled forward and jabbed. The tip of his sword met the flat side of Derrick's and pushed it just wide enough to miss Zarius.

Thrown off by the flurry of movement and a brief certainty that he was about to be skewered, Zarius brought his sword down in a haphazard swing that thudded off of Derrick's shoulder plate. The momentum took Zarius's sword into the grass, and his forearms sang as he tried to pull his weapon up and lunge backward at the same time. But Derrick had bigger aspirations.

DK's effort to save Zarius left him scrambling to get up from the ground, armor creaking and clunking as he tried to get up. Derrick went to stab into his chainmail and instead hit plate armor, so he resorted to brute force. He cranked back and landed two huge shots against the mail on DK's side, and DK gasped and sputtered and couldn't pull himself out of a heap.

Derrick's eyes scanned for an opening until DK let out an agonized holler and surged up. He brought his sword up with him, but Derrick sidestepped it. DK pushed the offensive. Zarius couldn't move, couldn't think as DK swung harder and quicker than ever. Caught on his heels, Derrick backed up, deflected a blow, turned away another, then ate one against the armor on his right arm. When DK swung again, Derrick tried to raise a guard, but his lame arm was a tick slow. DK swung his blade just over the top of Derrick's and drove into flesh.

Arterial blood spouted out of Derrick's neck. DK's sword almost took his head clean off, and as he tipped backward like a felled tree, it lifted off his shoulders. He hit the ground and his head bounced away only to snap back, still connected by a fraction of skin and tendons. Blood went everywhere. Derrick's eyes glazed over with shock, but he managed a glint of malice as, somehow, he focused on DK for one more split second. His mouth was moving, though no words came out, and he died with a nascent scream of anguish frozen on his face.

DK trembled where he stood, gazing down at the gore. Zarius

turned away in horror. Whatever he thought he knew or understood about Knighthood melted in Derrick's gushing blood. That almost-severed head. Stifled terror now came flushing through him, all the emotion he stuffed down during the fight. Tears welled in his eyes. Zarius had almost died. He was inches away from dying.

"You fucking *idiot*," DK bellowed.

Shocked, Zarius turned and saw DK with his helmet off, face bloodred, eyes alight with fury. "You almost got *killed*. You almost got *me* killed. I told you to stay back." He clamped his teeth together until he made little more than a continuous hiss. Zarius had never seen a look like that on DK's face, and he backed away, not even able to stammer.

"Where are you going?" DK asked, stepping forward. "*Huh?* Come look at what you did. *Look at what I had to do.*"

Zarius just shook his head and took another wobbly step back, but DK charged over and grabbed him by the chest plate. He dragged him toward the body, and Zarius dug his heels in.

"I *saw* it," he cried. "I'm sorry."

DK yanked Zarius clean off his feet and threw him. He landed right in the patch of muddy, blood-soaked earth. His face hit the ground and threw blood into the eyeholes of his helmet. It splashed into his mouth and nose. Groaning, Zarius scrabbled to get up and away, and Derrick's face appeared in his vision. Except it wasn't frozen anymore. It was blinking. The blood vessels burst in his eyes and turned his sclera red.

Zarius screamed and rolled away, and he heard the sickest, most gut-wrenching laughter even a nightmare couldn't imitate. He tore his helmet off his head. It had to be a mistake. A delusion. He wiped his face furiously, but when his eyes were clear, he saw Derrick's head tipping back and forth on the ground of its own volition, spilling laughter into the air.

"*What the fuck,*" Zarius screamed.

"Daaaayyyyy Kniiiggghhhtttt," Derrick drawled. "Come to where I can *see* you." His voice was different. Older and raspier.

It was all too much for Zarius. The fear along with the taste of another man's blood on his dry lips knocked him to the ground. He retched all over the grass as Derrick continued to giggle. His body began to flop and thrash on the ground.

"*Day Knight,*" he barked. "*Come here.*"

When Zarius picked his head up, he saw DK walking slowly toward the jostling corpse. When he got close enough, Derrick's body ceased to move, and the laughter became deeper and more demonic.

"There you aaarreeeeeee," he said. "I see you."

DK just stood there.

"Come home," Derrick cooed. "Come home or they *suffer.*"

In a flash, DK plunged his sword into the center of Derrick's face, and the foreign life evaporated. When DK withdrew his sword, he staggered back a couple steps, then went down on one knee, clutching his left side.

The first emotion to filter through Zarius's brain was unmitigated rage. The sequence of events played back for him, and a red balloon grew and grew in his head until it burst. He got up and ran at DK, who remained hunched over in pain, and speared into him from the side. They both went sprawling, and DK started gasping and kicking his legs in agony. Zarius scrambled up to his feet, blood on his face, blood in the creases of his palms, and screamed.

"*You fucking* bitch. *What the fuck was that? Why'd you do that to me?*"

Zarius picked up DK's helmet and spiked it into the ground, narrowly missing his master's exposed head. "*You fucking . . . You motherfucker.*" Zarius's eyes burned. His throat closed up.

As soon as the outburst began, it was over. The energy drained out of him. Zarius walked over, picked DK's helmet up again, and threw it as far as he could. With that, he made toward Ten-Berry all alone. Tears sprang from his eyes and streaked the dead man's blood on his face. He let out a couple heavy sobs, then stifled them. His head was on fire.

18

Anger lasted a short time, only a fraction of the journey back to Ten-Berry. What DK was left to walk with was the constant throbbing in his side and a massive specter of regret. Yes, the appearance of the bog witch terrified him, but somehow, it was he who created something even worse.

He relived those moments where fury took control over and over again. The way he dragged Zarius—his apprentice, his *friend*—over to a corpse and threw him down in a puddle of blood. Because DK was angry. It didn't matter if the anger was justified. Nothing could be so egregious to warrant a reaction like that. Every time he saw it, DK groaned and shook his head, as if somehow he could rewrite the past, if only he tortured himself enough.

Oh God. What if Zarius left? What if that loss of judgement and control cost DK everything? He couldn't be the Day Knight by himself. He knew that much. Having Zarius gave him confidence, a little more courage. The sight of that deer almost broke him. This—the witch *speaking* to him through a corpse—should have killed him. But that same fear couldn't find him now. The shame and guilt were so much worse.

When DK made it back to Ten-Berry, it was almost dark. He staggered down the street and pushed through his door. The hovel was dark and empty. Of course Zarius wasn't there, not even his armor. DK was certain that his apprentice was already on the way back to Endlin, where not even the lowest of street dogs would betray him in the way DK just had. DK groaned and hissed, and tears leaked out of his eyes.

Each strap of armor he undid sent pain shooting through his ribs. The whole process took half an hour, and when he finished, he didn't have so much as the energy to go get fresh water. He let himself down into bed, crying softly, and despite his anguish, exhaustion drove him straight to sleep.

When he woke up the next morning, he couldn't move. Even breathing cost him a sharp stab of pain. So that was all he could do. Lie there and take painstaking breath after painstaking breath. His tongue stuck to the roof of his mouth it was so dry, but his waterskin was empty and not even close enough to reach.

Hours passed. Someone knocked at the door. DK couldn't even grunt, but he wanted to scream. The knock came again, and the door cracked open.

"Christian?" It opened a little farther, and Ezekiel's head poked in. His eyes found DK, and he let out a little gasp as he rushed in and over to DK's side.

"Christian," he breathed. "Oh thank God." He scanned DK's face and body. "You're hurt. Zarius wouldn't tell me anything. Do you need a doctor, son? What do you need?"

"Water," DK croaked. The effort of that single word made his whole face twist up.

Without another word, Ezekiel hurried away. A few minutes later, he returned with a bucket of water. He filled DK's waterskin and tried to get it to his lips, but DK couldn't drink it from his position.

"Sit up," said DK.

Ezekiel cringed, probably because of the sweat already shining on DK's forehead, but he complied. He got his hands under DK's shoulders and managed to help him sit up. DK couldn't even gasp at the pain. The agony robbed every ounce of his effort and didn't cease as he sucked down mouthfuls of water with Ezekiel's help.

Cradling his wounded side, DK let the waterskin fall. "Zarius."

Ezekiel paused for too long, blinked too much. "Well, he said he didn't want me to tell you anything. But he's *safe*. I will tell you that much."

"Still in Ten-Berry?"

"Yes yes, still in Ten-Berry."

DK breathed a shuddering sigh of relief.

Ezekiel's face drooped. "Oh Christian. What happened?"

Now it was DK's turn to be silent for a while. He frowned down into his lap. "Fight. Bog witch."

"*Again?*" Ezekiel's voice cracked like a rusty hinge breaking loose. "But what did . . ." He shook his head. "I don't understand."

Rocking a little where he sat, DK motioned Ezekiel closer. He couldn't keep pushing out these single word explanations. He beckoned Ezekiel even closer until the old man was seated on the floor right next to him, leaning toward DK's face.

"We found some bandits," DK whispered. "About to rape some girls. We stopped them. I killed one of them, probably two. I . . . lost my temper, and I threw Zarius down on the body. Then the bog witch spoke through it."

"Through the *corpse?*"

DK nodded.

Ezekiel looked near panic. "What did she say?"

The voice played through DK's head and made him wither. "She wants me to go back."

Ezekiel shuffled to let his back rest against the wall as his face bled to a vivid pale. "That's what she said?"

Jaw clenched, DK nodded. A day ago, he'd been living in a petrified haze of terror over the same subject. When he saw that deer, that portent of evil, his mind broke down. All those memories from the past surged up like a fat, greasy gas bubble from the bottom of a swamp. They ran through him like wildfire, and he probably would have let it kill him, let it kill whatever identity he had just managed to reclaim. If not for Zarius.

Zarius marched into the burned forest and acted as though it had no right to burn, as if he couldn't see the damage. And when Zarius demanded answers, demanded progress, DK complied. That's what had kept him going, what had let him shake it off.

Now, though, he felt nothing but rage and disgust. He trembled where he sat. The bog witch took everything from him once, and it wasn't enough. When he clung to life and dared to show his face again, she came back. She'd been waiting, but she never interrupted his suffering. For years, she left him to waste away. Only when he dared to reach for life did she show herself again, and now he sealed her away in absolute hatred, a sliver trapped forever in his brain.

"Christian?" Ezekiel breathed, leaning forward. "Are you okay, son?"

DK squeezed his fists so hard that his overgrown fingernails pressed little half-moons into his palm. "I'm gonna kill her."

"*Christian*," Ezekiel snapped. "Don't go warmonger on me now. You're hurt. *Zarius* is hurt, and it sounds like you're the one who hurt him. You need to fix that and yourself. You've only *just* started doing this again. You've been through too much to go charging into the lions' den. I *know* you're wiser than that."

The anger ebbed out of him, leaving DK even more exhausted,

but the determination did not. He would not give himself up to fear, never again, but Ezekiel was right. The pain of his slight against Zarius was as fresh and raw as ever, and he knew that it would take time to right, if it could be righted at all.

"I need to rest," DK whispered. He guzzled down more water, this time without help, and slowly let himself roll back onto the pile of hay and blankets.

Without another word, Ezekiel got up and left. Late afternoon Sunlight filtered through the slats of the door, and DK gripped it with his eyes. He pulled the Light in and wrapped it around his head like a scarf. Let it protect him, let it heal him. He humbly implored the Sun to assuage his ailing mind and to ease Zarius's suffering.

19

The tavern rocked back and forth like a boat on a raging river. Zarius sat in a chair at a table with three men he didn't know. They were laughing and banging their mugs together, and each time they did, Zarius would sprout a wavering smile and hold up his own mug. Ale sloshed everywhere as they slammed their drinks into his, and they'd laugh and laugh as he tried to sip his drink only to spill half of it. The smell of ale pervaded his nose, probably because he accidentally inhaled some earlier. His ears were hot.

Finally, though, he wasn't thinking about the head that wouldn't stop talking even when its body was a foot away. Wasn't thinking about the blood that he kept seeing on his palms no matter how vigorously he scrubbed them. He drank the memories into submission, and that was enough, that was what he needed. He didn't care what happened after that so long as the memories stopped tormenting him.

Zarius kept stretching his face like he was waking up out of a deep slumber only for that grin to return. He'd slouch back down in his chair, and his head would start drooping and drooping until it snapped back. He couldn't follow the conversation; it all just sounded like "Blah blah blah, hah hah hah." But he'd nod his head or shrug his shoulders when it seemed like the appropriate response.

At some point, a new mug appeared in front of him, but when he took a sip of it, his lips pinched together, and he immediately dumped its contents onto the stone floor beside the table. His tablemates burst into uproarious laughter, and a figure materialized next to the table as if by conjuration. Zarius tipped his loose head up to one side and managed to distinguish Catherine, and she looked *angry*.

"You're hot," Zarius said.

The other guys at the table laughed so hard that they started choking, smacking each other on the back.

If her scowl were a blade, Zarius would've fallen to the floor in a heap of ribbons. "And you're wasted," Catherine said. "Time to go home, Zarius."

"FFFuck you, betch."

Catherine slapped him hard. One cheek stung like hell, and Zarius's body remained hunched to one side with the impact. The impact reverberated up and down from the top of his scalp to the base of his neck. Rage started growing within him, and he was about to stand up and confront her, maybe hit her back, when the laughter at the table turned to placating tones and apologies. A moment later, a couple pairs of arms scooped Zarius up under the armpits and walked him to the door and outside.

Zarius's new friends went so far as the threshold before they gave him a hearty shove that threw him into the dirt road. They chuckled among themselves as they returned into the tavern and shut the door. Apparently that was that. Zarius lay in the dirt for a while, breathing it in, letting off an errant belch here and there. He started to feel nauseous, so he sat up, got his hands under him, and fell over a couple times before managing to stand up.

The world rocked side to side, and so did he. He matched it like a seasoned sailor, and he made back for one of the three tavern doors he could see. A late stumble pushed him off course, though, and he went sprawling into the narrow alley between the tavern and another stone building. It reeked of piss, and that reminded him of something.

Using the wall for support, Zarius managed to stand up again, and he pulled his dick out and started pissing. Except the wall was directly in front of him, so his stream hit it and splattered everywhere, all over him. He noticed, but the force of pissing was so strong and so euphoric that he didn't want to stop, so he just kept going. It took a *long* time for it to stop, and his pants got soaked in the process. When it did stop, he just stood there, leaning against the wall with his dick out, smacking his dry mouth. After about a minute, he just plum fell over and passed out.

Zarius's eyes creaked open. As soon as he became aware, existence tortured him. A pulse throbbed so hard in the center of his head he thought for sure the vessel would split open and drown his brain in blood. His tongue was like sand, the rest of his mouth the desert. After somehow making it up to all fours, he vomited everything in his stomach.

Thin, watery chunks of puke puddled between his hands as acrid bile coated every inch of his esophagus. He retched again, torso scrunching with the effort, and only produced another few tablespoons of anything. Then the dry heaves set in. His entire body contracted only to eke out a series of choked groans. He shivered uncontrollably.

Zarius repeated this process for five minutes before the feeling resided, and even then, it only drifted far enough so as not to keep him on the ground. Clawing at the wall, he clambered to his feet. But how did he get here? Papery memories retraced his steps until fading out altogether. He didn't remember much, and the pungent odor of puke and urine didn't help. Banging into the stone walls on either side, Zarius staggered out of the alley. A weak violet on the horizon foretold dawn. Ten-Berry slept.

Before Zarius could orient himself, a wave of nausea sat him down, then put him on all fours again. He dry-heaved in the middle of the street like a sick feral dog. Pain emanated from every corner of his being; every cell threatened a mutiny.

From somewhere close, somebody opened a door and hollered, *"Fuck off."*

Jolted by the voice, Zarius managed to stave off another wave of retches. He forced himself to his feet and took off at a hurried stagger. He made his way along the outer edge of the town square to the next road and stumbled down it. Shortly on his left, he saw the shadowed pillars supporting the overhanging roof of the forge.

Detached from everything but the all-encompassing agony, Zarius managed to fumble through the big wooden door and complete one long fall onto the stone floor. As soon as he landed, he began to dry-heave again. He couldn't so much as find his hands and knees, so he just laid there convulsing while saliva and drops of bile leaked from his lips.

A rise of commotion entered the room as Ezekiel came in blind, sweeping his head in the darkness. "Who's there?" he asked. "Zarius?"

One retch stopped, and Zarius gripped the momentary reprieve as he gulped air. "Yes," he groaned.

"What happened?" Ezekiel cried, as if a barbarian horde were making for the front door.

Zarius wanted to die. "Drunk," he spat.

As Zarius started heaving again, Ezekiel returned to his bedroom and came back. Without a word, he deposited a bucket of water next to Zarius. Feeble, Zarius felt around until he found the bucket, and he dragged himself up to drink from it like a castaway.

Without another word, Ezekiel closed himself into his bedroom and left Zarius to his suffering. Eventually, after a couple hours of frequent and sporadic retching, Zarius's body wore out, and he lapsed into an exhausted slumber.

Zarius only slept for about an hour before slants of Sunlight crossed his face and brought him back to hell. Vicious cymbals crashed in his head every second. Every one of his senses was like a raw, open wound. He writhed on the ground, gasping, leaking tears and saliva. His body was empty, but his stomach revolted anyway.

More hoarse retches filled the room, long and resonant. He threw up the little water he'd managed to drink and then drank more. His body was a prison, his mind a shattered mirror. Every thought only pointed vile reproach back at him, and a heavy, uncertain anxiety took hold that he had ruined every facet of his life during one drunken stupor.

At some point, a reassuring presence came to Zarius's side, but he couldn't even lift his head. Ezekiel sat there, old bones on hard stones, and patted Zarius on the back as he twitched and writhed. For some reason, Zarius started to cry, and he hated himself for it. He hated everything, and he was sure that everything hated him. Everything except Ezekiel, and together, they sat there until the Sun was high in the sky and Zarius again collapsed into ragged slumber.

Full armor weighed on Zarius as he crept through darkened streets. Flies buzzed near him, settling on dark figures all around. If he stopped and listened long enough, he could hear the fleshy writhing of thousands of maggots. Corpses littered the narrow dirt road around him, swarming with larvae and insects, all tinted silver by a waxing gibbous directly overhead. Bright enough that Zarius could see his shadow on the ground, and he knew the cover of darkness would not conceal him.

Stealthy, Zarius crept between houses through twine clotheslines. Repulsive stenches emanated from every door and window. The incessant movement of flies and maggots invaded his ears, as if he were being consumed alive. Zarius came around one corner into a little clearing between houses, and he saw an emaciated red hound chewing at a corpse in the dirt.

"*Hey*," Zarius hissed.

The dog, slender like a greyhound, startled and backed away. Red hair bristled on its neck as it growled, and Zarius bared his own teeth as he lifted his sword. Missing patches of fur oozed black blood from the dog's flanks, and maggots fell from its long, narrow snout. The dog took one feinting step toward him, and when Zarius lunged to swing his sword, the creature scampered away.

Breathing hard, Zarius glanced down at a small, half-eaten body before he tore his eyes away and moved on. His heart thundered against his breastplate. Stars twinkled overhead. Banks of dark clouds made a lattice out of the black sky, and the moon hung perfectly in one open square. Zarius cursed it, panicking for cover as he ducked between another couple of hovels.

Finally, Zarius made it to the edge of the road. He peered out from the shadows, waiting. Seconds ticked by. A gentle breeze blew clouds of pestilence over him, and he barely stifled a gag. Moments later, the clanking of metal. Zarius shrank against the muddy wall next to him, pulling up a blanket of darkness.

A massive beast of a Knight walked across Zarius's vision. His armor was blacker than darkness, his whole shape a void, an anti-image. All Zarius could make out was the sheer size of him and pronged horns on his helmet. A moment later, the unknown Knight was gone, rumbling down the street. Zarius waited until the thunder of his footsteps faded before he slunk around the corner, raced a short distance, and stopped. The door to Zarius and DK's hovel lay in pieces on the floor, like it had been struck with a battering ram.

Fresh terror tightened every tendon as Zarius fell to his knees and scoured the floor with his hands. "*DK*," he whispered as he felt across DK's empty nest. He clutched up trembling handfuls of hay. Breathing hard, Zarius stood up. Foreboding despair gripped him by the throat.

Trying to think, Zarius crept to the door and stuck his head through. The faint glow of fire danced down the street. Zarius blinked and lifted his faceplate to wipe grimy fingers across his eyes. It was too dark to make anything out.

Fuck. Shit.

Zarius slipped out of the doorway and again took cover between the hovels, away from the main road. Trying to jog on silent feet, he wove through the firepits and makeshift play areas. As he came around one corner, his foot slipped in something wet, and his head landed in a pile of cold slop.

Almost shrieking, Zarius scrambled away, but he forced himself to stop as he heard his armor creak and groan. Holding his breath, he listened. Blood and flesh oozed down the inside of his helmet, against his face. Shit and decay flooded his lungs with every breath. Maggots rolled against his lips as he ripped his helmet free and shook his head so hard that stars burst in his vision. He wiped furiously with a chainmail sleeve and shuddered where he sat. When he saw the eviscerated human form he'd landed in, he could only force himself to his feet and leave it behind.

Ailing, Zarius pushed on. He needed to find DK. Zarius couldn't place it, but he knew DK had something important to tell him, something beyond urgent, essential to the very survival of the world itself.

Without his helmet, Zarius could see a little better. He approached the town square through the jumble of peasant homes, and after another minute, he had a vantage point, leaning around another daub wall and grimacing at what he saw.

Red hounds of all shapes and sizes trotted about the square, made spectral by the light of a dozen scattered torches. The malnourished beasts fed on a slew of corpses lying in piles all over. But Zarius focused on the very center of the square, where a shape was chained between the supporting beams of the well roof.

A thick pile of straw and wood lay at the base of this figure, and Zarius watched the massive, unknown Knight from earlier stride toward it, carrying a torch in hand. Terror rushed through Zarius, but he was frozen, panic rising in his throat.

As the black Knight arrived at the figure, the dim torchlight illuminated the victim's face. Zarius wanted to scream, to burst out of his hiding place and distract this demon even if it cost him his own life. That was DK out there, beaten to a pulp, but still recognizable. Black and purple bruises covered DK's swollen face, but Zarius thought he could see one blue eye glittering in the light as he raised his head to face the enemy.

"*Let us hear a round of applause,*" the huge Knight yelled. His voice was deep and metallic, but perhaps faintly human. "*From all the Day Knight's followers.*"

The square was quiet. Only the flies and maggots celebrated as they enjoyed a generational feast. Red dogs flitted through torchlight, blood dripping from their misshapen heads as they searched for untainted sustenance. The unknown Knight's ringing voice faded as he held the torch up to DK's battered head.

As if in reverence, the unknown Knight tilted the torch forward until the flames lapped at DK's face. DK's hair struck alight and began to burn, put out quickly by thick globs of blood. DK writhed and moaned as the fire singed his skin, and the unknown Knight laughed right into his face. He lowered the torch and held it close above the pile of wood and straw.

Zarius's heart stopped. He had to go. Had to *move*. If DK were to survive, Zarius had to burst out of hiding right *now* and stop this. But he couldn't. His feet refused to move; his voice refused to yell. He couldn't even breathe. For two crucial seconds, Zarius was a statue.

The unknown Knight dropped the torch, and the tinder surrounding DK's feet burst into flames. For a moment, all was quiet. Even the dogs ceased their padding, turning their noses up at the smell. Then, as the fire locked around DK's manacled ankles and began to eat his flesh, DK erupted with a horrifying scream, followed by a cannonade of laughter from his executioner.

DK's voice went hoarse as he began to jump, trying to throw himself free, but his arms jerked against the steel restraints. Zarius, engulfed in leaden dread, watched one of DK's shoulders pop free from the socket. Fire crawled up DK's dancing legs as the whole pile of fuel began to burn, and soon, it enveloped him halfway up the chest. But his head stayed free. His throat continued to work, as if stealing the necessary words from Zarius.

DK writhed and bucked and screamed himself out, and all the while, Zarius watched his master's legs turn to ash. Meanwhile, the unknown Knight stood so close that he, too, should have burned. Smoke rose from the front of his black armor, but he didn't step back. He studied the process of DK's death as the guttural screams and thrashing turned to dry spurts of shouting and a slow drain to nothing.

Exhausted, DK sank to his knees in the flames and disappeared. The fire grew brighter, consuming his body, and he struggled no more. Tears hung on Zarius's eyelids, and he shook like a leaf where he stood, watching his master burn. Eyes fluttering, Zarius glanced to the side and saw the unknown Knight gazing at him, two red dots beaming out from that horned helmet. The unknown Knight cocked his head to the side.

"Coward boy," said that metallic voice. It sounded like it was right next to Zarius's head. "Call me the Dead Knight."

20

DK entered the tavern with his right hand resting around his left side, more out of habit now than necessity. The pain was mostly gone, the once jet-black bruise now a mess of yellow and green. Thanks to Ezekiel's armor, DK avoided any broken bones. Though pain still lingered with him, mental if not physical.

He hadn't seen Zarius in almost a week now. DK couldn't even go to Ezekiel's forge for advice, because Ezekiel would shake his head and turn him away. DK had insisted on meeting Ezekiel somewhere neutral, but the old man—his closest friend in the world for years—arrived only to confirm DK's worst fears. Zarius was traumatized by what happened, and that torment had stoked a frightening anger in him. Even Ezekiel said he was worried, but he didn't think there was anything they could do except wait.

So here DK was, in the tavern alone for the first time in years. It was a calm night. The air outside got a little warmer all the time. The days were getting longer, the Sunsets larger. Grass and foliage across the land spread their newfound wings. The faces in the tavern weren't quite so hard, the bodies so hunched.

Morose, DK hovered near the entrance for a few minutes

before he wandered toward an empty table and slumped down. Conversation carried on around him, and a few looks did come his way, but he lost himself to his thoughts. To the same agonizing regret that swelled up every time he gave himself a moment to think. He sighed and imagined slamming his head into a bloody pulp on the table. Bare his contemptible mind for all of them to see.

Time passed in the constant flicker of the torches against the walls. The mind-numbing odor of ale wafted pleasantly around him, trying to penetrate his fortress. He let his hands drift over the rough surface of the table, and he pondered getting up for a drink.

There seemed to be a spot already waiting for him. DK walked up to the bar top and stood, fingering a couple bronze pieces in his pocket, still outside of himself. When Catherine appeared, it took him a beat to process the anger on her reddening face.

"I said *hey asshole*."

DK blinked. He glanced around. "Uh, what?"

She leaned forward, eyes hot. "Your little shithead friend came in here the other night and acted like a real fucking prick. That the kind of shit you're into now?"

Maybe it was the stoic absentness of DK's face that stole some of her thunder, or maybe his lack of response made her stutter.

"A real fucking prick," she repeated.

"I'm sorry." DK's face didn't change. "It was my fault."

She narrowed her eyes, examining him. "It was just him."

He grimaced. "Even so."

"What's that supposed to mean?"

"I said I'm sorry, alright? I'm sure he's sorry too. Can I have a drink or not?"

Scowling, Catherine reached for a mug and poured an ale through a spout in a barrel under the bar. When she set it on the counter, and DK reached into his pocket for the bronze, a couple pieces clattered onto the bar in front of him.

"That one's on me," said a high, smooth, unfamiliar voice.

DK turned and had to look down for the speaker. It was a slight girl with pitch-black hair and dark eyes to match, intensified by her fair complexion, though her face harbored an insistent sweetness. DK raised an eyebrow before shock dawned on his face.

"Holy shit," he said.

The girl laughed, a long watery sound that flowed gently into his ears. She added a couple more bronze pieces and looked at Catherine. "Can I have one too please?"

Catherine looked back and forth between them, beaming questions at DK, but DK only stared at the bar, suddenly uncomfortable. Catherine set another mug on the bar with maybe a touch of hesitation, and the girl whisked both of them into her hands and nudged DK with her elbow.

"Come on. Will you sit with me?"

"Sure," DK mumbled.

Together, they went back to the table he started at, and DK slid into a seat opposite the girl.

"I'm Caroline," she said right away. "What's your name?"

"Christi . . . er, well, Christian."

She tipped her head, smiling, and blew air through her nose. "Are you lying?"

"Well, I don't know. My friend calls me DK. And I guess I like it. I've kind of been thinking of myself as DK." He smiled, but it faded quickly.

"DK," Caroline repeated. It sounded nice coming from her. "I like it, too."

"Thanks." He looked off and shrugged.

"Well I guess I probably don't need to explain much to you. I've been looking for you to say thank you. And I mean *thank you*, from the bottom of my heart. Those words just don't feel like enough."

DK nodded solemnly. She was one of the girls they saved from Derrick and his band.

"You don't owe me any thanks," said DK. "I'm just glad we were there."

"I'll say," said Caroline. Her smile warbled, eyes going vacant for a moment. She shook her head. "Ugh, no. I don't even want to think about what would've happened. Seriously, DK, thank you. Whether it's *owed* or otherwise."

He smiled. "You're welcome."

"I told my parents about it. We're farmers. We have a few plots south of town, but I don't come up here much. That's probably why I've never seen you. But anyways, I told them, and we don't have much money, but they said they'd happily—"

"Please," DK interjected. He swiped the notion away with his hand. "Absolutely not."

The tavern was quiet this evening. Conversation carried on at regular volumes, and no one was plastered out of his mind. It *almost* could've been considered romantic. And the way Caroline was looking at him made DK squirm, though he took pains not to show it.

"I don't know what to say," said Caroline. She giggled nervously. "Like I said, thank you just seems so weak. You're very kind. And brave."

If only she saw what happened after she fled. In spite of her words and the smoke in her eyes, DK could scarcely focus. He wondered just how *kind* Zarius would say he was.

"I try to do the right thing," said DK.

"You're thinking about a lot."

He startled and gazed harder at her.

"You wanna talk about it?" she asked.

He looked away again. "I don't know." She was a stranger, after all. He didn't much trust strangers, no matter the first impression. Even when he found the words eager to come out, he took the first sip of his ale and savored the harsh flavor as it washed down his throat.

"You're an odd one." She grinned. "Definitely not how I was expecting you to be."

"What, did you think I was gonna be an asshole?"

Caroline burst into laughter, cheeks turning pink. DK smiled.

"Well, not exactly," she said. "Maybe in the neighborhood."

"Lucky for you I'm not an *Endlin* knight." He spat the words out like filth from between his teeth.

"Ohh, are they nasty?"

"Pretty much." He scoffed and shook his head.

"What does that mean you are then?" She leaned across the table, and their faces got a lot closer.

DK forced himself not to retract. "I'm just like . . . my own Knight, I guess. Basically that." *The Day Knight*, he thought, but that seemed ridiculous to say out loud.

"Wow," she said. "That's hot. I mean cool." Her eyes flashed.

DK almost choked on his own saliva. He let out a strained laugh, certain that his face was already bright red. "I mean, yeah . . . I guess so."

Fidgeting, he took a quick glance around just as the tavern door clunked shut. His eyes went wide as he stood straight up, forgetting Caroline altogether. There was Zarius. His face sat blank as he stared at DK, but he started moving immediately.

"Uh . . . Z," DK said, caught off-guard. All the innumerable apologies he'd thought up in the last few days mashed together in his head and left his tongue a useless slab. "How's it—"

Zarius ran the last three steps and shoved DK hard, launching him clear over his own table and into the next one. DK slammed his wounded side against the wood as the whole thing went toppling over, and a couple men burst into shouts and obscenities as they leaped out of their seats, ale flying.

"*Agghhh*," DK cried. He clutched his side and writhed on the ground, kicking a chair over. Fresh pain lit up old channels like a flood spilling down a shrunken riverbed. "Ahh, fuck *fuck*."

When he opened his watery eyes and saw Caroline's frightened face appear over him, he thrashed away and managed to climb up to a knee, panting. Fighting through the pain, not even looking to see if Zarius was still there, DK crouch-ran to the door and stumbled out of the tavern.

21

Sweat rolled down the sides of Zarius's face. He sat still, focused on a breath as he drew it in, then seeing nothing but DK's anguished face as he blew it out. He grunted and snapped his head back, then tried to focus again. Breathe in. DK's anguished face. He began to tremble, and he tried it again. Breathe in. Derrick's severed head. Blood in the thousand tiny valleys of his palms. Those red, rolling eyes as Derrick's head began to babble. Breathe out.

"You *fucking stupid bitch*." Saliva sprayed through Zarius's clenched teeth as he flew to his feet and started pacing in a circle. He wanted to punch the living fuck out of something, but all he had was the ground. So instead he went down and dug his hands into the earth, gripping soil and then flinging it as hard as he could back into the grass.

Just focus. Why the *fuck* couldn't he focus? How long had he been trying this stupid, pointless bullshit with not a goddamn thing to show for it? Stupid fucking mystical bullshit.

"Fucking bitch," Zarius repeated, throwing more soil. The wet smell of the earth filled his nostrils, and to him it smelled like blood, like soon the earth's essence would come gushing out of the wounds he'd made and drown him.

More than a week since the incident. Zarius attacked his training with a religious fervor. He attempted meditation every day to no end. He knew in the sparring pit that his footwork was sloppy. His strikes and slashes were slow and off target. He couldn't do fucking anything right, and DK wasn't there to correct him. All he did was toil and drive himself on mercilessly. Utter exhaustion was the only path to sleeping through the night, but nightmares now harassed him to no end. He was losing his fucking mind.

All at once, it became too much. Zarius collapsed straight to the ground like his spinal cord had been severed. He fell onto his back, arm twisted underneath his body, and the Sun seized upon his face. Hot rays drenched him, and all he could do was clench his eyes to keep his retinas from burning up.

The Sun painted his face in warmth even as he began to cry. Fat, angry tears splashed down his face into the grass. He dragged his arm out from underneath him so that his hands could tremble unencumbered, and he clawed more grass out of the earth.

"Fucking bitch," he croaked.

As quickly as they started, he forced the tears to stop. He jammed them back down and sealed the well. A Knight wouldn't sit here and fucking *cry*. Again, the memory flashed across his vision—him shoving DK, the pain on DK's face as he hit the tavern floor. Zarius groaned and climbed to his feet.

A sudden wild need hit him, and he took off running through the tall grass. He'd picked a meditation spot much farther from Ten-Berry to ensure he wouldn't run into DK, and as such, he wasn't too far from the badlands. That's what he made for. He beat the ground with force as he half-sprinted until rising exhaustion forced him to slow down. But he drove himself hard, not even completely sure what he was looking for.

When he saw the ground rising and balding to stone, a visceral reaction punched through his spirit. He almost turned around. He slowed to a walk but kept going. Even under the heat of direct Sunlight, goosebumps pimpled his arms and legs. His senses rose to a pinpoint focus, as if he were about to be attacked.

Zarius came over a low hill and stopped. There was Peter. Some of him. Scavengers had been after him—coyotes and vultures. Much of his carcass was picked clean, the bleach white of bone showing against the earth tones of the stone behind him and the green grass matted below. A thick blanket of flies covered him, and Zarius threw his hands up over his ears. He remembered his dream, and he did *not* want to hear the writhing of maggots. He saw the vague mass of their little white bodies and had to turn away, repulsed.

He wished they would've buried him. He wished he had a shovel now. To see a human corpse rotting out there in the open like that unsettled him in a way he'd never experienced. He'd seen dead bodies before, but not like this. Not left out in open country for a week, bare to the elements and the beasts.

Zarius got closer. He didn't want to, but he was still looking. He waded into the tallgrass on his left, trying to get a better vantage point, but again, he was forced to move closer. Where was Derrick's body? He came out into buffalo grass, now only a stone's throw from Peter's corpse. As he drew nearer, he saw the big black stain on the ground where Derrick fell. He saw the stain. He smelled the blood. But there was no body.

Goosebumps led a riot across all of Zarius's flesh. His scalp pulled tight, and his hands began to shake. Struggling to stay upright, Zarius kept looking around, as if Derrick might have been dragged off somewhere. Surely some band of coyotes pulled him into a corner to feast on him. But Zarius made a big circle around the scene and found no trace of him.

"Oh God," he muttered.

Like Derrick just got up and walked away.

Zarius's head snapped onto the rock corridor leading into the rest of the badlands. What if he was up there right now, waiting, head hanging down his back as he clutched a dagger and waited for Zarius to approach? What if he was looking for Zarius just as Zarius looked for him? Zarius drew his sword, heart pounding, and started backing away. He waited to see some flicker of movement or hear the dead creak of a voice drifting out to him, but nothing happened. When he got far enough away, he turned around and booked it as fast as he could.

Zarius didn't stop for anything, and he didn't sheath his sword. He ran through tallgrass, under trees, over hills, always throwing glances over his shoulder. Somehow, the panic almost got worse as he ran, like Derrick was back there gaining on him, just out of sight, and he'd catch up at the last moment and drag Zarius down right outside the gates.

After a while, Zarius blew through the gate past a startled Patrick Killington. Sweat ran down his face and back, soaking through his shirt, and he ran down the hard-packed dirt road and blasted into the hovel.

DK sent a bowl of stew all the way up to the ceiling, and warm broth rained down on both of them. Zarius stood there, panting, skewering DK with his eyes, and DK was frozen, one hand on the wall, eyes huge and confused.

"Where's his fucking body?" Zarius growled. Soup dripped from the thatch ceiling making *plip plip plip* sounds in the dirt.

"W-What?" DK asked.

"I went to look," Zarius snarled. "Derrick's body is *gone*. Where the *fuck* did it go?"

"I-I-I, well I don't know. There's—I mean coyotes and shit. They could have—"

"*No*. I looked. I looked everywhere. There was no trail. Peter's there, but not Derrick."

DK's eyes went distant. He sank down in the chair. "Peter died too?"

"Tell me where the fucking body is." Zarius said it through clenched teeth. His whole body shook. Tears welled at the corners of his eyes. The stress of the last week, the nightmares, the blood in his palms. It all rose up like a great wave conjured by the deep shifting of the earth, and it rolled toward him like a moving mountain.

Zarius fell to his knees. He squeezed his eyes shut, but the tears leaked through anyway. One hitching sob passed through him, then another. "You fucking bitch. Why'd you do that to me?"

"Z I'm sorry," DK cried. "It was terrible. I lost my—I lost everything. I never should've done that and I've regretted it every second since. I'm so sorry."

Shame radiated through Zarius. He couldn't believe he was in here crying, but he felt so alone, so afraid. The weight of what happened was crushing him, and he didn't have his closest friend to lean on.

DK took a step over and offered his hand. Zarius looked at it through blurred vision. He snorted a bunch of snot back, wiped his mouth with his wrist, and took DK's hand. DK pulled him right up into a hug, and for all the effort he could muster, Zarius couldn't stop a couple more tears from coming out.

"I'm so sorry," DK said, his voice thick. "I'll never do that shit again."

"I'll fucking *kill* you," said Zarius.

"I wouldn't blame you."

"Agh, *fuck*," said Zarius as they broke apart. He went and slumped down onto his blanket, and a little cloud of dust rose around him. He wiped his face and looked at DK, who remained standing. "I'm fuckin struggling man."

The sympathy on DK's face disgusted Zarius. He didn't want to be worthy of sympathy. He scrubbed his eyes, trying to banish the tears and any trace they left, but the egg was already broken, the yolk running everywhere.

"With what?" DK asked.

Zarius scowled at him. "What the *fuck* do you think?"

"I mean specifically."

"Specifically?" Zarius laughed. "Well specifically, I'm having nightmares every night about all sorts of shit. Mainly people getting slaughtered and cut up and coming back to life and their fucking heads rolling around talking to me. You know, like the shit we actually *saw, in real life*? I keep fuckin smelling blood. Jesus Christ. All that *shit* is just spinning around in my head."

DK nodded. Just nodded a few times and stood there, staring at the floor.

Zarius blew a bunch of air out. Saying it all out loud made it a little easier to comprehend. DK's constant calm rubbed off on Zarius. Maybe it wasn't as big as he thought, or at the very least, maybe he didn't have to see it as the end of sanity and reason. A few quiet minutes passed, as if DK were waiting to see what else might come out. Instead, Zarius found himself itching to change the subject.

"Sorry I launched your ass in the tavern," he said.

DK gave him a strange look that hinted at a smile. "It's fine. I had that coming. But I wouldn't say you *launched* me."

"Are you joking? What, you didn't see the table you flew over?"

"Maybe not. I just remember being glad you aren't that strong, cause I could have really gotten hurt."

"Okay, bet. We can find out about that in the sparring pit."

Now DK grinned.

Zarius tried not to let a smile of his own escape its cage. He was relieved to be home, but the dichotomy wasn't lost on him. Somewhere out there, a corpse was still missing, and now he was cracking jokes. Maybe nothing made any fucking sense and if his mind wasn't doing him any favors, he might as well lose it. "Who was that girl you were talking to anyway? The one who saw me launch you."

"Yeah, thanks for that by the way," DK muttered. "Great first impression. That was one of the girls from . . . the badlands."

Zarius jolted. "Oh. She wanna suck you off or what?"

"Jesus." DK's face reddened. "*No*. She was just . . . saying thank you."

"If what we did ain't worth at least a handy, I don't know what is."

"Well thank God it wasn't *you* she ran into. Oh, and you sure pissed Catherine off, whatever you did."

Zarius puffed his cheeks out before releasing a sigh. "Oh. Yeah. I, uh . . . don't honestly know what I did."

DK cocked an eyebrow. "You don't *know*? She was red hot."

"I don't, ah, remember."

After a moment, DK closed his eyes and nodded. "I see. Well, you might owe her an apology."

"Kind of awkward if I don't even know what I'm apologizing for."

"I bet she'd be *more* than happy to remind you."

"Lucky me."

The levity was so sudden it was almost shocking, but Zarius took shelter under it. It both confused and relieved him, but it was a hell of lot better than whatever he was feeling an hour ago. For all his flaws, DK was still his master and his friend. And he understood. He wasn't a douchebag. When Zarius could talk about his shit, it didn't seem so awful. He knew the memories would still bother him, and there were probably more nightmares to come, but DK had been down that road, too. To Zarius, that meant it was okay. Normal. Maybe even necessary.

"You wanna go spar?" DK asked.

Zarius sat still for a moment. "You asking or telling?"

DK grinned. "You're right. Grab your shit. Let's see how much worse you've gotten in a week."

SUMMER

SUMMER

22

Summer set in. Early mornings, hot days, and warm nights. DK and Zarius trained and trained, rain or shine, clouds or blistering Sun. Zarius grew accustomed to his armor—the advantages and limitations. If it was possible for him to work even harder after their reunion, he did it. DK was impressed, though he parsed his praise out carefully. Zarius didn't like hearing a bunch of "Good jobs." He liked knowing what he could do better. But DK still forced him to accept compliments here and there.

For DK, things normalized a bit. The immediacy of those encounters with the bog witch faded, as did the strong emotions attached to them. At first, he thought she would pursue them relentlessly, but she didn't. They went on a couple patrols—staying well clear of the badlands—and found nothing. Just long walks that turned into nothing but endurance workouts.

Zarius got frustrated—he told DK as much. He wanted to set things right after the last fight, where he felt he didn't perform well. DK told him to be patient, and they went back and forth with it. Really, DK was just relieved to have Zarius back. Zarius gave him structure and balance, and that brief separation had reminded DK of all those long, lonely days of solitude.

In the sparring pit, they sharpened each other's skills and toughened their constitutions. Soon enough, they could battle hard for five minutes without either of them giving in or calling for a rest. They got into combat shape, but DK continued to dance around increasing the frequency of the patrols. He knew they were lucky to escape the last one with the result they did, and he wasn't eager to test it. But he placated Zarius when he could.

The ultimate crucible, however, remained nestled in the lolling, grassy hills near Ten-Berry.

The Sun bathed DK in a silent stream of warm, invisible water. Washing out his pores, running through his blood. Sweat seeped out of him and soaked into the grass where he lay stark naked. Not even the crawling of insects over his skin stirred him. Each breath was deep, slow, and tranquil, the beginning forgotten by the end. No impetus, no detritus.

If his thoughts did exist, they were over such distant horizons as to be unreachable. They lived and died in unknown lands where they could not torture or comfort him. The flow of time flooded its channels and created one vast, unmoving plain where the Sun reflected trillions of times. The lines between the Sun and the Day Knight blurred. The god communed with the acolyte.

Strange experiences and sensations befell DK in these times, similar to dreams. Loose images that he viewed and released in the same moment. Singular words or phrases that he could really *hear*, as if spoken right into his ear. Buzzing, chittering sounds. Deep vibrations that massaged his heart.

The meditations sometimes lasted hours, sometimes only twenty or thirty minutes. DK never explained, never *had* an explanation.

They lasted as long as they did, and he didn't question it. To question would be to defeat the purpose.

When DK came to this time, his eyes split open like those of an infant kitten. The memory of his senses trickled in, and he flexed his hands on the grass, naked flesh cooking in the brilliant Sunlight. His eyes closed as soon as they opened, and he had to sit up and blink several times before he could focus on anything at all.

"Jesus Christ," said Zarius, a scowl etched on his face. "It's like watching the dead come back to life."

DK smacked an arid mouth and grabbed his waterskin, guzzling down a few mouthfuls and relishing the moisture. He focused on Zarius, still holding his waterskin.

"Alright." Zarius pointed his eyes up. "You can put your clothes back on now."

DK corked his waterskin and sat back on his elbows. "You nervous?"

"Eat me."

"Woah." DK put a palm up. "I'm not sure I'm ready for that."

Zarius grabbed DK's linen pants and threw them at him. "For fuck's sake."

Grinning, DK stood up and slipped his lightweight pants on. A breeze passed through and made them billow, and he stood tall to let it cool down his body.

"I don't know how you do that without passing out," said Zarius, who wore his shirt over his head to protect himself.

"It's because I'm strong."

"Shut the fuck up."

DK stretched. His skin was a deep tan, almost to the shade of leather. Sunburn after sunburn eventually made him nearly impervious to them. Wrinkles seemed to multiply overnight, but his eyes always sparkled.

"How'd it go this time?" he asked Zarius.

"Same fucking way," Zarius said.

DK sat down in a heap, exhausted and a little delirious. "That concerns me."

"Oh does it *concern* you?" Zarius asked. "Well it pisses me the fuck off."

DK resisted the urge to start lecturing him. He'd learned well enough by now that Zarius would stop listening after about five seconds.

"I know you know it's important."

Rolling blades of grass between his fingers, Zarius just nodded.

"And I believe you're trying," DK added.

"Fucking bullshit." Zarius shook his head and threw the grass away. "I don't know what's wrong with me."

"Nothing I'm sure. Nothing more than anybody else anyway. It doesn't have to work for you the same way it does for me, but it *does* have to work, you know? You might need to figure something out on your own."

"Great." Zarius rolled his eyes. "I'll just invent my own brand new type of 'meditation.' I'll call it . . . blahmuhblageration. Bog witch won't see it coming."

DK smirked and shrugged one shoulder. "She probably wouldn't."

Zarius tumbled backward against the grassy incline behind him. "I'm gonna fucking kill myself."

"That's the spirit."

He slammed his hands on the ground and bolted upright again. "I just don't *fucking* get it. Stupid fucking brain. Stupid thoughts. They're lucky they're trapped in my head or I'd beat their asses."

DK's smile faded, and he staved off frustration. "I don't wanna beat the dead horse, Z. You know where I stand on it."

"I know I know," Zarius muttered. "I'm gonna figure it out."

"I know right now it doesn't seem like a big deal. Or maybe it does, but I promise you, it *will* be a big deal. It'll be a huge deal. When I went to the bog, I could only do a fraction of what I can do now. But I still feel pretty sure that that's the only thing that let me survive. I got through to the Sun, or maybe the Sun got through to me. I had just enough connection."

Zarius shuddered. "God." He gazed off. "Is that where you think we'll end up?"

DK paused. "Yes," he said. "I know I will anyway. Eventually. Whatever that means."

"What, so you're just gonna leave my ass behind?" asked Zarius.

"I don't know what's gonna happen. I don't know what will be expected of either of us, only that I feel pretty sure right now . . . as scary as it is, honestly . . . pretty sure that I have to kill the bog witch. That's where this is going."

The wind stirred around them, pushing DK's thin hair around while Zarius's stood firm. They sat in silence for a while. A few critters rustled through the grass nearby, probably little field mice. The dauntless Sun dominated the sky.

"Why?" Zarius asked.

DK raised an eyebrow and thought on it.

"I'm a marked man," said DK. "Since that day. I think I always knew it. Even as I recovered my self and my senses. That's why I stayed hidden. And for a while, that worked. I stayed hidden, and the bog witch stayed dormant. I think in some way, I hurt her, too. Either before I escaped or by escaping at all.

"When I came back fully to myself . . . As in when you came to Ten-Berry and I accepted you as an apprentice, I caused something. A ripple that went all the way to her. I'm still marked, but now I don't think I'm the only one. I think she is, too. I think in some crazy, inexplicable way, we're bound together. And it won't be over until I face her again."

"Jesus fucking Christ," said Zarius.

DK didn't say anything, but he nodded in agreement. Yeah. Jesus fucking Christ.

Zarius looked hard at him for a moment, and when DK invited the question, Zarius grimaced. "What happened back then?"

DK held his gaze. "You really wanna know?"

23

Zarius shifted on the wooden chair, anxiety bubbling. "Man come on."

"I'm serious," DK said. "Apologize."

"Bro she's a bartender. It's probably water under the bridge."

"That's a terrible excuse. If you're gonna be a Knight, you've gotta have self-control. And if you slip up, you've gotta be able to apologize."

"Oh fuck me."

A lively tavern crowd bustled around them, enjoying a reprieve from a long day's work inside the cool stone walls. Torches flickered and crackled, and the hearth was cold—a true mark of summer. The smell of ale occupied its familiar place, but summer heat brought a newfound stench that lurked beneath the surface. The odor of arduous farming and hot days.

"Okay I *will*," said Zarius. "But not right now. It's fucking packed in here."

"Right now."

"Dude." Zarius tapped a fist on the tabletop. "Come on. Just go get us some drinks."

"Nope." DK sat back and folded his arms like a petty tyrant.

"You fucker," Zarius mumbled. Trying to hide his nerves, he popped up out of the chair and whisked away toward the bar.

The truth was, Zarius was embarrassed. He had avoided the tavern since that night after the fight with Derrick, even turning down DK when he asked about going. It was only so bad because Zarius didn't remember what happened. Not at all. And Catherine maybe kind of intimidated him. Just a little.

A wedge of bodies blocked the bar, and Zarius picked his way along the back like a vulture looking for a bite off some carrion. When he saw a gap, he squeezed into it. People shoved past him with their drinks in hand, and he edged closer until he found himself at the bar top.

Zarius didn't try to think of what he was going to say. He just traced his fingers through the woodgrain until he saw a figure appear out of his peripheral vision. Just as he was about to look up, two ales landed on the counter, and Catherine whisked away without so much as waiting for his coins.

Slack-jawed, Zarius looked from the ales down the bar to where Catherine was taking more orders. Confused and a little chagrined, Zarius hovered, not sure whether to stay or go. She came back down the bar but stopped a few paces away. It was loud, a ton of chatter. Lots of people were trying to get her attention.

"Catherine," Zarius whisper-yelled. He waved a little. "*Catherine.*"

Catherine took one single second to pause and give Zarius a miniature scowl with eyes so condemning that they stole the air right out of his lungs. Now embarrassment flooded through him, even though her rebuke was so subtle that nobody even glanced at him.

"Ah fuck," he said as he fished out some bronze and left it on the bar. He picked up the ales and began working back through the throng.

When he made it back to the table, DK eyed the ales with suspicion and cocked an eyebrow. "Well?"

"She wouldn't talk to me."

"Then how'd you get these?"

"She just put them in front of me and ran off before I could even say anything."

DK tipped his head forward, staring at him.

"I'm serious!" Zarius said. "That's what happened."

Frowning, DK didn't touch his ale. "You weaseled out of it."

"Bro I did not. I swear to God."

"Swear to the Sun."

"Oh for—I swear. To the *Sun*, if that really makes a difference."

"Well." DK finally picked his mug up and sipped it. "Guess you've got some legwork to do."

Zarius sipped his own, but it tasted like guilt. "Fuck. Agh. What, should I just go back up there?"

"Obviously not." DK widened his eyes. "That would probably just piss her off even more. But you need to apologize."

"*Durr*, no shit."

"Hey boys," said a new voice. Small and fluttering.

Zarius and DK both startled, and they found Caroline standing next to the table. Behind her, a tall, nervous-looking girl shuffled her feet and looked anywhere but at them. Both clad in simple, earthy peasant dress.

"Oh my G—gosh, Caroline," said DK. He stood up and just kind of hovered there. "Hey. How are you?"

"I'm good," she said. Her black hair hung long and straight down the front of her shoulders, gleaming in the dim light. She smelled faintly of lavender—a major standout in the current smellscape.

"I'm a little shocked to see *you* here with *him*." She gestured at Zarius in a way that blew a shot of steam through his head. "And I guess I'm a little hurt that you . . ." She shrugged and turned half away. "I thought you might call on me."

Zarius did everything he could to stifle snorts, laughter, a whole host of things. He stared at DK and watched the red rise to his cheeks as DK started stammering, and Zarius had to try even harder not to crack up.

"Oh jeez," said DK. "W-well, ah, jeez. Why don't you join us?"

"You sure?" asked Caroline. "You two aren't gonna start *fighting* or something?"

Zarius was glad those two black dagger eyes weren't gouging *him*, but he was also kind of annoyed. She sounded annoying.

DK laughed nervously. "No, no I think we got that out of our systems. Please, sit down." He pulled out their chairs for them and let them sit down before he came over and sat next to Zarius. Zarius pinched DK's thigh, and DK smacked him under the table.

"This is Gretchen," said Caroline.

A small smile crossed Gretchen's face, but she only looked at them for a moment before her eyes skittered away. She wore a short, thick shock of curly auburn hair that framed her round face and brought out her freckles. Zarius examined her, and she seemed to wriggle in her chair. Caroline nudged her, and Gretchen let out a nervous laugh.

"Hi," she said. She looked timid, but she spoke with confidence. "I had to see if Caroline was right, if you guys were really the same guys. Thanks for saving our asses."

"*Gretchen*," Caroline said.

"For saving us," Gretchen corrected with a goofy smile.

Zarius almost rocketed right through the tavern roof.

"Oh, it was nothing," said DK. "I'm glad we were there."

"She said thank you." Caroline leveled her eyes at him.

"Oh, right." DK nodded. "You're welcome."

"Well I'm curious about this." Caroline flipped a little finger back and forth between them. "Last time I was here, *you* were throwing DK across the bar."

"It really was across the whole bar, wasn't it?" Zarius said.

DK shook his head. "It wasn't that far."

Then Zarius dropped his smile and screwed his eyes up. "Wait. DK? Is that what he told you his name is?"

"He told me both," said Caroline. "He likes DK."

"Aww, he likes DK does he? You're welcome honey." He patted DK on the back.

Violence flashed in DK's eyes. "Why don't you go get our friends a drink, Zarius?"

"And introduce yourself," added Caroline. "Zarius, was it?"

Zarius stood up and pushed an open hand across the table. "Hi. I'm Zarius."

Caroline raised an eyebrow at him but took his hand and shook it. "Caroline."

He craned his arm to the right and looked at Gretchen, who still wore that nervous little half-smile, and her eyes flitted up to his. "Hi, I'm Zarius," he said.

Gretchen blew air through her nose and shook his hand. "Thanks for saving my ass."

"Oh goodness," Caroline sighed.

Zarius held onto Gretchen's hand a second longer than he did Caroline's, and she just kept grinning up at him like they were in on some joke at Caroline and DK's expense. And Zarius wanted to know what that joke was. He really wanted to know.

In a jolt, he snapped out of the moment, took his hand away, and forged into the mob again, thankful to have a moment to collect himself. He had to force himself not to look back to see if Gretchen was watching him. Thoughts swirling, he realized he was about to face Catherine, and that brought him back to Earth. But maybe she'd just keep ignoring him.

This time, he got right up to the bar, and to his frightened shock, Catherine appeared right there in front of him, this time gazing directly at him. His mouth turned into a desert.

"Uhhhh . . ."

"Alright," Catherine said. "What's the deal?"

He cleared his throat. "I'm—wait what?"

Catherine's eyes drifted over his shoulder before snapping back. "What? What is it, what do you want?"

He narrowed his eyes at her, and the moment hung. "Anyway," he said slowly. "I'm sorry. About, well, I don't actually know what happened. And that's embarrassing, I know. But I know I did some fucked up shit, and I'm sorry."

Head bobbing, Catherine didn't smile per se, but simply removed her frown. "Okay. Fine, it's fine. Whatever."

He cocked his head. "You sure?"

"Yes. Is that all?"

"Yeah—*oh wait.*" He made a strained smile. "Can I get two ales?"

Two ales appeared in seconds, and Catherine rushed off, but Zarius couldn't shake the feeling as he turned around that something odd had transpired. But he was heading back into something even odder *already* transpiring, so who had time to wonder about it? Not him. His eyes locked onto Gretchen as he approached the table again, and she side-eyed him with that thinly veiled smile. His heart double-clutched.

"There he is," said DK as Zarius slid back into his seat and passed Caroline and Gretchen their drinks.

"Here I am," said Zarius.

Caroline gripped her mug in her hand. "Thanks. We were just talking about your fight."

"Which one? Me and DK?"

She nodded.

"Oh goodie." Zarius rolled his eyes. "Sounds like you already have a favorite story. God forbid a couple friends ever hash out their differences. I thought this was a country village?"

Unfazed, Caroline gazed at him. "Well, why don't you tell me another story then?"

"Hmm." Mildly annoyed, Zarius kind of waited for DK to interject, expecting that he was about to, but he didn't. Zarius shrugged. "Well, there was that time we saw this rotten deer and—"

"*Alright.*" Now DK burst in, smacking Zarius under the table. "Maybe not *that* story."

"Oh, now there's secret stories." Caroline's eyes drifted to DK. "Very intriguing."

"Yeah why don't you guys talk about them?" Zarius asked. "I wanna talk to Gretchen." He pointed across the room. "Over there."

Gretchen just giggled where she sat, flushing a little pink. Caroline tipped her head at him with slits for eyes. "I think we're both okay where we're at."

"Alright." Zarius shrugged and stood up. "Well I think I'm okay in general then. I'm gonna go." He patted DK on the shoulder as he squeezed through a gap between chairs. "Good luck, tiger. I'll see you at home."

And Zarius did leave. The whole process unfolded in a sudden haze. But the idea of *stories*, and the way Caroline asked, struck a frayed chord in him. Stories? *Stories?* How could any of what they'd been through be relegated to such a meaningless word as that? Tell us some *stories*.

The fact was that Zarius couldn't sleep through the night without one or more of those *stories* waking him up in a cold sweat, clutching his sword, afraid of the darkness surrounding him. He still felt hot blood on his palms, slathered on his face. He could still smell it. Sometimes he could think of nothing else.

When Caroline appeared at the table, he'd tried to hold it together. He really tried. But normal conversation was beyond him. In Endlin, he would've drooled over an opportunity like that, a couple interested girls. He would've told them anything. Cutting throats, killing knights, whatever kept them drinking and got them out of their dresses in some dark alley in the middle of the night. But this was too real.

Something inexplicable followed him like a ghost through the dark street, across the torchlit square. The Beggar defied the stars, a shadow in the night. He made for home, winding back and forth across the road. Above him, millions of lights specked the dusty, phosphorescent belt cinched across the center of the sky. A fingernail of a moon clung to life near one horizon. The night abounded, and Zarius understood DK's draw to the Sun. The Sun gave Light. Excessive by day, precious by night. Zarius gazed at the horizon and hoped DK was right; he was in the process of believing it.

Somewhere out there, the Sun remained.

24

DK sat there, shocked, staring after Zarius, certain that he was about to pop back in through the door, laughing at them all. But he didn't. He was gone. Unease stirred DK's stomach as he focused his attention back on the table. Caroline and Gretchen were both gawking at him, Gretchen with a hint of sadness and Caroline with uncertainty.

"What's wrong with him?" Caroline asked.

"Nothing," DK said softly. "I don't know."

"Is it nothing or do you not know?"

DK gazed at her. "You'd have to ask him."

"Well clearly *that's* not gonna happen. But I hope he's okay."

"He—I'm sure he is, or he will be. Best to just leave him to it."

"Are you two on bad terms?"

"No, no, we talked that through. It's . . . hard to explain."

Caroline looked behind her at the door for a moment. "Does it have something to do with the deer thing he was just talking about?"

A little frustration bubbled. "I don't know, Caroline. I really don't. Best to just leave it be."

"I don't want to pry. But I do feel like there's something you're not telling me."

"There are a *lot* of things I'm not telling you. I barely know you. It's nothing *against* you, but shit. I mean, crap. Still."

A few moments passed. The chatter in the bar rattled DK's skull. He shifted in his seat, not sure if he'd just crossed a line or if he should have crossed it even further.

"I understand," said Caroline. "I'm sorry. It seems like I caught you on an odd night, maybe?"

DK snorted. "They're all odd nights. We actually haven't been here since the last time I saw you. So yeah, we haven't been taking it easy at the tavern all the time. I think it was just . . . unexpected."

"Shoot," Caroline said as Gretchen looked on with a shallow frown. "We didn't mean to spoil your evening. I just . . . wanted to get to know you better. And we came a couple times hoping you'd be here. Maybe I got too focused on myself."

"It's okay." DK reached across the table and patted the top of her hand. "Don't worry about it. We're just dealing with some shit. Why don't I walk you two back home? We can chat a little that way, and I'll know where I can find you."

"That sounds good," said Caroline.

With that, they left, and DK let them lead the way. They headed toward the southern gate at an amble, and the girls broke into a discussion about something to do with Gretchen's brother. Tension in the family because he didn't want to farm, something like that. DK zoned in and out and gave half-hearted answers when they tossed him something.

In truth, he didn't go quiet because he disliked them or anything like that. He was actually a little scared. They were heading out of Ten-Berry, into the farm country, and it was damn dark outside. DK hadn't been outside of Ten-Berry at night in a long, long time, not with his wits about him, anyway. Not since the day he went to the bog, in fact. And while right now, the girls kept it cheery and lighthearted, he knew that this would be a solo trip back. Alone in the dark.

All signs pointed to an excellent stroll through the countryside. The night was pleasantly warm, the air still and dry. The moon sank toward the horizon, the stars left to rule the sky. To DK, it was a gaping wound. The weeping light of a herd without its shepherd. Myriad insects chirped and chittered into the night, calling to each other, passing unknown messages. The croaking of bullfrogs ebbed and flowed from a pond somewhere nearby. So thick and loud was the collective noise that DK was almost hypnotized by it.

"DK?" Caroline asked, slipping back a couple steps to nudge him. "What are you doing?"

"Huh?" He looked up. "Oh. Just listening to the bugs."

They both laughed, and he just half smiled. Yeah, good one DK. Top shelf.

"You walk really slow," said Gretchen.

He shrugged. "I'm not in a rush."

They laughed again and went back to a conversation that had drifted far beyond DK's participation, but he didn't mind. His thoughts kept seeping out into the darkness all around him, poking around, sniffing about. Secretly, he was looking for signs of trouble. Whether it be trouble now or when he came back. But so far, nothing.

The first twenty minutes weren't too bad, but the second really started to make him fidget. Each step sounded like a gong in his head. That much farther from home. That much farther from safety. He wanted to ask Caroline and Gretchen which one of them was going to walk *him* home.

"Shoot I'm sorry DK," said Caroline. "Gretchen and I don't get to spend a whole lot of time together in the summer so we just talk and talk. We're totally ignoring you."

"Not at all." DK shook his head. "I'm enjoying myself."

"Oh? How so?"

He thought for a few steps. "It's nice out. And I like walking. I mean just look." He gestured up at the sky and stopped dead.

Above the horizon in front of them hung a peculiar, crimson star, as large if not a little larger than any others he could see. A black patch of space surrounded it, as if it had warded off all other stars. It wasn't particularly brighter or more imposing, but it snatched DK's gaze and held it long enough for dread to creep up inside of him.

"It really is beautiful," said Caroline. She and Gretchen stopped with him and craned their necks to look up. "It gets so easy to take for granted, you know?"

DK couldn't muster a response from a dry mouth. That red star glittered on the horizon, bright and warbling. Stomach turning, DK dropped his head and started walking again, but the star remained in his peripheral vision.

Caroline and Gretchen fell into step behind him, but he let them catch up. The darkness surrounding the road seemed to get darker, the tallgrass taller. A whole army could have been lying in wait, close enough to reach out and graze their shoes.

"Are you sure you're okay?" Caroline asked. "You *and* Zarius?"

"I'm sure we're about as okay as we can be," said DK, glad they couldn't see the strain on his face.

"Well that doesn't answer anything at all."

"And unfortunately it's the best one I've got at the moment."

"Have you two been going out a lot? You know like, when you saved us? Whatever you'd call that."

"Patrolling? I mean yeah. Kind of. But nothing's happened."

Gretchen chimed in. "So there aren't a dozen other girls out there moping around over you?"

"*Gretchen*," Caroline said, giving her a little shove.

DK managed to laugh, but to him it sounded like a chicken getting squeezed. "I feel pretty confident saying no."

"Sorry about her," Caroline said sharply. "She drinks one ale and this one just starts flapping her gums."

"And Caroline wants to start *rubbing* gums," Gretchen said.

"*I'm gonna* . . ." Caroline sighed, and DK heard her smoothing out her dress. "You know what? Fine, Gretchen. Fine. I'll remember this. That's us up there, DK."

For a moment, DK thought she was just pointing at darkness amid more darkness, but as he blinked, he could make out the dimmest glow of light coming through a door, still a ways off. From nowhere, clouds proliferated and submerged the world into tar. DK lost even the outline of the road under his feet.

"Oh my," said Caroline. "Well that got spooky. You can just leave the rest to us, DK. Get back home safely."

Before he could confirm or deny, she pulled him into a tight hug, and he put his arms around her. She held onto him for a couple extra seconds and then let go, and he couldn't even see her face. A hand poked into him from the side that almost made him scream.

"Nice to meet you," said Gretchen.

"*Jeez*," said DK. He took her hand and shook it. "Don't sneak up on me like that."

Gretchen snort-laughed. "Thanks again. For saving our asses."

"Oh brother," Caroline said.

"No problem," DK answered, itching to get out of there. "You sure you don't want me to walk you the rest of the way?"

"Definitely," said Caroline. "If my parents see me walking out of the dark with a strange man, well . . . yeah."

"Understood." He felt so awkward, but the nascent fear scrambled any attempt he made at effectively speaking like an intelligent human being.

"Alright. Well, bye."

With that, they turned and left. "Bye," he said as they melded into the shadows.

The darkness swallowed him up, and DK's heart ratcheted up a notch with each passing second. He turned and faced back the way he'd come, taking a deep breath, reaching out to the Sun. He set off at a jog. Better to get it over with. Hell, he would have sprinted, but that seemed dangerous in the pitch-black night. He could feel that red star on his back like a tick crawling under his shirt.

Trying to downplay his own fear, he hurried back toward Ten-Berry, picturing the Sun in his mind. Please God just let him get back to Ten-Berry. The chatter of the insects vibrated through his head, and the smell of summer vegetation intoxicated him. He had to stuff his senses down to keep his focus at the forefront of his mind.

About halfway there, with the Sun shining in a clear blue sky within his head, he slowed down to a walk and then halted altogether. He couldn't see anything, but he knew something was there. Goosebumps washed down his spine, and the fear he worked so hard to defeat routed him in an instant. He began to tremble as he took a step back, and two red dots appeared against the backdrop of impenetrable darkness. Two dots high off the ground, looking down at him.

"Clever," said a metallic voice.

It took everything DK had to stave off outright panic. No, he couldn't panic, not out here, alone, weaponless. He had to *think*. Fast.

The clouds broke up, and the faintest silver light shed down on the landscape. DK made out a hulking figure on the road in front of him, certainly too tall to be human. If his eyes could be believed, the figure wore a bulky set of armor with a horned helmet, and it held a massive blade in its dangling right hand. The tip of the weapon was inches deep in the surface of the road.

"Alone?" asked the figure. "No sword?" That voice clanged out of its helmet like mallet strikes on hot steel, and DK shuddered, heart racing.

"What are you?" DK gasped. All he could think to do was stall.

"I am the Dead Knight," said the figure, bringing his huge black blade to bear. "I will be your executioner."

"W-Why now?" DK asked, taking another step back. "Why does she want me *now*?"

"She?" asked the Dead Knight. He pointed his sword at DK. "It is *you*. The Day Knight abandoned himself to death. And I will vanquish your resurrection."

A double image appeared. DK saw the Dead Knight stalk forward but also remain standing still. DK blinked, frantic, grasping for the Sun. It was a trick. He knew it was a trick. As the specter drew closer, DK's feet wouldn't move. He couldn't think. Death crept toward him like a slinking cat, and he couldn't shake the terror.

"DDDKKKKK," a distant voice belted out.

That sound. That voice. At the last moment, DK locked in. He grabbed control of himself and dove out of the way as a shimmering black blade cleaved into the earth where he'd been standing.

"DDKKKK." Another shout, getting closer.

"*Zarius, run.*" DK screamed himself hoarse and took off up the road.

Thunderous footsteps approached from behind, and DK threw himself to the dirt. He heard the woosh of a blade passing overhead and hopped up lithely. The monolithic shadow of the Dead Knight wheeled on him from the left, bringing that huge sword around, and DK saw the figure running down the road cock back and heave something into the air.

"*Z, don't trust what you see,*" DK bellowed. He ducked under a big grasping paw, and his eyes just caught the outline of something fluttering down out of the darkness.

25

At home, Zarius tried to distract himself from his thoughts. He chewed on a chunk of beef from earlier and picked the dirt from under his fingernails by light of the weak, crackling fire. But his thoughts were persistent. They kept asking him why he had to leave, and he kept seeing Gretchen's freckled face grinning at him.

He grunted and got up, pacing with what room he had, which was about two steps. So he paced the two steps and turned around, again and again. Muttering to himself, eating the beef, building little piles of dirt with his feet just to squash them. Something was bothering him, besides the girls and Catherine and the tavern, but he couldn't figure out what.

Time passed, and he couldn't settle down. After a while, he started wondering if DK was okay. It was an odd thought. He told himself that yes, of course DK was okay, but was he? Zarius couldn't know for sure, could he? He finished the rest of his snack and decided to leave, and for some reason, he strapped both his and DK's swords around his waist.

When Zarius made it back to the tavern and found it clearing out, he searched the heads milling through the square and didn't find the right one. He broke up little clusters of conversation under the Beggar by staring hard into shadowed faces. He went to the tavern door and squeezed past some people to scan the interior. No DK. No girls. He tugged anxious fingers through his hair as he went up to the bar and barked to Catherine where she stood rinsing mugs in a big barrel of water.

"*Hey,*" he said.

She jumped and whirled around, eyes sparking when she saw him. "Damn," she said. "Don't holler at me like that. What the hell do you want?"

"Where's DK?"

She just furrowed her brow and scowled. "How should I know? He must have left."

"*Fuck,*" Zarius said.

"What's wrong?" Maybe a glimmer of worry in Catherine's eyes, but Zarius turned around and bounded out of the tavern.

Outside, he stopped for a moment to think. Where did DK say the girls lived? *Did* he say? Farmers, right? Farms to the south, but there were some to the west as well. Trying to calm himself, Zarius visualized the countryside from his many long runs with DK. Most of the farms were to the south. That was all he had to go on, so he went.

Zarius ran fast and hard. Certainty kept building inside him that something terrible was happening. DK was in trouble, and Zarius had to get there. Fast. *Now.* He broke into an all-out sprint, going up and down the little hills, barricaded in by cottonwoods and tallgrass, running more on instinct than vision. Sometimes he veered off the side of the road and crashed through grass and foliage until he found it again, but he never stopped running. He tripped over a mound of dirt and skipped like a ragdoll off the hardpacked earth, but he still came up sprinting without a moment's pause.

At some point, he smelled something putrid and awful—the

smell of death, and he poured on the speed. Clouds had just vacated the sky, and he saw figures on the road as it sloped down before him. One of them had to be DK. Again, it was more instinct than any kind of recognition. He shouted DK's name as he ran, and some muffled response came back.

Zarius pounded down the road. One of those figures was too tall, too big. The sight of it injected a chill into his hot blood. He screamed DK's name again, drawing closer, and without a second thought, he slung DK's sheath up and hurled it.

The smaller figure came toward him, dodged a slash from the big one. Oh shit, it was a fight. *"Z, don't trust what you—"*

The big shadow caught DK by the back of the head with one fist and slammed him into the ground as Zarius skidded to a halt.

Shcrulk. DK's head got smashed into pulp on the road, and the sound of it struck Zarius like a bolt of lightning. He collapsed right to his knees, jaw falling open as DK's sword thumped against the road with no one to catch it. Blood and gore dripped from the big shadow's mitt as it removed its hand and shook off the viscera. A buzzing, moiling halo closed in around Zarius's vision, filling his eyes and ears. Horror. Life and purpose gone to pieces before his eyes.

"You f—, fucking, you but I was . . ." Zarius trembled, muttering.

The big shadow came stalking toward him. Its footsteps shook the earth. Two red dots beaming out of a pronged helmet. And Zarius knew it. He recognized it—the figure, the smell, the eyes. He'd seen it in his dreams. The Dead Knight stepped out of the depths of his most vile nightmares and sullied the essence of the world with each thunderous step. When that black blade cocked back, finally, one drifting spark found a waiting morass of rage.

"You fucking bitch." Zarius erupted from the ground, drawing his sword in a fluid reprisal.

Schlanngggggggg.

The blades met and deflected. All of Zarius's power only pushed the Dead Knight's weapon off course while the bones in Zarius's forearms vibrated up and down from joint to joint. The Dead Knight grunted and flicked his weapon back as if it were made of paper.

Kannngggggg.

Zarius flipped his wrists and threw a guard that absorbed the shot but almost took him off his feet. He went stumbling off to the side of the road but steadied himself. Breath flushed in and out of him. Only instinct and training kept him alive, because his thoughts were lost in a ferocious inferno of bloodthirsty revenge. He wanted to wreak death and agony. His body revolted against the rotting stench of desiccation.

The Dead Knight laughed, like rocks shaken in a steel chamber pot. "Phony Knight."

They both moved in. But the sudden blast of inspiration began to wane as reality loomed. DK was dead, and where did that leave Zarius? What did he have to fight for besides vengeance?

The Dead Knight unleashed a devastating sweep of his blade, bringing it parallel to the ground like a horizontal guillotine. Zarius just managed to turn his sword up and contact the underside of the Dead Knight's. He pushed it up, and it sliced a chunk off the top of his hair as it whooshed past overhead. A cloud of that odious death scent followed the swing, but Zarius didn't see the true follow-up.

The Dead Knight only swung his weapon with one hand, and he brought the other around clenched in a fist as large as a basket. It caught Zarius flush on the side.

Schrunk.

Zarius's left arm shattered, and a few of the ribs below gave way. He left his feet and lost his sword as he went airborne, and he blacked out when his body slammed against the road. He came to seconds later, vision filled with a bleary darkness, a few shimmering spots. Dirt filled his mouth and nostrils; he could barely breathe. He was facing the sky, and as the ringing in his ears subsided, he heard the denigrating laughter of the Dead Knight moving closer.

A nightmare beyond terror appeared above him. Those two red eyes, towering over him, the giant shadow swallowing a swath of stars. And that awful stench descended upon him like a suffocating blanket.

"Weak fool," the Dead Knight rumbled. "Now you die."

That black blade rose into the air, cutting a thin fissure through the stars. As it came down, and the fissure widened, it was like the hell of empty death spreading through the vibrant sky—a giant, dripping maw opening wide to swallow Zarius forever.

A sudden cloud of dust blew over, and Zarius's eyes fluttered. Specks of dirt made his vision watery. The high-pitched grinding of steel on steel, power pushing on power. Two swords locked for a moment before they split apart, singing. And a new shadow rose above Zarius. Small but sure, every facet of its posture lined with tranquil confidence. The figure looked down, and Zarius gazed into two familiar eyes. Two tiny pinpricks of ethereal Light glowed in their depths, brighter and more intense than any of the stars behind them.

The Day Knight spoke. *"Hold on, Z."*

26

DK stumbled backward, narrowly escaping that grasping hand, but his eyes tracked something in the darkness overhead. He turned and leaped, catching his sheath and loosing his sword in one fluid motion. The presence of Zarius brought a ferocious and immediate counterattack, and DK set upon the Dead Knight in a frenzy.

Shcank. Schlank. Whanngggg.

They traded blows in quick succession. For all his size, the Dead Knight lacked no precision. He wielded his blade as an extension of himself, but DK presented no weakness and made no missteps. Strikes connected back and forth. The Dead Knight was immovable, too large, too sturdy. His powerful swings rocked DK, but DK didn't show it. He absorbed the shots and threw in a couple ripostes when he could, but he sensed himself losing steam. The adrenaline began to sputter, and he started losing ground, pushed off by sheer strength.

Whannggg. Whannngg. Woonnggggg.

The Dead Knight pushed the advantage. He cranked even more power into each swing, and DK's guard came back a little slower and weaker each time. But inside, he was thinking. Where was Zarius? He snuck a glance past the Dead Knight and saw the road empty, and he knew something was wrong.

No. He remembered. The bog, the visions. At once, DK knew it was a losing fight. It might not even *be* a fight. His mind fled past the horizon, and a charge rose up in his spirit. This wasn't him. Not fear, not fury. Not anymore.

Whanngggg.

Another huge blow forced DK back, but he planted his feet and dropped his weapon. Connection. Sunlight poured into his mind and spirit. Gentle warmth pervaded him, and he let the curtains fall away. The Dead Knight swung again, aiming to split DK in half at the waist. And that black blade found no resistance, no defense. It cut through the air, met DK's side, and passed right through.

DK stood there unharmed. Because his adversary was nothing but an apparition, and as soon as DK realized it, it melted into darkness. The real Dead Knight was a stone's throw down the road, stalking toward a ball curled up on the ground. Zarius.

Calm, DK burst into motion, and the ground seemed to vanish under his feet. He arrived just in time to slide under the Dead Knight's swing and catch it with his blade as if he'd stopped a falling leaf. Their swords grinded, and intention burned in DK's soul as he threw the Dead Knight back.

DK looked down and saw the physical signs of shock on Zarius's pale face. One side of his torso was dented, but his eyes were lucid; he stared up at DK. More intention and purpose poured into DK like flowing water as he saw the graveness of the situation.

"*Hold on Z.*" He moved on the Dead Knight.

The Dead Knight brought his blade to bear. "You can't—"

WHANNGGGG.

DK flashed forward and unloaded a strike that knocked the

Dead Knight off balance. Without pause, the Dead Knight reset his feet and swung, and their blades connected in the warm night air.

Kannggggg.

The Sun burned in DK's mind. He wasted no time on thoughts, left no room for feelings.

Shkank. Ting. Spinggg. Whannnggg.

He worked like a technician, probing the Dead Knight's defense. Each swing came faster, harder, as if he were *gaining* strength through his own exertion. The Dead Knight's red pupils warbled as he tried to stand his ground, but his feet began to slide and jerk backward as he weathered continuous assault. When he tried to work DK's power against him, though, DK remained a step ahead, prepared for the feints, aware of the tricks.

On the next blast of DK's sword, the Dead Knight's arms were thrown to one side. Without pause, DK started slashing into the center of the Dead Knight's armor. Bits of dust and stone showered to the ground. DK defeated the Dead Knight's reprisal, flinging his blade away again and setting in on the armor.

DK's arms moved in a blur, nimble and powerful. He pulverized the torso of the stone breastplate and began to hear the wet tearing of flesh. The Dead Knight groaned and lurched back, and DK matched his steps, never breaking the stream of punishment.

Blood sprayed and gushed out of the growing hole in the Dead Knight's armor. DK dislodged the Dead Knight's sword on another precise swing and immediately started stabbing into the gap. Like a wounded bear, the Dead Knight roared and swung a hand at him. DK stepped back not quite enough, and a big fist glanced off his chest. Even that weakened blow lifted DK a couple inches off the ground and pounded the air out of his lungs. Concentration broken, he fell and scrambled right back up, gasping.

When he reeled himself in, though, prepared for another

onslaught, he found no attacker. The Dead Knight stood on the road, drawing long, rasping breaths. The ground jumped as he collapsed to one knee and clutched his leaking stomach. He let out a rattling groan.

"Weak," said the Dead Knight. "Too weak."

As DK watched, the Dead Knight picked his sword up out of the dirt, and in one swift jerk, he drove it through the hole in his armor and skewered himself. Stone flew off the backside of his big contiguous chest plate, and he collapsed in a heap, writhing for a few moments before he went still. When that gasping, metallic breath went silent, the whole world seemed to go with it. Dead silence descended, and DK sprinted back to Zarius.

Zarius's eyes still shone. DK knelt over him, gently feeling over his wounded side. That momentary connection with the Sun had faltered when the Dead Knight punched him, and raw fear clawed through DK's thoughts as he realized the extent of Zarius's injury.

God please help him.

DK asked the Sun, asked God, would have asked anyone who might have been listening.

"Z," he said. "I have to pick you up. I'm sorry it's gonna hurt bad. I have to pick you up."

Without waiting, DK bent over and scooped Zarius up. Zarius let out half of an agonized squeal before his eyes fluttered and he passed out. DK hooked his apprentice over his back and set off at a jog toward Ten-Berry. He ran as fast as he possibly could, pushing beyond the limits of exhaustion. Terror drove him on. He was afraid he'd arrive home with nothing but a corpse.

DK burst through the door of Ezekiel's forge. With the last scraps of energy he could scrape from his weary body, he let Zarius fall gently to the ground before he collapsed and started writhing. Daggers filled his lungs with each breath as he choked and gasped, almost unconscious from the effort. Ezekiel came blindly stumbling into the room, crying out in confused fear.

"Who's-who's there?" he croaked.

DK couldn't answer. He rolled around on the floor, and Ezekiel fumbled a bunch of tools off the workbench. DK saw the outline of him raising a hammer over his head.

"*Who's there damnit,*" he barked.

"Ch-Christian," DK gasped.

"*Christian.*" The hammer clattered to the floor as Ezekiel hurried toward the moaning in the dark. "Christian what's wrong. What happened?"

"Zarius is hurt," DK said, forcing the words out. "Bad."

"Where is he?" Ezekiel cried. "*Where?*"

"On the floor," DK said, struggling up to one knee.

Ezekiel went feeling around in the darkness.

"We need light." DK ran over to the forge. Dim, red coals still glowed in its heart, and DK started working the bellows.

"Lord have mercy." Ezekiel had found Zarius, and after a moment, he rushed over and helped DK get a fire built.

"Mary Finnes," Ezekiel said. "You remember where she lives?"

"Yes."

"Go. I can do this."

Without pause, DK burst through the door and sprinted back into the square. He took off toward his own house but soon cut into the thick scatter of hovels. Mary Finnes was about the closest thing Ten-Berry had to a doctor—an old, wizened medicine woman who had tended his wounds plenty of times back in the day.

A couple dogs barked in DK's wake as he sprinted down the

street. He scattered clucking chickens and tore through clothes-lines. His knees threatened to give way, but he made it to the door of a hovel similar to his own and started banging on it. He tried to open it, but it was barred shut, so he banged even harder.

"Mary. *Mary.*"

"Who's there?" a terrified voice squeaked from inside.

"It's Christian Mary please, open the door. *Hurry.*"

The door flew open. Mary's confused, weathered face appeared in the slat of moonlight, eyes crazy, like she thought she was in a dream.

"Mary my apprentice is hurt. Bad. I need your help."

"Oh dear." Mary closed the door, and DK resisted the urge to scream as he waited an agonizing minute. Finally, she came out, dresses and hair all disheveled, a little wicker basket in her arms. Questions on her face, but she followed him as he led the way back to Ezekiel's forge.

When they went inside, Ezekiel had the forge roaring with fire, light lapping the stone walls. DK saw Zarius where he'd left him and immediately had to turn away. The blood ran out of his head. No. The sight of him in the light threatened to make DK vomit. Too many elbows, the skin rolling over lumps of bone. Like a bunch of pebbles in a sock.

"Oh my," Mary said as her eyes fell on the injured boy. "Is he stabbed? Cuts?"

"No," DK croaked, still not looking. "There's no blood."

"Oh my goodness," Mary whispered as she knelt down and straightened out Zarius's limp, wounded arm. Then she just knelt there, staring at him.

DK grabbed two fistfuls of his hair. "Well what can you *do*? Mary, *help him.*"

Mary stood up, solemn and pale. Her seasoned eyes filled with sympathy as she stepped over and grabbed DK's hand. Her palms were rough and sandy. "There's nothing I can do right now."

DK stepped back, shaking his head, blinking. The room started swimming. "Wh-What? What do you mean? You have to help him." His voice faded to a whisper.

"His bones are broken," said Mary. Her eyes flitted from DK to Ezekiel. The old man looked gaunt and small in the flames. His eyes drifted shut.

"I can't . . ." Mary's voice was strained. "I'm sorry. I can make a splint. I have the materials at home. But that's all I can do right now."

"Will he survive?" DK whispered.

Mary opened her mouth to respond, but Ezekiel interjected.

"*Of course he will,*" Ezekiel snapped, loud and angry. "That's your *apprentice*, Christian. Don't you put that doubt on him. *Of course he'll survive.* You need to believe that *now*. I won't hear you *asking*."

DK's heart hardened into steel. He wiped the tears from his eyes and reined in his breath.

"You're right," DK said. He nodded at Ezekiel and reached for the Sun. "Yes. He'll survive."

27

The first couple days, and especially the nights, were shaky and tense. DK never left Zarius's side. At times, when Zarius's breathing would weaken to the point of almost stilling completely, DK would bow his head and find the Sun. He tried to wash Sunlight over Zarius through his mind, filling the injured limb, empowering his body. It was all he could think to do. DK slept precious few hours, and Ezekiel couldn't so much as drag him to a bed. So they made a couple up right there on the floor and gently shifted Zarius to one while DK took the other.

Mary applied a splint to Zarius's arm. When she reiterated that there was nothing more to do, DK resisted the urge to scream in her face. She navigated the work with graceful, familiar hands, but she remained staunch and unyielding in principle. During another examination of Zarius, she and DK shared words.

"He's going to pull through," she said.

DK kept one hand resting gently on Zarius's good shoulder. He shook his head, grimacing. "But at what cost?"

"Didn't you hear me?" she snapped. "He's going to *live*."

At that moment, Zarius's eyes fluttered open. DK leaped straight to his feet like he'd been shocked, and Mary leaned over from where she sat on her stool. Zarius emitted a horrific, gravelly groan, eyelids flapping, and then he went still again.

DK furrowed his brow, whipping his head toward Mary. "Wh-What happened?"

She stared at Zarius's motionless face. "He's in a lot of pain. I think he passed out."

"Can you give him something?"

"We'll wait until he can stay conscious. It's probably best he stays under for now. It won't exactly be pleasant when he's awake."

Grim, DK nodded.

The tests of faith continued in much that same way. A few days after the attack, Zarius woke up and managed to hold onto consciousness. As soon as he did, Mary began feeding him a slow, steady allotment of herbs and poultices designed to numb his pain. DK watched Zarius's eyes glaze over the first time, and they remained that way for several more days. After another week, Mary let the medication flush out of him and waited to see how he handled it.

Poorly, it turned out. As Zarius's eyes sharpened, so did the grunts and groans. He struggled, but when Mary gave in and slid another green, pulpy spoonful toward his mouth, he clamped his lips shut. At first, Mary thought something was wrong, but DK put a hand on her shoulder and locked eyes with Zarius.

"He doesn't want it," said DK.

Mary started. "Are you sure?" She looked from DK down to Zarius.

Zarius looked at DK again.

"He's sure," said DK.

Another interminable week passed. Summer flogged the land

like a ruthless taskmaster. Mornings and evenings bustled with activities, and the whole village shut itself up to weather those hottest afternoons. A few older people died from exposure, cooped up in their hovels. Some oxen went down in the fields and couldn't get up for hours.

Life went on. Even DK—at Mary and Ezekiel's insistence—got back to some light training. Probably they just wanted him to get the hell out of the forge once in a while. In every free moment, though, he was there. He meditated in the forge, removing the ceiling in his mind and letting the Sun pour into the room, filling it to the brim with Light. He spent countless hours directing all that energy into Zarius, visualizing a healing arm, manifesting a complete recovery.

On one such evening, Mary entered the forge out of a dead, oppressive heat. Sweat pockmarked her frizzy hairline, and she wiped her face as she came into the darkness of the shuttered forge. DK knelt over Zarius, and Ezekiel occupied a stool nearby, his eyes closed. Somewhere in the far reaches of his mind, DK heard Mary walk over and stand beside him, but she pulled him to the surface when she spoke with a cracked voice.

"This doesn't make sense," she said.

After a moment, DK's eyes opened. "What?" he asked, without looking up.

Mary stepped back, and her voice rose a notch. "I've never . . . I don't understand what's happening. To his arm."

DK already knew. He'd been watching it. Zarius's arm was regaining its shape. The many undulations of flesh were almost smooth.

"A splint can't do that," Mary muttered.

"You don't believe in miracles?" DK asked.

"You don't believe in *God*," Mary said. "You rejected our one true savior. I just—I don't—it doesn't make sense. It shouldn't be possible."

"I don't believe the same way you do," said DK.

"*You don't believe at all.*"

"Mary," Ezekiel said gruffly. "Let's not have any shouting."

"Don't you see this?" Mary turned and pierced Ezekiel with burning green eyes. "This is *witchcraft*, Ezekiel. It's-It's paganism."

"Don't you invoke that in my home. This is a house of God. As much as yours."

"Then how do you explain *this*?" She threw her hands toward Zarius, whose eyes were now open, fixed on the ceiling.

"I've prayed, too," Ezekiel said. "Haven't you? Who's to say it isn't *our* prayers doing the work?"

Mary's hands fell, and her stout body sagged. She managed to shuffle over to the stool beside Ezekiel and plop down with a big sigh, thrown into the shadows of the forge.

"I'm sorry," she said. "I just didn't expect this."

"I did," said DK.

"As did I," Ezekiel added.

DK gave her a weak smile. "Guess that made it two to one."

Mary grimaced. "I feel as though I'm in the presence of black magic, and you're calling it God."

"You would have shut Lazarus back in the tomb," Ezekiel told her.

After a pause, Mary laughed, and DK laughed along with her. It echoed off the hard walls around them. The forge panted from the wall like an overheated dog, and they all sweated profusely.

"Maybe you're right," Mary said after a sigh. "But that would mean I *am* witnessing a miracle."

"It ain't no miracle," Zarius grunted.

DK almost went through the roof. They all jumped to their feet. It was the first time he'd spoken since getting hurt, and he followed up with a groan.

"Z," DK cried. Tears sprang to his eyes as he bowed his head. "Oh thank God."

"Well how about that." Ezekiel grinned so wide it almost carried off his face. "Good to hear your voice, son."

Mary went right over to Zarius's side. "How do you feel?"

Fire burned in Zarius's eyes. "Fucking terrible."

Mary jumped, and her leathery face went pink. "Oh my," she muttered.

"Hurts to talk."

"Well then stop," DK said, kneading his palms.

"No. Get me out . . . of this godforsaken room."

"Did he always talk like this?" Mary asked. She looked down at Zarius. "I'm Mary by the way."

"You doubted me." Zarius kept his eyes fixed on her, even as his face scrunched in pain.

Mary went even more red. "W-Well it's not that. I was . . . I just . . ."

"Leave her alone, Z," said DK. "She might just be the reason you're alive."

Slowly, Zarius's eyes drifted to DK. "Your eyes glowed."

"*Huh*?" DK asked. Now he thought Zarius might be confused.

"Your eyes glowed. When you fought the Dead Knight."

"The *Dead* Knight?" Mary and Ezekiel asked simultaneously.

"Okay." DK put his palms up and stepped back. "Maybe we need to let Zarius process a little here."

"Bitch I've *been* processing," Zarius growled. He spat out the whisper like a hunk of phlegm.

Mary shook her head profusely and walked away. "I think I might go home and take a nap. If he's, ah, going to keep swearing like that."

"He definitely will," DK sighed.

"Well, Zarius, it's nice to meet you," Mary said, the words tumbling out. "I'll, uh, stop by later to check in. Christian, Ezekiel."

"Mary," said Ezekiel.

DK raised a hand as she stepped through the door into the blinding Sunlight outside and shut the three of them in.

"*Damn*," said DK. "You about burned her ears off, Z. Was that really necessary?"

"She doubted me," Zarius said.

"She was *worried*," DK retorted.

"Doubted."

"Whatever."

"I'd like to hear more about this Dead Knight character," Ezekiel said, giving DK a scrutinizing glance. He twisted a black rag in his hands as if he might wring tar from it.

DK looked from Ezekiel to Zarius. "How did you know it called itself that?"

"I've seen it."

Raising his eyebrows, DK leaned down. "You saw it *before*?"

"In nightmares," said Zarius.

"How so?"

Zarius grunted. "Later. Too much talking."

DK and Ezekiel looked at each other, and DK shrugged. "Alright. Later."

"I smell like shit," Zarius added.

Glancing down at him, DK hovered for a moment. "Yeah. You do smell like shit."

28

Zarius jounced along the dirt road in a creaky wooden wheelbarrow pushed by DK. He rested on a bed of hay, already sweating not from exertion but from pain. Each bump in the road brought a stab through the side of his body, but he could move his head and good arm now. In fact, when he was alone at the hovel—he'd moved back in with DK about a week before—he even managed to stand up on his own. He paid a high price, but he did it.

Now, they trundled down the road toward the gate. A late evening Sun still kept a red-hot eye on the comings and goings below, and Zarius sensed it watching them, welcoming them. Near the gate, Zarius saw Patrick scramble to his feet out of the shade where he'd been dozing. He came bounding down the road toward them.

"Well *hell*," Patrick said, looking from DK to Zarius with wide eyes. "This some kind of exercise routine?"

"No," Zarius said flatly.

A little out of breath, DK set the wheelbarrow down for a moment. "Zarius got hurt."

"Slightly," Zarius added.

Patrick cocked a big red eyebrow and looked around, as if searching for the joke. "You got *hurt*? Well damnit to hell."

That much Zarius could agree with. "Damnit to fucking hell."

A grin snuck across Patrick's face as he shooed DK aside and hefted the rough handles of the wheelbarrow. "Here DK, let me get 'im through the gate at least."

"Uhh." DK glanced at Zarius. Zarius just tossed his head. "Sure, Pat. Gimme a little break."

The wheelbarrow lurched forward, and Zarius hissed through his teeth.

"Sorry," Patrick said from behind him. "You know I heard tell that somebody stopped some nonsense up near the badlands bout a month or maybe two ago. Never heard a name, but it sounded like the Day Knight if I ever heard it. That how you got hurt?"

"Sure," said Zarius.

Thin cloud snakes slithered across the sky as the Sun continued its descent. They reached a point in the path where DK patted Patrick on the shoulder and told him they could stop. Patrick let the wheelbarrow down more gently than he picked it up and huffed.

"Heavy son of a bitch," Patrick said.

Zarius couldn't keep a smile away, and Patrick burst into some heavy guffaws.

"Just teasin," he said. "Hate to see you laid up like this Zarius. Hope you'll find your feet again soon."

The smile vanished, and Zarius just clenched his teeth. Sympathy made him nauseous. "Thanks," he coughed.

"You're a good man, Pat." DK patted him on the back again. "We gotta forge on."

"Aye aye, sir." Patrick threw one of his usual mock salutes and went ambling back toward the gate in no hurry.

"Thanks for not calling him an asshole or something," DK muttered as he got the wheelbarrow moving.

This time, they veered off the road, and the path got even more unsteady. Whatever reply Zarius might have had vanished in a steady stream of gasps and grunts. DK tried to be careful, but a sea of tallgrass obscured all obstacles. Sweat poured down Zarius's forehead, and he gripped the side of the wheelbarrow with his good hand, knuckles white as he tried to brace himself for each little bounce.

"Fuck this is harder than I thought," gasped DK. "I'm sorry. Do you wanna go back?"

"No," Zarius growled. After all, it was his idea in the first place.

DK took a moment's pause and set off again. They climbed up shallow hills and descended the slopes. The ground smoothed out a bit, and the tallgrass gave way to more buffalograss, allowing DK to steer around rocks and divots. They still bounced off a few stones and broken roots, though, and Zarius almost bit his tongue off. When they made it to the little bowl in the earth, surrounded by knolls, they were both drenched in sweat. Zarius smelled it wafting out of the wheelbarrow and resolved to burn the thing when he could walk again.

Panting, DK slumped down to the ground on his bare patch of earth and laid against the hill. The evening Sun peeked over the western hillside and painted his face in brilliant gold. Those warm waves crashed over Zarius, too, and he examined the sky. The vibrant periwinkle lost the harshness of midday with each passing minute, and with all these long, thin cloud layers, the Sunset would be divine.

Zarius focused on the sky for a while, probably longer than he ever had before. Something about all those interminable days and nights in the forge affected him in a profound way that he still couldn't put words to. Nothing like long hours with only the company of pain to shake up your thoughts. He relished even the dim, dull thuds in his splinted arm and wrapped-up ribcage. They were a far cry from the agony of a month ago.

"My arm's getting better," said Zarius.

DK sat up and rubbed his eyes. They were a clear, clean blue as he fixed them on Zarius, and Zarius held his gaze.

"I know," said DK.

"I'm gonna do what you did." Zarius let his eyes drift back to the sky, as close to the Sun as he could put them. "I'm going to be like that."

"Like what?"

Zarius blew air through his nose—the best scoff he could muster. "You know damn well. How did you do it?"

Unspoken thoughts passed like clouds over DK's suntanned face. He didn't answer at first, and Zarius didn't press it. He knew there was no real answer. DK had already told him as much. But that didn't stop him from asking again and again because to Zarius, it mattered. It was like Zarius saw a vision of himself, what he could be—what he *wanted* to be—and that vision saved his life. A whole host of big ideas and emotions were trying to cram themselves down small enough to fit in his head, and it had been that way since he first regained consciousness.

"It had something to do with this." DK gestured to everything. The sky. The Sun. The grass. The clouds. Zarius. DK himself. "All of it."

"It's what you've been working toward," said Zarius. "Now I know what I wanna work toward."

"I don't know about that," DK said without affectation. "I don't know."

"I do."

DK lapsed into thought, and Zarius let it go. They'd already been through it from a dozen different angles. Still, those images loomed large and awe-inspiring in his mind. DK towering over him, pupils burning with Sunlight in a vast sea of darkness. Brighter and stronger than those of the Dead Knight. And it happened after Zarius thought DK was dead and his own life unalterably maimed forever.

To Zarius, DK defeated not just the Dead Knight but Death itself. Illusion, sure, but in that moment, Zarius had believed it with his entire being. Because DK was the kind of person and the Day Knight the kind of legend that he *could* believe in. He *did* believe in it, even when DK explained what really happened, the nature of the bog witch's tricks. There was no truth to the matter. Zarius experienced something, and *that* was true. In that moment—one that Zarius would hold forever—it would always be true. The Day Knight channeled the Sun and became something more than himself.

"Why do you think she hasn't come for us?" Zarius asked.

It took a few moments for DK to open his eyes, but he did so without irritation. "I've been wondering that myself."

"She must've known I was hurt."

"Of course."

"And she saw as well as I did what happened to you. What you did."

DK pressed his lips together. Whispers passed through the tallgrass. A couple of hawks looped through the sky above them on frozen wings.

"Now we'll fight for sure," Zarius went on. "Are we gonna go to the bog?"

"I don't know yet." DK's voice was heavy. "What makes you say all that?"

Zarius looked at him, expressionless, sure of himself. "She saw the Day Knight. I think she thought that night would be the end of it. I think that attack took her time and effort to carry out, to make something like the Dead Knight. She didn't expect you to do what you did. Now she'll gather her strength, and she'll do it again. The Dead Knight will come back. Or something else."

"You're really fucking freaking me out right now," DK said.

Face twitching, Zarius pushed his eyes back to the sky and nestled down into the wheelbarrow so that he could no longer see DK.

"That might all be true," DK went on. "But it doesn't matter right now. Whatever happens happened. You get me? If it's gonna happen, so it will. But right now, you need to focus on recovering. And when you do, because you *will*, we're gonna get back to training. This was a long time off, and I'm gonna push you hard. Don't worry about *then*, whether that's in front of or behind us. Be here right now, and work on what you can work on. Meditate."

Silence fell aside from the goings on of the earth. The heavy smell of summer pervaded the air. So much life and vegetation, the hot, acrid scent of a long day drawing toward its conclusion. The Sun continued to slide down the sky like melting butter. It passed behind the crest of the western hill and threw them into cool shade.

Zarius closed his eyes as the sweat dried on his skin. He took a few deep breaths, then a few even deeper. Blood and carnage bubbled up. He saw DK's head slammed into the ground, the volcano of gore. He heard that horrific *shcrulk* of bone and brain mashed into pulp. He saw Derrick's head, rolling around, babbling, bloodied tongue lapping at the grass and flitting across his face.

Goosebumps raised Zarius's skin, and his whole body tingled, almost vibrated. The Dead Knight's voice clanged through his ears. DK on fire. DK smashed in the road. The Dead Knight standing over Zarius, poised for the kill. Derrick standing up, head hanging halfway down his back, his body staggering across the grass, through the hills, over the plains of prairie, stumbling into a sea of narrow, black tree trunks, splashing through warm, fetid puddles—like urine excreted by the earth itself. Out of the bounds of the natural and comprehensible.

Zarius realized his whole head was trembling, he was clenching his teeth so hard. With a sigh, he released the pressure, but the thoughts remained, too large and too strong to force out like unwanted guests. They stood like giants across the landscape of his mind. So he let them stand, and he forced his focus to the Sun. The giants walked across his path, but he kept going back to the Sun.

29

The square bustled with chattering people. Dozens of them clung to the Beggar's shade like vampires. DK picked his way through the crowd carrying a basket already loaded with a few vegetables and a new linen shirt. All types of smells, including the standard proliferation of body odor, wafted through the air, directing DK to the proper stands even when he couldn't see through the crowd. With money from Ezekiel—the way he usually acquired it—DK browsed the salted meats at the butchery stall. He haggled with the seller and came away with a heavier basket and an emptier pocket.

Counting what he had left, DK milled through the throng in no particular direction, thinking he was probably stocked up. Lost in thought, he bumped into someone and muttered an apology, stepping to the side.

"Hey Christian."

DK jumped and whirled. "Oh, *Caroline*." His scrambled thoughts came back together in the wrong order. "H-Hey. How are you?"

She gazed at him with those dark, penetrating eyes. As if she could see that disorder in his thinking. "I'm okay."

Awkward panic rose in his throat like acid reflux. "Uhh . . . it's good to see you."

"Is it?"

He grimaced. They had to raise their voices over the general commotion. "Oof. Yeah I, uh, never called on you."

"You sure didn't."

Sighing, DK met her gaze. "I'm sorry about that. It's just that, well Zarius got hurt and he's—"

"Zarius got *hurt*?" Concern lit up her eyes. "Oh my gosh, I'm so sorry. I wasn't trying to be a bitch. I just, well I—" She hung her head. "I'm sorry. Is he okay?"

Thrown off yet again, DK stammered. "Uh-uh yeah he's, well he's getting better every day. He's back on his feet, but he can't do a whole lot."

"Oh my gosh," Caroline repeated. "So he got *really* hurt."

DK paused for a moment, chewing his lip. "Yeah. He did."

"Can we see him?"

"You, uh, you want to . . . You and?"

"Gretchen's here too." Caroline stood on her tiptoes and looked around as bodies filed past them. "Oh she's here somewhere." Caroline reached into her basket. "Here, do you want a couple eggs? My parents sent me to sell ours."

"Well sure. Yeah, sure. Thanks." DK took a couple eggs and nestled them in a cloth. "I don't . . . I doubt he'll want to see anyone."

"Well can we come find out?"

DK glanced off but finally shrugged. "Sure. Why not."

Without further ado, Caroline grabbed DK's free hand and started pulling him through the crowd. He complied like a docile ox. They came out in front of a plain stand consisting of just a few boards nailed together. A couple people loitered in front of it, coming away with eggs. They swung around the side, and DK saw Gretchen's lanky figure behind the stand.

A hot breeze blew through and ruffled DK's hair. His shirt billowed, the air vented by half a dozen sizable holes. When he looked down, he felt ridiculous, so he pulled the old rag off to don his new one. The morning Sun warmed the creases of his chest and abdomen. As he pulled his new shirt over his head, he noticed Caroline staring hard at him.

"Sorry," he said, trying to smooth out his hair. "I just realized how ratty that shirt was."

Caroline blinked and shook her head. "Umm . . ." She shrugged and stepped up to whisper in Gretchen's ear. Gretchen glanced back and threw a goofy, beaming grin at DK, and he raised a hand. Caroline stepped back over to him.

"We're almost through all the eggs."

"Good haul?" DK asked.

She snorted. "Well. We won't starve *today*."

DK laughed, and she smiled. He set his basket down and rearranged the contents to make sure the eggs wouldn't get smashed. For some annoying reason, his heart was riding high and unnecessarily fast. Stupid heart.

Composing himself, DK stood up and made sure to lengthen his breathing as Caroline twirled a loose strand of black hair, gazing at him with her head slightly tipped down.

"Sorry again." DK sighed through his teeth. "Ugh. Sorry. I feel awkward. I could've at least come by."

"If Zarius was hurt, I don't blame you at all," said Caroline. "Don't even worry about it."

"Thanks," DK said. "Yeah. It's been a long . . . it's . . ." His mouth pinched down to one side. "Well, it's just been long. I don't know."

He threw up his hands. A caged idiot couldn't have spat out worse drivel than that.

Caroline giggled, and he didn't know if it was at him or with him, but he honestly didn't care. "DK, it's okay. Seriously."

A few steps away, Gretchen got into a heated haggle with a rough-faced older man who seemed to be questioning the integrity of her eggs. Gretchen fired back at him with such intensity that DK startled where he stood, and he was getting ready to intervene when the action died down. The man ended up taking the rest of the eggs, and Gretchen turned around with a cheerful smile as she stuffed the bronze into the pocket of her white apron.

"Done," she said.

DK helped them lift the little stand and carry it over beside the wall of the church, out of the way, where they would leave it until next time. Together, they all made toward DK's hovel, and he was mentally approaching Zarius, trying to figure out what he'd say. Or rather, how he would end up telling the girls that Zarius said fuck no he didn't want to see anybody.

When they made it, DK asked them to wait, and he went inside. Zarius was lying down, uncovered, only wearing a set of linen pants he'd torn into very short shorts.

"Hey," DK said.

"What's all that noise out there?" Zarius asked. He turned his head to look at DK, and DK remembered not long ago when he couldn't do so much as that.

"Caroline and Gretchen are here."

"Oh really? That's great. Enjoy talking to them outside."

"They wanna say hi to you."

"Fuck no."

DK frowned. "I told them you got hurt. They're worried about you."

"Oh bullshit. They can worry about my dick. Caroline just wants to deepthroat your shit."

DK's face got hot as he closed his eyes and shook his head. "Well you're vulgar today."

"Your mama."

"What about just Gretchen?"

Zarius narrowed his eyes. "She ask for that?"

"Well not exactly. But I mean—"

"Fine."

DK cut himself short. "Really?"

"Yeah fine. Sure. So you and Caroline can go bone or what?"

DK hissed and feinted a kick. "Will you keep your voice down? Good Lord."

Zarius smirked. "Go on then. Send 'er in."

Rolling his eyes, DK left his basket under their tiny table and went back outside, where the girls stood whispering to each other. Women filtered in and out of nearby hovels with children and infants in tow, carrying water, hanging laundry. The smell of cooking eggs seeped out of the nearby hovels. Guess it was an eggs kind of day.

"Well it went about how I expected," said DK. "He, ah . . ." Well shit. He didn't know how to say it.

"He doesn't want a bunch of people in there," DK said. "Maybe just, like, one."

Caroline and Gretchen looked at each other. "Is three a lot of people?" Caroline asked.

DK's face warmed up again. "You know . . ." He glanced over his shoulder at the warped wooden door. "I mean, it's not a big place. Or a nice one."

"Does that *one person* he's okay with happen to be Gretchen?" asked Caroline. She gave DK a pointed examination.

DK chuckled. "Oh . . . Well. You know . . ."

"Interesting," said Caroline. "He's not like a pervert or something is he?"

DK pursed his lips. "Oh he's absolutely a pervert. But he'll be respectful with Gretchen. That much I can guarantee."

Gretchen giggled while Caroline continued staring down DK. She finally tore her eyes away to glance around at the peasants carrying on. "Isn't that a little scandalous? We can't just leave them in there alone."

"I stopped giving a shit about scandal a long time ago." DK shrugged. "That one's on you."

"Does everyone know he's in there?"

DK got exasperated. "Okay well it *sounds* like we're gonna be shooting for another time. We should think about some training anyway."

The door to the hovel banged open, and there stood Zarius, fully dressed now. A shirt on, at least. DK joined the girls in staring at him in surprise, and Zarius pointed right at Gretchen.

"Do you wanna go for a walk?" he asked.

"Sure," Gretchen said, smiling.

Zarius hobbled into the street like an ancient war veteran, and he took Gretchen's arm and led her toward the closest gate. Their progress was incredibly slow, but with each passing step, DK grinned a little wider.

Way to go, Z.

"What are you smiling about?" Caroline asked.

"He's walking," DK said. He turned to look at Caroline. "What do you say? Shall we do the same?"

30

Fat white clouds communed around a blue pool in the sky. DK led Zarius as he bounded down an obscure footpath that wound alongside a fetid pond. Little insects flitted all around, and they ducked to clear some branches. They came out on the other side in another stretch of flat prairie surrounded by tallgrass. Some cottonwoods lazed by the road.

"How you doin?" DK puffed.

Zarius bore down, churning his legs. Without answering, he passed DK and took the lead, breathing hard but relishing the exertion. He raced down the path, arms pumping in rhythm with his strides. The breeze on his face was cooler and sweeter than a whisper from heaven. Even the errant chirping from his ribs was music to his ears; those chirps were a far cry from the haggard wailing of weeks prior.

As they neared the wagon trail that designated their finish line, DK came abreast of Zarius, so Zarius poured it on. They both broke into all-out sprints, hammering down the path, jostling for position. At the last second, DK spurted ahead by a nose and went flying onto the road.

Horses screamed. Zarius heard a great creaking of wood as a brown shape clattered into his vision. Unable to stop, his legs twisted up, and he hit the ground in a half-slide half-fall. A cloud of dust followed him as he shot under the carriage and out on the other side, missing the rear wheels by inches. Pain flared in ribs as he tumbled into a ditch, scratched up by thistles.

"*What on God's green earth,*" a gruff voice hollered.

"Z?" DK cried from nearby. "Z, where are you?"

Zarius pulled himself upright, slightly bent to one side. Raw pain pulsed in his torso, but it wasn't debilitating. He stood up and rubbed the sore spots under his arm, wincing. DK saw him and crashed over through the vegetation.

"*Shit,*" DK spat, sweat streaming down his anxious face. "Are you alright?"

"What are you?" a man yelled from the top of a carriage in between calming words to his horses. "A bunch of fuckin lunatics?"

DK and Zarius stared at him, and he stared back.

"Move along," DK said.

"Sheeeiiitt," the man said. He snapped the reins, and his spooked horses got into motion again. "You go dig yourselves a couple of graves while you're at it." The carriage rolled on, trailing a cape of dust. DK and Zarius stood panting, catching their breath.

"Fuck me," DK said, shaking his head. Concern gripped his face as he patted Zarius on the lower back. "You sure you're good?"

"Yeah." Zarius rolled his shoulders back. Little pinpricks went into his ribs, but it was nothing he wasn't used to. In fact, it wasn't bad at all. He looked at DK with a crazy grin. "I'm fucking good, dude."

After a moment, DK smiled back. "Well thank God for that."

"I'm fucking *good.*"

Zarius took off back onto the road and started chasing the

carriage at a run. He ran through the fine filter of dust hanging on the lazy air. The clouds overhead turned a little grayer, as if preparing to let loose some rain. His shadow weakened on the ground. After thirty seconds or so, DK caught up to him.

"Don't tell me you're chasing this guy," DK said.

"I'm just *running*." Zarius said it like a crazy little kid. He flew down the road until they came up over a rise and saw the little smoke trails and buildings of Ten-Berry come into view. The carriage rolled on down the slope away from them, and Zarius coasted to a walk while DK matched him.

"Feels good?" DK asked.

"Feels fucking great." Zarius couldn't stop grinning.

They ambled toward town. Little birds scattered and resettled in the long, brown stalks of grass lilting on the sides of the road. Tufts of cotton drifted through the air, almost weightless. When they made it to a familiar point on the road, they veered off and headed into the hills, making for the meditation spot. Only now did Zarius's joy falter, but he forced his legs to keep moving.

When they made it and sat down, DK didn't set right into an admonishing lecture. He didn't even give Zarius a severe glance. He just closed his eyes, extended his breathing, and went somewhere else. Zarius watched him go, wishing that DK could just take him along, wherever it was. However he got there.

Uneasy, Zarius settled down and turned his attention to the world. The clouds had broken up but now gathered for another assault on the fortress of the Sun. A faint, swirling breeze stirred the grass. Birds like moving stamps silhouetted on the clouds. Cool, fresh air washed in and out of his lungs with each breath.

With the air, Zarius brought his awareness into his body. The grass scratching his legs. Those starbursts flashing in his ribs and arm. The beating of his heart, the wetness of his eyes. Zarius inhabited himself, but his mind flashed elsewhere like lightning in a thunderstorm. An aimless thought would light up a desolate landscape, and it was all he could do to turn away from it.

The Dead Knight loomed large and frightening. Bits of that metallic voice crackled in Zarius's ears. He remembered the punch that crushed him. One slip up. One moment of exposure, and the Dead Knight capitalized. Zarius remembered how he hit the ground, how the dirt filled his eyes and grouted his teeth. He let out an involuntary grunt at the viciousness of the memory.

Shuddering, he tried to bring his thoughts to heel. Be; don't *remember*. He wanted to live in *this* body, not the one so abused all those days ago. But it was hard. It pissed him off. He'd focus on the prickle of the grass on his legs only to remember how he kicked and squirmed through those first agonizing nights. He'd focus on the fabric under his hands only to feel his palms grow wet and warm as he caught a whiff of Derrick's blood.

Zarius never went to the fabled place he dreamed of, never brushed shoulders with DK's consciousness. No, he remained alone and distracted, firmly planted on and of the earth. No metaphysical escape for Zarius. No reprieve from these bloodsucking thoughts. The focus-killers accomplished their goal, as they always did, and Zarius only hated them more for it.

Unable to sit still any longer, he quietly got up and began to pace through the grass. He stayed on the shorter buffalograss so he wouldn't make a bunch of noise. Pacing pacified him. The thoughts couldn't zone in on him as easily if he kept moving. He walked in random lines before settling into a big circle that crossed the far side of the hill behind DK, and he focused on walking. He measured each step, checked for any hazards, noted the firing of the muscles in his legs as they propelled him along.

In this way, Zarius began to shrink. All that was Zarius didn't seem quite so Zarius. It lasted for almost a minute. He was just a collection of cells consuming air, expelling air. A group of muscles contracting and expanding. And that was all he was. No thoughts penetrated his mind.

After dozens of seconds, Zarius's head snapped back, and he came to a dead stop. Fuzz filled his brain like he'd just woken up from a nap. He blinked, frowned, raised an eyebrow, as if trying to find someone to interrogate. What the hell was that?

Stunned, Zarius took some time to reflect. The big, nervous clouds began to spit little drops of rain. They dripped into Zarius's hair, and he noticed the western horizon growing brighter, because the Sun was coming down. The first glimpse of evening. Zarius gritted his teeth.

Though still blistering hot, the days were getting shorter.

31

Dusk painted the western sky in brilliant reds and yellows, the colors fading like blood draining from the wound of the Sun's departure. DK walked alone down a narrow road through hovels in Ten-Berry. He covered his face against the stench of a freshly-dumped chamber pot and shuddered when he finally passed beyond it. The ground sucked at his feet from an afternoon rain, but he trudged on through the mud, almost at the southern edge of town.

Nestled against the low stone wall, near the southern gate, DK saw the long, squat wooden building. A crude fence of frayed wooden slats hemmed in a sloppy square of churned-up dirt. DK passed along next to the fence until he reached the door on one end of the building. Firelight flickered through one square window and through the gaps in the door. A voice bade him enter.

An older man, small and skinny behind a large desk, sat hunched in a chair, examining a few pieces of parchment. As soon as he saw DK, his eyes crinkled, and he stood up, jutting a hand out.

"Well I'll be," said Stanton Bainbridge. A sweep of coarse, gray hair on his head. Small, sunken eyes on a narrow face. He grinned wider. "You look like somebody I know."

"Hey Stanton." DK grinned and stepped forward to shake his hand.

Stanton hovered in front of his chair. "Good to see you, Christian. I thought you forgot the way down here."

"I got busy."

Stanton cocked a knowing eyebrow. "So I've heard. For the first time in . . . I don't even *know* how long, I heard some chatter about you. I think someone may have even mentioned the 'Day Knight' once or twice. Like as suddenly as the weather started warming up, you stopped coming around here and went a little broader. Didn't even deign to tell me you were planning on it, and all those times we chatted."

Despite a vague tone of hurt in his words, Stanton looked happy and congenial. DK put on a sympathetic smile and shrugged.

"Sometimes things just happen."

"Don't I know it." Stanton eased back down into his chair. "Well Louelle sure as hell misses you I'm sure. I've been taking her out on my own, keepin those legs strong, but I think she's been ticked I ain't you."

DK chuckled. "I'll have to tell her I'm sorry. That *is* what I'm here about."

Stanton's eyes lit up. "You wanna take her out?"

"Yes. Not tonight, but yes. I wanted to ask how she's getting on."

"Oh she's a peach." Stanton tossed a hand. "Going on eleven. Now she thinks she's smarter than everybody."

"You think she could handle two riders, in armor?"

Stanton stared at the parchment on the desk for a moment before lifting his eyes. "You take somebody on?"

"Yeah, an apprentice."

Stanton let out a hoot and slapped the table. "Well I'll be. How the hell you'd get wise enough for that?"

DK grinned. "I'm teaching him to fight, not to be wise."

That got Stanton laughing, and he tipped so far back in his chair that he almost fell over. A small fire crackled in the hearth to DK's right, so he stepped in front of the window to catch a cool lick of wind across his neck.

"For damn sure," said Stanton. "Louelle's gettin on, but she's still gettin on if you catch my meaning. Whatever you thought of her before is still true for now. Damn workhorse, still got that hot streak when she needs it. You won't win any races, and I hope I don't need to tell you to take it easy with two loafs on her back, but she could handle it. How far you ridin?"

DK's eyes wandered. "Just around."

"Around, eh?" Stanton bounced a pointy eyebrow. "If you're asking if she could make it to the bog and back under load, I'd say yes. At a nice easy canter, mind you. That's an estimation."

"Who said anything about the bog?"

Stanton put two hands up. "Nobody did. But you're asking about a horse I've been putting up for damn near five years now that you ain't ridden for war in what? Almost half that time? I remember what happened last time. Maybe you're not askin, but that's me tellin. If you're riding to the bog, she could make it. I hope to God you're not, but let's not play paddycake."

"Alright then." DK shuffled his feet. "What's the, uh, state of the account?"

Stanton snorted. "You think I'd be chattin like a butterchurn with you if we weren't square?"

A beat. DK furrowed his brow. "We're square?"

"Hell. Ezekiel paid that horse off two years ago, Christian." Stanton's face warbled, and he lowered it to his desk as his voice followed suit. "Was that supposed to be a secret . . ."

A stone rose in DK's throat that he couldn't swallow. He stood there for a few moments while Stanton anxiously leafed through papers, casting them all aside.

"Ezekiel paid her off?" DK asked.

Stanton groaned. "Well I think I might be a horse's ass. Look, don't tell the old man I told you that, will you? I don't remember if I was supposed to say nothin. It was a long time ago. But let's just say Louelle's yours, and you got that stable to your name long as you need it."

Curling his lips in, DK nodded. "I think I'll go see her."

"You do that." Stanton waved him toward the door behind the desk almost frantically. "Yeah go on and see her. I'll see about a double saddle next time you come through. Gimme a week or so. Go on, and let yourself out the back. Good to see you, Christian."

"Good to see you too," DK said softly as he exited through a door behind Stanton's desk. It shut with a final *thunk*.

As his eyes and ears adjusted, DK saw the row of stables stretching away. Snorts and quiet breaths puffed into the center alleyway, and the musty smell of hay permeated the air. In a trance, DK moved all the way down, past the big, swinging heads with glassy eyes. As soon as he made to the last stable on the left, another long face jutted out over the stall door, right up into his.

"Hey girl," DK said softly. He put his hands up and rubbed her snout and down her neck. Louelle snorted right into his face, and he laughed as his eyes flew shut. "Okay, okay, I'm sorry."

Louelle landed her head on his shoulder hard enough that it bent his knees.

"*Ow,*" he said. "Hey I'm *sorry*." He laughed as he kept petting her. "I'm gonna take you out soon, alright?"

Those big black eyes seemed to really focus on him, flashing only the faintest glimmer in the darkness. DK found a pile of hay and picked some up. Louelle ate it right off his palm and stepped back, munching. DK folded his arms on top of the stall door and watched her. When she swallowed the hay, she just stood there and stared back at him. He thought about the past.

"Big ol horse," DK said.

Louelle bobbed her head a couple times.

"You're gonna have to meet Zarius."

She snorted.

"Alright." DK patted the rough wood and stretched a hand out. Louelle put her head against it, and he rubbed her one last time. "I'll be back soon. Promise."

With that, DK left through the open doorway at the end of the stable. When he glanced back, he saw Louelle's long face shifting in the darkness, watching him go.

32

Zarius held the reins with white knuckles as the big, speckled brown horse named Louelle trotted slowly underneath him. He gripped the sides of the saddle with his legs and almost gave himself a charley horse.

"You look terrified," DK said from where he stood in the middle of the dusty stable yard. Louelle churned up soft dirt as she followed the perimeter of the fence, her legs and pace smooth and easy.

"Fuck you," Zarius grunted. He stared holes in the back of Louelle's head as if he could reach into her brain and control her from the inside. She continued her even trot around the yard.

"I'm not telling her to do this," Zarius said. The reins trembled in his hands.

"Well, she's doing it," said DK, pivoting where he stood to continue talking. "If you want it to stop, just make it stop."

"You mean make *her* stop," Zarius yelled. "You know damn well this ain't a magic carpet."

"*Ask* her to stop."

"Where's the damn translator?" Zarius continued watching the back of Louelle's head and tried to sneak a deep breath. He drew back on the reins, but she snapped her head once and forced him to relent.

"She doesn't *wanna* stop," Zarius said, a little higher pitched.

"Who's riding who here?"

Gritting his teeth, Zarius yanked the reins hard. The bit slammed into the back of Louelle's mouth, and she reared up, neighing. Sudden fear loosened Zarius's hands, and he fell right off and landed flat on his back. "*Unngghhh.*"

Louelle snorted once after he landed and walked off to the opposite side of the yard, throwing her head all over. When Zarius saw DK's face appear over him, he sneered and scrambled to his feet without aid. He glared at DK, searching for the tiniest shard of masked humor, but DK just stared flatly back at him, hair and face greasy with sweat.

"You're actually getting better," DK said as he finally cracked a grin.

Zarius shoved him and scoffed as he dusted himself off. He threw a menacing gaze at Louelle who stared at them from the far corner of the yard.

"Z, stop it," DK said. "You're on the same team."

"She's on her own team," Zarius said, rubbing a goose egg on the back of his head. "She's a wildcard."

"No she's not." DK rolled his eyes. "You're scared, and that makes her scared. She wants you to be confident."

"Oh is that what she wants?" Zarius looked at her again. Her tail swished, and he turned back to DK. "Well why don't you just tell *her* that? You know, since you can read her mind."

"Okay simmer down." DK flicked a hand and walked over to Louelle where she let him nuzzle right up against her.

An ebullient Sun wore a wide halo of light at the very top of the sky, like a preacher with both hands on the pulpit at the zenith of his exaltation. All of the clouds were keeping their distance, and the heat was unrelenting.

"Yeah, two peas in a pod, you and Louelle," Zarius said, scowling. A thin veneer of dust hung on the air. "Maybe she thinks you're her boyfriend."

"She knows you're not being nice," DK said. "Come over here and pet her."

Zarius pushed a pile of dirt over with his foot. "I'm good, thanks."

"Do it."

He spun around and did a big shrug, freezing with his hands up. "I'm . . . all tapped out for the day."

"Are you really scared of a horse?"

Zarius jabbed a finger at him. "Hey . . . She's big, alright? She just threw me."

"Come on." DK rubbed his forehead on her cheek, and Louelle just stood there, snorting. "See? She didn't even throw you. You just fell off."

"Did not."

"Zarius *come on*. Come over here and pet her. That's how you're gonna get more comfortable."

Zarius broke the sticky seal of his shirt on his back only for it to squeeze him again when he released it. "What difference does it make? We're not cavalry. You even said you barely know how to fight on horseback."

"Riding itself is a *skill*." DK beckoned him with both arms.

"You ride the horse. I'll sprint."

"It's an order."

Folding his arms, Zarius used his malcontent for the courage to storm right up next to them and stand there, pretending to be mad. Louelle jostled a little bit and shifted away from him.

"Alright." DK curled his lips. "That was extremely aggressive. Good job."

Zarius sighed and let his arms fall. "You said it was an order."

"Now *relax*, and let her sniff your hand."

"She already sniffed it."

"Let her sniff it again."

Scowling, Zarius raised his hand out and slowly pushed it in front of Louelle's hanging nose. She tipped her head forward and sniffed him and blew a couple puffs of air. Zarius watched her all the time, gazing at the large brown marble in her head. Her eye reflected the Sun, somehow looking at him and everything around him. Her brown head featured a scatter of white flecks on her face and a long, beige mane hanging down her neck. She was damn big.

"See?" DK kept rubbing her neck on the opposite side, and Louelle's head tipped away, but only a bit.

Zarius shifted his hand up and touched the side of one finger to her face. Her fine hair brushed against his skin, and she jolted an inch before settling. This time, he rubbed his palm on her cheek and gave her a couple light pats. That smooth brown looking glass captured him, and Zarius pushed his hand down her neck and applied more pressure.

Louelle stood there. She didn't spook or startle, and Zarius petted her for a minute while DK looked off and said nothing. There was some glimmer of wisdom in her eye, and Zarius felt sorry that he'd yanked the reins so hard.

"Alright," Zarius said quietly. "She's a good horse."

"Awww." DK hugged his arms around Louelle's neck as she snorted. "You hear that girl? Yes you are. Good horse. Very good horse."

"But I think she still has a little bit of a bastard streak in her."

"Then you two should get along great. Come on." DK swung

himself up over her and landed on the saddle before he offered a hand to Zarius. Zarius took it and hopped up onto the much smaller, much less comfortable rear seat.

"Where are we going?" Zarius asked. He examined the saddle. "Ah, what the . . . I don't even have a pommel thing."

"You're gonna have to hold onto me."

"Pause."

"I'm serious. Otherwise you're going down for sure."

"Oh now I'm *going down*?" Zarius grimaced and shook his head. "Yeah I'm not sure I signed up for all that."

"Fuck off." DK guided Louelle to the edge of the fence and hopped down to open the gate. It squealed like a dying mouse, and DK led Louelle through and closed it behind her before hopping on again.

"Fuck me." Zarius said. He wiped a slick forearm across his even slicker face. "It's a billion degrees out here."

The Sun bore down, still bullying the clouds. Everywhere they looked, air warbled and shimmered over the ground. The oceans of tallgrass sported no waves, and there wasn't a critter to be seen or heard.

"Feels good," DK said.

Louelle trotted down a wagon trail on the east side of Ten-Berry. About equidistant between the badlands and rocky outcroppings to their left and the stand of trees concealing Quail Creek way off to their right. Their swords made a steady thumping sound as they jostled against Louelle's flank. Zarius sat with both hands gripping the edge of the saddle, leaning back so as not to touch DK. The back of DK's shirt was so wet it was translucent, and Zarius grimaced.

"You're sweating like a pig."

"And you smell like a lavender breeze," DK shot back.

"Just saying." Zarius shrugged and let his eyes drift around. It was, after all, a hell of a lot better than walking. Without the artificial breeze from Louelle's movement, he thought he might just be dead already. He slung his waterskin around and sipped a single mouthful. It was already getting light.

"Can we go back now?" Zarius asked.

DK craned his neck. "Oh now you *don't* want to patrol?"

"I don't want to *die*, and the Sun is trying to kill me. Besides, this ain't no real patrol. You didn't make me put armor on."

"I did that for Louelle," DK corrected. "And maybe the Sun is trying to tell you something."

Zarius snorted but didn't respond. He tipped his head back and let the Sun blast him in the face. Even with his eyes squeezed shut, it felt like his eyelids might burn off and his eyeballs melt into the depths of his skull. When he brought his head upright again and opened his eyes, his whole vison swam in painterly waves. For a moment, he had no thoughts, only the memory of the Sunlight pervading his head, and then something hit him.

"Oh God." He yanked his shirt up over his nose. "What the fuck is that?"

"What?" DK's voice sharpened. "What is it?"

Zarius gagged. "That *smell*?"

As DK slowed Louelle down to a walk, he gagged, too. "Fuck me," he choked out.

Less than a stone's throw away, Zarius spotted a strange disturbance. Like a sprinkle of night left in the air, somehow escaping the Sun. But it was moving, morphing.

"Flies," Zarius said, pointing past DK's shoulder.

DK guided Louelle toward it, but she came to a stop on her own. He nudged her with his heels, and she just snorted and backed up a step. "Alright girl," DK said as he slid off. He tapped Zarius's leg, but Zarius just stared down at him, clutching his shirt to his face.

"You sure?" Zarius asked.

DK furrowed his brow. "What do you mean?"

Even Zarius didn't know, but his stomach was churning. "I have a bad feeling."

"Well then we better go check it out."

"Fuck," Zarius grumbled, but he slid off the saddle and joined DK on the spongy earth. They waded off the path into tallgrass, some of it almost chest high. It didn't take long to hear the buzzing of the cloud of flies.

"*Ow shit*," Zarius snarled as he swatted at something on his arm. "Fucking deerflies."

DK slapped a fly on his own neck but kept pushing forward. Zarius hitched for a couple steps but then chased after him. The buzzing got louder, and the stench got worse. It was death, but something else. A foulness Zarius couldn't describe, but not unfamiliar.

They saw something through the tallgrass, covered in a black carpet. DK paused for a couple moments, peering through the thin golden stalks. "Something's dead."

"No shit," Zarius said through his makeshift mask, clutching his sword in his free hand. "Fucking cooking in the Sun."

"But it's fresh. There aren't any maggots."

"Christ."

DK moved forward. It took everything Zarius had not to scream at him to stop. His revulsion intensified to a state bordering panic. He remembered this kind of foreboding. He had it before the Dead Knight almost killed him.

Staying close to DK, Zarius scanned the grass all around them, but he could barely see ten feet in any direction. Something creeping low to the ground could have gotten very close without detection. Sweat poured down his body, slickening his grip on his sword.

"Oh Jesus," said DK in a strangled voice. "It's a person."

Zarius squeezed his teeth together. He didn't want to look.

"What the fuck," DK muttered, pushing aside the vegetation to get a better view. "Maybe it's *not* a person."

Finally, the morbid curiosity outweighed Zarius's fear. With his heart hammering in his chest, he opened his eyes and stepped up next to DK as buzzing flies wreathed his face. A human figure laid on the ground on a flattened patch of tallgrass, as if it had just collapsed recently. Flies crawled all over it, but the mass of them seemed to be inside a gaping wound in the body's torso. It was just a small, malnourished figure, maybe five feet tall. Disturbed, Zarius noticed how the flies seemed to stop right at the neckline, leaving the face entirely clear.

And that was where he understood what DK meant. It didn't so much look like a human face as a deliberate but poorly executed *attempt* at a human face. It was too long and too narrow. The jaw jutted sharply down, and the mouth hung open, studded with errant teeth all over the inside. The eyes were wide open, glass-like, one blue and one brown, but the pupils were missing. Little lines of black sludge rimmed the border between the eye and the bottom eyelid. Patches of brown hair clung to parts of the bulbous scalp.

Zarius turned away and went crashing back through the grass. He ran all the way to Louelle's side and heaved himself up onto her back so roughly that she whinnied and stamped the ground. A moment later, DK appeared at his side, wide-eyed and questioning.

"What?" DK asked, as if he were afraid Zarius knew more than he did. "What's wrong?"

"Nah," Zarius said. "I don't like that shit. Let's get the fuck outta here."

DK's blue eyes shone in the blinding Light of the day. "What do you mean? Talk to me."

"Something ain't right, man. That shit ain't right." He looked up toward the cloud of flies as if they were about to start moving closer. "You remember the deer?"

One moment saw all the color drain from DK's face, and he hefted himself up in front of Zarius and got Louelle turned around. He goaded her up to a strong lope, and Zarius didn't say anything as he leaned forward and wrapped his arms around DK's torso. It took everything he had not to beg him to go faster.

Behind them, a set of dead, misshapen eyes blinked one time before the flies crawled over them.

FALL

33

Summer began to sputter. The stranglehold of heat loosened, and the mornings dawned with the hint of a chill. DK and Zarius trained endlessly and meditated diligently. They ate good meals and pushed each other past their limits. Several more patrols saw little meaningful action; most went entirely fruitless. They tracked a supposed group of bandits in the wilderness west of Ten-Berry only to find three half-starved young men who capitulated after a couple swings of their rusty swords.

As the leaves began to turn on the cottonwood trees, and the tallgrass slouched from the peak of its posture, DK noticed the restlessness in his apprentice. He tried to broach the subject, but Zarius kept mute besides some vague platitudes. Sometimes, the two of them met Caroline and Gretchen at the tavern for drinks, but Zarius seemed quiet and distant. Still, DK didn't want to press it. He wanted to give Zarius the space to process things.

Finally, on a cool night of ample stars and rustling wind, Zarius sat in his bed, alternately picking dirt from under his fingernails and gnawing on them. DK occasionally glanced over at him but mostly let his eyes fall into the morphing red and yellow tongues of the fire which he sat beside. Wood crackled and blackened, consumed by the flames, and the plume of smoke gathered at the ceiling, fighting to escape through the vent. Empty bowls of stew rested on the table, and DK's eyes were heavy after a long day of conditioning.

"I'm fuckin tired of this shit, man," Zarius said suddenly.

DK's eyes flew open. An icy edge of fear laced his thoughts, but he took a moment to breathe and let it melt. "What do you mean?"

"I haven't found a real goddamn fight. You always end up handling the baddies, and I get the morons."

DK's eyes drifted to Zarius. Firelight flickered against the uneven surface of the walls. "Be careful what you wish for."

"I know, I know." Zarius threw up his hands. "I just, like I want to pop the goddamn cherry, you know? I don't *want* to have some life or death shit, but I hate feeling like I'm waiting for that. Like it's sneaking up on me, and I don't know when it's coming."

"That's the nature of what we're doing. You can't know."

"And I don't *need* to know. I just wanna get the big one under my belt and get past it."

"You've done great so far." DK gave him a sympathetic smile. "You probably already know what I have to say on it."

Zarius let out a grumbling sigh. "Yeah. Patience. Discipline. Stay present. I'm trying my best."

DK chuckled. "And I know you are. It shows. You're a great swordsman now. You can actually give the impression that you know what you're doing when you're riding Louelle. We aren't running a race, and you're only competing against the you from yesterday."

"Agh, I *know* all that." Zarius tore a thread from his blanket and wrapped it tight around his finger.

"But something's still bothering you."

"Maybe it ain't the shit that *might* happen but the shit that already *has*." The words tumbled out. "I keep fucking having these nightmares and they're fucking up my sleep and shit. And I keep thinking about the shit we've seen and what it means but I don't *know* what it means so I just keep wondering and it's distracting and goddamnit fuck it all to hell."

DK was surprised to see a sheen come over Zarius's eyes. "I didn't know you were struggling so much."

"I'm not trying to," Zarius growled. His fingertip was purple, and he slowly unraveled the thread. "I'm trying *not* to. Fucking Derrick and that body and the Dead Knight, man. I keep seeing all that shit in my head. I wake up thinking it's the first morning after I got hurt and I have to go through it all again. And I guess maybe I feel like if I can get in a *fight* and just fucking do it right, something will change."

The fire crackled. DK looked away while Zarius scrubbed his face. He twiddled a piece of tinder between his thumb and forefinger, and he asked the Sun to help him find the right words.

"It won't help."

"Huh?" Zarius asked, almost in accusation.

"Killing somebody isn't going to help you deal with death. It would probably only make it worse. Nothing from outside is gonna fix how you feel. You need to accept it. That's how it goes away, whatever it is. You got hurt really bad. So did I, once. It sticks with you, but you can't focus on making sure it never happens again. You need to understand that it *could* happen again. You could do everything right and still lose, still get hurt. Or you could end up killing somebody who maybe didn't deserve it. You've gotta let it go, Z. You've gotta trust the Sun."

"The fucking Sun, man." Zarius shook his head. "You know that's just you saying God, right? Just your version of God."

DK shrugged. "So what if it is?"

"So you don't believe in God, but somehow you can believe in the Sun. You can believe in the Sun more than most of these motherfuckers do in God. I saw what happened to you, when you fought the Dead Knight. But I don't know how to believe like that. I *still* fucking suck at meditating." He gritted his teeth for a couple tense moments. "I feel like I'm not fucking doing anything right."

"Hey, you gotta go easy on yourself, man." DK went over and sat down beside him, and Zarius turned his head the other way. "You're twenty years old. I didn't know jack shit back then, either. Don't try to be me, okay? You just have to try to be the best *you*. It sounds lame, but it's true. You aren't gonna get there by trying to do the same shit as me in the same way I do it. You're gonna figure some of that out for yourself, but it takes time. You're doing a good job."

"Doesn't *fuckin* feel like it," Zarius hissed. "I feel like I'm goin crazy."

DK reached over and patted him on the shoulder. "You're already there."

Zarius snorted, but a smile snatched his lips as he shook his head. "Man fuck you."

DK grinned, but they both almost went airborne when a light knock sounded at the door. Jumping to his feet, DK stepped over and tried to peer through the gaps in the door, but the Sun had just dipped below the horizon and left only a small shadow on the doorstep. No, two shadows.

DK opened the door, and there was Caroline. Gretchen hovered a few steps behind her, already wearing that goofy grin. Caroline beamed when DK appeared, and he managed a smile.

"Oh, hey," he said. Zarius hovered behind his shoulder, and Gretchen's grin widened. "What's up?" DK asked.

"Do you guys wanna go to the tavern?" Caroline asked.

Before DK could even turn to glance at Zarius, Zarius blurted out a yes. So, they threw on their shoddy cloth shoes, and the foursome made their way to the tavern. The evening was cool, a shade short of chilly, and they passed around easy conversation. The road was hard packed from a late dry spell, and little snakes of dust slithered atop it like flowing veins. Firelight flickered through the many small doors they passed by, accompanied by the chatter of kids resisting bed and the clatter of housewares scrubbed and stowed away. Ten-Berry slipped into the dreamy lull of dusk, and a few other pedestrians meandered in the direction of the tavern. The musky smell of fall hung heavy on the air, but the Beggar maintained its voluptuous canopy for now.

When they made it into the crowded and lively tavern, DK locked in on an aberration immediately. Through gaps in the mob, he saw three men seated at the farthest end of the bar, all turned in toward each other as if discussing private business. Each man was larger than the last, and their clothing spoke more to nobility than peasantry, though they didn't appear stiff or uncomfortable.

"Knights," DK said aloud.

"The fuck you said?" Zarius started craning his neck, and DK jabbed him in the ribs.

"*Hey*," Zarius said.

"Don't start staring," DK said.

"Where are they?"

"Z, you better keep a lid on it tonight. I'm not joking."

"There ain't no *knights* here." Zarius tried to scan past DK's shoulder.

"Would that be a bad thing?" Caroline asked. Her light, summery dress flowed down her small frame. Her fair skin glowed, and her hair seemed to suck in and defeat the light of the torches. "Aren't knights, you know, *our* knights?"

Composing himself, DK took a breath and gazed at her. "If you sent all the knights in Endlin into the prisons undercover, it would only take a week before you forgot who was who. They're thugs."

"All of them?" Gretchen asked, cocking her head.

DK stared hard at them. "Maybe not *all* of them, but one bad apple spoils the bunch, right?"

"I don't eat apples."

Zarius laughed and nudged her with his elbow, nodding.

"It doesn't matter," DK sighed. "I'm just trying to tell Zarius not to cause any trouble or we'll all end up in the stockades."

Caroline's face clouded. "Well now you're making me nervous. Should we leave?"

Right then, Zarius beelined through the crowd and dove onto a table just as the last man was standing up from it. He ended up knocking the whole thing over, and a commotion stirred up around him as a couple drunks picked him up. The tavern dropped to a near silence for a few moments as Zarius righted the table and dusted himself off. DK and the girls forged after him, and DK resisted the urge to punch his apprentice in the kidneys.

"I'm gonna kill you," DK said.

"Yeah yeah yeah." Zarius straightened himself out, adjusted the table, and sat down. "You're welcome for the table."

Gretchen was snorting her head off as she sat down next to Zarius, auburn curls bouncing around her face. Caroline still looked worried as she and DK took their own seats on the opposite side. They were in the center of the tavern, now even closer to the men in question. Zarius took the moment to get a good look at them before DK reached across and dug a jagged fingernail into the back of Zarius's hand.

"*Man*," Zarius said, shaking his hand. "They sure got your pant-
ies in a twist."

"If you try to stare over there again I'm dragging you out of
here." DK glowered. "I'm dead serious."

"Okay okay." Zarius put his palms up. "I'm a peaceful young
man."

Meanwhile, DK started staring over there instead. No doubt
about it. The size of the men, along with their manicured beards
and well-groomed hair all spoke to military, and they had the dirty,
shitty reek of Endlin all about them. City-dwellers feeling like
they'd just squeezed their way down to the asshole of civilization.
DK watched the one nearest him, a square-faced man with short,
spiky blond hair, taking a disgusted glance around the tavern, and
that was all DK needed to confirm all his suspicions and then some.

"DK?" Caroline nudged him.

DK blinked and shook his head, focusing on the table. They were
all staring at him.

"Did you hear me?" Caroline asked.

Grimacing, DK shook his head. "No, sorry."

"I asked how it was going with Louelle," Caroline said cheerfully.
"I still wanna meet her. You made her sound really nice."

"She's very nice," DK said, unable to muster up much else.

"She's alright," Zarius muttered.

"Zarius just gets scared around her."

"I don't get *scared*," Zarius said. "She's just big. And she's like,
looking me in the eyes and shit, you know? Like she's thinking."

"She *is* thinking," DK said, shaking his head.

"She sounds scary," Gretchen chirped.

Zarius gestured to Gretchen with both hands, and they all
laughed. At the same time, DK's eyes drifted again, and he saw
Catherine standing in front of the three men. The laughter died

in his throat. He saw the blond man puffing his chest, prattling on about something, and Catherine was just standing there, staring at him without expression.

"I'll go get us some drinks," DK said, and he got up immediately.

A few moments later, DK squeezed in one person away from the trio of knights and focused through the din to listen, and he caught the rumbling train of the blond knight's voice.

". . . where I received the King's Holy Cross. So much travel and the many spoils of war, yet I am taken by you. I never could have imagined a . . . *remote* village such as Ten-Berry could house such beauty."

DK's heart jogged, and he stared at Catherine's blank face. She hadn't noticed him yet.

"Can I get anyone here another drink?" she asked simply.

The blond man smiled forcefully, showing his complete set of clean, white teeth. His face was red, and he looked drunk. "Perhaps I haven't made myself clear." He spoke slower now. "A knight of the Second Cavalry, an elite unit answering only to the King himself, has taken a fancy to you."

Another tense moment passed, and DK watched Catherine force a genial smile. "And how very flattered I am. Please, gentlemen, call if you need another refreshment."

Catherine turned to move down the bar, but her whole body snapped back as the blond knight lunged over and latched a meaty hand around her wrist. "You haven't been dismissed," he growled.

DK shoved somebody out of the way and stepped right up next to him. "Get your fucking hands off of her."

"*Let me* go." Catherine whipped her arm free.

The blond man remained frozen for a moment, hand still outstretched across the bar, before he turned slowly to DK, his face blossoming with rage. He stood up off his stool and rose a good six inches over DK, but DK didn't take even half a step back. Faded brown eyes sized him up as the knight leaned down and spoke, his breath repulsive.

"I think you must be mistaken, peasant. You accidentally spoke to me."

DK didn't flinch or even blink, but he couldn't stop his nose from wrinkling in disgust. "Touch that woman again and you'll pay with the hand."

The cast iron smile remained, but those brown eyes lit red with animosity. "Do you realize who you're speaking to?" The second of the three men stepped up next to the first, leaning toward DK.

"Stop this nonsense," Catherine hissed, trying not to draw attention. "Christian, get out of here."

No one moved. Everyone around them at the bar was holding his breath, eyes plastered to the confrontation. A wave of silence moved across the tavern as people pointed and whispered. The blond knight took one long glance at Catherine, eyed her up and down, and looked back at DK, teeth showing in a lascivious grin.

"I can't wait to fuck her like the peasant dog she is."

DK grabbed him by the throat and would have smashed his head against the bar had the second man not jumped him. A couple fists found his torso as DK went down to the stone floor. Commotion erupted around them, shouts and hollers cascading from every corner of the tavern. A boot narrowly scraped over his ribcage. He thrashed, but others from the bar nearby were toppling off their stools into the chaos.

Zarius flashed into the fray like a lightning bolt. He speared into the second knight with his shoulder, somehow finding him even amidst the melee. Now they, too, went grappling to the ground. The last of the knights, the biggest of them all, ripped Zarius off his comrade like he was nothing more than a ragdoll. Rather than brutalize him, though, he simply tossed Zarius back toward where he'd come from, and Zarius bowled through two tables and another assortment of hollering patrons.

"*Enough!*" the big knight bellowed, so loud and authoritative that even those on the far side of the tavern went rigid in their seats.

The other two knights froze where they stood. Groaning and bitching men picked themselves off the floor amidst clouds of dust. As soon as he was free, DK hoisted himself right up and resumed a staring contest with the blond knight. He supposed that made the big guy the leader.

"Fuuuuuck," Zarius groaned as he struggled to his feet, hunched over and holding his back. "So much for *me* causing trouble."

"I'll have none of this," said the biggest man. His name was Mark Whitestone, and he was the Captain of the Second Cavalry. "Paul, Kendall, these peasants are beneath you. Please, collect yourselves."

But Paul, with his spiked blond hair now partially flattened, giving him an air of insanity, was murdering DK with his eyes. They stared daggers at each other, silent and unmoving. DK's face was utterly expressionless, and that only seemed to enrage Paul more.

"I want this peasant dead by sunrise," he hissed.

"You're drunk," said Mark.

Finally, Paul broke his gaze from DK and fixed his small, hateful eyes on Mark. Paul stepped up to Mark, breathing hard. "He attacked a knight of the Second Cavalry. I'll have you charged with treason."

Mark's jaw tightened, and the slightest flicker of indecision shone in his eyes. But still, he did not demur. "Paul," he said, "if you kill this man in cold blood, I'll have *you* charged with *murder*. Let's take our leave. We should be taking our leave regardless."

Trembling, Paul watched Mark for another couple moments

before he glanced over his shoulder at DK. The look was enough to send goosebumps down DK's back.

"A duel then," said Paul. The torches pattered against the walls of the tavern. "What say you, *peasant*?"

Mark growled. "Paul—"

"I accept," DK said.

Next to him, Zarius sprouted a tantalized grin.

Paul glanced back and forth between them, shaking even harder now at these seemingly fearless peasants. "Take us to whatever worthless sparring pit this village has to offer."

34

The tavern stood empty, not a breath to be drawn. A crowd followed DK, Zarius, and the Endlin knights as they separately made their ways toward the sparring pits. For the time of night, the commotion grew to astounding levels. People ran up and down the streets, hollering to their friends and neighbors, drawing whole families out of their meager homes to see about the fuss.

Christian and a real *knight?*

Already, DK worked himself below his thoughts, beyond the reach of fear or panic. He chewed his tongue and tried to conjure up a Sunrise in his mind. Next to him, Zarius tugged at his shirt, picked his nails, dug at his thick hair. His eyes were wild, and a strange grin was frozen on his face.

"You got this," Zarius said, clapping DK on the back. "He's big, and he's pissed. He'll run out of gas before you do."

"He's also drunk," said DK. The crowd maintained a berth around them, as if afraid that a simple word of encouragement might send them to the stockades. DK rubbed a sore shoulder. "If this goes south, I need you to have my back. He won't take well to losing."

Lips pursed, Zarius nodded short and fast. "I hope he gives me the chance."

Despite his effort at stoicism, DK caught the electric anticipation of the hooting mob. His heart was already in the next gear, pumping extra blood to his muscles and brain. He kept seeing Paul's meaty hand fastened around Catherine's wrist. He didn't look back for his adversary, but the image gave him a hardy resolve. Whatever happened, it was a righteous engagement.

The sparring pits, dilapidated and unloved, saw the arrival of more people than they may have known in their entire existence. DK and Zarius, however, arrived at a second home. DK knew the sandy dirt of these pits like the back of his hand. These posts and ropes had seen him claw back from the abyss of idle hell, and he let his hand rest on one for a moment as he stepped into the ring.

Half or more of Ten-Berry mobbed toward the pit, already jostling for better views, children on their fathers' shoulders. Hastily dressed and bleary with broken sleep, mothers bunched together and muttered questions to one another. And it all came back to the single issue at hand: Christian—the resurrected Day Knight—was about to fight a knight from Endlin.

As Paul conversed with his cohorts, DK scanned the crowd, and lots of eyes stared back. Sneers and shaking heads were plentiful, but there were also a few nods and bright smiles of encouragement. Catherine was there, nearly right up against the ropes, her face unreadable besides duress. Patrick, Stanton, hell, even Cornelius was in attendance, looking more than a little concerned. Caroline and Gretchen must have been there somewhere, but he couldn't find them in the throng. Clamoring voices rose to a veritable roar, shouts of all different kinds. The crowd smelled blood. As Paul climbed through into the opposite side of the ring, Ezekiel wormed through the side of the crowd and rushed up to DK and Zarius.

"What on earth is happening?" he gasped, out of breath. He clutched at one of his hips. "I heard some people hollering about a fight. Of course I knew you two were involved." He reached through the rope and grabbed DK's shoulder hard. "What's this about?" He looked to Zarius. "What have you gotten him into?"

"It's necessary," DK said quickly. He glanced over at Paul's hateful face. Perfect beard and oiled hair. "Those men are thugs."

"What happened?"

"He disrespected Catherine's honor."

Ezekiel stared for a few moments. "Catherine?"

DK narrowed his eyes and took a half-step closer. "It wouldn't matter who it was, Ezekiel. I'd fight for anyone against him . . ." He sneered. "He said he'd fuck her like a dog."

A long sigh fluttered from Ezekiel. His defiance waned until he was nodding his head. "Very well. The mind only boggles that it will be *you* who gets yourself hanged and not Zarius."

"DK has this," said Zarius. "It won't even be a fight."

Ezekiel patted Zarius on the back but wore a frightening gaze. "It's what comes after that worries me, son." He turned back to DK. "Are you angry?"

"No," said DK. "He deserves this."

"That may be. But what he deserves could end with *you* on the wrong end of a rope. It doesn't matter how right you are. Hell, they killed Jesus."

DK stood tall. "I won't turn a blind eye, not for a knight or for the King himself."

"Very well, very well," said Ezekiel. His pale blue eyes glittered in the torchlight. The stress brought added years to his face. "We know who you are. Be him now."

A wave of tranquility washed over DK. He had all the support he needed, and his skill was beyond question. The Day Knight's name would ring through the ornate halls of the palace in Endlin, in reverence or disdain. Even the most distinguished of knights would hear tell of this.

DK faced Paul and cracked his neck, stretched his shoulders. Paul continued murmuring to Mark and Kendall, eyeing DK the whole time. They passed him one of the practice swords kept in the little shack nearby. Zarius handed DK a similar one. Torches came out in the crowd as people ran back and fetched more light. The mob morphed around the ring until it occupied every side. The roar had faded to a general clamor, and that dropped altogether as Paul stepped to the middle of the ring.

"People of Ten-Berry," he called. His voice was deep and full, resounding out of the pit. "Do you claim this man as one of your own?"

Some boos rained down. A few people shouted, "No!" and one or two might have half-heartedly voiced their support. For the most part, though, everyone was quiet.

"Your kin don't even want you." Paul pointed his sword at DK. "You're looking at a knight of Endlin, protector of the King, slaughterer of barbarian hordes. Do you, a mere peasant, truly wish to challenge me?"

"I'm no peasant." DK dragged some phlegm out of his throat and spit it on the ground. "And you're no Knight."

Paul was about to spout off again when another, shriller voice pealed through the arena with a ring of desperate authority. It was Cornelius, sweat shining in the flicker of so many flames. He held a knit stocking cap in his hands, wringing dust out of it as he pressed up to one side of the ring.

"Gentleman, gentleman, please," he called. "Is this any way to conduct yourselves? A knight of the King and a self-proclaimed one? We're all on the same side. Do we really—"

"*Self-proclaimed?*" Paul sneered. "I'll not hear such blasphemy. This man is a peasant. He stains the King's good name even speaking the *word* knight. He should be imprisoned for that alone."

Cornelius fidgeted. "Well, you see, he helps out around Ten-Berry. Just petty squabbles, you know, things we wouldn't bother you all about in Endlin. It really is a—"

"Any man who titles himself a knight is defying the King." Paul pointed his sword again.

"Why don't you show them, then?" DK asked. He raised his voice. "Why don't all of you watch? See what one of the King's knights can do against a lowly peasant."

Cornelius seized the opportunity. "Sure! Yes, why not a wager? If he wins, you'll leave him be. If he loses . . . well, I suppose you can do what you may. Try him, imprison him . . ."

A wicked grin slithered onto Paul's face. "Hang him."

"You fucking *coward*," Zarius shouted, twisting the rope between his palms.

"Z," DK hissed. "Cut it out." Ezekiel pulled Zarius close and whispered in his ear.

"I'll accept your wager, magistrate," said Paul. "For as an agent of the King, I may serve as his proxy. When this man loses, he will be put to death for assaulting a knight. After a month in the stockade for his wretched blasphemy, of course. Nothing less."

Cornelius bounced from foot to foot. "And if he, er, wins?"

Paul fixed a devastating glare on him and said nothing at all.

Silenced, Cornelius bowed his head and melted into the crowd, lest Paul decide one noose wasn't enough. Now, all eyes focused on the sparring pit as DK twirled his sword. He kept a blank expression, but inside, he went to work—centering himself, measuring his breath. Paul, meanwhile, grunted with animosity, face red and boozy, feet twitching on the ground like a bull ready to charge.

Still, though, DK was exhilarated as he turned to gaze at Ezekiel and Zarius. "Don't let them blindside me."

"Let him try," said Zarius through gritted teeth. Ezekiel merely offered a stout nod.

"This is it." DK shook his shoulders out one last time and took a couple steps forward, gazing at Paul.

Paul still hung onto his smile, although it looked pained now as the veins bulged on his neck and forehead. "Anything you'd like to say? An apology? Maybe I'd even think about letting you walk."

"I came here to fight." DK brought his sword to the ready. "You've done nothing but talk."

Paul's whole arm trembled as he squeezed his weapon. "I'll piss on your grave."

No fanfare met the clash of their swords. All the air was sucked out of the sparring pit—maybe all of Ten-Berry—when those first strikes rang out. Metal on metal. Strength against strength. The power in that sound reverberated through every skull in attendance, rattling teeth and silencing whispers. For the first minute, no one spoke, and no one could tear his eyes away. The sight unfolding was like something out of a play.

At first, Paul swung his sword like he was trying to fell a tree in one stroke. He wanted to hurt DK badly. As DK gracefully avoided these strikes and nearly caught Paul across the face a couple times, though, Paul backed off and started fighting like a real swordsman. The smile dropped from his face, replaced by expressionless concentration.

Fielding blows, DK knew this would be no easy fight. Paul had twice his power and extra reach. One haymaker could rip his sword free from his hands and end the fight right then. Of course, he was used to that. He trained that way—for bigger, stronger opponents. Even now, at a hefty weight for his frame, DK fought like a determined beanpole. His arms hugged his sides, his footwork impeccable, timing always on. Every time Paul parried one of his strikes, another came from somewhere else.

Paul, for his part, demonstrated that not simply *anyone* could make it to the King's court. It did take skill and dedication to earn the title of knight, but the character wasn't there. He didn't have a personal Sun burning in his chest. A lack of scruples left him loose and erratic.

DK had been down there in the mud, felt it clog his lungs, watched his vision tunnel away as his body grew cold. And he dragged himself out of it, out of desolation, mind shattered, soul scattered, raging all the time against death, against evil, against the infection in his brain. He raged and raged until even death could stand no more. Perseverance brought him crawling out of the bog, and now it sent him soaring into the clouds with a giant's stature.

Paul delivered what he promised: punishment. Many of his strikes were errant or parried, but he was too strong and too skilled to miss forever. Finally, a late block from DK saw Paul's blade pass within a whisker of his elbow and slam into his ribcage hard enough to knock the wind out of him. A smatter of jibes rose from the throng of spectators, some laughing, others cheering Paul on. DK staggered backward, gasping, then stopped and held his ground as Paul bore down on him.

Breathless, DK zoned in and saw every strike coming as if someone were whispering the next move in his ear. Block. Parry. Riposte. Dodge. Block. Block. Parry. Vigorous blows took his arms to each side, but they always snapped back into place just in time to absorb the next one. Sweat sprang out on Paul's face and soon poured off him in buckets. His silent intensity became a huffing outrage.

That was what separated DK from the rest, what made him a Knight among knights. He would do whatever it took, endure anything for however long necessary and still come out fighting. Stone lay below his skin, layers of it, too strong for a blade to crack. A heavy swing landed on his off arm and sent streaks of pain shooting up through his shoulder, but an iron door blocked them from his consciousness. DK's poise only hardened under the pressure.

That concentration came out in his hands and feet. He didn't gasp, shake, or even blink. And he saw in Paul's face as another strike connected with DK's thigh and failed to even move him that the wretched knight was surprised. Worried, even. The sudden possibility of exhaustion filled Paul's eyes and sent him on one last roaring assault.

The more anger that poured out of Paul, the more reserved DK became. He wouldn't lose to a conviction lesser than his own. Years of training flourished under his passionless tranquility. They could exert their lessons without being confused by fear or anxiety. They flowed through him like water through reeds, melding around everything.

DK finally landed a riposte, albeit a light one. It didn't so much as make Paul wince, but it was a warning. DK stopped being driven back and became immovable, claiming his half of the pit and refusing to give up an inch. Paul's strikes came slower now, less impactful, but DK was as quick and sharp as ever. Openings began to appear, and each one found a dummy blade swishing through it, connecting with Paul's torso, arms, legs. A few cheers rose from the crowd.

"Come on, Christian!" somebody shouted.

"Kick his ass, Christian."

"You ain't in Endlin anymore buddy."

Paul's cronies looked on in consternation. Mark stared at the floor of the pit, face tight, and Kendall craned his neck around, asking for a confrontation. But the crowd's intensity rose alongside that of the fight.

Paul held up admirably well. He had defensive skill of his own and managed to stonewall DK for a while, but the strikes just kept coming. DK was as fast and fluid as five minutes prior, and that was everything. That was the difference. Paul gasped for air. His feet staggered, form crumbling, and finally, his guard broke. DK started battering him, hammering every weakness with his sword.

"Too slow," DK grunted as he jabbed forward. "Too sloppy." He worked in a circle around Paul, tormenting him. "Too *weak*." A devastating downward slash caught Paul on the hands and stripped his sword out. It fell with a *thwump* into the dirt, and the crowd erupted. They actually erupted. Cheers and hollers rained down, and DK found a moment to feel shocked by it.

"*Yeahhhh*," Zarius shouted at the top of his lungs, beating on one of the wooden posts. "*Let's fucking go, DKKKKK. Yeeeaahhhhh.*"

Holding his sword at Paul's throat, DK finally let the rush of victory pass through him. Paul glared at him, trembling with rage, still gasping, eyes darting around as he searched for escape. Kendall stood against the ropes, ready to leap over and pummel DK. Hearing the cheers of his defeat must have snapped something within Paul, though, for the anger only grew more severe, his face red as blood.

"Worthless piece of steel," he said as he grabbed his sword off the ground and drove it into the dirt. "*That would never happen with a* real *weapon. I landed the first blows.*"

Boos lambasted him from all sides. His anger grew like an ingrown hair, coiling up beneath the surface until his whole body was just a tender vessel one bump away from bursting. Fists clenched, he stormed over to his side of the pit as DK turned to grin at Zarius and Ezekiel, holding a fist up. The boos flipped to cheers, and DK couldn't contain a beaming smile as he looked around. It was almost enough to bring a tear to his eye, to hear all these people supporting him. The people he had silently defended for so long, the crux of his Knighthood. He wasn't just the Day Knight. He was Ten-Berry's Knight. The Knight who bested a dreg from Endlin in a fair fight. A legend emerging before their eyes, before his *own* eyes.

"Grab your sword."

DK almost didn't hear Paul over the raucous spectators, but the waves of cheering came to an abrupt halt. Confused, DK turned around and froze. Paul was back in the center of the pit, only this time, he wasn't holding a sparring sword. He had his real weapon—an impressive piece of engraved, gleaming steel that looked like it could take the wings off a fly. Torchlight made it morph and breathe, and it looked as hungry and hateful as the man holding it.

"The fight's over!" Ezekiel shouted. "You lost. Show a shred of honor and leave."

"That was no fight," Paul seethed. "That was practice. Training. That doesn't count for *shit*."

"*You* agreed to it." Ezekiel stepped up and grabbed the rope, voice going hoarse. "It was *your*—"

"*Shut the fuck up*," Paul screamed. The crowd went dead silent. He fixed his beady eyes on DK, still panting a bit but quickly catching his breath. "Grab your fucking sword."

DK gazed at him, the rush of victory waning to nil. Fear loomed, but he didn't let it in. Instead, he regarded the sad excuse of a man before him. So full of rage and embarrassment at his own defeat in a *fake* swordfight that he was willing to risk his life against the same opponent in a real one. Apparently death was a preferable option to shame. DK shook his head, saddened, and for a moment, Paul thought he was demurring.

"*See?*" Paul screeched. "*He's a coward. Look at him refuse me.*"

The crowd murmured uncertainly, everyone uncomfortable. A meltdown was happening before their eyes, but this wasn't a drunk they could boot out of town. Whatever happened here could be spun in a very deliberate way to the authorities, and not a single voice in Ten-Berry would be able to undo the consequences. Everyone looked to DK to see what he would do. He was, after all, their Knight-in-residence.

DK, meanwhile, stepped back to the edge of the pit and gazed at his friends.

"What do you think?" DK asked, first looking to Ezekiel.

"He'll cheat," said Ezekiel, eyes cloudy. "Kick you in the groin and put his sword through your chest. He has no honor. Even if you won, I wonder what his friends would do. His death would not be taken lightly. Either they would skewer you or drag you back to Endlin to hang. You already won. That's enough."

Mulling this over, DK nodded and turned to Zarius. "Z?"

"You can't walk away." Zarius spoke without hesitation. "I mean look at this. The whole town showed up for you."

"Forget that." DK shook his head. "They'll go back to hating me tomorrow. Their opinions don't matter. What do *you* think I should do?"

Zarius glanced from DK to the jeering Paul and back again. "I think I'd fucking kill him, but you do you. God knows I've seen you win real swordfights out there without drawing blood. He's out of control, and I think you could smoke his ass again. Really bury him. But if he takes a cheap shot, I'm coming in there and finishing him myself, gallows be damned."

The decision made itself. DK gave one solemn nod, and Zarius passed him his sword.

Even more familiar with his own blade than the practice one, DK turned around with little trepidation. The crowd broke into newfound desperate cheers as he stepped forward and acknowledged them with a raised hand, and he couldn't help but feel appreciated. It truly was a marvel to him to hear Ten-Berry whooping and hollering for him. Even if it only lasted for a night, he would never forget it.

"Listen to the peasants bleat," said Paul. His eyes faded, as cold as frozen earth. "They think they've found themselves a hero."

DK twirled his sword and assumed his fighting stance. "Maybe just a villain."

Paul sneered at him. "As long as they see you bleed."

The crowd got rowdy as swords met in the darkness. The torches burned like ravenous spectators themselves, eager to see the first drop of real blood. Flames danced off the blades as they swished through the night. The Sun was long gone, forced to abandon its disciple, but DK's fight raged on. No amount of darkness could quell him now. The Sun burned within him, as strong and as hot as high noon.

Swishing swords met with force. They hissed off each other like raindrops on open flame. Paul fought with magnified fury, but DK was as stoic and placid as ever. One might have easily assumed him in the middle of a friendly disagreement instead of a fight to the death. His poise and confidence only seemed intensified by the heightened stakes, but it was the same for Paul's ferocity. Body odor and desperation wafted out of the pit.

Paul showed no deficit in determination. Perhaps the idea of humiliating defeat drove him harder than even death, but whatever the case, DK was stretched to his limit. Massive blows rained down one after another from every possible angle. A single break in concentration would've left him bleeding out on the dirt. The clash of their swords tolled like church bells on Good Friday.

"I . . . won't . . . *lose*," Paul growled as he battered DK's guard and broke it. His next vicious swipe still found a recovered position, though, and he snarled with rage. "You'll die for this. Hang for it. I don't *care*."

Again, DK fielded a hammer blow but managed to send it glancing away. His hands snapped back into position time and time again, weathering the storm. The fight was easier now as Paul bowed under the weight of his previous onslaughts, but still, the sour knight fought with desperation, battling for his life. Perhaps Paul sensed the enormity of the implications, but DK believed it was nothing more than calamitous hubris.

As he expertly defended himself, DK actually felt a pang of guilt. He saw something of himself in this man, in the utter desperation with which he fought. At one point, DK had been a similar person. Still, though, his life was on the line. All his goals were under threat until the duel was over.

Paul tried to kick him in the groin. DK saw it coming a mile away and simply stepped to the side. If he'd never fought a better swordsman, he'd fought many dirtier ones, and any paltry attempt at cheating had been seen a dozen times. The crowd jeered at Paul as DK backed in a circle, flinging blows away like Paul's sword was made of paper. He withheld his counterattack, biding his time, watching doubly close for another cheap shot. Criminals weren't the type to adhere to any sort of unspoken rules.

But Paul was no simple criminal. This was supposed to be the people's guardian, someone just as willing to put his life on the line for a peasant of Ten-Berry as a noble of Endlin. Instead, he was a pig and a lech. He probably spent many an evening in the bars and the whorehouses, and God help any lone woman he'd ever stumbled across. That much DK could see in his eyes, the way he carried himself. This was entirely out of the realm of possibility for Paul; he was likely kicking himself inside, trying to wake up from this blasted nightmare and escape this balding terror of a peasant. His final resort to assure victory in any confrontation would have been combat, but here he was, losing handily, in front of a crowd no less. The rage was tangible, shimmering off him in waves like a horrible fever, but so was the desperation.

DK did not generally take it upon himself to exact punishment. That was for the magistrates to decide. Sure, the system was corrupt, but DK didn't want that responsibility. He kept his head down and helped people, and that was all he desired. No fame, no medals, just to be left to continue his work. Knighthood fulfilled him, and to see someone make such a mockery of his ideals offended him deeply. As Paul drew on his last reserves of energy, DK flipped the fight and tightened his jaw.

This time around, he let the anger out—just a little. Enough for everyone to see just how much disdain he had for this false knight and just how much better DK was in every aspect of sword fighting. He humiliated Paul intentionally, dragging him around the sparring pit like a combat dummy. DK crushed Paul's sword out of his hands, let him pick it up, and did it again. And again. Every method he knew, he used with a vengeance, but he never struck the killing blow. To his credit, Paul never gave up, but he began to near the end of his bravado. His sword hung toward the ground, shoulders caving in, chest nearly bursting out of his shirt as he gasped for air.

By the end of it, the crowd was almost silent. Even Mark and Kendall had turned away, scowling at those who dared to meet their eyes. They knew. Everyone knew. The only question was *What happens next?* Would DK really kill him—kill one of the king's knights? He'd have a whole town of people to defend him, but he'd still hang for it. The swords met again in the torchlight. A cool rush of wind blew through.

When DK next slashed Paul's blade into the ground, Paul didn't move to pick it up. Instead, he lifted his eyes, filled with more bitter reproach than DK had ever seen in his life. He held his arms out and shrugged.

"Well?" he asked. "I'm tired of this."

"Are you?" asked DK, lowering his weapon.

"*Gut him, Christian!*" someone shouted. The crowd started to come to life again, pressing up against the ropes in anticipation.

"Fuck you," Paul snarled. Sweat drenched his face and shirt. "You think you proved anything here? Your life means nothing, and it always will. As soon as the King hears news of this, you'll be in a metal cage on the way to Endlin. You'll rot in the stockade for a couple weeks. They'll pelt you with rotten vegetables, stuff dogshit in your mouth. After that, you'll hang in front of a whole mob of people. Oh how they'll cheer as your neck cracks and your body swings. None of these little worthless peasants from your shithole village will be there to save you, and all your swordsmanship will be meaningless. That's all you are, you *cunt*. A worthless fucking peasant."

"More strong words from a weak fighter," DK said, sheathing his sword. "But you're still wrong about one thing. I'm no peasant."

Paul snorted, eyeing his sword on the ground. "Oh yeah?"

DK gazed at him, expressionless. "I'm the Day Knight."

Paul scooped his sword up, his whole body tensed to charge. But his eyes met DK's, and he stood there, frozen for a few moments. The crowd held its breath, eyelids plastered to their foreheads, glancing back and forth as fast they could. DK scowled and gripped his hilt. Behind Paul, his comrades fidgeted.

"Come on, Paul," Mark muttered. "Leave it be. Let's get out of here."

Paul stood his ground, but his sword drooped in his hand. Finally, he broke DK's gaze, mumbling under his breath as he turned and exited the arena. Paul and Kendall bunched up beside him as security, but the crowd parted like the Red Sea to let them pass. Once they vanished up the road, the whole mob—damn near every last person—burst into cheers.

"*Yeaaaahhhhh*," Zarius bellowed. "*You fucked him up, DK!*" He jumped through the ropes and barreled into his friend, shoving him hard in the chest. DK shoved him back, and Zarius's laughter pealed through the whole quadrant of town as he turned and flexed on the crowd. "*You see that?*" he hollered at them. "*You* all *saw that shit. Put some respect on the Day Knight's mother, fuckin,* name."

Errant spouts of celebration erupted like geysers around DK and Zarius as a mob surrounded them. When DK tried to slip off, Zarius clamped an arm around his shoulder, jabbing a finger into his chest, hollering louder than anyone else and really getting the throng into a frenzy. Most of the spectators filtered back toward their homes, but a decent group ended up back at the tavern.

Zarius planted DK at a table, and within sixty seconds, the top of it was clogged with free drinks. Men went around jabbering to each other about the fight, lording over all the pompous scum from Endlin, proclaiming the eternal victory of the farming man and his homely village. In no time, the script shifted more to a general win of Ten-Berry over Endlin, the country over the city, and Zarius's jubilation became a series of growling corrections. It was as if, in a measly half hour after the end of the fight, they had stripped DK of the victory and somehow bestowed it on *themselves*. DK remained placid at the table, but Zarius came back, smoking with indignation.

"What the fuck is wrong with these motherfuckers?" Zarius asked. A red cloud settled on his face from all the free ale. "They ain't done *shit*."

DK just sat at the table, looking more embarrassed than anything, shaking hands and accepting some drunken praise. Zarius turned it into a revenge tour. He sought out anyone who'd ever side-eyed them, any voice he'd ever heard whispering their names, and he made them eat crow. Of course, the Carmichael Blaine crowd was nowhere to be seen, and DK had to physically restrain Zarius from seeking out Carmichael's house.

After a while, DK broke down and told Zarius it was time to go. Shouting some renewed warnings and reminders at the tavern, Zarius let DK guide him by the shoulder to the door, and out they went into the chilled night air.

"Man *fuck yeah*," Zarius yelled, and he shoved DK.

DK just staggered a few steps and stopped, turning an enflamed eye on Zarius. "Get a hold of yourself, dude. Seriously."

"Mannnn come *on*. You just—you just whipped ass! Fucking showed his pig ass what the *fuck* is up. You need to—"

"*Hey.*"

They both stopped and turned around. Catherine came toward them, melting into a shadow as she left the light of the torches hanging on the tavern door.

"Uh oh," said Zarius.

She walked straight up to DK. "I could have handled that myself, you know."

DK's breath caught in his throat. He tried to clear it, but it was stuffed with stone. "C-Catherine, yeah, of course I know that. I didn't-I was just—"

She stood up on her tiptoes and kissed him. DK almost pulled back, but she put his hand on her waist, and she pressed her lips harder into his as his fingers spread over her lower back.

"Oh *shit*," Zarius cried.

Even that couldn't take DK out of the moment. As quickly as it happened, Catherine stepped away, blanketed by darkness. "But thank you," she said. "I appreciate it."

With that, she turned around and went back into the tavern. No final words or longing glance over her shoulder. She just vanished, and DK stood there dumbfounded, jaw hanging open, part of him still clutching that moment as time dragged him away.

"Lady killer," Zarius said out of the side of his mouth.

"Shut up." But DK smiled as he shook his head and turned around. He slung an arm over Zarius's shoulder, and they went home.

35

A rough shaking tore Zarius out of sleep. He groaned and rolled over, but a hand started jabbing into his ribs. He yelped and sat bolt upright, and through bleary eyes, he saw DK standing over him.

"Man fuck," Zarius said. He rubbed his eyes. "Morning already?"

"Sure is," said DK. "Get up."

Zarius collapsed back onto bed. "I'm tired."

"You're hungover. Get up." DK goosed Zarius with his foot and didn't stop until Zarius clambered to his feet.

"Alright alright *fine*." Zarius stood up, and a thunderclap of discomfort shook him. He bent over, head throbbing, but his stomach didn't like that angle, so he stood up again.

"Oh God," he said. "Don't tell me we're running."

"We're running," DK confirmed. "Eggs are almost ready."

"Fuck me in the ass."

"After we run," DK said, straight-faced.

"What if I *kill* you instead?"

DK stood up from the fire and shrugged, spreading his arms to either side. "Have at it."

Grumbling, Zarius sat down and massaged his temples while

DK scraped some scrambled eggs onto a broken piece of wood and handed it to him. The egg smell pervaded the whole room, and Zarius's head swam as he came to terms with the thought of eating them. Hand trembling, he pinched some up and brought them toward his mouth, but they quivered outside his lips.

"You *would* make eggs," Zarius said, his hand still perched above his mouth.

"They're good for you." DK set to work on his own eggs, shoveling them in. Zarius wanted to vomit just watching him.

Zarius released the eggs, and they fell into his mouth. Hot and chewy, they mashed up between his teeth, and he was all too aware of it. The sensation alone almost made him gag, but somehow, he managed to swallow. He followed it with a heavy gasp and a long pull from a waterskin, and DK just stared at him with an eyebrow cocked.

"You're pathetic," DK said.

"Fuck you egg man," Zarius shot back. "You're the Egg Knight." He prepared himself for another mouthful.

Weak Sunlight filtered through the door, but the flicker of the fire still painted all the walls. The dance of the flames hypnotized Zarius's sluggish brain, so he focused on that while he kept forcing down eggs. Fucking eggs, man. God. Every time he lifted some toward his face, he *smelled* them, too, and that was even worse than tasting them.

"Egg Knight," Zarius muttered. "I don't even like eggs."

"Well you're gonna like this run even less," DK said. Frizzy strings of hair made a haphazard halo around his head.

Zarius sighed hard and leaned forward until his head went between his knees. "Are you punishing me for being happy?"

DK rolled his eyes. "It's not a punishment. But you've gotta understand the consequences of your actions."

"I didn't even *do* anything."

"You got plastered on drinks you practically intimidated every-one into giving you."

"I didn't get *plastered*, bruh. So I indulged a little bit after prob-ably the biggest event in Ten-Berry's cousin-fucking history. I didn't forget that Catherine came out and stuck her tongue down your throat."

A pink flower bloomed on DK's face. "She didn't even . . ." He rubbed his forehead. "Don't be mad at me cause you're hungover."

"Whatever. Let me eat the rest of these *eggs* or the *Egg Knight* might give me bad dreams."

Through the grace of God, Zarius finished the rest of the eggs, and he halfheartedly threw on some clothes. A stitch ached in his head with every pulse, and he felt weak. Even still, he followed DK out the door and into the street. They walked toward the gate, and dread began to build in Zarius. He always dreaded the runs, but this was about to be a different type of hell altogether.

As they came around the last curve in the road and passed the last hovels, though, DK slowed down. Confused, Zarius looked around and then noticed Patrick sitting on the wall next to the gate, facing out. He was never here this early.

"Pat?" DK called as they walked up.

Patrick spun around and hopped off the wall. His red hair bounced as he came running over, and he smacked right into DK, pulling him into a hug.

"Well *hell*," Patrick yelled, a grin splitting his face in two. "Look at this guy, huh? Look at this *guy*."

Chuckling, DK broke out of the embrace and just nodded, smil-ing. "Thanks, Pat. Thank you."

"What a *show* that was, eh? I mean sheeiittt. You coulda cut his beard for him with that sword work. I'll be danged. Got the whole town in a ruckus. I ain't never seen nothin like it. That fella will be thinkin bout that all *year* I betcha." Patrick did some jabs with his spear, dancing around and blowing puffs of air. "Man, that was *sharp*."

"Why are you out here already?" DK asked. "Pretty early to stand guard."

Patrick's face soured. "Well don't I know it. Old Corny told us guards we had to post early, seein about all the *ruckus*. Wanted us to see them knights off and say good riddance to their sorry asses."

A strange, panicked look jolted onto DK's face, and it zapped Zarius like a shared electric shock.

"Wait," DK said. He clutched the hem of his shirt. "I forgot to even ask last night. What the hell were they doing here?"

"Ahh," said Patrick. His grin returned, but it was darker. "Now that might interest you. From what I could get out of Corny, they're headed to Terrell."

The color drained out of DK's face.

Looking back and forth between them, Zarius felt itchy. "Where's Terrell? What's wrong with that?"

"For what?" DK asked. "Why Terrell?"

No smile remained on Patrick's face. He gave DK a look that almost seemed sympathetic. "This is just hearsay. Take it with a grain of salt. But supposedly, there's been shit goin missin down yonder. Ain't just carriages and cargo, neither. They've lost 'em a couple of *people*."

Tension crackled in the air. "Somebody explain," Zarius barked.

DK turned to Zarius, gaunt and vacant. "Terrell's the closest village to the bog. Patrick, is that where they're going? Is that what you heard?"

"Aye," said Patrick, nodding. "Them fellas are meant to investigate."

"How long since they left?"

Patrick glanced toward the gate for a moment. "Nigh on an hour ago, I'd say. First light."

"We've gotta go." DK grabbed Zarius by the collar of his shirt and dragged him back toward the hovel. "Armor. Water. *Run*." DK took off sprinting, and Zarius chased him.

36

Louelle's hooves thundered underneath DK and Zarius as she galloped down a beaten wagon trail. They couldn't speak over the cacophony of hooves and clanking armor, but soon enough DK let her slow down to a canter to catch her breath. She was, after all, supporting two armored men, and to whip her on made DK cringe.

Even at a slower pace, DK kept a death grip on the reins. His armor seemed to be shrinking around him, trying to crush him into a ball. Dreadful images kept flashing through his mind, and his thoughts could only scatter like birds whenever he looked their way. He wanted to scream.

"We're going to the bog?" Zarius asked.

"Yes," DK said.

"*The* bog?"

"*Yes*," DK snapped.

Silence held for a bit. Louelle made steady progress down the path, and DK counted the seconds until he'd goad her into another burst.

"Don't be scared," DK said.

"*You* sound scared," Zarius replied.

"I'm not scared." But of course, he was scared. Against his will, DK was on the road back to the bog. It was impossible not to be scared. But he turned his mind to the Sun climbing the sky and tried to give it all his attention.

"Are we gonna go in?" Zarius asked.

"I don't know. I don't know."

A new fear rose in DK's mind, centered solely on Zarius. What if they *did* have to go into the bog? Could he really, in good conscience, allow Zarius to take so much as one step in there? DK thought about himself in the past. How fast it all broke down. Part of him thought that backup was crucial, but another told him Zarius wasn't ready. He didn't know what he'd be in for or what they would come up against. Frightful, unfamiliar ambivalence tortured him. In any case, they were already on the way. He could leave Zarius with Louelle if it came down to it.

DK prayed they would catch up to the knights before the bog, but they had an hour head start, and the bog was only four or so hours' ride. Terrell maybe four and a half. Maybe they'd start at the village, but DK had a horrible feeling that they wouldn't. They were headed straight to the lion's den.

Asking Louelle's forgiveness, DK jabbed her up to a gallop again, and they roared down the deserted paths. Zarius asked no more questions, and while DK wanted to reassure his apprentice, he couldn't even reassure himself. In just one short conversation with Patrick, it felt like everything was spiraling out of control. The tempered jubilation of the previous night was gone, the victory dead and rotting.

After a long stretch of following one road and then another, shorter stint on a barely visible footpath through a screen of tallgrass and thistles, DK saw a familiar rise ahead. The whole horizon seemed to slope up like a vampire bunching his collar against the Sun. As if the ground itself were hiding something.

Louelle rode up the gentle incline, and soon enough, DK saw the black fingers rising out of the ground. The highest reaches of the bog's many treetops. The fingers lengthened into branches as Louelle went up the rise, and when they reached the top, the bog revealed itself below them.

The bog occupied a big depression in the earth, where rainwater and God knew what else gathered with nowhere to run off. The ground at its core was sloppy, more liquid than solid. A variety of trees grew like mold in the wetness and gave the canopy a hypnotic undulation. Black gum, bog spruce, red maples. The unsettling joints of thick, ancient alder trees and even the sprawling orbs of a few industrious willows. Many wore capes of moss, and dead men's fingers poked out about their trunks. Roots slithered over the top of the ground and plunged in wherever they found purchase. Stunted patches of bog rosemary and witch hazel clung to the earth like tumors. No birds circled the trees. No squirrels foraged the grasses at the rim. The whole blob of growth looked dead, black, and lifeless. But not empty.

Scanning the perimeter, DK saw distant flashes of gunmetal. Clouds had moved in, and the little knights in the distance looked like soldiers of the sky. Hope soared in DK's chest, the very first since leaving Ten-Berry. They weren't inside yet.

Without a second thought, DK sent Louelle down the opposite side of the hill at full gallop. She complied, and her legs moved with fluid, powerful grace as she assaulted the ground. They roared across the carpet of buffalograss, riding parallel to the bog.

Dark energy snapped at him like a whip. DK's head actually glanced to one side like he'd been struck, and a vicious pain flashed through his head. Decrepit fingers tried to pierce into a scar and rip it open. DK's stomach rolled, and Zarius yelped behind him.

"*Dude are you okay?*" Zarius gripped DK's torso like a log in a raging river. That was all that kept DK from going over.

DK fought it. He locked his jaw, and as fast as that strike came, he latched onto the Sun. His mind punched through the clouds into clear air and melded with the Light. DK righted himself, and Louelle galloped on uninhibited.

"*What just happened?*" Zarius yelled over the roar.

"Close your mind," DK barked. "Don't look into the trees."

An icy block of fear began to boil in a rising tide of intention. Not so much a rage as a convicted inspiration, not at all dissimilar from how he felt fighting Paul when the real swords came out. DK slashed back and recaptured his thoughts, but they all bounced around in a disconcerted mess.

The knights grew as DK approached them. All three of them went running back to their horses as Louelle barreled toward them, as if they expected an assault. As the knights mounted their impressive, armored steeds, Louelle began chopping down to a stop.

A thin trail of dust blew over Zarius and DK, but no other breeze moved through the basin of the bog. The air was as fetid as the water and laden with unease. Goosebumps ran up and down DK's arms and legs as he stared at the knights for a moment. In his armor, they didn't recognize him. They held their swords at the ready, poised in a loose triangle.

"*Who goes there?*" one of the knights barked. DK recognized Paul's voice.

DK lifted his faceplate.

"You." Acid melted the word into little more than a hissing accusation. Paul pointed his sword at DK. "I'll slaughter you."

"What's going on?" Mark revealed himself, lifting his faceplate on a silent hinge. His helmet was detailed and ornate, the steel polished and gleaming. All three of the knights wore armor so complete that DK saw not one exposed patch of skin. Interlocking plates provided near-total defense and remarkable flexibility. Even the tops of their feet and hands were protected. Their mounts were no less well off.

"You can't go in there," DK said. His thoughts formed slowly, the words even slower. All that time on the ride over, and he drew a blank for what to say.

"*Get off your horse*," Paul shouted. "I'm slitting your throat."

"*Paul*," Mark snapped. "Control yourself."

The third knight, Kendall, hovered uncertainly at the rear of the triangle.

Mark turned back to DK. "Why? What's wrong?"

"There's evil in that bog," said DK. "I've seen it myself. You need to get as far the fuck away from here as you can. Fast." Tension strangled DK's voice. He kept his eyes firmly on the knights, not even glancing toward the bog. But alarm bells blared in his head, like time was ticking down, though he didn't know why.

"Peasant scum," Paul seethed. "You're interfering with a royal investigation. I'll have you hanged for treason."

Slowly, Mark turned toward Paul again, and he removed his whole helmet. "Paul," he said. The words flowed out of him, deep and resonant. "Stand down. That's an *order*."

Face hidden, Paul trembled where he sat on his horse. DK could almost see the vitriol bulging in his throat, but somehow, he kept it down.

"What was your name?" Mark asked DK.

"Chr . . ." DK's face twitched. "It's DK."

Mark cocked an eyebrow and paused for a moment. "Well DK, you've ridden a long way to find us here. You don't strike me as one to gloat. Did you really come here to warn us? After last night, I wonder why you'd do that."

"I'm not in the business of watching innocent men die." DK scowled. "And I only know for certain that one of you *isn't* innocent."

Mark looked at Paul and waited, but Paul contained himself. He was a mystery, still hidden behind his faceplate.

"We're knights," Mark said. "You think the danger here is that grave? I've heard of no such thing."

"No one wants to tell an Endlin knight about a *witch*. But she's in there, and she'll kill you all. She almost killed me two and a half years ago."

"He's lying."

Zarius clutched DK so hard that all the air gushed out of his lungs, and DK went ramrod straight. That voice had come from their left. Instant terror gripped him by the throat. All the men turned toward the bog.

A bleeding human face gazed out from behind a skinny, black tree trunk several paces within the tree line. DK didn't so much as find it as it found him. His eyes locked right onto it as if by force, and the figure moved out from behind the tree and came staggering out into the open where even God could not deny it.

DK's eyes bulged. He felt every ounce of the armor on his head and back, like an anchor trying to drag him off Louelle. His breathing hitched, but he withdrew to the Sun. The bog witch wanted him to be afraid.

Paul's horse reared and screamed. He just managed to hang on before it landed and went shooting off in the opposite direction as he hollered for it to stop. The other horses got skittish, scampering back despite the weight of their armor and riders. Only Louelle maintained her composure. She took a few steps back, snorting, and stamped the ground.

The thing looked human enough. Blood leaked down its face from thin scratches, and a gray mass of intestines hung to its knees, spilling through a huge slit in its torso.

"What the fuck," Zarius whispered, but DK barely heard him.

Hunched over, the humanoid lifted its head and gazed up toward the sky through a curtain of long, oily black hair. Its eyes were smooth and glassy, no pupils, no irises. It turned its face to the sky and made a strange moaning sound. Large hands kneaded haphazardly in the air, as if the thing weren't quite sure how to use them. Its arms and legs were stick-thin, the joints knobby and small.

"DK?" Mark's voice came out choked.

"He's lying." It was a raspy sound, like the crunch of dry leaves. The creature tried to take another step forward but collapsed to one knee.

"What are you?" DK asked. An injection of adrenaline sent him off Louelle's back. He stalked right up toward the ailing creature and stopped just a couple steps away.

It lifted its empty eyes toward him, and a grin spread over its thin, cracked lips. "Have you forgotten?" It let out a long, giddy groan. One of its hands went into the hanging ropes of its intestines and started kneading the flesh with a terrible wet, writhing sound.

"God Almighty," Mark said. "Explain yourself. Wh-who . . . who are you?" Mark's voice shook like a newborn kitten.

"You're all going to die. You, Mark Whitestone."

"*Silence devil.*" Mark's voice went hoarse. "What evil is this? *DK, what is this?*"

"The bog witch," said DK, as still as stone.

"Wrong," the thing said. Its body drooped toward the ground as it rifled through its own guts. It came out with a wet fist of colorful string and held it up toward the sky like an offering. "The Thread Knight." With that, it pitched forward and died.

Stunned, DK gawked at the twitching corpse until it went still. The smell of blood and death infested his nostrils.

"What did it say?" Zarius cried. "Did it say the *Thread Knight*?"

"I don't . . . I-I don't know." DK didn't speak loud enough to be heard.

"DK," Mark said after another couple moments. "DK, please. What in God's name is that? Witchcraft? Are you serious?"

Gaunt and pale, DK turned slowly around and looked up at the big knight on his big horse. Genuine fear spotted Mark's face like the pox. DK walked over and mounted Louelle.

"Worse than witchcraft," DK said. "You need to go home. Now."

"You'd have us leave?" Mark asked. His eyes hadn't moved from the corpse, sword still at the ready. "We're here to . . . We're supposed to answer to the King. About peasants and carriages missing from Terrell."

"They're almost certainly dead."

Mark shifted his horse to one side. Paul was off in the distance, beating his horse with vengeance. Kendall hung close to Mark's back, scanning the tree line.

"I'd say we should go in . . ." Mark's voice weakened as he spoke. "Normally."

DK scowled and shook his head. "There's worse than that in there." He nickered at Louelle and got her turned away, ready to depart at a gallop. "Meet me in Ten-Berry if you really wanna talk. But right now, we all need to get out of here."

Without waiting, DK pressed Louelle and got them headed toward home. He didn't let her slow down until they put a good mile between them and the bog, but he and Zarius threw constant glances over their shoulders. As if the whole bog might have gotten up and come stumbling after them.

37

Zarius sat next to DK's motionless, sweating body. Tallgrass drooped in big clumps around them, succumbing to the onset of fall. The thin patches of buffalo grass lost their color and grew scratchy and brown. He was so distracted that it was impossible to even reckon with the idea of distraction. Thoughts exploded in his head like giant thunderheads and wreaked destruction on the scarred landscape of his mind.

Over and over in his mind, he saw the Thread step out of the trees. The guts hanging down its torso. Empty eyes searching through an invisible plane. And the black, putrid energy washing out of the bog like a tide of sewage to fill their lungs and clog their throats. Fresh nausea welled in Zarius's stomach, accompanied by the lashings of ineptitude.

Worse than what he saw in the bog, Zarius saw cowardice in himself. That whole time, and he moved not a muscle, said not a word. He locked up, practically from the moment he and DK left town. Shame radiated from the core of his spirit and made even his fingertips hot. It took all he had not to audibly groan as his horrific shortcomings paraded through his mind.

When foreign footsteps approached their position, Zarius whipped up to his feet, eyes wild like a feral dog's. He prepared to charge just as Mark came into view, and the shock made him stutter. Finally, though, his rage found a new rod to latch onto, instead of himself.

"Get the fuck out of here," Zarius seethed.

Mark raised his hands and tilted his head in confusion.

"Zarius?" DK asked. His eyes fluttered open. "What's going on?"

Hands shaking, Zarius looked from Mark to DK and back again.

Mark kept a watchful eye on Zarius. "I, uh . . . was coming to talk with you. As you said."

"Z, what's wrong?" DK stared at his apprentice.

"They're all thugs," Zarius said, his voice raw. "You said it yourself. We can't trust him."

A thin layer of clouds, like a threadbare blanket, laid across the sky. The Sun probed its golden fingers through but couldn't quite grasp the men below.

"Z, it's okay," DK said slowly. "I know what I said."

"I'm sorry about Paul," Mark said, still gazing at Zarius. "I understand that . . ." He dropped the placating tone and scowled. "He *is* a thug. And a lech. I never asked to have him in my unit, but he's a distant cousin to the King. It's out of my control. I sent him and Kendall back to Endlin ahead of me. I understand that you may not have the best opinion of knights, but I'm here as a man and maybe, in turn, as a friend."

"We don't need friends," Zarius spat.

"What the hell, Z?" DK stood up and got between them, searching Zarius's face. "What's wrong with you?"

"What's wrong with . . ." Zarius ached inside and out. "Did you not *see* what we . . . Weren't you *there*? Didn't you *see that shit*?"

DK put a firm hand on Zarius's shoulder. "Of course I did. But we don't know Mark yet. Let's just hear him out. It's okay. We're safe here."

"Oh we're safe?" Zarius asked. "We're *safe*? You saw that god-damn *thing*, talking about *another* Knight. The Dead Knight, now the Thread Knight? *Huh?* Derrick got up and walked off *months ago*. But you think we're safe here? He could be *one of them*."

"I understand your fear," Mark said.

Zarius leered over DK's shoulder, eyes on fire. "No you don't," he seethed. "And who said I was afraid?"

Mark locked eyes with him. "No man is above fear. Certainly not me. I was frightened by what I saw out there, and that's why I'm here. Paul doesn't like me. He'll go straight back to the King and tell him I abandoned my post to talk witchcraft with a couple of peasants, and I'll have much to explain when I catch up. I'm not your enemy."

"Knock it off." DK grabbed Zarius's shoulders and forced him to sit down, and as soon as it appeared, the fight went right out of Zarius. He lapsed into a blank stare, and Mark winced as he looked at him.

"Sorry if I surprised you here. A guard directed me, though not without an interrogation and some indirect insults, I might add. I'm not sure what I'm expecting. I know hoping for an explanation would only leave me disappointed."

"The only explanation I can give you is a vague one," said DK. "You basically already know it."

"A witch," Mark muttered. "I would have . . ." He shook his head and slowly sank to the earth. His short, flat face caught a stray beam of Sunlight, and he closed his big, brown eyes against the glare. "Well, I saw it with my own eyes. Whatever that was. Did it call itself a knight? Did I hear that correctly?"

"I don't think that's what it meant," Zarius mumbled.

They both looked at him.

"What do you mean?" DK asked.

Zarius stared at the ground and ripped out blades of grass to send floating away on the breeze. The earth smelled dry and withered. "I think . . . something is making things. That body in the field . . ." He gazed at his friend. "I have a horrible feeling."

Frozen, DK could only blink. "Making things . . ." He grimaced. "The deer."

"What does that mean?" Mark asked.

No one answered him. After a few moments, DK muttered, "We're not sure yet."

"In any case," Mark said, glancing between them, "I'm not sure what to tell the King. He might hang me for heresy if I stick to the truth, and I think he considers me some shade of a friend."

"What about Paul and Kendall?" DK asked.

Mark scoffed. "Bloodsuckers. I told you Paul doesn't like me. And Kendall's more of Paul's ilk than mine. If they saw an opportunity to take me out and replace me as Captain of the Second Cavalry, they would do it."

"Second Cavalry?" DK cried. Even Zarius jolted where he sat. The Second Cavalry was known across the Kingdom of Endlin as the most formidable fighting unit, decorated in every war Endlin had ever fought.

"Aye," said Mark. "We didn't wear our colors, as if a bunch of knights on armored horses would fool anyone. The King feared some kind of foreign espionage, out here on the edges of the territory, but I was never convinced. The tone of the letters coming out of Terrell was . . . fearful. And now I think I know why."

"What do you mean?"

"I mean those letters their magistrate sent sounded flat out desperate. Like he was afraid not only for the missing persons but for *himself*. If they've seen anything like what we just did, I can understand."

DK sat back, shaking his head.

Mark made a slight grimace. "I suppose you don't have any better intel to offer."

"I don't." DK glanced at Zarius, who sat there like an anthill. "That bog *is* dangerous, but even I don't know exactly how. What we saw might be a symptom of a larger disease, or it might have been a posture, a big flash to demonstrate strength without much substance behind it. The only way to know would be to go in."

Mark's eyes fluttered like he'd been struck. "And you think that's what's happening to the goods from Terrell? This . . . *witch* . . . is taking them?"

"She has something to do with it, for sure. But the exact nature of it will stay a mystery."

Interest faded to defeat on Mark's face. "I have to admit, I came here hoping for some kind of plan. At least some insight besides more fuel for my nightmares."

Zarius jostled, and Mark and DK both glanced at him.

"I appreciate it," DK said slowly. "Really I do. At least you care. That's . . . Well it's more than I would have expected."

"My duty is to *all* the people of this Kingdom, wherever they are." Mark sighed. "I only wish I could say the same about my comrades. If you think it's wise, I could try to convince the King to dispatch a real force of men. Up to a regiment, perhaps. But he would want a detailed explanation of why we'd be setting up a supply train well within our own borders. I'm not sure what we've got would suffice, even if the whole village of Ten-Berry or Terrell attested to it."

"And they wouldn't," DK said. "Besides that . . ." He looked off at the horizon for a moment. A chilly breeze meandered through the shallow divot where they sat. "Well, I think this is up to me, Mark. I've been there. I've seen the witch, and I survived. I'm training Zarius, here . . ."

Zarius didn't react to his name, and DK scowled but went on. "And I think it will fall to us to see this through."

"Two men . . ." Mark muttered. "Even if Zarius is as skilled as you are, that . . . *thing* didn't look like a conventional target to me. I can only imagine what else lays inside. Frankly, it sounds like suicide."

"I have faith," DK said. "I've been nurturing it for years, and I think that's my greatest resource. That's why it's up to me, and it's why I'll succeed. I have the faith."

Mark examined him. "For some reason, I feel you aren't referring to God."

DK returned a strange look. "Maybe I'm not. Would that make you think less of me?"

Brow furrowed, Mark took his turn to look off into the distance. He moved like he was always wearing armor. "I suppose not. Hearing you speak, you sound like a good man. A man of conviction. I'm faithful to Christ through and through, but you give me the air of a true believer and a proponent of justice. You're a braver man than me for trusting faith alone, though."

"I think in the end, that's all we've got." The Sun finally broke through the clouds and put a golden cap on DK's head.

"Very well." Mark grunted as he rose to his feet. "I can't say any of this has mollified my unease, but I respect you. I sense . . . Well, maybe it's something like you said. Something about faith. I sense a purpose here, perhaps one that I'm tied to. For now, I'm going to return to Endlin, but I'll leave my personal address in your magistrate's office. Send a pigeon if you need me. When the weather turns, I'll come back, or I'll notify you otherwise. We can catch up then, see about those forces. In the meantime, if something happens, good luck and godspeed."

Mark put a hand down. DK grasped it and shook it without standing up, and Mark nodded as he turned and departed back the way he came. DK sniffed and watched him go, and then he leaned back on the grass. Sunlight fell over his face.

"What'd you think of that?" DK asked. After a few moments, he sat up and stared at Zarius's unwavering face. "Z?"

38

Something cold and wet slathered over Zarius's eyes. He came up sputtering, flailing his arms, and a thin, red dog leaped away, growling. Zarius bared his teeth and snarled, and a quick lunge sent the hound scampering away.

A bright Sun bore down out of a vapor-blue sky. It was sweltering hot, and Zarius's clothes were dark and sticky. He craned his neck and saw a wooden fence where there should've been a stone wall, and the hovels beyond were squatter and squarer than those he knew. He wasn't in Ten-Berry.

Confused apprehension passed through him as he scanned through the fence. He saw no people, heard no sounds, and even the mangy dog had disappeared into the streets. Unsure what else to do, Zarius followed it.

Where was DK? Where was anybody?

The Sun pressed on his head like a crown of molten iron. Sweat seeped out of every pore, and Zarius was shocked to scratch his face and find the bristle of a patchy beard. He'd never been able to grow more than a black mist under his chin.

Zarius saw a dark lump on the side of the road ahead, lying half out of a hovel doorway. A carpet of flies undulated over it, the lazy drone reaching him even at a distance. His stomach flipped. Fear hit him like a slap in the face, and he checked over his shoulder.

Someone was standing at the gate he'd come through. A single figure, a shadow, somehow invisible even in the ocean of Sunlight. Insectoid panic chattered in Zarius's throat as he started backing up. As soon as he moved, the figure matched him, coming down the street, a stone's throw away.

"What the . . ." Zarius whispered. He squinted and shielded his eyes against the Sun, but the figure defied perception.

Dread collapsed on him. He passed the body, bugs writhing and fizzing. White, fleshy maggots squirmed through the dirt. Zarius struggled to focus his vision, and when his eyes flitted back to the figure, it was running toward him.

Zarius took off at a dead sprint in the opposite direction. Half a scream scrambled out of his throat, and the hot wind slashed against his wet face. He tore down the narrow street until he came out in a square, again similar but not identical to Ten-Berry's. There was no Beggar to shield him from the Sun, and what he found repulsed him.

Corpses littered the ground, some alone, others in piles. A few of them looked charred, flecks of papered skin drifting away on the breeze. The smell of burnt hair invaded his nostrils, and the sheer intensity of it all overwhelmed him. He ran for the first building he fixed his eyes on, sprinting through the death and mutilation. Limbs littered the churned-up earth. Red dogs loped around the edges of the square, hugging the shade if they weren't feasting. Maggots rode along inside gaping wounds in their flanks and faces. A few of them snarled at him. Two were in a vicious fight, ripping each other to pieces, barking and howling.

Zarius barreled through a wooden door and slammed it behind

him without so much as checking to see if his pursuer was still there. He boarded the door and backed up, and a new, fetid odor of putrefaction made his tongue writhe.

Rotting corpses lay bloated and stinking all around him. Shrunken, withered eyes stared out of leathery faces. Mouths hung open in frozen expressions of pain and misery. Flies by the thousands. Maggots squishing under his bare feet. Zarius let out a strangled cry, then hushed and listened. He squeezed his eyes shut and clamped a hand over his nose and mouth. The seconds ticked by.

A heavy dragging sound started up outside, and it was all Zarius could do not to scream. It was slow, and he stood frozen as it approached the door. Every once in a while, it would stop, and he'd hear a few heavy clunks. Someone started whistling.

"Here boy," a jagged, wet voice said from outside. "Where are ya? Where are ya, boy?" It laughed. More dragging. It got closer to the door. Closer, closer, until something was scraping through the dirt right outside. The door rattled as someone tried to open it. More long guffaws.

"Locked up, eh?" the voice asked. Right through the slats of the door. "Found yourself a kennel?"

Zarius said nothing. His vision swam. His thoughts broke down.

"*Zarius*," the voice barked, suddenly vicious. "*Open the fucking door.*"

Zarius opened his eyes in darkness and curled up into a ball as if waiting for a boot to find his ribcage. He quivered where he lay, even as he tried to be motionless. He listened, but his ears were ringing. Dry straw prickled against his face. After a few moments, he made out DK's long, measured breathing, but even still, he trembled. His face was wet with tears. He imagined that thing from the bog on its way toward him, right then. Stumbling over the fields and through the grass. Knowing where he was. Maybe it was at the gate. Maybe it was down the street.

Maybe it was standing over him, waiting for him to look.

Gretchen swung her legs out and let them bump back against the stone wall beneath them. The evening Sun painted a complementary backdrop to her fair, freckled face, and it turned her auburn curls into a ring of fire. She looked at Zarius with a plain, innocent curiosity, and still he found damnation.

"Have you told DK?" she asked.

"No," Zarius said. He turned to face the horizon. The eastern sky produced a rich violet as it shooed away the last vestiges of Sunlight.

"Maybe you should."

"He'd think I'm weak."

"Would he?"

Zarius scowled. "How would you know?"

"I'm *asking*."

Still scowling, Zarius kept his eyes averted. "I'm supposed to be a *Knight*."

Gretchen waited for a beat. "And what does that mean? You can't be scared?"

"Are you fucking with me?"

"I'm asking you."

"I'm supposed to *handle it*. Not go fucking crying about it, especially not to my master."

"But is that what *he* told you?"

"Shut up," Zarius growled.

Gretchen winced and dropped her eyes, and a lance of pain stabbed Zarius in the chest. A few moments passed. Stray breezes blew a chill through, and they both shivered. Gretchen scooted closer until she nestled against him, but they didn't embrace, and she didn't say anything.

"Sorry," he said.

"You look really tired," said Gretchen in her quiet, thoughtful voice.

"Thanks," he muttered.

"How long's it been?"

"Since what?"

"Since the bog thing."

"A few weeks." Zarius pulled his woolen overshirt up around the collar.

"You aren't sleeping good."

He scoffed. "You think you would?"

"No. But you need to sleep. Maybe you should talk to DK."

"I'm talking to you."

She turned and waited until he met her glittering green gaze. "I can't help you. I can listen, but I can't help."

"*Fuck* do I need help for?" Zarius said. "I'm not asking for help. Goddamn."

This time, Gretchen set her face, even looked a little angry. "Well you're . . . don't be *mean*. Why are you mad at me? You tell me stuff and then you get mad at me."

Grimacing, Zarius growled at himself and shook his head. He leaned way back on the wall until he almost fell off, and he saw the stars coming out like the waking eyes of distant giants. When he sat up again, he put his hand on Gretchen's and said nothing.

Both their hands were cold, and they were still for a moment.

On top of each other. Then Gretchen's fingers twitched, and she rolled her hand over. Zarius took it in his, and another lance went through his chest, this one more nebulous.

"I'm tired," he said. His voice almost broke. "I'm scared that I can't do this."

"Talk to DK," she said. "Or Ezekiel." After another moment, she squeezed his hand and leaned in just an inch. "I believe in you."

39

Hands stuffed into scratchy woolen pockets, DK hurried down the street with Zarius at his side. They walked against a real edge of cold, and the warmth and coziness that enveloped them as they let themselves into the tavern provided a beautiful respite. Rubbing his hands, DK grinned as he and Zarius picked their way over and sat down at a table. The tavern was only half-full. The weather put off some of the irregulars, and the farmers were pulling long hours at harvest, though some of their ruddy faces still hunkered around the joint. Flames flickered in the hearth and from the torches on the wall. The cold air had cleaned out some of the smell of summer, so the swaddling scent of ale prevailed.

"You wanna grab the drinks?" DK asked.

Zarius shrugged and got after it. It only took a minute, and he returned and placed one in front of DK. They knocked their mugs together and tipped them back. DK let out a big sigh and eased back on the creaky chair. Quiet conversation reverberated off the walls.

"Gettin chilly," he said.

"Hadn't noticed," Zarius said.

"Soon it'll be *real* cold."

"All the same."

DK widened his eyes and glanced off. "You're really getting that twist and parry move down. I could barely find anything wrong with it today."

"Bout time." Zarius sighed and took a couple big pulls off his ale. "I can't suck ass forever."

DK rolled his eyes. "You haven't sucked ass in a long time."

"Balls?"

DK snorted. "No."

Zarius nodded and let his head loll. "I feel strong."

"You are strong." Bitter ale washed over DK's tongue. "Stronger every day."

"Hopefully there's enough days left."

Narrowing his eyes, DK waited a moment. "What do you mean?"

Zarius shrugged. "Y'know. Before the Pope takes a shit, or whatever they say."

"Huh? What makes you say that?"

Zarius cocked an eyebrow. "*You* say that shit. You're always talking like we're on a countdown. The fucking bog shit. Fucking . . . *Thread Knight*. Whatever the fuck."

Dubious, DK kept his face nonchalant. "I guess I probably do make it sound like that huh."

"Yeah. Pretty much all the time."

"Does that bother you?"

"Bother me?" Zarius lifted one hand, then looked around as if he expected someone to place something in it. "Stepping in shit *bothers* me."

"Hey, uh, sorry to interrupt."

DK and Zarius both snapped their heads to the side and found Catherine standing next to the table, face made rosy by the dancing flames. They stared at her.

"Christian," she said. "Do you, uh, have a minute?"

Zarius stood bolt upright out of his chair. "I just realized I have to piss. Maybe for a long time. Catherine." He nodded at her and walked off to the other side of the tavern.

DK was glued to his chair as Catherine sat down opposite him. Her hair fell unbraided around her shoulders, bangs curving into and then away from her face. A warm, hazel gaze met his own.

"Hi," she said.

DK swallowed a mouthful of dust. "H-Hi. How are you?"

"I'm good. How are you?"

"Good . . . I'm great." He leaned back and looked at the bar. Catherine's father meandered this way and that, giving shit to a couple of the regulars, all of them laughing. "You got the night off?"

"Sort of," she said. A half-smile crossed her face but vanished just as quickly. "I guess I wanted to talk to you."

"Uh okay." DK nodded and managed something resembling a grin. "What's up?"

Catherine looked off for a moment, smoothed her skirt, shifted in her seat. Then some words tumbled out. "Remember when we used to go for walks? Back before . . . Well, you remember?"

"Yeah," DK said. Of course he remembered, but his voice made it sound shady. "Yes." He cleared his throat. "I always liked that."

"Me too." She met his eyes for only a second. "I guess . . . Well, what happened?"

"With what?" he asked.

She leaned forward. "With *that*."

"Right . . ." DK's lips twitched. Suddenly he found the tabletop very interesting. "I'm sure you heard the stories."

"I did," said Catherine. "I heard stories. And that's all I ever heard, because you never came around and told me yourself. Poof. One day you stopped showing up, and all I got were *stories*. They gave me shit about it, you know? Carmichael, those guys. Gave me shit about you. Because even they thought something was up, and so did I. But you just . . . you never came back. Somehow, in a place like this, you managed to disappear. And that means you tried really hard to."

Stunned, DK stared at the lip of his mug as he sank lower in his chair. It almost gave the impression that he was looking at Catherine, but not quite. DK didn't even make an attempt at a response before she went on.

"And then, *years* later, here you are. Waltzing around, starting fights, talking shit with your new friend. And he's getting drunk and calling me a *bitch*? Where the hell do you get off? You come back, and you still don't say anything to me. I'm just the bartender now? I don't get it. And I guess I'm finally asking."

Catherine grabbed DK's ale and took a couple big glugs out of it while he just stared into space. When she set it down and wiped a sleeve across her mouth, she reached over and poked the top of his hand a couple times.

"I need you to say something. I don't care what it is."

"I'm thinking," DK said.

She snorted. She looked half cross and half anxious.

DK let out a sigh, eyes closed as he shook his head and dug a fingernail into the table. "I don't think you understand what happened to me, Catherine."

A few moments passed. She was waiting, but he held back.

"Oh, that's it?" she asked. "Well no shit, Christian. You know what might have helped? An *explanation*."

"I wasn't in a position to explain." His jaw locked.

"Because of why?"

"Because I almost *died*," he snapped. "I almost . . . I lost my fucking mind, Catherine. You don't understand because you can't. I fucking . . ." He clenched his teeth for a moment. "I went to hell and back. For nothing. I was embarrassed, hurt . . . I was *dying*. You think I wanted to come and tell you that? You think I was even *capable*?"

Her eyebrows dropped as she gazed across the table at him. DK felt a sting behind his eyes and cursed himself under his breath, muttering and shaking his head. He cleared his throat hard and put his eyes on hers.

Catherine wore a pained frown. "You were all alone. You could have talked to me."

"I wanted to," he said. "Believe me, I wanted to. But I couldn't so much as make myself *eat* at first. Like I said, I almost died. When I was even cognizant enough to think about you, all I felt was ashamed. And then every day I didn't come to see you added another pound to what felt like this godawful weight, trapping me in bed. It was just too much. I'm not proud, but I just couldn't do it. And then I had to do a whole lot of work to even get to a point where I forgave myself. For everything."

The murmur of conversation washed over them. Warmth from the fire stirred through the room like a gentle ghost. DK eyed his ale but didn't drink again, and now it was Catherine staring off. He resisted the urge to prod her.

"I understand," she said finally. DK's heart jogged. "But still," she added, "after all that, then you come back, but you still didn't say anything to me."

"You're right, and I'm sorry. Maybe I just . . . didn't know what *to* say."

A beat of silence, and then Catherine nodded. "Okay. Are you with that girl who keeps coming around? Caroline?"

"W-What?" DK asked, taken aback. "Oh, no, no we aren't to-gether. I mean, well I don't know, we've drank here together a few times. Walked around a little. But that's it."

"Are you *going* to be together?"

DK raised an eyebrow. "Uh . . ." He thought about it. "No."

"Come by sometime late, then. If it's not past your bedtime. We can talk."

Her eyes pierced him, and DK just stared back as she stood up, adjusted her dress, and walked off. A few moments later, Zarius zipped back into his seat, leaning forward, eyes wide.

"Holy shit," he said. "That took forever. What'd she say what'd she say?"

"Uh . . ." DK's mouth hung open, and he shook his head. "I guess, she kind of told me we should hang out?"

"*Damn.*" Zarius swung a hand out, and DK just managed to field the dap. "She's hot," Zarius said. "Is she still mad about the bitch thing? I told her I was sorry."

"I-er-no I think she's fine. I just . . ." DK shook his head again.

Concern leaked into Zarius's face. "Jesus, dude, are you good? Did you cum in your pants or something?"

That snapped DK out of it. He scowled and rolled his eyes. "Fuck you. No. I'm just, well I sure as hell wasn't expecting that."

"The Day Knight's getting *bitches.*"

"I'm not *getting bitches.*"

Zarius's eyes shown above a wide grin. "There ain't enough bitches in Ten-Berry for this guy. They're gonna start carting 'em in from Endlin."

"Shut the hell up." But DK finally cracked a smile, and Zarius burst into laughter, thundering a fist on the table hard enough to make everybody look at them. "Dude, shut *up*," DK hissed, snickering.

"Sorry, sorry." Zarius put on a placating smile and waved at all the wary faces as they turned back to their conversations. "I'm just excited for you."

"Well don't be. I probably won't do it anyway."

Zarius's face fell apart as he leaned over. "*What*? Catherine Plester wants to 'hang out'—" He made air quotes and then shoved a finger into a half-closed fist a couple times— "and you *won't do it*?"

"I don't know if that's the type of thing I should be putting my energy into right now. For both of our sakes."

Zarius soured, eyes going vacant. He leaned away, and his voice trailed off. "I'm not sure I even wanna know what you mean by that. Because what? You don't think you'll be around?"

DK's eyes dropped. He didn't want to say it. "I don't know. You want another ale?"

40

A half-moon hovered off the horizon like an ethereal fingernail. Silver light cascaded across the chilled prairie, the tallgrass gleaming. Steam puffed out of Louelle's nose as she trotted them across a flat road. Zarius clamped his hands over his ears to warm them up, his own breath steaming against the back of DK's armor. His ass was already sore, his nose wet. His sword thumped against his thigh in rhythm with Louelle's hooves. Zarius exaggerated a yawn.

"You awake back there?" DK asked.

"Hardly," Zarius said.

"Z."

"I'm *awake*. I was just telling you how *boring* this is."

"You need to be alert. Remember what happened at the bog."

A cold wire brought Zarius upright. Fingers of fear reached into his thoughts as he scanned either side of them, but the ground was mostly flat, his view unobstructed. They were two or three hours outside of Ten-Berry to the west-southwest, drawing closer to the small village of Cawville. Another patrol, and so far, another snoozer. But Zarius forced himself to stay above the looming lethargy.

Up ahead, Leopold Creek drew up near to the road and nurtured a long stretch of trees and foliage that led right up to the border of Cawville. Thick cottonwoods towered into the dark, their branches mostly naked. Dry leaves scattered on the ground, swirling with the wind as if attempting to conjure something. After another minute, they passed into the shelter of the trees. The darkness was instantaneous.

"We'll hit the edge of the village and turn back," DK said. No disappointment, no jubilation. He just said it like he was reporting the weather, and Zarius held back a disgruntled sigh.

They rode along the path. Louelle was as steady as an ox, as placid as an old dog. She clopped along the beaten trail, breathing steadily. Zarius let his hands fall and rub against her warm flanks.

Maybe Zarius heard it, maybe he felt it, but he clamped a hand on DK's shoulder and told him to stop. DK pulled up on the reins, and Louelle stuttered to a quick halt.

"You hear that?" Zarius asked.

It was a low rumbling sound, coming toward them, rising in volume. After a moment, DK leaned forward. "Now I do."

They sat there in the middle of the road, and soon enough, it was unmistakable. A carriage was coming down the path from up ahead, and that was so unusual as to be alarming. No one in their right mind moved cargo through the bandit-infested countryside in the dead of night. Zarius's heart kicked up a gear. Maybe it wasn't a fight, but it was something. Action.

After another few moments, the carriage rounded a bend, and two swinging lanterns came into view. DK put his fingers in his mouth and whistled long and loud, and it must have been just enough to cut through the commotion of the two horses and heavy wheels. The carriage driver shouted and yanked on his reins, and a second man stood up on the bench with a sword already brandished. DK and Zarius whipped their weapons out simultaneously, and Zarius vaulted off Louelle's back and dashed into the trees.

"*Woah, woah,*" DK shouted.

The carriage stopped, and they all started hollering at each other. After a few seconds of confusion, things calmed down. The carriage men weren't looking for a fight.

"Come on out, Z," DK said, though he didn't sheathe his sword.

Zarius plodded out of the trees, sword hanging by his side, eyeballing the carriage. A loose link of chainmail dug into the back of his left shoulder.

"What's going on here?" asked the carriage driver.

"Looks like knights," said the other.

"Ain't no knights out here. Fuck are you fellas? Inbreds?"

"For your sake, we might as well be knights," DK said. "What are you doing out here?"

"I could ask you the same question," said the driver.

DK stared at him. "I hope you don't have anything important in there." He gestured at the carriage with the tip of his blade.

The carriage men looked at each other, and the driver sneered. "Fuck sake. You swear you ain't gonna rob us?"

"I'm in the opposite business, actually."

Again, they shared a glance. The passenger said, "Does that mean you're, like, *sellin?*"

Zarius dropped his head and shook it, scoffing.

"No," DK said flatly. "It means—well look, we're Knights, alright? Just go with that. We aren't gonna rob you. But I sure am curious why the hell you're out here right now."

"Jackass magistrate in Cawville," groaned the driver. He was bald on top and stocky, bundled up in wool, and his partner had a big hooked nose hanging under buggy eyes.

"Say *one* word he don't like and he's *all* up in your business. Transcripts. Transaction logs. He's reading over them five times and finding something wrong on the fifth that makes him go back and do it all over again. Got them damn inbreds poking through all our shit just to hold us up, rantin and ravin. We're supposed to be in Endlin by tomorrow sundown. Fucker held our asses up, so now we're beatin feet in the dark tryin to get to Ten-Berry so we can *maybe* get a couple hours of sleep. Fuckin arrogant prick."

DK and Zarius looked at each other. The passenger on the carriage toyed with the sheath of his sword. "I mean you did insult him. A lot."

"Oh my." The driver rocked back. "You're right. I shoulda told him to spread his legs and lift his balls so I could—"

Shoooschlegth.

An arrow whistled through the air and punched straight through the driver's throat and out the other side, sticking halfway. Instant adrenaline hit Zarius like a slap across the face, and he threw himself to the ground. The passenger let out a strangled yell as he started to stand up, and the driver's body toppled forward. It landed on the horses and set them screaming, and they reared up and took off. The passenger fell, and the driver tumbled through the ropes and bindings, hitting the ground only to be run over by the carriage. A thick crack echoed through the air as his femur snapped under the weight. The only source of decent light went clattering away down the road as Zarius crawled into the trees and DK took off after the carriage.

"Z," DK called, his voice shrinking. "*The guy.*"

"Buddy, *hey buddy*," Zarius hissed from where he lay on the far side of the road. The passenger groaned on the ground, just a shadow, and rolled about. Nearby the driver writhed a couple times before going still. Blood gurgled out of the wound in his neck, and the passenger just kept groaning.

As his eyes adjusted, Zarius saw the man get up to one knee, holding the side of his head where he'd hit the ground. "*Come here,*" Zarius hissed.

Heart thundering, Zarius made a call. He darted out of his defilade and snatched the passenger under the arms. He was a big guy, so it took a burst of effort for Zarius to haul him off the road and then tumble back into the ditch. They both laid there, gasping, as Zarius scrambled to put eyes across the road again. He couldn't see anything. The trees were dark and nebulous.

Trying to control his breathing, Zarius looked for some sign of DK, but the carriage was around a bend down the road. No DK. Fuck.

"Hey." Zarius turned and prodded the passenger. "*Hey.* You good?"

Lying in the dirt, the man just grunted.

"We gotta move."

"Fuck no," said the passenger.

"Get your ass up," Zarius growled.

"You go get yourself killed. I'm staying right here."

"It's your funeral."

Zarius bear-crawled farther into the trees before he stood up and started running parallel to the road. Cold air swished through the eyeholes of his helmet. Every creak and clank of his armor made him wince as he navigated through the trunks and bushes. In no time, he was panting, weighed down by all the steel. But his conditioning kept him going, and he ran until he could see the lights of the carriage where the horses had stopped halfway off the path.

Slowing down, Zarius scanned around the lanterns. He saw nothing and nobody. No sign of Louelle, nobody trying to break into the locked hold of the carriage. Opting for silence, Zarius picked his way through brambles and bushes, always watching and listening. His mouth was dry, but his waterskin was on Louelle. Adrenaline gave him tunnel vision. He felt like he could only focus on one sense at a time.

After a minute, Zarius drew close to the carriage, still hidden well within the trees. He crept low to the ground, expecting at any time the whistle of an arrow or the shout of a leaping assassin. Where was DK? Think. Where would he go? Zarius stopped behind a tree trunk and peered out from behind it, observing the ground on his side of the road. After many long seconds, he caught a misplaced gleam of moonlight on something shiny. He stared at it hard for a moment until he could make out the shape of a figure lying on the ground.

Dropping to his stomach, Zarius crawled forward, still trying not to rustle all the dry leaves. He moved like a centipede, straining with the effort in full armor. At this angle, he lost DK's shape, so he went by memory. When he thought he was near enough, he called DK's name just barely louder than a whisper.

"Shhhhhhhh . . ." came the response, so quiet that Zarius had trouble distinguishing it over the breeze. He moved forward, heart cranking up a gear. What if it wasn't DK?

When Zarius's hand closed around something warm and soft, he almost screamed. He'd just grabbed DK's foot. A silent hand moved back and tapped Zarius on the helmet, and he crawled up alongside his master.

"Where's the guy?" DK whispered.

"He wouldn't move," Zarius said.

"Was he hurt?"

"Banged his head. I got him off the road."

"Okay. Good." DK glanced across the road. He was just a silvery apparition in the shadows. "You see anything?"

"Nope," said Zarius.

"Me neither. We'll wait them out. They have to move on the carriage at some point."

Great, Zarius thought. Wait them out.

And it turned out to be quite a wait. Zarius thought his sense of time was distorted, but it felt like an hour they laid there in silence. The lanterns on the carriage flickered and rocked, and the horses munched on the grass at the side of the road. The land was quiet. An owl hooted somewhere nearby. Whenever some little creature rustled through the undergrowth, Zarius's heart tried to explode backward out of his chest.

The sound of movement came from across the road. Zarius and DK tensed at the same time, and they saw a shadow flit out into the clear. Before DK could even give the order, Zarius launched forward, straight up onto his feet, a nightmare of gleaming gunmetal. He let out a bellow, heart thundering, and the figure on the road skidded to a halt just behind the carriage. The sword that came flashing up in the figure's hand was slow and half-hearted at best, and Zarius was too quick. He could have jammed his blade right through his adversary's chest, but instead, he hammered down on the weapon and threw it straight into the dirt. He let his momentum carry him through the attacker, and he drove a light body straight into the ground.

"Pwaahhh," the figure gasped as all of Zarius's weight and armor came down.

Zarius scrambled back to his feet and hauled up what turned out to be just a skinny, long-faced kid. Zarius held him around the neck and maneuvered him like a shield aimed at the other side of the road.

"*Come out,*" Zarius roared. "*Now.*"

"Cece," the kid cried out. He grunted and groaned but didn't fight the hold.

More rustling from the side of the road, and a small, slender shadow emerged into the flickering light of the lanterns. A girl. Olive-skinned with black hair tied up in a tight bun. Neither of them could've been any older than Zarius.

"What the hell," DK growled. He stormed out from behind Zarius, straight up to the girl. He ripped her bow out of her hands and stomped it into pieces on the ground.

"What are you *doing*?" DK shouted into her face.

The girl, Cece, recoiled, and now the kid in Zarius's arms tried to squirm free.

"Let me go," he spat.

"I'll tear your fucking guts out," Zarius seethed.

"Nice job *Keaton*," Cece said as she scowled at the dirt.

"Wha—" Keaton stopped writhing. "*Look at them.* I didn't know there'd be fucking *knights* out here."

For a moment, DK stood there motionless. As he slowly removed his helmet, though, even Zarius felt a jolt of fear at the white-hot anger pulsing in his face.

"You think this is a joke?" DK asked. He put his face right up to Cece's. "Huh? You think it's a game?"

"You stopped a couple of poor kids from robbing a carriage." Cece sneered. "Congratulations."

"*You killed a man*," DK bellowed. The force of it pushed Cece back a couple steps, and her face morphed to shock, then confused agitation.

"No we didn't," she said.

DK gawked at her. Zarius winced.

"You did," DK said, deathly calm now. "A man *bled* to death back up the road because of *you*." He stomped the bow again. "You shot him in the neck."

Color drained from Cece's face, but she maintained her defiance.

"That's—I didn't. That's impossible. It was a warning shot. To *spook* them."

DK grabbed her by the front of the shirt. "It *killed* him."

"Cece?" Keaton asked. His voice went high. "Cece you said we weren't gonna hurt anybody."

"We didn't," Cece said.

"Z, get a lantern," DK growled.

"You gonna bolt?" Zarius asked Keaton.

"No."

Zarius released him and hurried over to unhook a lantern from the carriage. He brought it to DK who handed it to Cece. She just looked at it.

"What do you want?" she asked. "You gonna hang us? Huh? Just a couple kids trying to feed their dying mother?"

"Take it," DK said.

After a moment, Cece grabbed the lantern. DK turned her around and kept a hand on her shoulder. "Walk."

They walked. All four of them made their way back up the road.

"Cece," Keaton said. He was paler than the moonlight. "What's happening?"

"We'll probably be executed by a couple of do-gooders. Cleaning up the streets by killing all the poor kids. You know how it goes."

Anger flared through Zarius, but he waited to see what DK would say. Turned out, nothing.

"You said it was a warning shot," Keaton said.

"*It was*," Cece snapped. "They don't know what they're talking about."

"We weren't gonna kill anybody. They can't hurt us if we didn't kill anybody."

"Keaton, shut the fuck up."

They walked in tense silence. Bats flitted over the treetops. Thin strips of cloud bandaged the moon and made a haze out of the silver light. When a shape appeared at the outer edge of the lantern's glow, Cece came to a dead stop.

"Go," DK said.

Her voice weakened. "It was just a warning shot."

"Walk."

"I didn't do it. It wasn't me."

"Cece?" Keaton asked uncertainly.

"*It wasn't us*," Cece said, turning around.

DK caught her arm and yanked her back. "You're gonna look at him."

"*I won't*," Cece yelled. She tried to break free, but DK kept an iron grip. He squeezed her hand until she cried out in pain and stopped resisting. He took the lantern from her and started dragging her forward, and she erupted in ferocious opposition.

"Do you wanna live?" Zarius asked Keaton. "You want your sister to live?"

"Yes," Keaton whispered.

Zarius shoved him forward. "Make her look."

As if in a trance, Keaton walked forward and grabbed Cece's arms, pinning them behind her back. She started thrashing and screaming, cursing her brother, and he walked her forward in big, staggering steps. DK walked a couple steps behind them, pushing the ring of light farther, and the details of the body came into view. A twisted, broken leg. The black pool of drying blood. The pale, livid face, frozen forever in agonized terror. Cece started screaming like a banshee.

"*Keaton. Stop. Please. It wasn't me, okay? I said. I told you we—Keaton stop. Stop. Please.*"

Keaton threw her forward. She almost fell right on top of the corpse. Her hands made a wet squelch as they plunged into bloody mud, and she screamed herself hoarse as she lunged away and curled up on the ground. Keaton accepted his fate and gazed at the corpse for a few moments before he drifted a couple steps, turning green.

Disturbed, Zarius could hardly watch. Visceral memories flashed through his brain, and he felt the warm wetness on his hands as if he were the one coated in mud and blood. He remembered. The smell returned to his nostrils, the nausea to his gut, and he knew just what kind of torment lay ahead for these kids.

"You killed this man," DK said. "His family is fatherless because of you."

Cece was hysterical, sobbing her eyes out. "I-I-I'm so-so-sorryyyy," she wailed. "I s-s-swear I didn't me-me-me—"

"I don't give a shit," DK snarled. "Remember this."

DK came toward Zarius, passing Keaton's pale, motionless statue, and put a hand on Zarius's shoulder, turning him around.

"Wait, we're leaving them?" Zarius asked, stopping. "But, but they killed a guy. Shouldn't . . . I mean shit, shouldn't she *hang*?"

DK gazed at him. Those blue eyes shone even in the dimness of the moon. Zarius removed his helmet and let his concern show, but DK's face remained the same.

"What do you think?" DK asked.

Zarius looked back. Cece was in a fit on the ground, bawling and shuddering, and Keaton stood next to her, staring at the corpse. Just kids.

"His family . . ." Zarius said.

"Her death wouldn't undo his. Now tell me, do we take them in? Let them hang? What's justice?"

Zarius thought. He saw the image again of Keaton throwing his sister onto the body, heard her frantic shrieking. If it were him in their shoes, he knew he'd never consider robbing another carriage or even so much as pilfering a coin out of the collection basket.

"I don't think they're bad kids. I don't think they meant to do it."

"You think they've been punished?" DK pointed at them.

Tears rolled down Keaton's face as he tried to get Cece off the ground, but she was a mess of snot and tangled hair.

"Yeah," said Zarius.

"Then let's look for the other guy, and we'll get this carriage back to Ten-Berry."

"Thank you." Keaton's voice was grave, his face gaunt, but he held his chin up as he gazed at them.

DK offered a single nod.

While Keaton finally got Cece up and led her back toward Cawville, DK and Zarius probed the woods, hollering for the passenger of the carriage. After several minutes, though, he hadn't turned up. They came together on the road after combing the trees on either side. The skin on Zarius's scalp tightened, and he shivered in a chilly breeze.

"Where the fuck would he be?" Zarius asked.

"I don't know." DK's voice was hard and quiet. He held his helmet at his side, sword in his other hand.

"Why the fuck would he just run off?"

DK shook his head. Thicker clouds drifted over the moon. A stiff wind picked up and blew a curtain of leaves across the road with a dry clatter.

"The fuck man?" Zarius muttered.

"We should get out of here."

Zarius jolted. "*What*? We're just gonna leave his ass out here?"

"You wanna keep looking?"

Zarius looked around. They'd already shouted their way up and down the road to the carriage and back. He had a bad feeling. "Fuck," he said. "Okay."

They headed for the carriage, walking fast, though they didn't speak on it. More clouds gathered at the moon like acolytes eager to absorb their dim, dying icon. A blast of wind whipped down the corridor and dried out Zarius's eyes. His hands knotted into fists.

"DK." He had to spit the word out.

"What's up?"

"Something's off."

DK turned to him, face fraught in the errant glow of the swinging lantern. "Okay. Let's go."

They took off running. Around the next bend in the road, they saw the lone lantern on the carriage, waving wildly in the wind.

"You take Louelle," DK puffed.

They reached the carriage. As DK clambered up to the bench seat and Zarius vaulted onto Louelle's back, Zarius heard a distinct, shrill whistle from deep in the trees on his right.

"Oh fuck," Zarius said. "*DK.*"

The whistle sounded again, cutting through the wind.

"Help . . ." a distant voice called.

All the hair stood up on Zarius's neck, and his spine crackled.

"What the fuck," DK said, gazing into the trees. He looked back at Zarius. "What do you think?"

"Help . . ." The voice was closer. More insistent.

Louelle stamped the ground and snorted. Zarius put a hand on her neck.

"Ain't no way that's him," said Zarius. "Why wouldn't he answer earlier?"

Harsh wind growled down the road. A host of leaves blew up all around them as DK snapped the reins and got the carriage moving onto the road. Before DK could shout at the horses to speed up, though, Zarius came abreast of the carriage on the opposite side and saw a shadow walking onto the road, barely visible against the darkness, a good distance in front of them.

"*Shit*," Zarius shouted over the wind. "You see that?"

As soon as it kicked up, the wind died in the branches. The trees ceased to rattle, and the land grew deathly quiet. The thin veil of moonlight hung on by a thread under the massing clouds.

The figure was tall. Too tall. Skinny and lanky. It raised its arms to its face and whistled down the road at them.

"Come here." It clapped big hands together. "Here boy!"

Louelle whinnied and turned sideways, as if she were thinking about taking off. The carriage horses neighed nervously.

"Easy girl," Zarius muttered, keeping his eyes locked on the figure.

"Come on," the figure yelled. It was a bassy, resonant voice. "Come here boy! Dog Knight! Come here!"

Zarius's eyes twitched. "What the fuck did he just say?" he asked. "DK?"

DK also remained locked on the figure on the road. "That's not the carriage guy."

"*Come here*," the figure bellowed, so loud that Zarius jumped. "*Dog Knight. Come.*"

Zarius and DK sat motionless. The horses stamped and neighed. Zarius's heart was about to beat itself into pulp.

"Is it saying *Dog* Knight?" Zarius cried.

The figure cocked an arm back and threw something. A shadow hurtled through the air and landed with a *whumpf* about halfway between them. Louelle snorted hard, and the carriage horses were ready to rear.

Laughter belted down the road. The figure bobbed up and down as it laughed and laughed, and it fell down on the ground and started rolling around, laughing its head off. After a few moments, it started dragging itself off the road, cackling all the way, until it disappeared into the trees. They listened to the laughter fade, and the ensuing silence swallowed them whole.

"We gotta go *now*," DK said.

At the same moment, he snapped the reins and got the carriage rolling, and Zarius followed suit. They passed the shadow in the road, and Zarius gazed at it as he rode by. A half-squeezed fist, bent wrong at the wrist. The white of bone showing through the red flesh at the top of the forearm. It was a human arm.

41

Strong Sunlight penetrated the gaps in the hovel door. Zarius stared at the ceiling. He didn't know if he'd fallen asleep; he didn't think he had. They had arrived in Ten-Berry just before dawn and roused a grouchy Cornelius Flember who shortly grew elated at the security of some important cargo and the future gratitude of some bigwigs in Endlin. After that, DK and Zarius returned home, where they collapsed into bed. DK set to snoring almost immediately, but Zarius lay there and watched the ceiling until the Sun relieved him of the perverse darkness.

All night, he replayed it all in his head. Everything. Forwards and backwards. All the way back to Derrick, back to Endlin, before he ever set out on this journey. How little he knew back then. How little he knew now. The specter of the bog witch had grown to a towering giant in his mind, beyond comprehension, impervious to encapsulation. Fear hung in the rafters of his heart like so many bloodthirsty bats.

Eventually, DK woke up, and he got up, built a fire, and started making porridge. Like nothing was wrong. Like it was business as fucking usual. Zarius wanted to scream.

"You awake?" DK asked, peering over at him.

Zarius grunted.

"How you feeling?"

"Me? Oh you know, just Sunshine and rainbows. Kicking my feet and twirling my hair and shit."

DK smirked, then lost it. He turned back to the bubbling pot. "That was a lot."

Zarius just scoffed. Black clouds of smoke gathered at the ceiling and filtered through the vent.

"You handled yourself well. Really."

For some reason, Zarius felt his throat closing up.

"Especially with the boy. Keaton."

Zarius closed his eyes and shook his head, face still pointed at the thatch ceiling. "He didn't even swing his sword."

"I know that." DK sniffed. "And you responded with the exact right amount of force. You could've killed him, but instead you just disarmed him. That showed restraint and presence of mind."

"I wasn't even thinking. That's just what happened."

DK sighed. "You should give yourself more credit than that. I'm telling you you did good."

"Thanks."

"Dog Knight." DK looked over at him, grinning.

Now Zarius sat up and met his gaze. "Yeah. What the fuck was that all about?"

DK shrugged, a mischievous glint in his eyes. "Hell if I know. Best I can figure is that she—well, whatever that thing was, but you know—was trying to insult you. Calling to you like a dog."

Anger boiled up under Zarius's skin, even cutting through the latent fear. "Fucking cunt."

DK laughed as he stirred the pot. "I think it's kind of funny. I don't know. The Dog Knight isn't half bad. You've got that dog in you, right?"

Slowly, Zarius unclenched his jaw, even sprouted the trappings of a smile. "You ain't wrong about that."

"Would you wanna be the Dog Knight?"

Something about the tone made Zarius pause. His smile vanished. He stared at DK from where he rested against the wall, and DK met his gaze.

"What do you mean?"

DK cracked his neck. "I mean do you want to be the Dog Knight?"

"Are you . . ." Zarius leaned forward. "Are you saying what I think you're saying?"

"You're proving yourself every day. I'm not bossing you around anymore. I trust your judgement, and I've thought of you more as a partner than an apprentice for a while now. Sure I'll still correct you here and there if I need to, but you've corrected me too."

"But, but . . ." Zarius shook his head like he might wake up. "You're still a way better swordsman than me. And I—you *trust* my judgement? I feel like an idiot most of the time. Like I . . . you think I'm *ready*?"

"Hey." DK tossed a hand. "Nobody ever came up and told me, 'You're the Day Knight now.' I just kind of decided. What do you think?"

"I . . ." His tongue was heavy. "I don't—I don't know. I hadn't thought about it. You want me to be what that *thing* called me?"

"I think the Dog Knight sounds badass. Plus, it's an extra *fuck you* to whatever that was. They wanna call you that shit like an insult? I say put it right back down their throats."

A spark of inspiration went through Zarius. He latched onto the idea. The Dog Knight. Cause fuck you, that's why.

"You really think I'm ready?" Zarius asked.

"I'm asking *you*."

At first, he wanted to say no. Of course he did. He was comparing himself to DK, and that seemed an impossible bar to reach. But maybe he didn't have to be the Day Knight. What if he could just be the Dog Knight?

"I still feel like I have a lot to learn," Zarius said.

"So do I." DK mixed the porridge.

Eyes wandering, Zarius picked at a hangnail before setting his jaw and bunching his blankets up in his fists. The bog witch thought he was a *dog*, huh? A fucking street dog. A pet. Well maybe he was a dog. Maybe he'd always been a dog.

"Fuck that bitch," Zarius said. "I'll be the fucking Dog Knight."

42

DK's heart thudded in his chest, and in the streaming fall Sunlight, it was a bizarre sensation. The culprit walked alongside him in simple peasant dress, but she wore it all like a princess headed to a feast. Sunlight painted a glow on the edges of her hair as she tossed her head and looked at DK, hazel eyes sparkling, brown rimmed in green. Yep. His heart was beating his sternum for lunch money. When they made it to the stables, DK let himself into the yard through the gate and chuckled as Catherine bunched up all her skirts in her hands and slopped through the mud.

"Sure you're okay with this?" DK asked. "You might get all dirty."

"Oh *no*. *Dirt*?" Catherine put a hand over mouth and feigned horror. "You mean that's not j-just a w-w-wives' tale?"

"Alright smartass. Just you wait."

A brave fall Sun fell over them. DK was almost hot in his wool overshirt, but the heat was so fresh and reassuring that it didn't bother him. He took a moment to close his eyes and turn his face up to the Sun, soaking up the Light. There wouldn't be many more days like this. It wasn't so much a conscious thought as a haunting dirge playing in his soul. The moment dragged.

"What are you doing?"

DK opened his eyes and found Catherine right next to him. She let her own face tilt up toward the sky, but she kept her eyes on him, and he had to remember how to use his vocal cords.

"Just . . . thinking," he said.

They stood side by side, hands on the rough wooden fence boards, looking at each other. The faintest breeze stirred Catherine's hair, and without thinking, DK reached up and tucked a loose strand behind her ear. The air crinkled around them as DK's breath caught in his throat, and he put his hand back on the fence. Catherine waited a moment, her eyes absorbing all of his vision like two holes from which he cared not to escape.

"What are you thinking about?" she asked.

DK collected a big sigh and released it. Now he let his eyes fall into the sky. A lurid blue plain. Tufts of cloud like God's beard shavings floating on the cleanest, clearest water.

"About what's going to happen."

She smiled at him. "I thought you were all about the present."

DK laughed. "I'm supposed to be."

"What's got you out of it?"

His smile faded, and his eyes hardened. DK stared up at the closest cloud, a gray-bottomed slipper scooting across the sky. "You know what? Whatever it is, it's not worth it. I'd rather be here anyway."

With that, DK turned around and picked his way around the mud patches, disappearing into the dark cavern of the stable. As his eyes adjusted, a long face poked out of a stall and stopped right in front of his own. He laughed as he reached up and stroked Louelle's big brown head, and she snorted her approval.

"Good horse," DK said. "Who's a good horse?"

Louelle snorted louder, and a mist of what he hoped was just saliva sprayed him in the face. DK spluttered, laughing and mopping himself with his shirt. Louelle was a good horse.

"Is this her?" Catherine asked in a small voice from the doorway, as if she were speaking into a church.

"This is her," DK said. "You remember."

Catherine inched into the darkness and brushed shoulders with DK. She raised her hands to Louelle's eager face and gently stroked her. DK rubbed her on the other side, and when Catherine's hands drifted over and mingled with his, he froze up and dropped them. Catherine paused, cleared her throat, and continued to pet Louelle. Louelle let out a little bluster.

"She's so sweet," Catherine said. "Hi Louelle. Remember me?"

Louelle's head bobbed a couple times, like she was nodding emphatically, and Catherine burst into long, hearty laughter that made DK's face heat up.

"Here, let's get her out." DK swung the stall gate open, and Louelle plodded right out. The big, dappled horse made her way out into the yard of her own accord, without waiting for her companions.

"Guess she was ready to get out of here," Catherine said through a smile.

DK fetched the double saddle off the wall and hefted it over his shoulder, lugging it out into the yard after Louelle. Louelle had stopped in a patch of dirt, swishing her tail, tossing her head. She looked like she was basking.

"Maybe she can be the Day Horse," Catherine said.

DK gazed at Louelle, grinning. "She already is."

The Sun fell over Louelle's chestnut coat and the swath of white dots splashed across her back and hind flanks. Her beige mane swished as she swung her head, and DK walked up to her and tossed the saddle on her back. Louelle allowed him to fuss over her, cinching straps and buckling clips. She didn't resist the bridle on her head or the bit in her mouth, and he stroked her for a long time.

"Alright," he said, craning his neck to find Catherine still at the edge of the yard. "You doin this or what?"

A wagon clattered past the stable on the road out front, the earth trembling as it went by. Catherine shifted from foot to foot and scratched her head.

"Why don't you go first?"

"Oh come on." DK beckoned her and held out his hand. "We can go together."

Toying with her skirt, Catherine slowly made her way across the dirt. She took his hand and gazed at him for a moment before she faced Louelle.

"Now what?" she asked.

DK released her hand, hooked a foot in the stirrup, and hefted himself up over the saddle in one fluid motion. He put both his hands down, and she took them right away.

"Alright so do what I just did. I'll pull you up and give you a boost."

"Okay," Catherine said.

"One, two, three."

They executed the move flawlessly. Catherine landed in the saddle right behind him and immediately wrapped her arms around his chest like Louelle was about to go off a cliff. And they just sat there, motionless, in the middle of the stable yard.

"You good?" DK laughed, very aware of her hands around his torso.

"Oh shut up," she said. "I don't wanna fall."

"You won't, not with me driving." He would've turned around and winked at her, but now her head was pressed against his back, and he struggled putting a string of thoughts together.

DK took the reins and gave Louelle the smallest prod, and she started walking across the yard. Catherine squeezed him so tight that he belched out a gasp.

"Jeez," he squeaked.

"Sorry," Catherine cried, releasing the pressure.

Louelle plodded forward like the smoothest, sturdiest carriage. They barely even jostled on her back, and DK patted her on the side of the neck.

"You're so smart, Louelle. Such a good horse."

Louelle snorted. They traversed the perimeter of the fence, and DK goaded her up to something between a walk and a trot. Catherine loosened her grip and sat up higher. The wind whooshed around them. Pieces of Catherine's hair fluttered around DK's head. When he glanced back, she was leaning back, face up toward the sky, grinning.

"You wanna go faster?" he asked.

Catherine's head tipped down, eyes going wide, and a mischievous grin spread across her face. "Hell yeah."

DK guided Louelle to the gate, let her out, then hopped back on and made down the road. They passed disgruntled pedestrians and sent a couple chickens flapping away before they made it out of Ten-Berry and found an open dirt road in front of them.

"Fast?" DK asked.

"Do it," Catherine said.

He grinned. One snap of the reins, and Louelle understood. In seconds, she kicked up to a full gallop, and silence became a roar as the wind lashed past their ears. Catherine let out a long holler, squeezing DK, and DK beamed as his hair flapped around his head like a tattered flag. They tore down the road, Louelle's hooves thundering below them, like they were chasing a lightning strike.

Badarumbadarumbadarumbadarumbadarum.

The sides of his vision blurred as Louelle hit top speed. They flew over the road, and DK half-expected them to float up and take off. If any horse could do it, Louelle could, and for a moment, with his eyes closed, it felt that way. Like they were leaving the ground, thundering through the sky, challenging even the stature of the Sun.

After maybe half a minute, DK pulled up on the reins ever so gently and let Louelle start coasting down. When they finally came to a halt, Catherine let out a whoop and gave him a hard squeeze. He spun halfway around on the saddle, grinning at her, and she grinned right back, hair in crazy twists all around her head.

"*Wow*," she said, cackling. "I haven't done that in forever."

"You're a natural." He smiled.

They locked eyes. Catherine's smile faded, and vague shadows clouded her eyes. She leaned forward and pressed her lips against his. For a moment, DK lost himself. He let it happen. He let her hands drift up to his face, and he returned her kiss. After that one moment, though, as she leaned farther into him, DK broke the contact and dropped his head. Catherine sat there, frozen, then let her hands fall.

DK shook his head. "I'm sorry, Catherine. I just . . . I, uh—"

"No I'm sorry." She closed her eyes and turned away. "That was stupid. I should've—"

"It wasn't stupid." He took her hand, and she let him hold it. Finally, she opened her eyes, and he gazed at her. "It wasn't stupid," he repeated. "I just . . ." He took a deep breath and set his jaw. "I don't know if I'm gonna . . . if I'm gonna be here. For much longer."

Shock and confusion lit up Catherine's eyes, and she leaned away. "You don't . . . What the hell do you mean?"

DK tried to hold onto her hand, but she pulled it away. His

throat turned to stone, and he struggled to swallow. They shifted to and fro as Louelle meandered down the road.

"What do you mean?" she asked again. She bore into his eyes, face flashing through emotions. "Oh no," she said, blinking. "You don't think, you're not gonna—"

"I'm gonna have to go back," he said.

"To the bog?" she asked, breathless. "*Why* would you do that?"

"It's not that I *want* to. But it's . . . she's not gone, Catherine. The bog witch isn't gone. In fact, I think . . ." His eyes went vacant. "I think I woke her up somehow. She's coming after us, and we aren't gonna be able to wait forever. If something happens, I don't want it to hurt you. Any more than it has to."

"But, but . . ." Catherine's whole face arched in horror. "You think you're going to *die*?"

DK didn't answer. That question had been looming in his mind, shapeless and unspoken. He didn't know exactly why, and he didn't give any power to it, but it loomed, nonetheless. When he came out of his meditations, when he lay down to go to sleep. And there was a frightful node somewhere within it, an answer that forced the question to be asked. It was frightful, but it wasn't fearful. DK wasn't afraid, but yes.

He thought he was going to die.

"You didn't . . ." Zarius gawked. "Bro what? You didn't go for it?"

DK dug a splinter out of his palm, looking away. His stomach rolled; it hadn't stopped rolling since he walked Catherine back to the tavern.

"Nah," DK said.

"Why?"

"I just . . . I don't know if that's the right move right now."

"Why wouldn't it be?"

"Because, man." DK dug into his left eye with the heel of his hand. "I don't know how shit's gonna go."

Zarius was quiet for so long that DK finally looked up.

"Z?"

"You mean with the bog witch?" Zarius stared a hole through DK's head; DK could barely hold that gaze for even a second.

"Yeah."

"So what then?" Zarius's voice snapped like a whip. He stood up and bore down on DK. "We're just supposed to fucking *die* then? That's what you think?"

DK leaned away and forced himself to look up, to catch that scorching gaze and let it burn him. "I don't know. It's possible."

"Oh it's *possible*," Zarius spat. "Dying is *always* possible motherfucker. We could've died eight months ago. But you're gonna . . . now you're gonna what? Stop living? Cause you might die *soon*? What the fuck is that?"

"I don't want to hurt her."

A vein grew and trembled on Zarius's forehead. His eyes shone against the dim Daylight from outside. "So might as well pretend to be dead already? Sick fucking plan, bruh. Don't you *want to live*? Don't you wanna *win*? I mean what the fuck. I don't wanna fucking die, bitch. As if you know shit. *Fuck you*."

Zarius stormed out and slammed the door so hard it shook dust off the walls. DK stood up to go after him but only managed half a step before he collapsed back into the chair and bowed his head.

43

Bitter and tired, Zarius hunched over on a stool in the hypnotic heat of Ezekiel's forge, a thick blanket over his lap. His chest ached from hundreds of pushups, legs weary from miles of running. When doubt or fear tried to take hold, Zarius trained and conditioned beyond the brink of exhaustion. These days, sometimes it was DK running ragged around the sparring pit by the end of the day.

Thick clouds had covered the sky for days. The Sun was nowhere to be found, only present in the ambient Light it could squeeze through the blanket above. Still, Zarius followed DK to meditate and ground his teeth when his thoughts inevitably assailed his fragile house. But he tried. He thought about it. Day in, day out, the idea of meditating, separating from his thoughts or maybe just rising above them, antagonized him, sometimes to the point of preoccupation. But he tried. He tried hard.

"Sorry I haven't finished up that armor yet." Ezekiel pursed his lips. "This order for Endlin is taking longer than I thought. Maybe my hands aren't as quick as they used to be."

"It's alright." Zarius shook his head. "You've done more than enough for me already."

"Glad to hear it." A gentle smile crossed Ezekiel's face. "What's on your mind, son?"

Zarius told him. Everything. All of what was bothering him, particularly what DK had said about Catherine. It still bothered Zarius even a couple weeks on.

"He really said that?" Ezekiel asked, frowning as he sipped a hot cup of tea. The forge glowed red behind him, like a portal to the most temperate corner of Hell.

"Yeah," said Zarius.

Ezekiel sighed. His wizened face was exaggerated by the firelight behind him. Every wrinkle seemed to cast a shadow, and his wiry white hair was thinner than ever. "I won't pretend to like it," he said in a tired voice. "But Christian is a man, and so are you. I don't think he's a nihilist. I won't deign to tell him what's right or what's wrong. I can only give my advice and trust his opinion."

Zarius gritted his teeth so hard that his jaw trembled. He forced himself to relax, but only just. "But, but it's like giving up, isn't it? To just . . . to like, not do something because he's afraid of what might happen?"

"It's a very particular *something*," Ezekiel said. "Romance can be a nebulous beast."

Gretchen's freckled face flashed through Zarius's mind and sent his heart reeling. Each word Ezekiel spoke threw a shovelful of dread on him.

Ezekiel cleared his throat. "I don't think he's right, mind you," said Ezekiel. "If anyone can go into that bog and come back out, it's Christian. We both know that. But I don't think he's wrong to prepare for the worst. Maybe it's not for Catherine as much as it is for him. Maybe he doesn't think he can reach the pinnacle of his focus if he has her in the back of his mind."

Anguish radiated from the tips of Zarius's toes to the crown of his skull as he sank even farther forward, staring at the dusty stone floor. The red breath of the forge made him feel like his feet were planted on brimstone. The rough wool blanket scratched his palms.

"Isn't it possible to do both?" Zarius croaked.

Ezekiel took another small sip of his tea and leaned back in his chair. "Are you prepared to fight, Zarius?"

Zarius looked up at him.

"Are you prepared to put everything on the line?" Ezekiel asked. "If Christian, if *DK* asked you, would you go? No matter what?"

"Of course I would," Zarius snarled. "I'll fight to the end with him."

"Because who are you? What are you?"

"I'm the fucking Dog Knight."

Ezekiel nodded. "I'm not going to sit here and tell a young man not to listen to his heart. You have a girl you're thinking about, I'm assuming?"

The sudden energy rushed out of Zarius like a sneeze, and he deflated, nodding.

"You need to be you, Zarius," Ezekiel said. "Christian's going to do what he thinks is best, and so should you. If you want to pursue this girl, then you better make very sure that you and especially *she* knows what that entails. What might happen. If you think it would be a distraction, then weigh that as well. Think on it, and be intentional. Don't just go stumbling down this path because it feels good. That doesn't mean it's wrong, but it does mean you need to be careful. You have tall tasks ahead of you. You're the Dog Knight now. But I have full faith in you. I believe in you."

Emotion snatched Zarius's throat and brought water welling to his eyes. "I wish I felt that way. What if I can't do it, Ezekiel? All this shit." Images rolled through his mind like a column of cavalry. Derrick. The corpses. His nightmares. The Dead Knight. The

Thread Knight. It all ballooned in his head until he thought his skull was about to crack.

"I'm fucking struggling," Zarius said. "I can't even sleep. I see all this shit and everything I've done wrong . . . and I just . . . I have so much doubt."

"That's what you can give up to God, Zarius. Struggling is natural. Doubt is natural, and it absolutely doesn't mean you'll fail. Not a single great man ever walked this earth without doubting himself at least once, at least for a moment. You're a remarkable young man. Far beyond where I was, at your age."

"What difference does that make?" asked Zarius. "You didn't have a battle looming. People weren't counting on you."

Ezekiel's eyes glinted. "Well you're mighty wrong there. I had a wife already, and she was with child. People certainly *were* counting on me, and I was bouncing around trades with no end in sight, terrible at practically all of them."

"Really?"

"Yes." Ezekiel shifted in his seat, wincing as he rubbed his hip. But his eyes remained on Zarius. "My name bore a black mark on every scroll in Endlin. Tradesmen wouldn't hire me, so I tried to learn on my own. During harvest season, I worked the fields from dawn to dusk just to bring home a single loaf of bread to share with Marie and our still unborn child. I'd get a few hours of sleep and spend the pre-dawn hours begging yet more tradesmen for an apprenticeship. I resented my condition and the lot I felt had been cast for me. I'm ashamed to admit I spoke in anger against my wife, far too many times. Drinking, gambling, just despicable behavior. But then our son was born."

Zarius sensed the intensity behind these words, and he was afraid to speak. All he'd ever known Ezekiel as was a blacksmith. No wife, no family. Ezekiel continued on, old blue eyes shimmering against the darkness. A chill touched the room as night whispered through the cracks in the wall.

"Our son, Jeremiah." Ezekiel smiled, eyes distant. "My goodness, if ever there was a more handsome child . . . So beautiful, so curious. Docile as a lamb. Rarely did he cry. Rarely did he take ill. He absorbed everything this world could offer through his big brown eyes. The way they would shine in the Sunlight . . ."

Afraid to even move, Zarius kept his eyes on Ezekiel's chair, and Ezekeil continued, kneading his thick hands.

"When he was still young, moving from toddler to child, I *finally* caught on with a much-reviled blacksmith in Endlin. He couldn't keep an apprentice, and I couldn't keep a master. We seemed fated to be stuck together forever, working for pennies. But it was something I could finally hang my hat on. I actually enjoyed it. I was a blacksmith, and I was filled with ambition to get better and better.

"That took *years*, mind you. Years of working harvests and spending winters begging in one form or another." Ezekiel grunted and shook his head. "To say I was humbled doesn't even approach the true magnitude of the experience. But with Jeremiah waiting for me every night, it all seemed a little more bearable. My relationship with Marie improved daily, and we bonded over our love for our wonderful son.

"With a purpose, a family I loved to provide for, I threw myself into my work. Very soon, I eclipsed my master in skill, but I bided my time. His reputation took off on the back of my efforts, and he lorded over me and anyone else who would listen, as if he truly didn't understand the reason for his sudden good fortune. Still, I saved my money. When Jeremiah was ten or eleven years old, we moved here, to Ten-Berry. I purchased this building and the forge and that was that.

"I could see it all laid out before me. I could enjoy a modest and quiet life with my beloved wife and son away from the bustle and treachery in Endlin's slums. People here were kind. They took to me right away, impressed by my burgeoning reputation. I even brought business to this town, a few contracts from larger villages and soon even Endlin. I foresaw the business growing long after I was too old, when my son could take over and achieve absolute security. Our posterity would be safe and comfortable forever. Never did I believe so strongly in a vision. It began to consume my thoughts, and when Jeremiah turned twelve, I got him right into the forge. Posthaste."

The air was deathly still. Zarius's muscles were tight and cold, but the silence held as he waited for the story to continue. He stole a glance up, but Ezekiel's eyes were drifting toward the ceiling, seeing another time. Perturbed, Zarius watched him, and Ezekiel turned and caught his eyes. They gazed at each other for a moment, and Zarius couldn't read his expression. Finally, the curiosity was unbearable, like a stone hovering in mid-air. It simply had to fall.

"What happened?" Zarius asked.

Ezekiel settled back and reaffixed his gaze on the wall. "Jeremiah wasn't a blacksmith. Not in his heart. He disliked the idea of it from the very beginning. He'd rather spend his time gallivanting around the rocky hills, making up stories, playing pretend. For a while, I tolerated it, but I grew increasingly frustrated, then angry. When he was fourteen or fifteen, we entrenched ourselves as adversaries. I forced him to work long hours with me at the forge, and our relationship deteriorated. Marie tried to reason with me, but I thought *I* was the only one with any reason.

"Our son needed to learn a trade. He needed to have an income. If I couldn't teach him that, I was a failure as a father. If I couldn't impress upon him the cold harsh reality of this world, I was a failure as a mentor. Anger at myself transformed into anger at my family.

They weren't helping me, weren't meeting me halfway. Jeremiah snuck writing lessons behind my back and began to write stories—a stark indication to me that he was grabbing on more firmly to his whimsical, fruitless fantasies.

"I thought I was losing him to some kind of slothfulness, so I forbade the stories. I worked him longer and harder in the forge and tolerated no dissent whatsoever. From him or Marie. Our home was a knot of tension ready to explode at any moment, and it frequently did. I shouted my son into tears, even his mother a couple of times. I had so much anger that they wouldn't listen to me, wouldn't understand that I knew best for all of us.

"Of course, that was my folly. I had no say over them. They were my family, my dearest loved ones, not my subordinates. But I couldn't understand that at the time, no matter how they tried to explain it to me. When Jeremiah turned eighteen, he disappeared. Off to Endlin, his note said. Somewhere people might let him be himself, might understand him. He wanted to join an artists' guild.

"I was beside myself. In a rage, I pursued him, but I couldn't track him down. I searched high and low, anywhere I thought he might set up camp, but I found nothing. Within a few days, my anger was scorched to despair. I became terrified that something had happened to him, and I begged Cornelius's predecessor to send word to Endlin for a search party. After a couple more days, they dispatched one."

Again, Ezekiel stopped. He just stared at the wall, lower lip jutting out, wrinkles as deep as they'd ever been. He stared until his eyes closed. Fat drops slid down his cheeks and dripped onto his bony legs. He made a strange hitching noise as his whole body jumped, but he held back the sobs. Unsure what to do, Zarius scooted his chair over and put a gentle hand on Ezekiel's shoulder.

"My only child," Ezekiel whispered. Tears lacquered his face.

"The greatest blessing God ever granted me. I still remember him like he was here yesterday. They found him in a stand of trees off the side of the road. He hadn't even made it to Endlin before some thieves killed him for the pennies in his pocket. And it had been days. The scavengers had already picked most of him away. They brought me to Endlin to confirm his identity, and what I saw in that box haunts me to this day. Half of him was just bone, but I could still see Jeremiah, still see my son. I just wanted to hug him, to somehow give my life to restore his."

A fit of crying overtook him, and he sucked in rattling breaths until he staved it off. Zarius labored in frozen silence; his heart ached for his suffering friend.

"You're a good man," Zarius said quietly. "One of the best men I've ever known."

"Thank you," Ezekiel said, sniffling. "I only wish God had given me the opportunity to learn as much without losing my son and his mother. She left, of course, too overcome by grief to bear being in the same room as me. I haven't seen her since, but I got word that she passed away some years ago, an old maid for some family in Endlin. I lost everything. I was all alone. I had no choice but to change, lest I lay myself down in the forge and wait until the flames took me away."

"And you did change," said Zarius. Grief made his voice thick. "You're the father I never had, a father for DK. We wouldn't trade you for anything."

More tears leaked out, and Ezekiel didn't bother to wipe them away. "I can only hope you're right, son. God knows I've tried my best to make up for my horrible mistakes. That all goes to say, though . . . Please, Zarius, please be yourself. You have no reason to feel doubt. Acknowledge it as a human feeling, but allow it to pass. You and Christian burn so bright. You're both more incredible than you know. Be the Dog Knight, Zarius. That's who you're going to be, and that's who you *are*. No matter what happens, God is with you. Allow Him to guide you, and you'll never move astray.

"I only wish Jeremiah had gotten the opportunity to embrace his dream. I did nothing but harp and hold him back. I tried everything I could to destroy his ambition, but he held onto it anyway. I have so much respect for what he did." His gnarled fists trembled on his knees. "I-I only wish I could tell him so. But I'll settle for you and Christian. You're the Light of this whole town, this whole country. Together, you can do anything. You can defeat the bog witch, and you will. You can be the Dog Knight, the Day Knight, and you *will*. So long as I'm here, I won't allow you to be anything else."

Emotion swelled in Zarius's chest as he stood up and pulled Ezekiel up into a hug. The old man sank into the embrace, crying his eyes out. He felt so frail, like he might just crumble to dust in Zarius's arm, so Zarius held on tighter. He held Ezekiel up until the sobs faded, reduced to just sniffles.

When they separated, Zarius gazed into Ezekiel's eyes with as much conviction as had ever blazed inside him. "I won't let you down."

Ezekiel managed a weak smile, and he tugged Zarius back into another hug. "Oh, Zarius," he said, each word cracking. "Don't you understand? You never could."

44

Breathing hard, Zarius watched DK's blade come swishing through, and he threw a guard at just the right angle.

Skannngggg.

"Nice," DK said. Sweaty strings of hair clung to his forehead.

They traded a few blows. Clumps of cold dirt flew about their feet as they maneuvered for advantage in the confines of the sparring pit. Sweat trickled down Zarius's back as dug his feet into the ground, always ensuring firm purchase, searching for extra leverage.

Shclannggggg. Whannngggg.

A couple big shots connected between them, neither gaining the upper the hand. No thoughts wheeled through the sky of Zarius's mind; every facet of his attention was absorbed in the fight. But a deep-seated awareness still resonated in the back of his head: Gretchen was watching.

Caroline and Gretchen hung over the ropes of the sparring pit, ogling as DK and Zarius went back and forth. That much Zarius couldn't push out of his brain, and a moment later, he missed a slash from DK that came so close it rumpled his shirt.

Gritting his teeth, Zarius planted his feet and refocused. Again, the whining of steel on steel screeched through the sparring pits. Thick gray clouds lay slothfully across the sky, giving no indication of movement. Days of cloudy skies had become over two weeks without the Sun, and the horizons showed no sign of any impending reprieve.

The Knights went around and around. Shaping strikes paved the way for big, swishing haymakers, but no one landed a winning blow. Occasionally, one of them ate a quick slash or caught the tip of a jab as they leaped away, but the fight raged on. Ragged, Zarius saw a flash of auburn hair over DK's shoulder and pressed into an attack.

Shkank. Schwank. Slannnggg. Kannggggg.

DK tried to squirm out of the advance, but Zarius moved to block his way. They traded three blows in quick succession. Zarius took a chance and slashed down at DK's legs, but DK jumped straight into the air like he saw it coming the whole time. Caught standing still, Zarius tried to whip his sword up, but DK was too fast and too agile.

DK's sword came down on the cleft between Zarius's neck and shoulder, and he crumpled to the ground, his own weapon falling straight to the dirt.

"Agghhhh, *shiiiiitttt*," Zarius moaned, clutching his shoulder as he rolled around in the dust.

Panting, DK stood with his hands on his knees for a moment before he offered Zarius a hand up. Instead, Zarius swept DK's legs out and brought him to the ground. They started wrestling, rolling around, trying to pin each other. Hissing through his teeth, Zarius tried to crush DK's left shoulder against the earth, but DK quivered as he kept his back up, then sprang into a sudden roll. He flipped Zarius off and scrambled after him, and now it was Zarius caught face-down in the dirt, fighting as DK tried to roll him over. Caroline and Gretchen giggled, and that cut through Zarius's concentration enough for DK to slam him over and pin him.

"You fuckin bitch," Zarius seethed.

Face bright red, DK sat back on his knees, gasping. Zarius sat up, hair all clumped up. They were both covered in dirt, but Zarius couldn't even muster the energy to speak for a minute as he caught his breath.

"That was strangely erotic," Caroline said, and she and Gretchen burst into more giggles.

"I know I'm turned on," DK said as he struggled to his feet. This time, Zarius allowed himself to be helped up.

The girls were framed against the hazy glow of the overcast sky. Zarius met Gretchen's gaze for a moment, then looked away. Bitterness surged up his throat. He stared the other way, at the nearby scatter of earthen hovels that turned into a labyrinth of filth and family.

DK cocked an eyebrow at Zarius for a moment, then turned back to the girls. "Well, clearly we're going to wash up after that. Would you wanna meet us at the tavern afterward, maybe?"

Both the girls nodded emphatically as they huddled deeper into their thick, wintry dresses. But Zarius killed DK's grin with a vacant stare.

"I'm good," said Zarius.

DK frowned. "What do you—"

"I don't want to."

Gretchen's face turned pink, and she quickly looked away. Caroline just arched her eyebrows.

"What's wrong?" Caroline asked. "Are you hurt?"

"I don't feel like going to the fucking tavern," Zarius snapped.

Caroline's eyes widened. "Oh. O-okay."

"Why don't you two just head over there anyway?" DK said. "I'll talk to Zarius, and I'll be there either way."

Quiet, Caroline just nodded, and Gretchen didn't so much as spare a glance back as they trudged off out of the sparring pits. DK watched Zarius, but Zarius just started gathering his shit and dusting himself off. He climbed through the ropes, dummy sword in hand, real sword sheathed around his hip, chainmail slung over his shoulder.

"What's wrong?" DK asked.

"*Nothing*," Zarius said.

DK jolted. "You sure sound angry."

"Are we leaving or not?" Zarius started walking off without him.

Half a minute later, DK caught up with all his own stuff bundled in his arms, and he bumped into Zarius as they made it to the main road and turned toward home.

"Hey man," said DK. "Did I piss you off? If I did, I'm sorry."

"I don't get it, bruh," said Zarius. "Half the time you're doom and gloom, now you're ready to go get a drink with them. I don't fucking get it."

"What do you mean?"

"Dude." Zarius turned to him, indignant. "You're gonna . . . Here you told Catherine . . . like, all that shit. Whatever the *fuck* you said. But you wanna go drink with Caroline and Gretchen? What the fuck is that all about?"

DK blinked. They walked in silence for a minute. A baby wailed from a hovel nearby, and a dog yapped as if trying to shush it. People filed past on the street, carrying buckets of water or baskets of groceries. Distant chatter in the square reported the last big sales of the fall harvest being hauled off. The Beggar towered over all the hovels, even the church. The sweat that had soaked into Zarius's linen shirt grew cold and slimy.

"I guess I don't see them as the same thing," DK said. "With Catherine . . . it's different."

"You ain't the only one who's got it different, motherfucker."

For a moment, DK looked confused, and then sorrow leaked into his eyes. "Shit. You and Gretchen."

"Yeah." Zarius clenched one hand. "How am I supposed to . . . here you're making it sound like you're gonna fucking *die* and shit. And—"

"I said I was sorry."

"*And* . . . you're basically setting me up on another date with this girl. Maybe it ain't like that for Caroline with you, but it is that way with Gretchen for me."

"Damn." DK hung his head. "I'm sorry dude. I didn't . . . I guess I wasn't thinking. But what, you don't wanna see her?"

Incredulous, Zarius gawked at DK. He almost slapped him across the face. "Are you joking? You won't even *kiss* Catherine, and you want me to get all wrapped up with Gretchen? When you're talkin bout 'the end of times' and *shit.*" Zarius spat the last word. He was heating up.

"I never told *you* not to do it," said DK. "I had to make that call for myself."

Anguish twisted up in Zarius's gut like a malevolent parasite. "Man I don't *know* what to do. I *like* her. I want . . ." He squeezed his jaw and shook his head.

DK looked hard at Zarius for a long time, and Zarius returned it with fire in his eyes.

"So is it the end of goddamn times or ain't it?" Zarius asked.

"I don't know what's gonna happen," DK said.

Zarius tipped his head up to the sky. The clouds covered his vision like a thick, gauzy bandage. Part of him thought he could just get lost up there. His mind would wander and lose track of his body, and that would be that. He spoke no more, instead just grumbling to himself. They made it back to the hovel, and DK stripped down and started washing himself with a rag. Muddy water ran to the floor and collected in a puddle, and Zarius built up a liberal fire. Steam rose from his clothes as he huddled close to it. When DK finished, he threw on his woolen shirt and pants and yanked on his muddy cloth shoes.

"I'm gonna go over there," said DK. "You sure you don't wanna come?"

Trying not to tremble, Zarius stared into the fire. The flames licked at each other, charring the wood, crackling in conspiracy together. Zarius thought of Gretchen. Her auburn curls, toothy smile, and his heart creaked. He wanted to go, and that was exactly why he told himself he couldn't. For no reason other than that he was trying to understand what DK said, why he did what he did with Catherine. Zarius didn't know what to do, so he followed the only example he had, and part of him hated DK for it.

"Okay," DK said. "Come by if you change your mind."

He went out and closed the door behind him. As soon as the wooden slab clunked home, Zarius went over to his bed and got down on all fours. He pressed his face into the musty hay and covered the back of his head. And he stayed like that for a long time.

WINTER

WINTER

45

The clouds held on for weeks. And when the Sun finally did re-appear, it did not bring the tempest heat of summer or even the quiet warmth of fall. It dawned over a bleak, dormant landscape that struggled to remember its own colors after so long under the gray boots of the clouds. The Sun hugged the southern sky as if too afraid to peer directly into Ten-Berry, into the land so long aban-doned. No leaves adorned the trees, and the conifers clutched their needles. No, the Sun brought little heat, but it did bring harsh, daz-zling winter Light.

On the first day of Sunshine, DK spent every hour on his bald patch of earth, absorbing every photon. In the morning, he shiv-ered, but by afternoon, he took his woolen shirt off and let the Sun rub out his goosebumps. He laid on the grass and did not move for long periods of time, and his thoughts became shapeless mysteries.

Zarius spent some time with him. For a while, he sat on his own frayed spot of dirt, and then he stood up and paced in silent consternation. At some point, Zarius left for a long time, then re-turned as it was getting on toward evening. Somewhere deep in his mind, DK sensed his friend's presence, but that was about the extent of it. He was somewhere else, beyond thought, beyond consciousness. The Sun lapped his face like an eager puppy, and DK cherished every precious minute. When the glow of Sunlight disappeared from his eyelids, and the cold air cinched up around his neck like a noose, DK opened his eyes. And for a moment, he was shocked.

The imposing figure of Mark Whitestone sat across from him. Mark met DK's gaze and sat in silence for the first few moments, like he understood the surprise. Zarius sulked next to Mark, eyes lost in the darkness marching over the eastern horizon.

"Mark," DK said flatly.

"Hello." Mark gave an almost reverential nod. A massive fur coat hung around his equally massive frame, with thick woolen pants and fur-lined boots to match. He wore a short, even crop of brown hair over his square jaw and shapely beard, but his large brown eyes emanated uncertainty. Maybe even fear.

"I'm . . ." DK shook his head. "Here you are."

"Indeed," said Mark. "I told you I'd be back."

"How'd it go in Endlin?" DK picked his threadbare wool coat up from the ground and threw it around his shoulders.

"About as well as I expected," Mark said, slowly shaking his head. "Paul and Kendall didn't *refute* the story, so to speak, but they didn't bolster it either."

DK grimaced. "And what does that mean?"

"It means the King was—is—skeptical. Their bizarre behavior around the whole incident was enough to stir his intrigue, but without any firm, assenting voices, he didn't exactly trust me either."

DK took a deep breath. Zarius remained quiet, ripping up handfuls of tan, dormant grass.

"And so?" DK asked.

Mark tucked his lips for a moment, and his hands tangled up in his lap. "I didn't receive permission for troops."

No emotion showed on DK's face. His eyes remained only watchful, and he gave a solemn nod.

"But," Mark said. His lower jaw swung side to side. "I haven't stopped thinking about all this for hardly one moment since I went back to Endlin. I know something's wrong, and to know someone like you is out here, ready and willing to face it alone . . . That just doesn't sit well. I'm going to offer you my allegiance. As in, I'll break the rules. I'll *bring* troops from Endlin, regardless of the King's orders. It won't be a substantial number. It'll have to be volunteer only, and even then, I'll need God's grace in preparing the right speech to sway them. They'll want to know what they're up against, and I . . ." Mark sighed and looked off for a moment. "God only knows I won't be able to lie to them. Don't expect much, but it might be something."

Fascinated, DK gazed upon this man in his fancy clothes, speaking with the prim and proper precision of a noble. But the words were all guts, all devotion. And Mark looked serious. His eyes were heavy and clouded, like he knew what was at stake. A swell of gratitude filled DK's heart.

"Mark," said DK. "I don't know what to say besides thank you. I'll feel a lot better knowing Ten-Berry has men of the Second Cavalry coming to her defense should it be necessary."

"And you think it *will* be necessary?" Mark ventured.

As DK sat back to chew it over, Zarius spoke up in a harsh, commanding voice. "Of course it will be."

Both DK and Mark startled as they looked at him. His eyes burned with black fury. "It'd be fucking idiotic to think otherwise. The Dead Knight. The fucking . . ." Zarius gripped a handful of his pants. "*Thread Knight*, whatever the fuck. Whatever was in the forest the other night." He stared at DK for a second. "We've seen shit, man. And she wouldn't show her whole hand to us. No way. There's gotta be more in there."

For a moment, they were all quiet. Mark readjusted his coat as the darkness swarmed the sky overhead. It smelled cold out there, the air itself. Hardening in preparation for the long months ahead.

"I guess that transitions into my one request," said Mark. "Before I really put my neck on the line. I want to go back."

"*What?*" Zarius barked, wheeling on him. "Last time wasn't enough? Are you fucking dense?"

"I'd be betting my entire *life* on this," Mark snapped back. "Not just the possibility of death. I've lived in that thought long enough. No, it's the mere matter of bringing men down here without the King's knowing. I would be dishonorably discharged, almost certainly sent to the stockades, and potentially *hanged*. I need to see it again for myself. I need to feel it. I'm trying to discern what the right thing is."

"The right thing is staying far the fuck away from there," Zarius said, looking to DK for support. "Forget about a battle. We might not even make it back from a field trip."

"If that's what you need, Mark," said DK. "So be it."

Zarius's jaw almost fell off. "*What?* DK, are you serious? You really think it's worth—"

"You'll stay behind," said DK, turning to Zarius.

A raging inferno couldn't have charred the expression off of Zarius's face any faster. "What?"

"If something happens," DK said, speaking carefully. "We can't all . . . we can't all go. Someone needs to stay here."

"And you want it . . ." Zarius threw his hands, stood up, and stalked off.

They watched him go. Mark turned back to DK, gaunt and serious. "Are you sure it's wise?"

DK narrowed his eyes. "What?"

"He's just a kid."

Leaning forward, DK put his eyes through Mark's head. "He's a Knight by his own merit."

"Very well." Mark grimaced. "I'm sorry. I don't . . . This isn't in my wheelhouse. Any of it. I'm nervous even being away from Endlin . . . I have a wife, and a daughter."

A flock of small birds flittered past overhead. DK glanced up at them, then let his eyes linger near the trailing red ropes of the descending Sun.

"Mark, you're gonna want to think long and hard about all this. Obviously I don't know for sure, but lately . . . I've been feeling like it's gonna be a one-way trip."

Mark paled but kept his face steady. "I'm prepared to do what's necessary to keep my country safe. I swore an oath, and I don't intend to forsake it out of fear."

Gentle relief soothed DK, but only for a moment. "You're an honorable man."

"I'm a man of my word."

"Alright." DK patted his thighs and stood up. "Are you sure you wanna go back out there?"

Now Mark's face did tremble, but he spoke clearly. "I need to be sure."

46

A harsh Sun glittered in a periwinkle sky. Thin patches of cloud roved the expanse like pirate ships stealing Sunlight. Big slanting rays of morning Light painted the hills in gold as DK, on Louelle's sturdy, steady back, followed Mark on his grand black stallion, Buck. Buck somehow dwarfed even Louelle, and Mark looked like a gunmetal giant atop his back. His armor gleamed in the Sun, perfectly fitted, engraved with ornate flames around the edges. He was a devil dressed in silk.

They rode in silence, pushing the horses hard to make the trip as quick as possible. DK sank into an improvised meditation as he bobbed on Louelle's back. Anything was better than lapsing into thought. The journey passed too quickly. Suddenly, the Sun was overhead, and the terrain became eerily familiar. Out in front, the ground rose like a makeshift wall, and beyond it laid the bog.

DK shouted at Mark, and they both trimmed speed down to a walk. Louelle and Buck moved a little closer together of their own accord. DK and Mark both let their helmets sit on the pommels of their saddles, and they gazed at each other. DK saw the fear laced in the lines of Mark's face, but the figure he cut was so imposing that DK thought if *he* were the bog witch, he might find himself intimidated.

"We don't know what might happen," DK said.

"We know what *might* happen," Mark replied.

DK widened his eyes and shrugged. True. A lot of bad shit might happen.

Before they started moving up the hill, DK brought Louelle to a halt. "Are you sure about this, Mark? Last time wasn't enough?"

"I wasn't ready last time," Mark said. "I couldn't get over my shock."

"And if we see nothing?"

"I'll know," Mark grunted.

They moved the horses onto the hill. The mass of thin tree branches came into view, like a black cobweb that fell from outer space. As soon as he saw it, DK's heart dropped into his stomach, and he started sweating. For DK, one look was enough, but Mark started down the opposite side of the hill.

It was about a hundred yards of dormant tallgrass and yuccas between them and the outermost trees. The faintest of footpaths offered vague guidance as the horses plodded along. About halfway to the trees, Buck came to an abrupt halt, swishing his tail.

Mark dropped his head in confusion. He jabbed his heels into Buck's flanks, but Buck didn't flinch or take one step. He let out a disgruntled snort, and Mark widened his eyes at DK. Solemn, DK moved Louelle around Buck, and she flicked her tail as they took the lead. A moment later, Buck cautiously followed.

"That can't be good," Mark muttered.

"It isn't," DK said flatly. "How close do you want to get?"

About three quarters of the way to the tree line, Louelle came to a halt. She stamped the ground twice, hard enough to make

DK jump, and he started stroking her neck. "Okay, girl. Okay." He turned back to Mark. "That's as close as she gets."

Mark was pale, made even paler by the gray plating of his armor. "Does she—she knows?"

"She feels it," DK said. "Don't you?"

Tendrils of nefarious energy caught them like the suction cups of a tentacle. DK felt a cold stirring in his mind, the bubbling of thoughts that were not his own. Mark blinked. His eyes shimmered.

"Yes," he said.

"We shouldn't stay here." DK fought the rising fear.

"Hold on." Mark cleared his throat and tugged at the collar of his chainmail. His eyes were fixed over DK's shoulder. "I think my wife is walking toward us."

All of DK's hair stood up. It took him a second to summon the courage to turn around, and when he did, sure enough, a figure was coming toward them. But to DK, it was no woman. Or maybe it was. Hard to tell by a headless, rotting corpse.

"Mark," DK said. Louelle started backing up on her own, whinnying. "We have to go. Is that enough?"

"She looks—is that my wife?" Mark asked. "*Alice*," he called.

"*No*," DK barked, now parallel to Mark. "*Snap out of it. Mark, we have to go.*"

"Oh my God." Mark's face twisted. He clamped both hands over his ears. "She's yelling. It sounds just like her."

The headless body was getting closer, picking its way over the lumpy ground, falling and getting back up. Greenish skin sloughed off its body with every step, revealing blackened, rotting tissue underneath.

Mark whipped his head to DK without dropping his hands from his ears. "How could she know what my *wife looks like*?"

DK shook his head wildly, heart crashing in his chest. "Mark, *we have to go.*"

Slowly, Mark lowered his hands. He turned back toward the figure stumbling toward them. Only a stone's throw away now. It was picking up speed.

"What's my daughter's name?" Mark asked, leaning forward. He called out louder. "Tell me you don't know her name."

A moment later, Mark's face went so white that he almost disappeared. As if broken from a trance, Buck let out a terrified whinny and turned around, bolting in the other direction. DK kicked Louelle up to a gallop and gave chase, cold air rushing against his face. Tears leaked from the corners of his eyes, such was the fear that swelled within him. He pursued Mark all the way back to the hill and caught up to him at the crest.

Mark's face contorted like he was being tortured. He flashed through emotions, always pale and sallow, until his eyes just blanked and finally focused on DK. "That looked like my wife," he croaked. "She knew our daughter's name."

DK shook his head. "I only saw a corpse, Mark. It didn't even have a head."

"What?" Mark whispered. He trembled on his impressive steed, and even Buck fidgeted nervously. "She . . ." He put one gloved hand on his head. "She got into my head."

"That's what she does," DK said.

"And you're gonna go in there?" Mark's gaze drifted back toward the bog below, and his eyelids almost tore off his head. "Oh look. She's still coming."

DK flipped his head and saw the corpse sprinting over the open ground, making a break for the hill. For a moment, they watched, and it was like a dream. Even all the way out here, beyond that malicious cloud of energy, they weren't safe. When the corpse made it to the base of the hill, DK and Mark took off again.

"Will it follow us all the way back?" Mark asked.

"I don't know," DK said.

"Couple of fucking idiots," Zarius said, glaring at them. "Just *had* to go back."

DK sat in his rickety chair and stared at the fire. Mark stooped against one wall, head brushing the ceiling of their hovel; DK was half-afraid the structure wouldn't hold his weight. Mark had barely spoken, and his face was so empty that DK couldn't look at him.

"Now he knows," DK said.

"Like he didn't know before." Zarius threw a scathing look at Mark.

"It wasn't just that," Mark said suddenly. DK and Zarius both jumped. "I wanted to know . . ." He cleared his throat and slumped to the ground. The whole hovel vibrated. "I thought maybe I could help you . . . in there."

"Mark," DK said. "I never would have asked that of you."

"I would have asked it of myself." Mark fixed his jaw and gave them each a pointed glance. "If you two are willing to do it, why not I? But now I know that . . ." He shook his head. "I can't. I don't have the ability. So I'll do what I can on the outside. And believe me I will do *everything* I can. I'm afraid for the both of you."

DK gazed at Zarius. When Zarius caught him looking, he sneered. "What?"

"Nothing," DK muttered. His thoughts were a mess.

Zarius stood up, eyes catching fire. "What? You think that's gonna happen to me?" He jabbed a finger at Mark. "*Huh?*"

DK grimaced. That was exactly what he was thinking. "You've never been in there either. And what about Ten-Berry?"

"That's what *he's* for." Zarius threw both hands at Mark. Hurt slashed his face. "What? You seriously . . . don't you believe in me?"

"Yes," DK snapped, and he skewered Zarius with a glare. "Don't even go there. I'm trying to think about what's *best* here, Z. Should we really risk both of us in there? With you going in for the *first time*? I mean look at Mark. You can't tell me you don't think he's a brave man, and he's shaken up like this? No offense, Mark."

Mark waved a hand and smiled weakly. "None taken."

"You aren't going in there alone." Zarius glowered at DK, face painted by the dancing flames.

"What if that's our best option?"

"*It isn't.*"

"We can't let emotions win out here. We have to think—"

"*Fuck* your logic. As far as I'm concerned, *you're* the one talking crazy."

DK gazed at him. "It's worth consideration."

"Consider my ass." Zarius balled his fists so hard they shook, and he looked ready to erupt.

"Hey, look," said Mark. "We're all in this together. We're a team."

"You're a fucking pig from Endlin," Zarius seethed. "What do you know about a team?"

Mark stood up. For a moment it looked like he'd just keep going until his head was in the clouds. He had to bend his knees just to tower over Zarius, and Zarius didn't so much as take a step back. He tipped his head up and kept his eyes glued to Mark's.

"I'm the Captain of the Second Cavalry," Mark said. "I've drilled teamwork since before you were—"

"Guys, *quit it*," DK pleaded. He gripped a handful of his hair and bounced his head off the wall. "For fuck's sake. Who is this helping?"

"You're just a big fucking pussy." Zarius took a step right up to Mark's chest. "Why don't you go find an innocent woman to rape?"

In one easy movement, Mark threw Zarius into the wall. *Thrunk.* Zarius hit it so hard that the wall cracked and left a sizable dent. He fell to the floor and moaned for a moment before he came up like a raging bull. As DK started shouting, Mark grabbed Zarius and threw him again, this time straight down. A cloud of dust flew up as Zarius choked and rolled around, gripping his side. Mark stepped right through the door and slammed it shut, but DK chased him outside.

"Mark, please," said DK. "I'm sorry. Don't go."

Mark wheeled on him, eyes glinting. "I'm trying to *help you.* What doesn't he understand about that? I'm sorry DK, but I won't tolerate that kind of disrespect from some child. I'd think twice about who you keep in your circle, especially at a time like this. In the meantime . . ." Mark shook his head and threw a hand as he strode off. "I guess I'll be in touch."

47

A week later, DK and Zarius waddled down the road toward the gate, laden with all the blankets they owned. The cold pressed in on them; winter bore down. Ten-Berry languished through gelid nights and short, windy days. The breeze cut Zarius to the bone, and it agitated a tremor in the depths of his spirit that had been bothering him for days, since Mark left.

Thankfully, the Sun was out, though a bank of clouds was gathering in the west and preparing to march. Besieged by the slashes of wind, Zarius peered out from behind his mound of blankets and saw Patrick scrunched up in a meager guard box they'd built during the fall. It was scarcely large enough for him to stand in, and when he saw them, he unfolded out of it like a resurrected spider unfurling its legs.

"Well I'll be," said Patrick. His teeth started chattering, and he hugged himself with his spear in one hand. "I-I-If it ain't the D-D-Day Knight."

"And the Dog Knight," Zarius added.

Trembling as he was, Patrick managed his trademark gap-toothed grin. "G-G-Got that right."

All of Zarius's bones ached. He wanted to resent Patrick for making them stop, but he just couldn't arouse any dislike for that grinning, wind-burned face.

"Hey Pat," DK said, shifting his own mound of blankets down so he could see. "How you holdin up out here?"

"F-Feels like one minute it's too got damn hot," said Patrick. "Next th-th-thing you know, too got damn cold." The redness deepened on his face, and he turned away from a blast of wind. "If Satan knew about wind, methinks he would've made Hell a tundra."

DK and Zarius both grinned.

"I think you're probably right," said DK. "You been havin any trouble lately besides the weather?"

"Aww, nah," said Patrick. He gazed off for a moment, long enough that Zarius and DK shared a glance.

"What's up, Pat?" DK prodded.

"I just been havin the weirdest dreams," Patrick said. He looked around like he was afraid of being overheard. "Weirdest damn dreams."

"What kind of dreams?"

For a moment, Patrick seemed to consider something, then he just shook his head. "Nothin good. All sorts of *bad*, really. Any which way. Junior ain't been sleepin well neither. Got me a case of the heebie jeebies, to be honest." He stared hard at DK. "You've been in some of 'em."

DK stared back at him. He waited for Patrick to explain, but Patrick just waved them on.

"Go on then," he said. "Go sit out in this gale you loonies. I'm gettin back in me box." Get back in the box he did, hustling over and stuffing himself right into it.

Perturbed, Zarius followed DK as he set off again. They made it out of town and down the cold dirt road. When they turned off and forged into the grass, Zarius closed his eyes and clenched his teeth. Gusts of wind caught them in every patch of open ground. Wrapped up in nearly all of his clothes, Zarius still winced as the wind cut through. Goosebumps covered his body. When they finally made it into the little divot of ground where their bald patches of earth awaited, he slumped right down on his and piled his blankets on himself.

DK, on the other hand, took his time getting settled, and Zarius watched in something close to awe as he left all but one blanket on the side. DK adjusted his seat on the ground and let his head tip up toward the sky. A few warm rays battled through the frigid atmosphere and collected in that hidden valley like a warm pool. Warm against the razor-sharp teeth of the wind, anyway. Zarius still shivered under his blankets, but he, too, basked in the Sunlight. Unease still circled his gut, though, and he knew he wouldn't get any peace if he let DK slip off into a reverie without addressing it.

"I'm sorry," Zarius said. The words jumped out of him like a man on fire. "I'm really sorry."

DK opened his eyes. He blinked once, focusing on Zarius. "What?"

"About Mark," Zarius said. Saying it made his throat hurt. "I'm really fucking sorry, man."

"Z," DK said, eyes softening. "We've been over it. It's alright."

"It's *not* alright," Zarius snapped. He clutched the blankets. "I fucking jeopardized our shit, man. I might've jeopardized *Ten-Berry.*"

"Look," said DK. He took a deep breath, palms open and facing the sky atop his cris-crossed legs. "You lost your temper, and you pissed Mark off. He said he would still be in touch. I know you know it was wrong. I'm not gonna beat you over the head with it, and you don't need to do that to yourself either."

"Well I have been," Zarius said. His nose hairs were freezing one by one.

"Well stop." DK gazed hard at him. "Remember what Ezekiel said."

"I feel like I fucked up."

"Dude, let it go. Shit happens, right? Look, we're right where we're supposed to be. The Sun is still here." DK pointed up. "That means we're good. For some reason, that needed to happen. I know you feel shitty, and it seems bad, but all you can do is be better *now*, right?"

Glum, Zarius nodded.

"Right. You just need to do what you can *now*. I know you wouldn't go off like that again, so you learned something from it."

Kneading his fists, Zarius held DK's gaze. "But I don't have *time* to be learning fucking lessons *now*, do I? Not when it's, when you're . . ." He had to stop for a moment. His eyes stung. "You think you're gonna die, and I'm just fucking shit up."

Sadness pulled on DK's face, and the Light faded from his eyes. "I shouldn't have said that. I'm sorry."

"Oh you don't have to *bullshit* me."

"No, for real. I shouldn't have said that. I don't . . ." DK shook his head. "I don't know why I did. I don't think I'm gonna die, it's just . . . I want to, like, be prepared, I guess. Maybe I wanted you to be prepared. I don't know. But that wasn't the right way to go about it. I shouldn't have given you a reason to feel any doubt, or even to worry about me. You need to be the best you, and I need to be the best me. The Day Knight and the Dog Knight. If we can just be *them*, everything is gonna be . . . Everything is going to work out how it's supposed to."

Warmth stirred in Zarius's chest. He grasped those words and didn't let them wriggle out of his brain. His vision blurred, but he didn't look away. He wanted it to be true. He wanted to make it true.

"I'm scared, man."

DK nodded. "So am I. I'd be more worried if you weren't."

"Are you gonna make me stay here when you go?"

DK sighed. He looked up into the sky, face screwed up against the harshness of the Light. "I don't know what the right call will be. I think we cross that bridge when we come to it."

"I feel like it's coming up fast," said Zarius.

DK grimaced. "It might be."

They spent every last moment they could under the shelter of the Sun. As Zarius stewed in his thoughts, he watched the placid calm on DK's face. Zarius tried as hard as he ever had, and he thought he achieved some semblance of tranquility. His thoughts never really went away, but for a while, it felt like he was beyond their reach. For a precious while. Then he got dragged back to the surface like an air bubble released underwater, and when he popped, the dread came surging back.

When the Sun dipped below the western hillside, the cold assaulted them. It took no time at all before they were back on their feet, picking their way to the road and heading back for Ten-Berry. Patrick was gone, replaced by another guard who didn't so much as look up from the guard box as they trudged past. As soon as they made it to the hovel, Zarius dove at the fire and built it up beyond reason.

Flames nearly brushed the walls, and DK and Zarius both huddled next to them, absorbing the warmth, heating their blankets. They made a hot stew, more broth than anything in these lean times, and wolfed it down like prisoners. Zarius's muscles ached and creaked like the rigging of a ship on frozen seas, and he was relieved for the day off. Tomorrow would bring more training, more conditioning, more punishment. But he was stronger, faster, and hardier now than he ever had been. And that was good, because as the weather got colder, every trip outside felt like a war in itself.

After resting by the fire for a while, DK stood up and stretched, groaning. "I think I'm gonna go see Ezekiel."

"I'll go with you," Zarius said. But he didn't get up.

DK smirked at him. "Just stay there you slug."

Zarius let his head fall to the warm dirt, and he yawned. "If you say so."

"Maybe we can hit the tavern after?"

"Sure." Zarius yawned again. The fire lapped his face like a friendly dog. "Just kick me when you need me."

DK snorted as he pulled his thick, gray wool overcoat on. "Will do."

48

Catherine dunked a couple of mugs into a bucket of water before hanging them on wooden pegs under the bar top. She half-listened to a man barking a drink order at her and started pouring ale into dry mugs. By the time he finished bleating, she had five full mugs in front of him. The man looked down and furrowed his bushy unibrow.

"Those are mine?"

She nodded.

"Thanks gorgeous." He showed a few missing teeth as he set some coins on the bar.

Catherine just swept up the change and moved on, scooping empty mugs up and dunking them in strategically placed buckets. When someone whistled or called her name, she usually spared them one single glance before she went to work, made their order, and collected her payment. When one barrel of ale ran dry, she tapped the next with a spout and a wooden mallet as easily as stepping into a shoe.

One brief moment of silence let her stand up and survey the tavern. The place was rocking. Bodies crammed up toward the bar, hands waving, and the smell of body odor wafted over to her. She wiped a wrist across her forehead and narrowed her eyes for a moment. Her gaze shifted back, past the line of people at the bar. Someone was staring at her. A chill ran down her spine. She shuddered and shook her head as she noticed someone at the bar, jaw flapping.

"Sorry, what?" Catherine said.

"Can I get two ales?" an older woman asked, smiling.

"Sure." Catherine flashed a smile back and poured them.

"Thanks." The woman paid and carried off her drinks.

On a streak, Catherine completed another half dozen orders. When she paused again, the commotion pressed into her ears and rattled her skull. She absentmindedly redid her ponytail as more hands started flapping and more voices started chirping at her. But the pause lingered. Her jaw felt tight. Something made her look back toward those staring eyes from earlier, and somehow, even through the thickening crowd, she found them again.

It was a short, bald man up against the perpendicular wall of the tavern. All by himself. Not in a chair, just leaning against the flame-scorched stones. Flickering torchlight grazed one half of his face. At first, he looked normal enough, but Catherine stared back at him, and something just wasn't right. His face was a little lopsided, one eye lower than the other, mouth in a permanent half-frown. Even as they locked eyes, Catherine didn't feel like they were sharing a glance. His eyes were sort of vacant, but they followed her. Most unsettling of all, though, was that Catherine didn't feel so much as a vague flare of recognition.

There were no strangers in Ten-Berry.

Disgruntled faces bunched up and broke her view. Grimacing, Catherine went into work mode again and fired off a bunch of ales. The crowd continued to thicken, the din continued to rise, but

Catherine kept messing up. She dumped two ales across the bar—two more than she had in the last month. She lost a piece of silver into a rinse bucket and had to fish it out while people snapped at her. Her hands were sticky, and annoying strands of hair got caught in her eyelashes.

Carmichael Blaine appeared at the bar. His face was already red, maybe from the wind, maybe just permanently marked that way. His beady brown eyes met Catherine's, and he nodded. Catherine nodded back and poured four ales. As she set the last one down on the bar, though, and Carmichael reached out a closed hand with his payment, Catherine met his eyes again. Carmichael cocked an eyebrow.

"Can you sit at the bar for a little bit?" Catherine said, tipping her head toward an empty stool a couple spots down.

Carmichael squinted his whole face. "Me and the boys got a table."

"Carmichael. Just for a few minutes. Please."

The confusion didn't abate, but Carmichael nodded. He disappeared for a few moments and came back to the bar with his one ale. He took his spot at the empty stool and just leaned forward and sipped his drink like that was where he'd meant to be the whole time. Another body squeezed into the spot vacated by Carmichael, and Catherine backed up. Cold fingers wrapped around her spine.

It was the stranger. Up close, there was no doubt. Something was wrong with him. His whole face slanted down to the left, and his left ear was a good two inches below his right one. Normally, Catherine would've been embarrassed to be so fixated on some physical abnormalities, but the chill flowing through her blood told her to beware. Her stomach churned.

"Um." She cleared her throat and locked eyes with him. His were two different colors—one blue, one brown. They looked wet, almost oozy. His lips were so pale they were almost white, and they were covered in deep, dry cracks. A misshapen shock of brown hair sat on top of his head. Bangs hung down only one half of his forehead.

"Can I help you?" she asked. She stayed a step away from the bar.

The stranger just held up one finger.

Catherine furrowed her brow. "You want an ale?"

He dropped the finger, then raised it again. Catherine glanced down the bar at Carmichael, and Carmichael was watching her.

The stranger's smile widened. She could almost hear his lips cracking even deeper. Flakes of dandruff stirred off his head. He held up a finger again.

"What do you want?" Catherine growled.

Carmichael's stout frame appeared next to the stranger, brown eyes glittering like a vicious rat's. Carmichael bumped his chest into the stranger's shoulder, and the stranger turned up to look at him.

"Who the fuck are you?" Carmichael asked.

49

A few steps from the door to Ezekiel's forge, DK paused. No smoke billowed from the chimney—not even a trickle. Of course, it was getting late, but he couldn't remember the last time he'd seen it dead. Perturbed, he stepped up and knocked a few times. His cold knuckles ached at the impact, and he stuffed his hand back under his thick woolen coat, hugging himself.

No answer. DK's heart jolted as he knocked hard again, this time numb to the pain. He put his ear up to the expertly crafted slats and listened. From inside, he heard a throaty voice bid him enter. Relieved, DK yanked the door open, stepped through, and pulled it shut behind him.

The forge was as dark as he'd ever seen it, but all the familiar smells were there. A cold piece of half-worked steel rested on the workbench next to the forge's charcoal heart, and Ezekiel sat next to it. He rested on a small wooden stool, curled in on himself like a flower losing the battle against decay. Blankets were heaped over him, obscuring nearly all of his body save his old, gnarled hands clasped on his lap.

"Ezekiel," DK said. Worry tickled him. "What's wrong? Are you sick?"

"No, no," said Ezekiel. He was quiet, almost impossible to hear. DK had to take a few steps closer. "Just tired, son. Old and tired. This winter came on so fast."

"I'll say," DK agreed. He hovered where he stood. "Done with work already?"

Ezekiel didn't move. "Like I said, I'm tired. If the Lord can take a day of rest, why not I?"

"Fair." DK shrugged and glanced around for a seat. He headed toward the table against the wall. Rather than grab a chair, though, he simply stood and leaned against it. Normally, he would've taken himself right over to sit by his old friend, but it just seemed right to stand.

Anxiety surged in DK's mind, and he wanted to release it. "I'm worried about . . . well all of this, Ezekiel. I haven't heard anything from Endlin."

"Endlin?" Ezekiel asked.

"Yes. From Mark."

Ezekiel's face was hidden in the cold shadows. The blankets drooped over him like layers of excess skin. When he readjusted just a bit, though, a slant of torchlight caught him, and DK saw all those familiar wrinkles, more numerous by the day.

"Ah yes," said Ezekiel. His voice was slowed, perhaps by the cold, as if it took effort to produce any noise at all. "Mark. He's to help you?"

DK stared at him, or rather stared at the blankets covering his head. "Well, yes. That was the plan. But then Zarius . . . don't you remember?"

"I'm sorry, Christian. I feel cloudy today. My thoughts don't want to connect. Perhaps I have taken ill after all. Mark is supposed to help you."

"Ezekiel, are you sure you're okay? Some people have been really sick in the last few weeks. Why don't I build the fire for you?"

"Yes, yes," said Ezekiel. "But just give it a minute. My old bones are comfortable right where they are. I just . . . Can you bring your chair over, Christian? I'd like to look at you more easily. Not to speak so loud."

Despite an odd twinge inside him, DK grabbed the back of the closest chair and carried it over. He set it a few feet away from Ezekiel's thick, moccasin-clad feet and sat down, though he remained bolt upright. Ezekiel didn't move a muscle, just continued his quasi-hibernation.

"That's better," the old man said. His head bobbed up, just a bit, and again, DK caught a glimpse of him. His eyes were cold. The sight of them made DK shiver. His friend was clearly sick, yet he had not even a fire by which to warm himself. He had to be freezing.

"Ezekiel," said DK. "Please, let me build your fire. I'll make you some stew. You're sick."

"In a minute," said Ezekiel. "I've got all the time in the world. As much as I need, anyway. But I'll only have you for a short while now, won't I?"

DK's heart thumped along in his chest. Those words floated across to him like poisoned cotton, heavy and foreboding. "I'm . . . Well I'm not sure. I think there could be a battle any day now."

"Yes, the battle," said Ezekiel. "You must steel yourself. Embrace your help. I only wonder if Mark will be enough."

Frowning, DK gazed at him. The illness was clearly thick in Ezekiel's mind. He was probably burning up under those blankets, consumed by fever. Perhaps that was why the forge was so dead and the house so gelid.

"That's if we can get him here at all. In fact, I'm going to send a pigeon tomorrow. Mark said he was going to bring as many men from the Second Cavalry as he could. I only hope he didn't change his mind."

Ezekiel was silent. The seconds ticked by, and DK began to lean forward, consumed by worry. He considered fetching Mary, but just then, Ezekiel shifted in his seat. He looked uncomfortable.

"The Second Cavalry?" the old man asked.

"Ezekiel, you must have a fever. We've discussed all of this. I can hear sickness in your voice. I'm going to get someone."

"*No,*" Ezekiel hissed, just as DK was about to stand up. The violence in his voice froze DK in place. "I have no need for such things," he added. "I want to sit with you. I want to look at you."

Before DK could process the words, he heard something else behind him, just a faint sound. It never should have really caught his ear at all, but it did. Footsteps outside, close. It sounded like someone was walking up to the forge, and he turned his head halfway around to listen.

50

In his nest of blankets, Zarius tried to relax but couldn't. A deep uneasiness bloomed in his gut and only seemed to grow stronger the more he tried to ignore it. He kept flashing back to his stupid, rash words to Mark. Chagrin tortured him, and he rolled around under his blankets, unable to get comfortable.

It started with his dumb outburst to Mark, and then Zarius's thoughts trickled down a path surrounded by every mistake he ever made. Every misstep in every duel, every reprimand DK had given him. Not good enough, not fast enough, not strong enough. Winter was on, the bog witch was stirring, and Zarius had pissed off their only hope for help. He clenched his teeth so hard that his jaw trembled.

So many fuckups. And time was winding down. Would he able to do it right when it counted? Would he step up when he needed to? Images of failure traipsed through his brain like marionettes painted as denigrating caricatures of the Dog Knight.

Gritting his teeth, Zarius lashed himself. What would DK say? Or Ezekiel? Even Gretchen? They would tell him to believe in himself, and he did, didn't he? Otherwise he wouldn't be here now.

Otherwise his never-ending nightmares would have shaken him out of his Knighthood. But he was still trying. Still striving, determined that none of this would hold him back from what he knew he was and would still continue to become.

The Dog Knight.

The thought of his friends brought his mind back to Earth. DK was out there, fighting the bitter cold, still trying to be there for Ezekiel, still being human. Even when Zarius screwed up and sent Mark away, DK forgave him. An opportunity squandered, but DK didn't hold it against him. Tears welled in Zarius's eyes.

Yes, the nights were frigid and long, yet here Zarius was, alone, without even DK at his side. A tingle went down his spine as he clambered to his feet. No, it was DK who was alone, out there in the cold, black night. Questions around every corner. Darkness breathing life into the impossible. How could he have let his friend go out alone? This was the Day Knight for Christ's sake. If they didn't have him, they had nothing at all.

Cursing himself, Zarius threw on all the clothes he could find and instinctively grabbed his sword before he burst through the door. He loped down the street, embattled by freezing wind, and went through the town square. A couple people stood cloaked in winter garments, fishing water out of the nearly frozen well. The Beggar made its stand against the winter, stripped naked but indefatigable. Besieged by cold and anxiety, Zarius rounded the corner, passed the bustling tavern, and made straight for the forge. The smokestack was barren. Thick blankets of clouds made for a black night.

Zarius threw the door open, and as soon as he picked up one whiff of the air inside, his whole body tensed like a muscle preparing to fire. He had only a fraction of a moment to process what he saw. DK was sitting in a chair, neck already craned to peer at the door. Just a few feet away from him was something ungodly. Vaguely familiar but tinged with wretchedness. The same, putrid smell from the bog.

And Ezekiel, too, was looking at him. Except it wasn't Ezekiel. As the old man's head appeared from a mound of blankets, Zarius saw the insanity in his eyes, the dearth of all humanity, no soul to be found within. They locked eyes, just as Ezekiel's mouth began twisting up into a vicious grin.

Something happened to Zarius, inside or around him, as if the air and gravity touching his body began to warp. The next moment seemed to string out far beyond the limitations of time. Zarius bolted forward instantly, without a flicker of pause. At the exact same time, Ezekiel, a Thread, lunged forward, dagger flashing from concealment. And DK was none the wiser.

Zarius had only one singular second, and it wasn't enough. How could he hope to cover the length of the forge before the Thread covered a measly arm's length? He couldn't, and the unfairness of it enraged him. Like a chemical reaction, rage enveloped him, separate from time. Rage against defeat, against failure. Zarius hated the thought of it and rebuked it, rebuked the next second that would force it upon him.

No. The Dog Knight would not fail. The Day Knight would not perish. If time was not an ally, it was an enemy, and Zarius would slay it with all the rest. And so he did. A fragment of Light in his eyes as he flashed across the room. In Zarius's mind, it all played out in slow motion.

One moment, Zarius was in the doorway. The next, he was gone, and the sound of steel on steel echoed through the stone room. A thin cloud of dust blew over as Zarius strained to hold back the dagger. It hovered inches away from DK's neck. With one great sweep, he threw back both the blade and the attacker. Ezekiel's imitation

stumbled backwards a couple of steps before he found his foot-
ing. The animosity in his eyes was so bright and violent that Zarius
could scantly hold his gaze.

"I won't fail him," Zarius snarled.

The hatred glowed brighter in Ezekiel's reddening eyes, so
bright that Zarius's own eyes began to burn just gazing upon it.
He screwed up his face but refused to turn away. No attack would
catch him by surprise. He refused to let his mind be consumed by
the violence.

"The Dog Knight," Ezekiel muttered. He flashed a sneer as he
lifted the dagger and slit his own throat. As his neck split open,
blackish blood began to bubble out like thick sludge. He tipped forward and landed facedown on the stones with a chilling *thwock*.
Shining in the ooze coming from his wound were a few strands of
brightly colored thread.

51

By the time Ezekiel's body ceased to twitch, DK had not moved. He was still sitting, right where he'd been. Part of him still existed before, before he watched it all unravel right in front of him. He could still see his friend sitting there, not just today but a thousand times before, fatherly mirth and concern twinkling in his eyes.

"Ezekiel," said DK, as if the utterance of his name might raise him from the dead like Lazarus.

But Ezekiel did not stir. His body began to decay before their eyes, skin shrinking until it pulled tight against his thin bones. His eyes melted in their sockets and leaked onto the bricks. The stench of rot filled the air, and Zarius stepped away and vomited. Ezekiel shriveled like a squashed insect.

"Oh my God," Zarius said, collapsing to his knees. Rivulets of snot hung from his nose as he convulsed again, gagging—long hoarse sounds that would've struck fear into the most seasoned medicine men. "He's dead."

DK did not move, did not speak. The reaction was slow. A black tree on a charred plain bore a single seed that dropped into ruined soil and somehow took hold. No amount of mental effort could kill it—the anger that sprouted from the ground.

Rising to his feet, DK shook as he gazed upon a life going to pieces before him. That corpse was not Ezekiel. He could only hope his friend's death had been quick, but nausea greeted the thought. Fighting not to vomit himself, DK pulled Zarius up by the back of the shirt and turned him away from the ghastliness.

"We have to get out of here," he said.

Fires burned inside the Day Knight's chest, and the bells tolled for war, for vengeance. This would be the bog witch's final mistake—her last miscalculation of him. She tried to assassinate him, like a coward. She bastardized the only father he knew. He would scour the very essence of her from the earth.

"He's dead," Zarius sobbed, clutching his face.

"*Zarius,*" DK roared.

His voice was like an explosion, the crack of a dam giving way. The shock of it managed to halt the tears on Zarius's face.

"Don't submit," DK said. "Avenge him."

Perhaps it was the words, perhaps just the proximity to such boiling intensity, but it worked. Zarius stopped crying and turned to stone. He glanced back at Ezekiel's crumpled form. Black sludge covered the floor. Tendons popped and snapped as his body twisted into a grisly visage of death.

"I'll kill her," Zarius snarled, his voice still thick. "I'll kill them all."

"Let's go." DK ran out of the forge only for his stomach to turn to lead. Screams echoed out of the tavern down the street. Bodies came pouring through the door, and DK sprinted toward them. As he approached, the fleeing tavern patrons got caught up in a crowd crush in the exit. Those who escaped turned around and started pulling their friends and loved ones, trying to break up the jam. Those caught in the door screamed like trapped goats.

"*What the fuck,*" DK shouted as he slid to a halt just outside the door. He joined some of the others in trying to pull bodies free. "*What's going on?*"

No one answered. There was too much screaming, too many flustered words of encouragement as those outside continued pulling on those who were stuck.

"*What's happening?*" DK bellowed.

He gave up on pulling arms and ran to the window. What he saw struck his cursed mind like lightning. A lone figure inside, stabbing a corpse on the ground. Upturned tables everywhere, a couple starting to burn from scattered torches. Bodies on the floor. Bloody footprints. The figure doing the stabbing looked up as if DK had called its name. DK grimaced as a misshapen head and lopsided face came bounding right up to the window, inches away. The Thread threw an arm through the window and slashed with a curved dagger, and DK leaned away just in time. When the strike missed, the Thread withdrew its arm and just grinned at him. Black blood leaked out of a couple bruised cuts on its face. Someone had put up a fight, but it wasn't enough.

"You can't even protect your own," said the Thread in a rasping voice, grinning wider. "Come to the bog, DK. Come home." It showed its missing teeth. "Part of you is already there."

DK stepped back, pervaded by disgust, nauseous in every fiber of his being. The Thread began heaving tables and chairs toward the door. People cried out from inside as smoke began to billow.

"*No,*" DK screamed, his voice going hoarse. He tried to throw himself through the window, but it was too small. He scrabbled anyway, getting only his head and one shoulder inside, enough to see the Thread as it threw torches toward the legs and backs of all those trapped in the doorway. Fire spread over the piled furniture. Somehow, a thought worse than even this unfathomable reality smashed his mind to pieces.

"*Catherine*," DK shouted, suddenly hysterical. "*Catherine*."

The heat from inside soared, as did the smoke. Soon enough, the clothes of everyone piled in the exit began to catch fire, and the screams that tore out of them cut straight through DK's soul. The Thread glanced over at DK, still grinning. It pranced over to the bar, stood on its tiptoes, and peered over the far side.

"Ohhh, sorry," it said. It turned around and shrugged at DK. "I don't think she's gonna make it."

It raised a torch to the ceiling, and the thatch caught instantly.

52

"Dear God help please."

"Zarius pull me. Pull me. Please!"

Flames gnawed on the people in the doorway, and their screams benumbed the frozen air.

"DK," Zarius shouted as he jumped at the pile, trying to rip someone out, but DK was gone.

It took less than a minute for the whole tavern roof to go up like a tinderbox. Red and orange tongues coated the rafters, which began to crackle in protest. The screams from the doorway filled with agony, and Zarius sobbed as he latched onto grasping arms and tried to yank them free. Other men and women surrounded him, still fighting to save the others. Fingernails pulled chunks of flesh from Zarius's arms, and the smell of burning hair and flesh filled his nose.

Zarius tugged on helpless arms and shoulders, managing to free not a single one of the writhing mob. The church bell began to ring ferociously, each bang like a steel mallet striking his heart. He found himself face to face with Carmichael Blain, brown hair plastered to his face, eyes as wild as a stricken rabbit's. *"Please,"*

Carmichael bellowed. The sheer volume and intensity of his voice punched Zarius in the stomach, and he wrapped his arms around Carmichael's rotund shoulders and tried to pull.

What furniture was left began to burst into flames as the tavern turned into an oven. Fresh, intensified heat exploded through the narrow opening at the top of the door and sent Zarius reeling, coughing, choking for clean air. His vision blurred with smoke as he stumbled and fell. Carmichael called out like a bellowing steer, and the voices of those in the doorway began to weaken. The blur of hot color intensified behind the windows. It was all going to hell.

"Don't leave me," Carmichael gasped. His eyes were streaming, spinning, his voice cutting through the awful commotion. Somehow, through all the chaos, he and Zarius locked eyes. "Please, Zarius. I'm sorry. Don't let me die."

Beyond reason, Zarius leaped back into the fray and grabbed Carmichael again. The flames lapped at the top of the doorway, and the writhing mass of bodies moaned in agony. Those inside were dead or unconscious, but the ones in the door still drew clean breath from outside. Their collective anguish rose in the air like an incantation, and the searing heat finally forced Zarius to pry himself free. Carmichael resisted his efforts, holding on with all the strength he had.

"*Let go*," Zarius shouted, out of his mind. "*Let me go.*"

Zarius ripped himself clear with bruises and gashes on his arms, but Carmichael just kept reaching out, as if Zarius were a long-lost friend. Tears gushed from Carmichael's eyes as his face suddenly contorted in agony, and when he started shrieking, Zarius had to clamp his hands over his ears and turn around, as if by getting all this out of his sight, he might take it away. He could make it untrue. Black smoke billowed into the stars. The tavern roof belched as it gave way, and the crowd outside shrieked in stupefied horror.

Hoarse name-calling turned to nothing but tortured screaming. The flames chewed through anyone still alive, and Zarius was snow-white, unable to withstand their writhing faces. DK appeared, his face red and burned from the heat, arms torn up like Zarius's. He looked as lost and insane as Zarius felt, and they watched the silhouettes of so many people they knew turn to ash.

Slowly, the screams fell away as fire consumed the doorway. The hair on their heads burst into flames, and their skin began to char and crack. Again, Zarius set to retching, and even DK was forced to avert his gaze. The last mewls of desperation ceased, and only the fire's consumption remained as it stripped the bones of the people and the tavern.

Citizens of Ten-Berry came running from all directions. Men mustered into a firefighting force and began passing buckets from the well, but the damage was done. The dead remained stacked in the tavern doorway, and the buckets of water only made them hiss like burning snakes.

Gaunt, pale faces languished in abhorrence as the men continued fighting the fire, and a gaggle of women clustered nearby, calling out names, sobbing on each other's shoulders. Cornelius appeared, and his initial crossness and indignation bled to tremorous disbelief. He gazed upon the burning husk of the tavern—now a blighted sepulcher—and began to weep.

"The bog witch," Zarius groaned as he looked around wildly. "We're under attack."

A few others heard him say it, and the words spread faster than the fire. Before any time at all, the square was teeming with shocked and horrified peasants, roused from slumber by commotion turning to tragedy. Some met the notion of attack with disdain, but a few others had seen it—the stranger in the tavern, murdering their friends. Soon DK and Zarius were trapped in a writhing mob of vitriol, a mob calling for blood. Zarius and DK leaned heavily on one another, caught in a maelstrom of grief and hate.

Cornelius, with much effort, hoisted himself onto the well in the middle of the square, still clad in his nightclothes. "*People,*" he screamed. The armory was emptied of the guards' weaponry. Torches were being brought out, chairs broken to make clubs. "*People, please.*" The clamor faded, just enough for him to be heard. "*What happened?*"

"The bog witch!" some of them roared. "A fire," said others uncertainly.

"The *witch*?" Cornelius cried in disbelief. His round, cherubic face betrayed his fear as it grew red in the cold. "What on *Earth* do you mean?"

"A stranger in the tavern," someone said as the din quieted more. "He started killing everyone."

A roar of indignant terror. Cornelius waved his arms wildly to settle them, but his own fear was plain. Sweat began to pour down, even in the tundra of the night. "Are you sure?"

Verging on a riot, the crowd near DK stilled when he put a hand in the air. The wave of quiet passed to the outer edges. A circle cleared around him, and Cornelius's tortured face locked onto DK from where he stood on the well.

"*Christian,*" Cornelius breathed. "What's happening?"

DK looked up with tears in his eyes. "The bog witch has attacked us."

Instead of chaos, this time the mob seemed shocked into paralysis. DK went on. "Ezekiel is dead because of her. Everyone . . ." He squeezed his eyes shut for a moment. "Everyone in the tavern, too."

A few people burst into sobs. They clung to each other, mothers clutching their children. Some peasants still paced outside the tavern door, feebly calling names as the structure burned down to a crackling mass, hissing as the firefighters continued throwing buckets over it. Suddenly, more screaming. A blackened figure came stumbling out of the ruins of the tavern, and it staggered toward the mob at the square.

DK fled from Zarius's side and tackled the shape. He got it behind the arms and carried it forward. Shocked murmuring fell to pin-drop silence. A bigger clearing was made, and DK threw the charred Thread down in the center of it. Bits of flesh stuck to DK's skin and clothes as the body fell in a heap, but when DK came and took Zarius's sword, the Thread reared up like a frightened horse. Everyone screamed.

Its face was black and cracking. *"You're all going to die."*

DK sprinted over and plunged Zarius's blade straight through the Thread's torso, in one side and out the other, skewering it. Black sludge leaked from the wounds, and the body collapsed. Women went screaming down the streets, fleeing to their homes, ready to abandon the village itself. Commotion surged, and Cornelius bellowed from the well, trying to wrangle the crowd. When there was some semblance of quiet again, this more just a general state of absolute shock, Cornelius put his pained eyes on DK and Zarius. A huge ring remained around the Knights and the shriveling body.

"What do we do?"

DK looked at Zarius. Such anguished determination poured out of DK's eyes that Zarius couldn't help but be roused by it, but he felt like he had just taken a shovel to the head over and over again. His skull rung like a bell, and he couldn't formulate a single thought. It was all fucked.

"We'll strike back," DK said.

The crowd erupted in a roar of defiance. Bodies surged around DK and Zarius, propelling them forward, up to the base of the well. Some remained behind and trampled the Thread into pulp. Zarius couldn't do anything but watch as DK climbed up next to Cornelius. The sheer ferocious intent in his eyes cast a spell over everyone. When the quiet gathered again, DK's eyes scanned over every face and drifted to the smoking tavern.

"The bog witch dies *tonight*."

Vicious jubilation exploded in the square, louder than anything before. As quickly as he was foisted up onto the well, DK was brought down, and he and Zarius were harried toward their hovel by a bloodthirsty mob. When they made it home, Zarius stepped up to follow DK inside as DK opened the door. A second later, though, he slammed it shut, and he looked back, pale and crazy-eyed.

"What is it?" Zarius asked. The words almost choked him.

"He's in there," DK croaked.

Goosebumps flushed over every inch of Zarius's body. "What?"

"We need our armor," DK said. "Don't look. Just armor up."

Zarius's stomach dropped. DK opened the door and slipped in, and Zarius followed him. The fire Zarius had built was down to just a murmur of short red tongues fussing over charred logs. Of course, he looked right away. He couldn't help but look.

Ezekiel. Barely recognizable. His naked body was heaped in the chair against the far wall. Gashes and bruises covered his swollen face. Thin scores covered his flesh from head to toe, and he was almost entirely black with dried blood. Zarius took one step and squished something soft and wet underfoot. He looked down. It was the end of a trail of ripped-out intestines. Something was drawn on the wall over the corpse, though in the dim light it took Zarius a moment to puzzle out. His stomach fell into his shoes. It was a drawing of the Sun.

Zarius crumpled. On all fours, he stared at the ground. A ribbon of intestine lay pink and glistening in the dirt. His own arms were shredded, leaking blood. DK started pulling on his armor, and he gave Zarius a few moments before he barked at him to get up. Like a zombie, Zarius rose to his feet and stumbled into his corner. He began strapping up pieces of armor, feeling like he had to be dreaming. It had to be a dream. The metallic scent of blood was pungent on the air.

"Z," said DK.

Silent, Zarius fastened his chainmail.

"Z."

"What?" Zarius asked. He looked at DK with wide, red-rimmed eyes.

"I need you to stay here."

Zarius stopped buckling his armor. He gazed at DK, then through him. His vision swam. "What?"

"I need you to stay behind," DK said through gritted teeth. His eyes were on fire.

"You don't . . ." It had to be a dream, right? "You don't want me to go?"

"She *attacked* us," DK said. His voice shook, but he got the words out. "Something did *that*." He pointed at Ezekiel. Anguished rage seared his face. "There must be more of them here. We waited too long," he muttered. DK punched the wall so hard that the whole structure shook. "God fucking damnit."

Zarius watched in dismay. "What if there's more of them out *there*?"

DK threw his head away. "I can handle it." He squeezed his fists, arms trembling. "I'll fucking kill them all."

"But DK—"

"*You need to stay and protect Ten-Berry,*" DK snarled.

Zarius reeled back like he'd been struck. His mind was going to pieces, and DK stomped on whatever he could find.

"I'm supposed to go with you," Zarius said weakly.

"You're supposed to do what I say." DK looked at the bodies and began to shudder like a leaf in a hurricane. "We waited too goddamn long. I'm gonna fucking annihilate her."

"DK, wait." Zarius couldn't jog his mind. It was all so torn up, so twisted. Maybe it burned away with everyone in the tavern.

"We don't have time," DK said. "There could be more on the way. They could already be here. Somebody needs to protect Ten-Berry."

"That wasn't the plan."

"There *was* no plan. The plan was to figure it out. Now we're figuring it out. We can't leave them here defenseless."

"But, Mark . . ."

"Mark's not coming." DK glowered at him. "You made damn sure of that." He finished the last buckles and straps on his armor. Zarius wasn't even halfway dressed. He fumbled a buckle, fumbled it again. His fingers were cold and unresponsive.

A minute later, DK came over and roughly helped Zarius finish his armor. Zarius barely did more than stand there, in a haze. He kept hearing the screams from the tavern ringing in his ears. He could still feel the heat burning his face.

"There," DK said. He went straight to the door. When they went outside, the crowd hadn't disappeared. As soon as the Knights appeared, the energy swelled again, cheers and vile requests raining down.

"*Day-Knight, Day-Knight, Day-Knight,*" they chanted.

Zarius stood wobbling as DK mounted Louelle. A few men had gone and fetched her for him. Zarius went up to her side as if to follow him, but DK shoved a hand down on Zarius's helmet and stopped him. Zarius looked up. He put a hand on Louelle's flank.

"Stay here, Z," said DK. "Protect them."

"But what if you—"

"*I said stay here,*" he hissed.

Agony ripped through Zarius's soul. He really meant it. He didn't want Zarius to go. Lost for words, Zarius just stepped back, but his fingers stayed on Louelle. When DK snapped the reins to get her moving, she resisted. She even backed up a step.

"Louelle," DK said firmly.

Louelle snorted, swinging her head. She moved her flank more firmly against Zarius's palm. He was pretty sure she looked at him.

"*Louelle.*" DK dug into her sides with his heels, and after a dragging moment, she started forward.

In a matter of seconds, Zarius watched DK vanish into the darkness. He watched his best friend ride toward what Zarius could only envision as certain death. His brother, taking the final road alone.

53

Mark knocked softly on the door to his daughter's room, a gentle smile already resting on his face. Without even opening the door, he could see her in his mind's eye, curled up on her pallet mattress, blonde curls strung about her face, thumb tucked in her mouth. Little Shailene. A spitting image of her mother that never failed to squeeze his heart. She would never understand the simple comfort of her present or the pure joy he felt when she screamed his name and trundled into his legs.

Finally, he pulled the door open, soft and quiet on oiled hinges. Light from the main room poured through the opening and slanted across her bed, but her covers were pulled up over her, just a little slumbering lump under a blanket. The smile grew on his face, and he crossed the stone floor quietly on stockinged feet.

Gingerly, he grabbed the top of the blanket and rolled it down, but it was not his daughter's angelic face that greeted him. It was a pulsating mass of organs and viscera. Mark ripped the blanket from the bed and saw nothing but bleeding, oozing gore. His breath caught in his throat as tears leaped from his eyes. He tried to cry out but gagged. Finally, a scream thundered through the halls of his home.

In a panic, he fled to his own bedroom, hollering for Alice all the way, but when he threw open his own door and ran sobbing to the bed, he threw back the covers to find only more horror. Chunks of mangled flesh, not even the recognizable form of his wife. Finally, he vomited everywhere, covering the writhing tissue with more repulsiveness.

A searing pain forced his eyes down, and he found a seam split from neck to navel, spilling his guts to the floor. He collapsed to his knees, eyes wide, still screaming. He grabbed handfuls of pink rope and tried to stuff it all back in. The pain was blinding, the grief corrosive. He sensed his mind being rent to pieces.

Mark gasped awake, leaning over his daughter's bed. Something was poking him from behind, and he let out a cry as he whipped around and nearly catapulted Shailene across the room.

"Daddy?" Shailene cried as she stumbled and fell on her butt. Fear bloomed quickly on her face. "Daddy?"

Mark couldn't catch his breath. Even the sight of his daughter unharmed couldn't seal the wound of terror from his dream. Tears welled in Shailene's eyes at the distress on his face, and she tottered out of the room, crying for her mother.

A moment later, Alice appeared in the doorway, youthful face creased with worry as she rushed across the room and knelt beside him. "Mark," she cooed. "Mark, what's wrong honey? Are you okay?"

Mark clutched onto her like a solitary life preserver in the middle of the ocean, and he shut his eyes and let out a couple sobs as he breathed in the smell of her. His whole body shook, but after a moment, he managed to pull himself to his feet.

"I . . ." He shook his head, trying to remember before the dream. "I came to . . . Somehow I fell asleep."

Alice stroked the stubble on the sides of his face, eyes shimmering with concern. "You fell asleep? Did you have a nightmare?"

"Yes," he choked. "A nightmare."

Even so, it didn't make sense. He never fell asleep like that, not in the middle of the morning. He remembered now what he'd been doing. Foreboding had been eating away at him the last couple of days, and he simply went to Shailene's room to surround himself with reminders of her, hoping it would settle his spirit. Instead, he fell asleep, and the nightmare greeted him instantly. A wave of dread crashed over him, and his heart crawled into his throat. Dear God. It could be a coincidence, but could he really believe that?

"Alice," he said, gazing at his wife. "I think I have to go."

She pinched her mouth. He'd told her only pieces of the mission to be executed in Ten-Berry, none of it good, all of it frightening. "Now?" she asked. "But, we were about to leave for the park."

Mark battled his dread, and he settled back on old methods he'd used to ease his mind before combat. Ground himself in the present, dwell within his body, not his mind. He kneaded his hands together and focused on the sensation, letting the fear pass. Fear was his enemy.

"Now," he said. "I have a terrible feeling that I might already be too late."

Shailene appeared next to them, big tears stained on her little face. "Daddy okay?"

"Yes baby." Mark scooped her up and clutched her to his chest as if she might crumble to dust. "Daddy's okay baby. Daddy loves you. I love you. I love you, Shailene." His eyes flitted to Alice as he enveloped her too. "I love you both so much."

Now Alice began to weep softly, and Shailene followed her mother. They cried in his arms, and he couldn't fight back a couple tears of his own. The shock of the nightmare still chewed on his mind, and he wondered what was to come.

"I have to go now," he said.

"Promise me you'll come back," Alice cried. "What conflict is there for you in Ten-Berry?"

"I have to go," Mark whispered. He passed Shailene to Alice, using every ounce of energy not to choke up. "I'll be thinking of you always."

Unable to endure the anguish any longer, Mark left them there. He left them because he had to, because he would do everything in his power to keep that nightmare from coming to pass. Before he left the house, he took a deep breath and wiped his tears away. As soon as the front door opened and he stepped outside, he was the Captain of the Second Cavalry.

Mark sprinted to the messengers' building and latched onto the first aide he saw. "You," he barked, pointing a finger that froze the boy to the ground. "I need the Second Cavalry mustered *now*. Send them to the barracks. *On the double*."

Like a soldier, the boy dropped all the scrolls in his hands and fetched a bell from a shelf. He flew out onto the street already ringing it.

All the aides, boys of twelve to fourteen, stood staring at him. Mark pointed out another. "Men and materiel to Ten-Berry from Endlin. What's the fastest we could get it done?"

The boy started stammering. Mark ripped a gaze across the room. "*Anyone*," he barked.

"Th-three days, sir" one boy piped up. He stepped forward, a head taller than the rest, probably the oldest. "We could set up fresh horse teams at every waypoint to drag the armor wagons through the night. You could push your own horses harder and farther if the armor goes separately, but . . ." He looked off for a moment, eyes flitting about in thought. "Probably a dozen men. They only have a few horses at some of those waypoints. Could probably only get one wagon, armor for a dozen."

"I need *pigeons*. I need *messages*. King's seal, utmost urgency. This is life or death, *go, go, go*."

All the boys scrambled into the next room to fill out the messages. A couple went sprinting through the front door. Mark lashed a finger at the boy who'd spoken. "What's your name?"

"G-Godwin, sir."

"You're in charge, Godwin. Get it done."

Godwin lifted his narrow chin. "Yes sir."

It was midmorning as Mark took off running toward the barracks. God willing, it wasn't too late. God willing, that nightmare had arrived right on time. He ran all the way down the road to a big, square barracks of hewn stone. Inside, he was at home. A large training area with various weapons and wooden dummies. A row of mahogany tables and benches, gleaming in the pale winter light coming through the high, open windows. Most impressive of all, the indoor horse track of moist, dark earth.

Men began to report almost as soon as Mark got there. Mark walked out onto the big field of dirt, and the men began to circle around him. All of them were built and stocky, muscled from years of endless training and conditioning. They didn't question Mark as they began to gather, but they did murmur amongst themselves. Groups of them came flying in, bundled up in their big winter cloaks, eyes full of questions. Still, no one addressed Mark as the crowd formed. There were two hundred and fifty men in the Second Cavalry, and Mark waited only for about the first hundred before the anxiety forced him to begin.

"Men," he said. "Brothers. I know we're still short. The call to report was unexpected, and I thank those of you who responded so quickly. More will surely arrive, but I'm going to address you now."

The murmuring fell in an instant, and the whole barrack dropped to silence except for the occasional clunk of the door admitting more cavalrymen.

"Allow me to alleviate any confusion," Mark said. "Time is of the essence, so I'm going to make this brief. I take it as a given that every man in here knows evil. Maybe you've had the good fortune not to see it for yourself, yet. Maybe you've seen it on the battlefield or in Endlin's own slums. Maybe you've seen it in a comrade."

Mark gazed hard at them as he paced before the growing crowd. In the role of Captain, his thoughts settled. The doubts fell away, and his voice got stronger. "Evil is the strong preying on the weak they could just as easily protect. Evil is the absence of honor. Evil is subterfuge and dishonesty. Evil is Satan and all his unholy works. It can be any of those things, all of them, or a host of others. So please, men, take me at my word that recently, near the village of Ten-Berry, I came face to face with true evil of a sort I have never before witnessed in my life. Not as the Captain of the Second Cavalry or as a humble Christian layman.

"I haven't found the right words for the King. I haven't even found the right words for myself, but I know what I encountered, and I know it's a threat. Today, I have received word that this evil is on the move. It's seeping outward from a remote bog near the village of Ten-Berry. Far off, I know. Probably unknown to most of you. That's where I'm about to ride. As soon as this meeting is over, I leave for Ten-Berry. Whether it's alone or with the whole of the Second Cavalry at my back."

Mark continued to pace, projecting his voice. Snowflakes drifted in through the high, rectangular windows and filtered around the men. Over half the company was present now, all breathless, eyes fixed on their leader.

"This isn't an official mission," said Mark. "I could very well be put in the stockades for undertaking it. And that's a risk I'm willing to take because I *know* in my heart, I know through God's grace, that this is important. It's *worth* the risk. It's worth my life, and that is what I assume the cost to be." He paused, gazing at them, and let those words sink in.

"The Second Cavalry knows no strangers to courage, but I'm not here to give you an order. I'm here asking. I won't swear off any man with a family, but just know, if it were me in your shoes, I wouldn't go. I'd urge you *not* to go. Because this, in my most honest estimation, is not a journey from which I will return. It's a suicide mission, and it's a suicide mission that *needs* to be completed."

He glanced up at the windows, saw the precious, dim Light filtering in. "We're already out of time. I have to go now. Eleven volunteers. That's all I can take and all I can ask for. There are no orders in this mission. I believe this goes beyond the realm of man. This is a row with evil. Satanic forces have invaded our land with the hope of spreading from coast to coast, and I intend to stop it. There's no time for questions. We leave in ten minutes. That's how urgent it is. Now, would anyone like to come with me?"

Out of the hundred and fifty or so men who ended up as part of the crowd in the barrack, Mark moved off to the dressing room with his eleven volunteers. Among them, his most trusted, noble Lieutenant—the scar-faced Spiro. Spiro's presence simultaneously gave Mark a boost of composure and a black streak of dread.

"Mark, what's this all about? Really?" Spiro asked as they directed the squires in gathering the proper gear.

"I've just told you," Mark said. "Are you sure you don't want to stay with Elizabeth and Michael?" He locked eyes with his friend.

Spiro looked off for a moment, arms out as a greatcoat was draped around him. "The devil?" He gazed at Mark again.

"That's all I can call it."

Spiro's face hardened. "Then they can tell my son his father killed the devil."

In three days and a handful of hours, the Thread would enter the tavern in Ten-Berry.

54

A quiet roar, above even the wind, filled DK's ears as he thundered down the road. His perception of his body faded to almost nothing. Instead of grass and bushes, he rode down a path lined by grinning, drooling memories. Horrors unforeseen. Shortcomings as tall and as mighty as any he'd ever had. The sight of each one triggered a physical, groaning reaction.

Ezekiel was dead. Catherine, dead. His oldest friend and most trusted confidant. The woman for whom his unspoken feelings were now sealed forever. Tortured, murdered, burned, dishonorably displayed in DK's own home, an affront as such his spirit had never endured.

Where was the Sun now? Gone, lost. Perhaps it would never rise again. Boiling rage steamed out of his helmet as he flew across the desolate landscape. Flakes of snow began to drift around him, glowing in the light of the lantern he carried. Yes, the Sun was gone. Darkness prevailed.

The ride was torture. Questions loomed, and when DK tried to lapse into a meditation, he found that he couldn't do it. His mind wouldn't quiet. Dread began to fill the cavern of his gut like black oil, and fear seized the opportunity to slink inside. He was going to die. Probably wouldn't even find the bog witch.

Louelle's hooves thundered against the ground. Gelid wind punched through the eyeholes of his helmet. He only wore it now to combat the freezing cold. DK flexed his fingers to keep the blood in them, but his legs were beginning to ache. Billions of stars hung over him like so many watching eyes, heavenly gazes turning down to the Day Knight's ride into darkness. He longed for the Sun. He longed for a sign.

Could it all have really come to this—one frantic expedition into the bog? No forethought, no planning. Just the drop of a hat, and he was back in it? Years of training, years of meditation, the pursuit of a command over his mind to pale all others. Yet, in this critical moment, DK felt as lost as he did on that first ride to the bog. Ezekiel, *dead*. Catherine, *dead*. Along with so many others. And whose fault was that? Who clung to the vestiges of a life in Ten-Berry while a devil gathered power?

If he never went to the bog all those many months ago, would they still be alive? If he never decided to throw on a helmet and call himself the Day Knight, how many people would have just avoided a hellish, fiery death? What more could be laid at his feet? There were too many crosses to bear. All the bravado of anger and vengeance were short-lived. Now, it was cold and dark. He forgot to bring extra water. Worst of all, he was utterly alone.

Already over an hour outside of Ten-Berry, much too far to turn back, DK wished he had Zarius.

Zarius stood outside of the hovel for a long time after DK rode off. The crowd milled uncertainly, some of them filtering back to their homes, others streaming toward the square where

Cornelius's shrill voice could be heard squawking out some semblance of orders. A few people came up to Zarius and started asking him questions. What was happening? Was he going to protect them? Were there more of those *things* going to attack? He didn't offer a single response, and he didn't look at anybody. At a certain point, he just began wandering aimlessly down the street.

When he came out into the square, a chunk of the previous mob remained. Their ferocious energy was gone, though, and Zarius smelled the fear lingering about. Even in the bitter cold, some people dressed only in pajamas, they remained outside, listening to Cornelius. The tavern continued to smolder behind them, and everyone was afraid.

As Zarius stood there, fully armored, he attracted the more nervous of Ten-Berry's citizens like a magnet. They saw armor and a weapon, and they wanted to be close to it. Soon enough, he had his own little throng around him. People chattered to each other. More questions came his way, and Zarius answered not one of them. He just sulked with his head down, helmet on. It almost looked like he was praying.

Really, he was languishing. The pain of DK's rebuke didn't subside; it actually got stronger, until it throbbed in his heart like a lodged arrowhead. He spent a lot of time forcing back tears, and when he tried to conjure the Sun in his mind, he saw only darkness. A black, empty void. No help was on the way.

"Zarius? *Zarius?*"

Coming out of a daze, Zarius saw a familiar, painful face. Gretchen swept up to him and threw her arms around him with Caroline hot on her heels. Tears splashed down Gretchen's face as she leaned back.

"Zarius what happened? We saw the fire. Where's DK?"

Head swimming, Zarius just stammered. "He's . . . It's a . . . There was . . ." He trailed off.

"What?" Gretchen said, gently shaking him. "Are you okay?"

"Where's Christian?" Caroline asked nervously, stepping up beside Gretchen. Tears in her eyes as well. "Was he in the tavern?"

"No," said Zarius. "He's gone."

"*Oi*," said a voice. Somebody grabbed Zarius's shoulder plate and almost yanked him off his feet, and Zarius looked up in a rage.

"The fuck?" the same voice asked.

After the red veil lifted, Zarius saw Patrick Killington, bundled up in a ratty wool coat.

"I said the fuck?" Patrick asked again. "Where's DK?"

"Going to the bog," Zarius said flatly.

"The *fuck*?" Patrick asked again, leaning in to peer through Zarius's eyeholes. "And why the hell are you here?"

"He told me to stay back. To protect Ten-Berry."

Patrick looked around. He hefted his rusty spear and eyeballed Zarius again. "What the hell does he think I'm here for?"

"It's not that simple."

"It ain't? Way I understand it is, some *things* lookin like people killed my friends. Sounds pretty *damn* simple to me, eh? And you and DK are supposed to be, you're the spearhead. *I'm* the armor. You know we got more guards in this town than just me. Plenty of able-bodied men to boot. Why the *hell* ain't you with DK?"

Uncertainty tainted Zarius's thoughts. "He *ordered* me to stay back."

"I thought you was the Dog Knight!" Patrick snapped. His eyes glistened, his voice was rising. "I thought you two was a *team*." He gripped his spear in both hands and twisted, gritting his teeth.

"Zarius," he said. "You might not think much of me and the other boys out here. But this is our village, too. These are our people. I can muster a good twenty men, and I'll do it." He put a hand down hard on Zarius's shoulder and swept the other over the crowd. "You know I'll give my life for 'em, if that's what it comes down to."

Goosebumps spread over Zarius's neck and back. His thoughts began to churn. "You mean—"

"For God's sake, son," said Patrick. "You could still catch him."

He looked at Gretchen and Caroline, the grief plain on their faces as they huddled together. But Gretchen stepped up and took his free hand, squeezing it. "You can do it, Z."

Sparks flew, and a buried pile of tinder went up in Zaruis's mind. *Shoosh.* He took off sprinting out of the square, toward the stables. When he got there, he found Stanton Bainbridge pacing around in the little room at the front of the building.

"Oh no," Stanton said. His face drained white when he saw Zarius. "I knew those damn *buffoons* would screw something up when they took Louelle. *Damnit.* You got left behind?"

"I need a horse," Zarius said.

Stanton got serious. His eyes went distant for a moment before he nodded. "Very well."

They went through the back door into the stables, and Stanton retrieved a compact black horse out of one of the stalls.

"His name is Comet," said Stanton as he rigged up a saddle with amazing efficiency. "He's not as strong as Louelle, but he rides like the wind."

In no time at all, Zarius was on Comet, ready to take off. In front of the building, though, Stanton stopped him and clutched a hand around Zarius's wrist.

"A lot of good people died in that tavern," Stanton seethed. "Pay her one back for me."

Zarius nodded, and Stanton released him. A minute later, the Dog Knight was out of Ten-Berry, riding like the devil was on his heels.

55

Mark led a short column of men on their towering horses. He was tired and gnawed by anxiety. One night in a decent inn, two nights on meager piles of hay, packed into tiny waystations with his men sleeping practically on top of each other. He prayed constantly that he wasn't too late, and part of him wondered if he was just flat insane. If this turned out to be a fool's errand, he might well hang for it, and he thought it might just be deserved.

The dozen men of the Second Cavalry caught their armor wagon on a hill several miles north of the village, and Mark opted to have the men dress right then and there. Under the lazy gaze of the moon, they filed through the northern gate of Ten-Berry and headed toward an ominous glow at the center of the village. They passed between the scant, lacking houses of Ten-Berry's merchant class and shortly found themselves among hovels. Astonished peasants began to follow them along the road. Boys walked with their mouths hanging open. Women clutched babes to their chests, swaddled in blankets. As they approached the town center, Mark detected the foul odor of burnt hair, and his stomach did a flip. He lifted his faceplate and glanced back to see Spiro doing the same.

"Smells like death," Spiro said. He wore the gaunt, strained expression of a man learning that the tale Mark spun for them might have had substance to it.

"Aye," Mark said.

They continued in a uniform line, all the way to the town center, where Mark saw a throng of peasants standing in nervous clumps under a single, towering tree. On the other side of the square, women in and out of the town hall, tending to the wounded. The fat-faced magistrate, identifiable only by his posture atop one of the wells, turned flabbergasted eyes onto the knights of the Second Cavalry.

"W-W-What's this?" Cornelius asked. He jumped down off the well, landed with a huff, and scurried over. Mark signaled for his men to stop.

Buck snorted and bobbed his shining head. The dim glow of the dying embers in the tavern played against the knights' seemingly endless pieces of armor. Their horses turned red like chariots of fire.

"My name is Mark Whitestone. I'm the Captain of the Second Cavalry."

"S-S-S-Second Cavalry?" Cornelius asked. His face was bright red, and he tried to pull his collar up far enough to swallow his head. "What on Earth . . . you mean Endlin knows? How did, what about—"

"I'm here through the grace of these brave men behind me," Mark said. "This is no official mission. I gave my word to DK that I would defend your village in the event of attack." Mark turned a bitter gaze onto the ruined tavern. Regret rattled his soul. Even a cold wind couldn't seem to blow away the stench of suffering. "It appears that I'm too late."

"Ch-*Christian*?" Cornelius asked. "Christian brought you?"

"Where is he?"

"He and Zarius are on the way to the bog." The skin around the red patch on Cornelius's face went stark white. "You mean this whole thing is *real*?"

"*Shit*," Mark snapped. He turned his head away and found Spiro's curious face in his view. "The Knights are already on their way to the bog," he said, more to himself. He faced Cornelius again. "What happened here?"

Cornelius shook his head, shivering. "Well . . . As far as I can put it together, someone or some*thing* was in the tavern, and it started stabbing people. Then it set the whole blasted thing on fire. As many as two dozen fatalities, and plenty injured." Tears brimmed in his small, wide-set eyes. "Everyone's in shock. They think we're under attack."

Mark flashed straight back to the bog. Straight back to that rotting figure stepping out of the trees, the one that almost looked human. Almost, but not quite.

"God help us all," Mark muttered. He turned around. "Spiro. There might be impostors in this village. Things that look human but aren't. But the Knights are on their way to the bog, where they'll surely find a fight. There could be enemies on their way. What do you think?"

Spiro went pale, but he didn't hesitate, and he didn't stutter. "We have a dozen men. We leave three or four here, and the rest of us ride on." His eyes flitted to the tavern. The sobs and moans of grieving peasants besieged them. "We'll search for a fight of our own."

A small crowd began to gather around the mounted knights. A few voices called out to them, hoarse and bloodthirsty, asking for vengeance.

"Agreed," said Mark. "Thomas, Arthur, Kent, Viggo. You're to defend this village with your lives. Ask the locals about what they saw. Learn what you're watching out for. Stay vigilant. If anything happens, you send five pigeons to Endlin on the double and get the whole fucking army down here."

All four men barked their understanding.

"The rest of you," Mark said, "follow me. The devil might yet be waiting."

Eight knights of the Second Cavalry left the square after watering their horses. They followed the path of the Dog Day Knights, but Mark slowed when he came to another, much smaller mob hovering near the doorway to DK's lowly, slouching hovel.

"What is it?" Mark asked with a flare of alarm. He fixed his eyes on a skinny, hunchbacked man. "What happened?"

"Devil's work," the man grunted. His eyes were red and puffy. "Lost me a good friend."

Mark dismounted Buck and pushed through the group to peer through the open door. He saw an old man inside. Naked, brutalized, displayed in disgrace. But it was the bloody shape scrawled above his swollen face that froze the blood in Mark's veins.

A crude mockery of the Sun. A declaration of war if he'd ever seen one.

"Jesus Christ protect us," Mark muttered. He made the Sign of the Cross and returned to Buck and his men. He climbed onto Buck, and they set off again.

"What was it?" Spiro asked.

"Darkness," Mark said. As they made it to the end of the road, they found one last group of men, these armed with spears and short swords, just a helmet and a single breastplate to share among almost twenty of them.

"Ho there," called a strong tenor voice. A lanky, redheaded man scampered up to Mark's horse but didn't make him stop as he walked alongside him. "Who're you?"

"We're the Second Cavalry," Mark said. He lifted his faceplate.

"Ah, you," said Patrick.

Mark gazed over the meager weapons and armor among Patrick's men.

"I know we ain't look like much," Patrick sneered. "But this is our village, and we'll by God fight for it. I only feel sorry for any one of those damn cretins tries to come through us."

"You look like soldiers to me," Mark said. "Ten-Berry is lucky to have you."

A flicker of pride crossed Patrick's face, but it quickly melted to uncertainty. "You goin to help DK?"

Mark nodded.

"Don't let him die out there."

"I'll give it everything I've got," Mark said.

Patrick offered a flimsy salute, and Mark paused before he returned one. With that, the knights passed through the gate, and Patrick remained behind them, holding that salute until he was swallowed by darkness.

"Pass those lanterns up to the front," Mark called. "Fall in, on the double."

Eight knights of the Second Cavalry roared to life, thrusting into the darkness.

56

Through the light of the half-moon, utter desperation, and perhaps sheer divine intervention, Zarius saw the vaguest shape of a horse and rider moving off the road up ahead of him. For hours now, he'd been terrified that he was lost. He resisted the urge to whip Comet into a mad gallop, instead only lightly snapping the reins. Comet responded with a hard canter, following the dim path in the moonlight as the ring of light swung out from Zarius's lantern.

After the longest, most patient minute of his life, Zarius saw again the shape of the rider, this time from behind. His heart palpitated as the rider slowed down, and he fell into the most dreadful relief when DK's helmet came into view. DK dismounted Louelle, and as soon as Comet halted, Zarius did the same.

"*Damnit Z,*" DK barked. His eyes glinted as he threw open his faceplate. "*Damnit.*" DK put a quivering hand up to his face and bowed his head. "I told you to stay back. I told you to *protect them.*"

Zarius braced his entire being. "Patrick's gathering the guards, and you're not going in there alone."

Wind howled down the road, a cold blast of air that made Zarius lean into it.

"Don't you *understand*?" DK seethed.

"I understand you're *pissed off*," Zarius hollered, so sudden that DK jolted upright. Zarius took off his helmet and stepped toward DK. "You're fucking *furious*. But you don't get mad, bro. You never get mad, and I don't want you to die in there, man. I know dude. I know." His face quivered, and despite his best efforts, his voice choked up. "We lost Ezekiel, man. We lost . . . we lost so many."

DK hung his head, and for a moment it looked like he might go all the way to the ground. Teardrops made gray craters in the snow, so Zarius steeled himself. They couldn't both fall apart. DK took a step forward and grabbed the front of Zarius's breastplate, still staring at the ground. Finally, he let out a huge sigh, and it was like all the rotten anger just went right out of him.

"You're right." Snot rattled in DK's nose. "I-I'm sorry. He wouldn't want me to be upset."

DK kept his grip on Zarius's breastplate, kept staring at the ground. Finally, he raised up, the vague sheen of tears still on his cheeks. His eyes glowed in the lantern light. "But he'd want me to keep going."

Zarius grabbed the front of DK's breastplate in return. "He'd want *us* to keep going."

"There were . . ." DK looked down again, but only for a moment. "There were a lot of people in there."

Zarius shook his breastplate. "You're the fucking Day Knight."

DK's face hardened. He nodded a couple times as scathing, frigid wind rolled around them. Tiny snowflakes fell like frozen stars.

"What about Ten-Berry?" DK asked.

"Everyone told me to come after you," Zarius said. "Patrick said he'd organize a defense. Stanton gave me this horse." He pointed.

"They all sent you," DK muttered, as if telling himself. He looked up at the black bellies of the clouds. "You're supposed to be here."

"For Ezekiel. Catherine," Zarius said. "All of them."

DK nodded and turned around. "We'll do it for them."

When Zarius approached Louelle with DK, Louelle did a few tippy-taps with her big hooves and snorted. She swung her head into Zarius, and Zarius managed a smile as he reached up and stroked the sides of her face.

"Hey girl," he said. "You know you can't get rid of me."

Louelle left her head nestled in the crook of Zarius's neck for a moment before DK mounted up and extended a hand.

"What about this guy?" Zarius asked. He pointed at Comet.

"I wouldn't tie him up," said DK. "We don't know . . . when we'll be back."

Clearing his throat, Zarius nodded. He jogged to Comet's side and put his arms around the horse's slender neck. Comet didn't stir.

"Thanks buddy," he said. "I'll remember you for this one."

Zarius came back over, gave Louelle one last pat, and accepted DK's help in vaulting up onto her back. They found their familiar spots in her compact double saddle, and their armor clanked and hissed as they got situated.

Onward they rode. Not far to the bog, now. The drifting snow-flakes thickened, little tufts of concentrated fog. They scraped over the Knights' armor and collected in Louelle's mane where they melted against her warm flesh. Every puff of steam from their breathing was sucked away into the darkness. The wind hissed and moaned, warning them to turn around, go home. Don't you know what's out there?

During this final trek toward the bog, Zarius made what was per-haps his most ardent and honest effort yet to connect with the Sun. Even under a black, hollow sky, embattled by frigid cold, envel-oped by sticky darkness. He tried to kick any nascent or established notions out of his head, good *and* bad. He wanted nothing. Just intention and instinct.

Of course, it wasn't that easy. The fear held onto him with a million barbed claws. Ripping it out was painful, and it seemed to leave wounds that bled and bled even when he tried to focus. He was headed for the *bog*. Straight into the witch's lair. How could he be tranquil about that? The only instinct he could feel was fight-or-flight, and it was already kicking in, still well short of where the axe would really meet the lumber.

But he tried. He tried his best, and he sowed no doubt in DK with any fearful questions. He waited, gathering his courage, measuring his breath, trying to be at peace. The Sun was out there somewhere. If it was lost, he would find it. If *he* was lost, well, he believed that it would still come up tomorrow.

In no time at all, he felt DK guiding Louelle down to a slow walk. That sensation alone hit Zarius like the rush of a winter river. All his muscles locked up, and goosebumps washed down his spine. They were almost there.

"Alright," said DK without turning around. "This is as far as Louelle goes."

When DK slid off, it took Zarius a moment to follow him. The snow continued to fall, painted by the lantern. A ring of white-gold fluff covered the ground around them. Zarius slung his waterskin from around his back, thankful he'd remembered it, and DK eagerly slurped down a few mouthfuls after him.

"I guess we can just eat snow," DK said as he turned over the empty leather skin.

"Yeah," Zarius breathed.

DK tossed the skin into one of Louelle's small saddlebags and fidgeted with her reins. In the end, he just let them fall, and he patted her on the side of the neck. He let his hands linger there for a bit. "I'm not gonna tie you up, girl. Do what you need to do. Run if you need to run."

Louelle scraped the ground a couple times, tail swishing. When DK moved away, she took a couple nervous steps toward him and snorted hard. It came across plainly to Zarius: she was scared.

Zarius's ears began to ring as DK started forward. He took one last long look at Louelle, but she seemed to be watching DK. A mournful look if ever a horse could have one. Heart aching, he bowed his head and turned into the wind.

To Zarius, they were simply walking into a wall of darkness. DK carried the lantern, and Zarius followed it like a moth. They trudged toward the bog, the invisible screen of black tree trunks. Zarius walked a step behind DK, only half abreast.

"You're gonna see shit," DK said. "Shit's gonna talk to you. Whatever you do, *don't* talk back to them. If you talk to them . . . if you *acknowledge* them, they'll get in your head. They'll touch you."

"What the fuck," Zarius breathed. "Okay."

His heart reared. Snowflakes skittered across his helmet. Their breath fogged out of their helmets and evaporated in a dead sky. The few visible stars overhead ceased to twinkle, a graveyard of frozen worlds.

"What do you mean by shit?" Zarius asked. It took conscious effort to keep his teeth from chattering in the cold. Even under so many layers, his skin ached. His nose hairs were frozen, his throat sore, and snot leaked onto his upper lip.

"It doesn't matter." DK's voice was harsh and strained. "Don't even look. Talk to me if you need to." He paused for a beat as wind whistled through the gaps in their armor. "It's gonna be bad."

Zarius swallowed hard. The trees came into view ahead of them. Clouds drifted away from the moon and brought everything into focus for a few moments. Zarius would've sworn the bog was twice as wide, the trees twice as tall. It towered in front of them like a bristling tumor, a burr stuck deep in the flesh of the earth. In the silver light of the half-moon, Zarius thought he could see the glow of eyes waiting in the tree line. All his hair stood on end, and the goosebumps were so bad he had trouble moving his arms.

"Alright." DK turned around and faced him. He banged both fists down on Zarius's shoulders. "*Alright?*"

"I'm good," Zarius said, breathing hard. He didn't feel good, but he steeled himself anyway. This was it.

"Who are you?" DK asked.

"The Dog Knight," Zarius said immediately.

"Who?" DK turned his earhole to Zarius.

"I'm the Dog Knight," Zarius seethed.

DK faced him again. Heat rushed out of his eyeholes as he barked, "*Who?* I don't think they can fucking hear you."

"*I said I'm the fucking Dog Knight bitch.*"

"*That's right,*" DK shouted. He snatched Zarius by the chest plate and banged their helmets together. "She thinks you aren't a Knight. She thinks you ain't *shit. Remember*? Remember what she did to us." His voice got heavy. "Remember why we're here. We won't turn back, and we *won't* fail. This ends tonight. For Ezekiel, for Ten-Berry, for *us.* We'll take the best she's got, and we'll wipe her off the face of the goddamn Earth."

"Goddamn right," Zarius snarled.

DK faced the bog as a long, smoky shadow stepped out of the trees and waved at them. Fired up as he was, Zarius still felt the fear.

"It's alright to be scared," DK said, like Zarius had said it out loud. The figure beckoned to them. "Just remember who you are. Be with the Sun. None of this is real."

"You know where we're going?" Zarius asked.

The long shadow melted back into the trees. A faint cackle of laughter drifted across to them.

"I'm gonna figure it out."

"Fuck me," Zarius muttered. "Okay."

DK started forward again. Not far at all now. A matter of seconds. "Don't talk to them," DK said. "Talk to me. I might not answer, but I'm with you. We got this. *You* got this. Believe in the me who believes in you."

"Zarriiiiuuusssss . . ." a hoarse voice called.

Zarius almost broke his own jaw he clamped it so hard. He focused on relaxing his breath. Myriad thoughts scattered like birds because of course they would. Of course, when he *wanted* a distraction, it was a barren wasteland between his ears. There was no hiding. The bog opened wide to swallow them.

They passed the first trees. Darkness fell like an instant, total eclipse, like the trees were eating all the moonlight. Zarius heard frantic footsteps rush from a distance right up next to him.

"Oh Christ," he hissed. He just managed not to leap away.

"Christ? Christ?" A shrill soprano voice spoke right into his ear. "You don't believe in Christ."

Zarius struggled to breathe. He peered straight ahead through slitted eyes, and when a gaunt, pale face loomed into his vision, flickering in the lantern light, Zarius squeezed his eyes shut altogether and hooked a hand on the back of DK's armor.

"Oh what's wrong, Zarius? Can't even *look*?"

It was DK. DK's voice. Zarius almost opened his eyes but stopped himself. No. It *sounded* like DK.

"Z, help!" DK called.

Zarius heard the thrash of a vicious struggle, heard someone being dragged away. DK's voice screamed and screamed, and now came the wet tearing sounds of a body being ripped apart. Zarius grimaced. He just kept his head down, kept a hand hooked on DK's steady, bobbing collar.

"They're imitating you," Zarius said through gritted teeth.

"Imitating?" a voice asked. It had that metallic ring, as if it were coming out of DK's helmet right in front of him. "How do you know? What if that *was* DK? What if you're following someone else?"

Zarius opened his eyes. It was DK's armor all right, but he couldn't see his face.

"You could still turn back," the phantom voice said. "You could still make it out alive. Before we—"

"Z, Z, Z."

Zarius snorted and shook his head. He snapped out of a trance, hand still hooked to DK's armor.

"You good?" DK asked. His familiar voice.

"Fuck," Zarius said. Sweat began to gather under his armor before immediately freezing in the cold. "I'm good."

"Good. I'd hate for you to lose your mind before I make you suffer. I'm going to flay you alive. Let you heal. Months. Years."

Zarius trembled. He dropped his head again as what sounded like DK kept babbling on. But they continued moving forward. The steady movement of DK's armor gave Zarius some semblance of safety. His feet knocked together. Sometimes he stumbled over exposed roots, and they both went toppling to the ground in a heap of clanking metal. But every time, DK rose back up in silence, and Zarius never lost his grip on his brother's armor. They were still moving.

He stepped through huge puddles, freezing water up to his calves. Mud sucked at his feet. Even as voices assaulted him and gory images manifested in his mind, Zarius forced his legs to keep churning. He didn't know what he could trust, so he trusted

nothing besides the sense of forward progress. But the sheer violence and intensity was already grinding him down. It wasn't his
physical prowess being tested. No, his mind was under siege. How
much could he take?

57

DK heard only whispers. He saw flashes of shadows, nothing more. As they moved through the bog, though, he knew the witch's evil was upon them. His flesh reacted, pimpled with goosebumps. The hairs on his neck quivered. But he was only vaguely aware of those sensations. He retreated to a sturdy fortress in the depths of his mind, designed for this exact moment, informed by his first, disastrous foray into the bog.

In that fortress, the Sun was King. It sat on a golden throne, casting golden Light, filling golden goblets. DK traversed the familiar halls, considering nothing and everything. His thoughts were just a steady, fuzzy hum. He stayed in enough contact with his body to keep himself moving. Those voices tried to reach him. Faces tried to materialize in front of him, but he simply passed through them and turned them to mist.

As he walked, though, the one fear that did manage to leak into his castle walls was for Zarius. He could feel the iron grip Zarius had on the back of his armor, could just hear him panting and muttering. But DK couldn't answer. If he did, it would put him right there. It would invite all those terrors behind his defenses. He trusted that Zarius wouldn't break, but he worried nonetheless. When Zarius tripped over a root and took them both to the ground, cold, dirty water splashing into his eyes and mouth, DK didn't miss a beat. He got himself back up and got his legs moving, and the palisades around his castle only quivered.

Stoic, DK continued forward. He didn't know where he was headed, but he knew he would find it. Or it, him. It was almost relieving, in a way. This was it. No more wondering about when, how, why. Here he was, in the bog. The notion dripped molten steel into his blood.

"Christian."

A boulder struck his placid pond. A familiar knock on the fortress door. It was maybe the only voice that could cut through his peace, and she found it.

Catherine spoke again. "Christian, please."

That voice dragged him into his body, forced him to *look*.

A charred, womanly figure lay on the ground a few feet ahead of him. DK almost broke step, but he didn't.

"Christian," she moaned. "Help me."

DK almost tried to step over it, but no. That would be acknowledging it; that would be admitting it was real. Instead, he stayed measured, and his foot passed right into the burnt corpse. It dissipated. Then it was walking right beside him.

"You let me die," Catherine sobbed. "You let her bring me *here*." She hissed and snarled. "You fucking *idiot*. You fucking *coward*."

His steps got a little wonky, but DK kept walking. Zarius's hand remained clamped on the back of his armor, but the Dog Knight had gone silent.

"You never got to fuck me," Catherine whispered into his ear. "Because you're a pussy. Why don't you fuck me?"

She licked the side of his helmet. He heard the wet, slimy sound, and she moaned right into his ear.

There she was, on the ground again. This time lying on her back. Half-melted face tipped up, one hazel eye locked onto DK. Parts of her skin stuck to the ground. A spider-web of oozing wounds cris-crossed her from head to toe. Ribs showed through her charred torso. She lifted her black, ashen legs, and he heard her skin cracking as she spread her legs open in front of him.

"Stop and *fuck* me, Christian."

Sweat dripped down DK's face and back, under his armor. It took real exertion to stay steady, to fight off these horrific visuals. He kept walking in rhythm, and again, his foot turned the image into nothing. Just more frigid puddles and lumpy tree roots snaking in and out of the ground. DK took a deep breath and swallowed in a dry mouth.

"We have to keep going, Z," he said.

"I'm gonna kill you," Zarius said from behind him.

DK didn't turn around, didn't answer.

"I'm gonna rip your throat out," Zarius said. He laughed. "You were never man enough for Catherine."

"Ohh, that's right." Catherine's voice again, right behind him, right next to Zarius. "He never was, was he?"

DK heard them kiss, heard it get sloppier. In no time at all, Catherine was moaning, grunting like an animal, and DK could hear the friction of skin on burnt skin. Like hay being rubbed together. Zarius started moaning too, and DK just kept walking, kept sweating.

"Oh yes, fuck me Zarius, fuck me, oh, oh, yes, yes."

DK's vision got cloudy. He imagined himself at his meditation spot, back in the dead heat of summer, massive Sun boiling the water out of the sky, bearing right down on him. So hot he couldn't think. So hot he couldn't see. There was nothing but scorching heat, cooking his body, drying him to leather. The sounds continued behind him, but he stayed with the Sun as best he could. They faded a bit in his ears, and he took a rattling breath.

None of it was real.

Trudging on, even DK began to feel the strain, and he worried about Zarius. But he couldn't ask Zarius how he was or if he was holding up because the voice that answered back always said something heinous. DK didn't even know if Zarius was still with him, but that hand on the back of his armor never let go, and that gave him hope. They were lost, but they had each other. DK began to lean on that sensation as much as the Sun—the feeling of company in this godforsaken wasteland. At least he wasn't alone, not like last time. They could do this if they stuck together.

"Yeah," DK muttered to himself. Things passed in front of his eyes. He refused to focus on them. "We can do this."

Zarius's voice started babbling behind him about how they certainly could *not* do this, and wouldn't they just keep walking because they were almost there, almost somewhere. Keep walking, keep walking. You're sacrificing yourself for nothing.

A distant anxiety loomed. DK thought some sense of direction would find him, but so far, nothing. Only suffering. And he knew that if he himself was struggling, Zarius was probably at war in his spirit. Maybe almost to his breaking point. If that hand let go of DK's armor, he had no doubt that all would be lost. How much farther could they go without so much as an inkling of a destination? Everything looked the same. Same trees, same bushes. New faces and voices appeared at times, but mostly Catherine. Like the bog witch knew it was getting under DK's skin. He was breathing hard, like he'd been running for miles. His skin itched under his armor. The cold burned his eyes.

Fuck.

Where was he supposed to go? What was he supposed to do? An

idea appeared on the distant horizon of his mind, and it rattled him straight to his core. He grimaced and stowed it away. He could only go there as a last-ditch effort.

58

The long road to the bog offered much time for introspection, but Mark found little more than dread to pick over. He tried to think of his family, tried to feel the love of his wife and daughter, but it came out only as twisted fear. The men followed him unquestioningly, and that, too, made him afraid. Because for the first time in his career, the first time in his life, he didn't know what he was leading them into. He had only the slightest idea, and that was so perverse and unconscionable that, again, he could feel nothing but dread.

Wind roared down the road. The quiet clink of armor followed him like a chain tied to his ankle. When Mark saw the dark shape of a horse in the distance, he slowed down. Spiro trotted up beside him, atop his own towering, fully armored stallion. They didn't speak, but they watched the same target drawing nearer through a flurry of snow. Warm, flickering fire washed over the pale white blanket on the ground. A glance back showed Mark a train of such lanterns like a string of ants trying to find their way out of the belly of some giant beast.

They drew up on the horse. A black, skinny thing, just standing off the side of the road, looking nervous. Mark pulled Buck to a stop and gazed at this horse as if he could command it to speak. Mark glanced ahead, trying in his mind to fill out the vaguest outline of a map.

"We're close," he said.

"Whose horse is this?" Spiro asked.

"I don't know. But I know it means we're close."

In fact, as Mark looked closer, he saw the faintest footprints in the snow, just barely visible. The wet smell of snow tickled Mark's nostrils as he took a deep breath. They weren't far behind the Knights, and that meant if action was coming, it was coming soon.

"Move out," Mark said simply, and he started forward again.

Spiro dropped back and barked some encouragement to the men, and they followed Mark like a doomed tribe past the brink of extinction. As they moved into open field, the moon broke through a layer of clouds and imbued the air with cold silver. Pale light cascaded down from an inhospitable sky, and shadows thickened on the ground.

Here, Mark finally succeeded in some reflection, a little nostalgia. He thought of Alice, her slender form, her small fingers playing through his hair. And he thought of Shailene. Precious Shailene. The way she would thunder his name down the halls of their home followed by a sweet cackle. He took in these images like a last breath before plunging into frigid water. In his heart, he knew something was coming toward them.

About halfway to the bog from the point where they left the road, the eight knights of the Second Cavalry crested a hill that overlooked a relatively flat plain. Snow everywhere, sparser now, but the layer on the ground seemed to glow as it reflected the moonlight. And in the distance, hundreds of yards away, Mark saw figures moving down a farther hillside onto that same plain. A battlefield being born.

Goosebumps washed down Mark's arms and legs. He cleared his throat, and Spiro walked his horse up next to him. Together, they gazed at the dark figures in the distance.

"Cavalry," Spiro said. Half question, half statement.

"It appears so," said Mark.

"But . . . cavalry?"

Mark grimaced. Some thoughts sparked off in his head, and their embers lingered. Even at such a distance, Mark would have thought it was his *own* men coming toward them, such was their shape and stature. A couple dozen, maybe thirty of them in all. And that was the source of his distress. Of course that's what it would be. The witch saw them, after all, didn't she? Along with the so-called Thread Knight. They saw Paul, Kendall, and Mark himself when they went to investigate the bog. Saw them and remembered them, well enough to imitate them. They were going to be fighting some demonic recreations of themselves, and they were outnumbered almost four to one.

"*Men*," Mark barked, wheeling Buck around to face his troops.

The men were gathered side-by-side a few steps behind Mark and Spiro, already in a nascent battle line. All of their helmets were pointed toward the distance, tracking those figures. They all saw it. The shapes of horses and riders.

"The time has come," Mark said. "What you see out there is no earthly adversary. Those aren't men. I'm not sure what they are, but I know who they fight for. You're gazing upon the skirmishers of hell. The probing arm of an unholy invasion. First, us. Then Ten-Berry. After that, Endlin."

Mark dismounted his horse and began striding up and down the line, and the men removed their helmets to return his gaze.

"That's right," Mark said. "Endlin. Your homes. Your families. You're fighting for them now. *Right now*. You're fighting for your brothers. For all of Christendom, that our Christian Kingdom will *not* be lost to darkness. That our faith will *not* succumb to the pressure of evil. We're going to fight, and we're going to die."

He let those words hang. Snow drifted out of the sky. The figures in the distance gathered at the base of the far hill, organizing en masse. They'd seen the Second Cavalry, and they were waiting. The hard, frostbitten faces of the knights in Mark's command followed him as he walked.

"There are *men* inside that bog, inside the source of the evil you see before you. *Men*, like us, already on the counterattack. They did it without knowing we were coming. They thought they had no reinforcements, and they went in anyway. Rest assured, they will succeed. I have the ultimate faith in them. But they need *us* to hold the line. They need *us* to buy them time, to contain this infection while they root it out at the source. They and all of Endlin need the Second Cavalry. As much as we've ever been needed."

Somber and stoic, Mark climbed back onto Buck and donned his helmet. But his chest was on fire. His heart roared like a mountain lion. Blood began to rush through his veins. This was it. Fight and survive.

"*We can win,*" Mark shouted. It was so loud and sudden that all the horses jostled. "*We* will *win. We'll fight them until the end. We'll slaughter them where they stand. I know you, each and every one of you. These things aren't* knights. *They aren't* men. *And so help me God, they won't take one ill-fated* step *beyond this field.*"

The knights erupted in support. Anger blotched their faces. The rising heat of incipient combat buzzed in the air around them. Across the field, the enemy formed a line and began to advance. In turn, Mark started down his own hill, letting Buck walk slowly. They reached the floor of the plain and flattened out.

"Maintain order," Mark said as the men took their positions behind him. "Fight in your combat pairs. No man left behind. We fight together, and we die together. We kill them all, *together*."

The Second Cavalry barked their assent as they cast their lanterns aside. A few of them hooted and waved their great, gleaming swords. Steam puffed from their helmets and the horses, and Mark thought that never before or again would eight men strike such an imposing force. From across the field, they heard the thunder of hooves. Drive and anxiety welled up to the very top of Mark's spirit, pushing him into a frenzy. He wheeled around for the last time, and the men stopped. He tore off his helmet and sized them up for the last time.

"*Endlin is watching,*" he bellowed. Buck began to jostle below him, pulled up by the soaring energy. "*Your brothers are watching. God Almighty Himself is watching. Ride for them all, and ride that all our women and children might yet spend one more night free from the boiling cauldrons of Hell. Knights of the Second Cavalry, charge!*"

Mark turned Buck headlong into the field and charged. Seven men roared like a whole company behind him as the Second Cavalry thundered into motion. The boom of hooves on frozen ground resounded like the heartbeat of the earth itself, urging them on, goading their conviction. And across the way, the dark shapes of the enemy, maybe a hundred yards now, closing in seconds.

Lost to the delirium of battle, Mark tossed his thoughts to the wayside, and his training and instincts over. He lifted a long, eight-pound maul from his back and switched his sword to his off hand. Buck rode without direction, pounding the earth, flying forward like a runaway wagon down a hill. The enemy took shape, and he was right. They looked like the Second Cavalry, only their armor was black. Their horses showed bone through rotten flesh. Mark let out a roar at thirty feet per second. Five seconds to impact. He cocked back the maul and locked in on a gleaming target.

God be with us.

59

Panting and drooling, Zarius stumbled after DK. His fingers ached terribly where he still had them hooked into DK's collar. Removing them might take them right off. The voices were constant. Right next to his ears at all times, never stopping to breathe. Ghastly, visceral images penetrated his mind as he refused to open his eyes. He saw all manner of gore and abuse, and the voices described it in tandem. Snot covered the bottom of his face. Occasionally, he bumped a forearm against his helmet, trying to wipe it off, forgetting he was in armor. Little trace of the original objective remained. He knew he was somewhere bad, and he knew he had to follow DK no matter what. Besides that, his only goal was one more step. One more step. Bear one more second of this horrific onslaught. But even he knew he didn't have long.

When DK stopped, Zarius slammed right into him and then just stood there, gripping his armor. It took several seconds for Zarius to really process that they were no longer moving. When he did, dread welled in his heart like a geyser pushing out of the earth. He still didn't dare open his eyes. What if it wasn't DK?

Through a thick, fuzzy din, Zarius heard his name being called, as if from a long distance. The abhorrent voices in his ear trickled away as that familiar one drew nearer. Warmth enveloped Zarius's free hand, warmth of the Sun, like he was holding it through a tiny portal into a summer afternoon. That voice kept getting louder, and Zarius knew it. It was DK. The *real* DK.

"Z." DK gave Zarius's arm a shake as he held his hand.

Zarius made a weird, wet, blustering sound, and he lurched back. He would've fallen if DK didn't catch him. When he steadied, Zarius went straight down to one knee, gasping for air like they'd just surfaced from a frozen lake.

"Fuck," Zarius said. His mind was in tatters. "What's happening?" He finally opened his eyes and looked around. Only the faintest moonlight managed to sneak through the cris-crossing branches above, and the treetops looked a mile high. There was no other light; DK must have lost the lantern somewhere. "Did we find her?"

"No," DK said. His own voice was hoarse, though he sounded better off than Zarius.

That warmth continued emanating up Zarius's arm, and Zarius looked down. DK was holding his hand. Zarius stared at it. It was as if that simple contact, that fleeting heat had banished all the evil, if only for a moment.

"How are you doing that?" Zarius asked.

"Doing what?" DK asked back.

"Never mind." Zarius tried to gather himself, but it was like building a fire in an ice storm. He was all scattered, and he couldn't even tell which piece was supposed to be gathering the rest.

"Z," said DK. His voice was tight, strained. It sent a shock down Zarius's spine.

"What?"

"I have to meditate."

Silence for a few moments. Deathly silence. The bog was like a tomb, but Zarius knew the ghosts weren't gone for long. He lifted his faceplate and wiped the snot off his chin before picking up a handful of dirty snow and shoving it in his mouth. Then he grabbed another and rubbed it harshly over his face.

"Say it again."

DK grimaced as he lifted his own faceplate and ate some snow. "I have to meditate."

"Here. Now."

"Yes. I don't know where we're going, and we can't make it much farther like this."

Zarius looked around. So many tree trunks. So many hiding places. In fact, he started seeing faces peering out. Red, rotting, sunken-eyed. He blinked and looked at the ground.

"Why don't I hear shit right now?"

"I don't know," said DK uneasily. "Maybe because we stopped."

"You're gonna meditate."

"I think that's our only hope of finding out where to go or just . . . what to do."

So we came all this way just for you not to know what to do?

Zarius wanted to ask it, burned to ask it, but then it withered away. What did it matter? They were already this far. Did DK rake him over the coals when he pissed Mark off? No. He didn't.

"Okay," said Zarius.

"I need you to protect me," DK said.

Zarius nodded as he lowered his faceplate. "I know."

"Okay." DK stood there for a moment, gazing at him. After that pause, he just sat right down on the ground. Back straight, he settled into a spot and lowered his own faceplate. "Stay with the Sun. That's where I'll be."

"I know," Zarius said again.

The warmth faded from Zarius's arm as DK folded his hands in his lap. In just a couple long breaths, Zarius watched him go. DK's posture changed ever so slightly, and Zarius knew he was sinking or maybe rising out of his body, going somewhere else. And Zarius was staying behind, alone in the bog.

Protect DK at all costs.

When he heard something start muttering in his ear, Zarius stood ramrod straight and crushed it in his mind. He crushed the very notion of the voice to dust, and it disappeared. When he saw those slimy, dripping faces peeking out from behind the trees; those lanky, naked bodies slinking toward him from the distance, he banished them too. And it was easy now. Not because he *found* strength, but because the moment *demanded* strength. DK needed him. The Day Knight was defenseless here, in the heart of the witch's lair. Pressure brought the Dog Knight out into the open. Moment by moment, Zarius inhabited the Dog Knight because that's what was required. Every second was the most important one of all time, and it all hung on him. He would not let his brother down.

Zarius realized that he could see better now, a little farther. At first, he thought it was a trick, but when he looked down at DK, he saw an inexplicable glow shining off his armor. As if the Day Knight himself were emitting Light. Goosebumps covered Zarius's arms. This was it. This was what they had been training for.

A new figure materialized in the distant darkness, striding forward, different yet familiar. The blood ran cold in Zarius's veins, and his left arm throbbed. The Dead Knight walked toward him, red pupils burning in a horned, steel helmet. His armor was black and shined like obsidian, his blade almost invisible in the darkness. He wasn't as massive as before, but that was no relief. He looked stouter and more agile. His armor—studded with small black spikes—fit him perfectly, not a gap to be found. Complete, polished black steel. Interlocking plates from his neck to the tops of his feet. The bog witch had remade him.

The fear was there, grabbing, but Zarius pushed those frozen fingers away from his throat. Let the Dead Knight come. Let him discover what Zarius had learned since their last encounter. The bog witch thought this was it, the winning play, an ace up her sleeve. Zarius gritted his teeth, fuming at the implication of his own weakness. Fine then. Let them find out who the real Knight was. Show her who should be afraid.

"Hello, Zarius." Gravelly bass notes vibrated the air, and the sound plucked the hairs from Zarius's neck.

"Thank God," Zarius said. He pulled his helmet down snug. "I was worried I'd never get to kill you."

The Dead Knight laughed. "Manners maketh man."

"Fuck you."

"It is poetic, isn't it? All your effort. All your sacrifice. Only to run into me. I was surprised to hear you survived our last encounter. Saved by the Day Knight, I'm sure. I know you have no such strength of your own. Make no mistake—this time, I'll be sure."

Zarius scowled and began to tremble with rage. "You should've killed me when you had the chance."

"Aye." The Dead Knight lifted his weapon. "And you, me."

They crossed the ground together and met with the devastating ring of crashing steel. Blows traded like cards, almost too fast to see. The Dead Knight's force was unreckonable. Each blow fell like a boulder from a cliffside. But Zarius was enflamed, invigorated by the presence of a lame DK mere yards away. Doubt was nowhere to be found. He could not and would not fail his brother, and he would slit his own throat before he let himself fall to the Dead Knight.

Flashes of that first encounter sprang across Zarius's vision.

His helplessness, his fear. All those agonizing seconds spent in recovery, blacked out with pain, gasping himself to sleep. And here was his tormentor, back to scour every iota of effort he'd put into bettering himself. Rage, rage against his would-be killer. Rage against the injustice of failure. Zarius was not the same person he was back then.

Whannnggg, whanngg, shlink, shkank, skinngggg.

Lightning blows met between them. Neither fighter moved back nor forward, but their feet danced in place as they jockeyed for inches of advantage. The ground was hostile, littered with jutting roots and slippery puddles, but Zarius created leverage out of nothing, grinding his feet against the turf. He matched the Dead Knight strike for strike until a massive impact sent them both reeling backward.

Huffing, Zarius reset his stance and stared down his adversary. The two Knights observed each other, searching for weakness and exhaustion. They both breathed hard, and as if in unspoken agreement, they came together again.

Iron met iron. Counters. Ripostes. Dodges. Evasion. Every manner of carefully constructed feints and deception. Attack and defense were on display, flipping back and forth at a speed that should have been impossible. Zarius caught the Dead Knight in the torso with a quick swipe, but the beast didn't so much as stagger before he brought his black blade sweeping through. Zarius ducked under it and swiped at his adversary's legs, thwarted by the dense and well-fitted armor. He looked up just in time to catch an overhead strike inches away from his face.

Skannnggggg.

Their swords squeaked and trembled as they pushed against each other. The Dead Knight swept a leg out and unfooted Zarius. Zarius hit the ground on a thin patch of ice that broke through to a few inches of frigid water below. As soon as his body touched the dirt, he rolled, and the Dead Knight's sword put up a cascade of droplets that twinkled like floating jewels in the Light emanating from DK. Safe by a hair, Zarius pushed himself to his feet, aching from the gnarled roots and stones that caught his fall.

"You've improved," said the Dead Knight. He shook off his sword. "Mere humans must fear you."

"Shut up bitch," Zarius seethed, dripping with sweat and gelid water.

He charged forward, and they locked blades again. Three minutes had passed already, but the Dog Knight fought as ferociously as when they began. Exhaustion was unacceptable, missteps unconscionable. Opportunity would come; he just had to be alive and able-bodied enough to find it. The Dead Knight was cold and indefatigable. And there sat DK, motionless, totally unaware of the momentous duel happening right before him.

60

When DK opened his eyes, he was not in the bog or his meditation spot. Blinding Light obscured his vision, and it didn't diffuse even when he shut his eyes again. It was harsh and unbearable, but moment by moment, it began to subside. For a few seconds, he couldn't tell if his eyes were open or closed, and he quickly settled into the thought that it didn't matter.

Where *was* he? The ether? Space? These were his first semi-conscious thoughts, and they seemed to float beyond the confines of his mind, like there were no barriers. They drifted out into the Light where they gently burned away, and the pressure of unknown answers gave way. He didn't think of any more questions; they were useless.

Instead, DK sat there, and the Light continued to fade. As it went, he found himself longing for it to stay. He didn't want to be alone, without the Light that had been his guide and comfort for so long. But even as it grew dimmer, the richness of it still inspired and reassured him. Everything was okay, and everything was going to be okay.

Finally, DK opened his eyes again, and he found himself in

a meadow, lusher and more vibrant than any he'd ever seen. No
thistles or tallgrass here. Hills in every direction sported luxuri-
ous green blankets of grass, and throughout these blankets waved
stunning, colorful veins of wildflowers. Colors he'd never seen before. The freshest, most fragrant scents imaginable. A faint, warm
breeze that caressed his face like a loving hand and set the flowers
bobbing as it passed.

Tears flooded into DK's eyes. He immersed his hands into the
grass, plush blades rubbing under his palms and fingers. He tried to
breathe deeper and deeper, pervading his soul with that smell, that
purest of air. When he gazed up, he was confused to find a kaleido-
scopic sky masked by shimmering shapes way up above him. These
seemed to mirror the grass. Mostly green, specked with patches of
all different colors. His eyes traveled toward the horizon and came
down to a single entity, way off in the distance.

A giant tree. Its leaves made up the entire sky. The ground rose
and fell, following the undulation of its massive roots. More tears
leaked out of DK's eyes as he gazed at it. It brought him the exact
same relief as the Sun, only stronger, and he could gaze directly at
it without having to shield his eyes and look away.

While he didn't understand it, and he couldn't bring himself to
really *wonder*, he knew what it meant. The Sun, the Tree. Here, in
this meadow, they were one and the same. Here, where only flowers
and grass laid any claim to the land. No chamber pots or stables to
foul the air. A vast emptiness so full of life that DK felt he was in a
massive banquet hall brimming with dear friends. He was another
blade of grass, another artful flower. And to him, it felt like home.

DK breathed in the longest, slowest breaths of his life. Eons
passing in moments, yet the meadow remained unchanged. Maybe
time *was* passing; maybe there was no time at all. This felt like the
destination he'd been walking toward his entire life.

When he was deep in the lowest valleys of shit, it was this idea that brought him slipping and sliding out of it. After the bog witch destroyed him, on all those dark, frigid, lonely nights, in the sparring pit, climbing around the badlands outside of Ten-Berry. Here was where he meant to go. Here were the sights he longed to see. And now that he was here, he wanted to stay forever. Free of pain, free of suffering.

At the same time, though, something nagged him. He wasn't dead. That wasn't how he arrived here. But he could die very soon. And he was sure that death *would* let him stay forever. Just let go, release the worry. There were no devils here. Yes, DK could lie back and wait until he rotted, turned to compost, fed the grass and *became* the grass. And it was the most tantalizing choice he'd ever faced in his life.

Footsteps approached from behind him, and DK felt no fear. As he lay back and gazed at the sky of leaves, all bobbing and shimmering in a mesmerizing pattern, somebody sat down next to him. After drinking his fill of the sky, DK sat up again and turned.

A wooden being sat on the ground beside him. All wood, dark, like mahogany. Black whorls and interconnecting lines cris-crossed its body. Its hands were finely crafted, feet just big, rounded blocks. Rounded balls held the shins and the forearms to the thighs and the upper arms. All of it dark, glossy wood. DK gazed upon it without judgement of any kind. He didn't wonder what it was, and he still felt no fear. The mannequin gazed out across the fields at the Tree, and DK joined it.

For several moments, they remained that way. DK's bliss, though, did begin to bubble with questions. Who was this being? Why was it here? He saw no other such creatures anywhere over the vast expanse of visible land around him. DK turned to it again, and this time, he found the smooth sheen of its face pointed back at him. They regarded each other.

As if through osmosis, DK began to understand something. This mannequin was like him. The way it gazed across the landscape. Not just gazing, but *watching*. Looking. It began to dawn on DK that this was some kind of guardian. The protector of this meadow and the Tree. Maybe it was a Knight.

This single realization brought goosebumps to DK's skin, and his mind began to harden. It pulled out of the grass, out of the sky, away from the Tree, and it centralized within his head again. Even in a place like this, there was a Knight, and that meant he or she or they hadn't given in to the grandiose splendor. Maybe it meant there was more *to* this place than grandiose splendor. Maybe this Knight knew pain and suffering of its own.

The notion of rancor in a place like this offended DK, but he knew it must be true. It was always true, wasn't it? There was always pain. Always trials. But what would this beauty be without it? Would DK be sitting here, appreciating it as he did, if he didn't go through any of his past ordeals? Surely not. Maybe it would mean nothing at all.

So much suffering. So much effort. The weight of his own life ceased to press down on him, and he allowed himself some pride. He fought so hard, trained so long, committed himself to an ideal that *was* good and *was* important. That commitment beat him to his knees and ground him into pulp, but he always came back. Even after the bog witch tried to erase him, tried to extricate the very fabric of his being. At one point, he thought he'd given up, but he never truly did. He came back. It took years, but so be it. Here he was, living proof of himself, of the Day Knight. DK gently sobbed, raising a hand to wipe the tears.

And what about all those who believed in him? Everyone who gave him grace? Ezekiel. Catherine. Zarius. Patrick. Even when he fucked up. Even when they didn't see eye to eye. People believed in him and in what he could do. They supported him. Somewhere out there, Zarius was protecting DK, defending him, giving him the chance to be *here*, so what was *here* about?

DK looked over again, and that wooden Knight was gazing at him. It reached an ornate hand out and patted him on the shoulder before wrapping its arms around its knees and returning its gaze to the distance. That one piece of contact sparked something in DK.

This was a beautiful, awe-inspiring place, but he had to keep going. These sights were ones he hoped he would see again, but that time wasn't now. He had to keep going. If this was just another piece of what he was fighting for, he would keep going and fight for it. But somewhere out there, a whole village of people needed him. A whole country, whether they knew it or not. And most of all, his brother was alone in the hellscape of the bog. DK had to get back to him.

Light began to grow in every particle he could see. He looked for the Knight but quickly lost it in the rising haze of Light. DK squinted his eyes shut, nodding, and he muttered out some thanks anyway. Here came the Sun. Brighter, hotter, bigger all the time. Yes, here came the Sun, because after all, it was coming from the Day Knight.

61

Impact.

Mark's maul punched straight through an enemy breastplate as wind screamed through their ranks. The force of the blow shook the maul loose from his hand. He heard the abrasive, resounding crash of steel on steel behind him. A sword swished over Mark's head as he ducked and leaned, shielding himself next to Buck. The clatter of weapons coming together reverberated down the line, and in a moment, Mark was through, back into open grass. He threw a glance back and saw six of his men passing into the clear behind him. Someone was down.

"*Shit*," Mark snarled.

Buck carried forward and started coming around in a long arc. The remaining knights followed Mark to where he stopped to regroup at the opposite end of the field. One lost Cavalryman. Three downed enemies.

"What the hell are those things?" one man asked. "I didn't even hear them breathing."

"I don't know," Mark said. "We lost a man."

"Elgin," Spiro grunted. "And we only took a few of them."

The enemy started back across the field. Mark's heart clanged in his chest. His ears rang. He fought against the disorientation of combat.

"Who's got a hobble?" Mark barked.

The men were already fanning out to charge. A couple raised their hands.

"Use them," Mark shouted. "The horses are weak." He dug his heels into Buck and snapped the reins. "*Go.*"

The men with hobbles held back and followed the charge. Brave horses pounded across the earth, and Mark's heart climbed into his throat, firing away. He grinded his teeth and cocked back his sword. Here they came.

Shkuunnngggg.

Mark blasted a rider straight off his black horse, but an enemy blade caught Mark across the chest. For a moment, it was like he froze in mid-air. Buck shot out from under him, and Mark landed flat on his back.

Gadarumgadarumgadarooommm.

Hooves flew past a foot from his head.

Shkannggg. Whunk.

Weapons clashed. Somebody screamed. In a flash, it was over.

Mark gasped, trying to recover his breath. He pushed himself up to his knees and looked up. A couple of enemies rolled around on the ground, bleeding black, viscous blood into the snow. Head throbbing, Mark heard a couple hobbled horses shrieking with broken legs, and their frantic breath puffed out in clouds of fog. Their riders, in their black, shimmering armor, climbed to their feet. One of their helmets had been knocked off, and Mark saw cratered, torn flesh in silhouette against the moon. The bare-faced enemy locked eyes with him, and Mark saw a visage of Hell.

Finding his sword in the snow, Mark rose to his feet and stepped forward just in time to deflect a blow slicing toward him.

Whanngggg.

Mark launched a shot of his own but ran up against the enemy's guard. In an instant, the second Thread came forward as well, wobbling on unsteady feet. Two swords began to flash toward Mark in the moonlight.

Skink. Shink. Shinnngggg. Skanngggggg.

No thoughts passed through his head. He analyzed the assault as a second nature, a primal directive. Block. Slash. Parry. Riposte. He threw back the attack and managed to cut the helmet-less cretin across the face. It stepped back, grasping at its neck, whining like a dog, then snarling in a rage. A roar rushed toward them like an approaching tornado.

Mark blocked another blow from the second enemy, breathing hard. Just as the first surged up again, a gray blur flashed through and hit it dead on. A disgusting wet belch saw the Thread burst into pieces, and the rest of the tornado surrounded them.

Horses again. Riders towering in the moonlight. Somehow, Mark and his grounded adversary continued to trade blows as brutal chaos reigned around them. The ground shook as big hooves rumbled past. All around, the sounds of death and destruction. In the corner of his eye, Mark saw one of his men riding step for step, side by side with an enemy. They dueled facing sideways on their saddles. Horses stamped through the viscera of slain bodies and threw up fine mists of blood.

Skannngggg. Whannngggg.

Mark cocked back and prepared to deliver another strike when another blur came through and half-crushed the helmet of his opponent. The Thread left its feet and hit the ground a few yards away in a writing heap. Mark looked up and saw a black mass bearing down on him, and he dove out of the way. A sword barely missed him, and snow flew in through Mark's eyeholes. He sputtered and threw his faceplate up, wiping furiously at his eyes. The storm subsided again.

When he could see, the field was in utter disarray. Bodies were strewn about. Horses galloped in circles with no riders. Clusters of action erupted in pockets as his comrades and enemies took turns playing pursuer. Men dueled on their horses or down in the snow where they'd been dislodged. Mark could only see four of his silver-armored knights still in action. A vicious gale of grief swept through him, but he was inspired by their tenacity. At least a dozen enemies lay dead in the snow, a few more staggering aimlessly.

A sputter of hooves flew up and skidded to a halt behind Mark. He wheeled around and saw Buck, breath steaming, black eyes gazing at him. Mark grabbed a maul out of the snow and ran over to him, muttering praise as he hefted himself back onto his mount. As his eyes passed over two of his slain men, snow flitting across their armor, his heart burned for revenge.

Back into the fray. Mark locked in on three enemies chasing a knight. He goaded Buck to a mad dash, and they bolted over the cold ground. Mark wielded his sword as he caught up to the last of the enemies. As soon as the Thread turned and saw him, Mark lashed out with his sword and caught the top of the horse's left rear leg. Its next step failed to connect with the ground, and they both went down in a cloud of white dust. Another enemy turned back at the commotion and slowed down, raising his sword.

Whannggg. Skannnggg.

They dueled over inches of open air between two horses galloping at full speed. Mark defeated a blow, and when the Thread went to pull back, Mark grabbed his enemy's sword by the cross guard and leaned heavily to the side. Buck instantly veered away from the other horse, and Mark brought both the weapon and the fighter off the saddle. The Thread hit the ground hard at blistering speed and cartwheeled ten feet off the ground. Pieces of armor flew off into the air, and Mark turned his attention to the last enemy.

The knight being chased was now engaged with the last Thread. They fought side by side like Mark just had, and Mark pushed Buck to the limits of his exertion, bringing the horse up on the opposite side. With the enemy distracted, Mark produced his maul and gripped it in his left hand. He steered Buck to the left and swung the maul down, as low as it could reach.

This time, he broke the horse's front leg outright. It let out a scream, and the rider vanished as they smashed into the ground. Panting, Mark let Buck slow down, and his comrade slowed down with him. They turned together, making an arc to face the field.

"Thanks Captain," the man gasped.

Mark said nothing as they came around. He focused on what he could see, trying to read the fight. Pockets of cavalry moved in random directions across the field, trajectories constantly changing as the soldiers all jockeyed for positions. Mark tried to count his men but found his vision hazy. His heart rattled.

"How many can you see?" Mark asked.

"Two," his man croaked.

"We have to help them. *Come on.*"

62

Seven hard minutes of battle pushed Zarius to the brink of exhaustion and insanity. His thoughts fell away, followed by the trees around him, until even the Dead Knight himself was just a spectral presence in his vision. All Zarius saw was that black, shimmering sword, sweeping through the air like the Reaper's scythe. It was all he could do to throw up another block, scrape out another parry. The Dead Knight bore down on him, relentless. But even he was slow and dogged. The shudder of their unrepentant blades sounded through the trees.

No insults passed between them. They were too tired now, too focused on surviving. But Zarius found joy in it, elation in drawing even a shred of weakness from the Dead Knight. He wasn't invincible. In all that armor, with his frightening sword, he failed to land a decisive blow against the Dog Knight. As far as Zarius cared, that was a victory. Every breath he drew from here was another score against the bog witch herself. It was a battle of attrition. Surely, DK would get up. Until then, though, Zarius had no choice but to fight on, to push his body past the point of collapse and demand from himself unthinkable exertion.

Zarius's feet knocked into each other; he just managed to lean back and avoid a strike coming down at an angle. The Dead Knight's blade shattered a divot out of a tree, and he snarled with rage as he ripped it free and pressed the attack. Gasping, Zarius somehow managed to deflect the next heavy slash. He stumbled backward, then set his feet and gnashed his teeth. DK was right behind him, steps away. No retreat. No surrender.

Determined, Zarius managed an attack, but the Dead Knight blocked it with ease. They traded another blow, another, swords crying out like wounded predators in an agonizing dispute over shrinking territory. Zarius was slipping. His body was giving out. He missed a strike. When the counter came sweeping in, he tried to dodge but could only collapse forward, just out of the way.

When he hit the ground, the terror found him. Oh no. Oh God. This was it. That sword was coming, he was sure of it. It would plunge straight through the chainmail on his lower back, and that would be it. All the rage and conviction in the world couldn't keep him on his feet. DK was right there, soon to be strung up and paraded through the bog like a hated effigy. Or worse, he would simply endure the first round of malicious torture, the first step along an eternal path of suffering.

In a panic, Zarius went to scramble to his feet, but he just didn't have the energy. The Dead Knight, huffing like a whole team of ragged horses, looked down at him. A moment later, the beast unloaded a devastating kick that would've shaken the teeth out of someone standing ten paces back.

Stars exploded in Zarius's vision, a mesmerizing eruption of color that stunned him for a single blessed moment before the pain came rocketing through. *Wham.* Another kick landed before the first could even be processed. No amount of armor stood a chance against the demonic force of those impacts. Most of the ribs on his left side shattered into pieces. Chunks of bone pierced through his lung. An errant thought passed through the wasteland of his mind.

Not again.

Zarius was on the ground, his right cheek in freezing water. Delirious, he went to pick his head up just in time to catch a boulder of a fist that pulverized the left side of his face. His orbital and cheek bones cracked as his nose shattered to the side. Teeth exploded down his throat and into the dirt. Flecks of mangled flesh slapped against the hard earth. His vision went black as his left eye ruptured in its socket.

The Dead Knight staggered backward from the Dog Knight's motionless body, gasping. After a moment, he lifted his sword and pumped it one time in the air. He let out a monstrous roar, a bellow that wreathed his face in steam.

Get up.

Zarius's right eye creaked open. A thick, hazy film gradually receded until he could just make out the Dead Knight's silhouette. The impact of the punch had spun him around, and the ruined half of his head lay gushing blood onto frozen soil.

Whatever rage he thought he had was swallowed by the maw of a gigantic, scorching-hot fury. A fury that surged through every fiber of muscle, every tendon, every broken bone. The Dead Knight was gloating. The fucking cunt bastard. Through a bombardment of agony, Zarius clawed to his knees and took a breath that wheezed through his punctured lung. His helmet was in pieces, left on the ground. Another breath, and he forced himself to his feet. Blood and water ran down his body, dripped from his hair, pooled in the haunted caverns of his face.

Gasping, he leaned back and ripped his whole body forward; a bark exploded out of him. *"HEY."*

The Dead Knight froze where he stood bent over, catching his breath. Slowly, he turned around, just a few paces away. His red eyes warbled as he examined Zarius's wound, the crumpled armor on his left side and the mangled face. Light burned in the Dog Knight's intact pupil, pulsing with each ragged heartbeat. The Dead Knight's eyes glittered with abhorrence.

"You think I'm finished?" Zarius snarled.

It was unintelligible through the broken gash of his mouth, but the sentiment rang through the shuffle of guttural sounds. The effort of it made him stumble backward, a step away from DK. Bloody drool oozed from his gaping mouth in strings, and that acrid, metallic scent flooded the broken passageways of his nose. "You think that's all it takes?" His words were strong, but below the molten lake of indignation was a quiet, desperate understanding.

I need help.

The Dead Knight stalked toward him. Zarius bared his teeth, hunched over as he was. The rage faded until it was a scowl of nothing but pieces of broken sorrow. He could see DK's shins through his own spread legs.

The Dead Knight towered over him, a step away. Zarius could only just manage to crane his neck up to gaze into those hateful eyes. He was utterly spent, beyond exhausted, beaten to a pulp, but still standing. As time slowed to a crawl, and the Dead Knight reached out to grab a fistful of his hair, Zarius had to marvel.

He *was* still standing, wasn't he? After more punishment than any mortal could withstand, Zarius was still upright. His heart still thumped in his chest. And what did that mean, not just for him but for everything around him? Impossible adversaries. Impossible odds. Yet here he was. Zarius. All of twenty years old. Human, restless, but still here. Gazing into the red eyes of evil. But what kind of Dog, what kind of *Knight*, gave up? Even when all his cards were on the table, even when his body failed him.

"Petulant mutt."

The Dead Knight slammed Zarius into the ground like an asteroid. A small crater formed around his body. His skull should have been crushed, but it wasn't. His brain should have burst, but it didn't. Even buried in the ground, his lone pupil burned on. The Dead Knight crouched down next to his victim and tasted the air.

"I can smell you dying."

Rising up, the Dead Knight stepped to DK and examined his motionless form, still perfectly seated on the cold bog floor. He blinked, tilted his head, studying the Day Knight as none ever had. Joyous drool dripped from the Dead Knight's helmet.

Zarius's body was motionless, but his mind churned, retrieving some semblance of awareness. He had only the dimmest recognition of the world around him. He knew he was dying. He knew his breath was running out, but he wasn't gone yet. If he could drag out so much as one more tiny gasp, he was still alive. And he was still enraged.

How could this be it? How could he not be enough? To come so far, through so much, only to fail in the end? No. He refused to believe it. It couldn't be over. DK *needed* him, goddamnit. His brother fucking *needed him*. He had to be there. Smoke trickled from his ruined eye, crawling through the cracks and crevices of the dirt surrounding his head.

No. He wouldn't go, wouldn't let Death take him into the abyss. Not with DK still there, not with so much still resting on his shoulders. The Dog Knight rebuked it. He slashed off Death's reaching hand. The Dead Knight raised his sword, stepped behind DK, aimed the tip of the blade at the tiny gap between his helmet and the armor on his back.

"I am the father of the Dog Knight," he said. "I am the slayer of the Day Knight. Let it be known: the Dead Knight alone has secured this victory."

The Dead Knight's body shifted, and Zarius felt it. He felt it through the vibrations in the ground and could see it without sight—the Dead Knight leaning forward to skewer DK through the neck and ruin them all, ruin everything they'd worked so hard for. Ten-Berry in flames. Innocence running through the streets. A land choked off from the Sun's life-giving gaze.

I won't abandon him.

The Dog Knight snapped out of the ground in a blur of white-hot fury. Just like in the forge—he did it because he had to, because there was no other choice but to *do it*. He had to be there, and he shook off the crushing chains of death and injury. Bits of rock and dirt seemed to float around the crater of his body as the Dead Knight's sword flushed down.

Shkank.

That black blade deflected backward, checked by another. It missed DK's neck by inches and buried itself in the soil. The Dead Knight looked up, and as he found the glowing mass of Zarius's ruined eye, Zarius saw fear. For the first time, he saw fear. He tasted it, and his whole body trembled with rage and bloodlust. The energy of a dying Sun burst out of him.

"You ain't the father of shit."

All that really came out through Zarius's lolling tongue and shattered jaw was "Yatttthhhttt."

For a moment, the Dead Knight was frozen. And Zarius's ruined eye glowed brighter as the realization struck him. He *was* the Dog Knight. The Sun burned in him as it did in DK. Nothing was impossible. He survived the darkness, escaped Death's inescapable grasp, and the energy flowing through him compounded itself like fire catching a dry forest.

"Demon," whispered the Dead Knight.

Zarius cocked back and delivered the strongest blow he'd mustered all night, and the Dead Knight barely caught it.

Whoonnnngggggg.

The enemy staggered back a step, and Zarius sidestepped DK to press the attack. Another devastating blow almost ripped the Dead Knight's sword free, and the Dog Knight mounted his assault.

The Dead Knight continued stepping back, rocked by each successive swing, and Zarius pursued him with newfound fuel flowing through his veins. He slashed, jabbed, attacked with everything he had, and the Dead Knight was driven away from his prize.

Finally, the shock wore off, and the Dead Knight stepped into the next strike and met it full force with the sound of a massive gong blasting through the trees. The Dog Knight threw the guard off and snarled like a hellhound.

Skrank. Thkank. Shtingg. Shinngg.

They battled harder than ever. The Dead Knight seemed to sense the precariousness of the situation, the power exploding from his adversary, and he fought back ferociously. Their blades flashed through the darkness, a blur of blocks and counterattacks. The Dead Knight deflected Zarius's blade into the ground and followed with a haymaker from his left fist, one that had pulverized Zarius's bones mere moments before. But this one Zarius absorbed; he ate it on the broken side of his face and didn't even stagger. Blood sprayed out of the crater in his head before he ripped his sword up and resumed the attack.

Inside, there was no more Zarius. Thoughts did not exist. The Dog Knight was all of himself and nothing less. The Sun pushed him on. But so too did the Dead Knight rise, and their fury burned together like two infernos gnawing at the same share of fuel. Which would give out first? Which would die and be feasted on by the darkness?

This time, Zarius caught the Dead Knight's blade and forced it to the ground. In a flash, he grabbed the front of that black steel breastplate and ripped it clean off like tugging out a splinter. Hideous, rotten red flesh was exposed, and Zarius defeated a frantic guard to cut a slash through that torso. Black blood gushed through a massive wound, and the Dead Knight roared like a wounded bear.

The Dead Knight leaned into the next strike and absorbed it with a shoulder plate as he grabbed Zarius and threw him away before charging in pursuit. Zarius, still embattled by dazzling agony, lost his sword in the fall and just managed to flop away from that slashing blade as it chased him. The Dead Knight's sword hit the ground and wedged itself into a tree root, and when he struggled for just a split second to rip it free, Zarius was there.

This was it. No wondering left to do. It was him and the Dead Knight—him and the *bog witch*—in a battle to the death, and that was a relief. All he had to do was be here, just be present and be everything he'd always known he was capable of being. Dawn would break over this godforsaken wasteland, and the Day Knight would be there to welcome it home. So said the Dog Knight.

Zarius flew into the Dead Knight like a jouster, hooking one of his legs under one arm and driving him into the ground. Water leaped from a cratered puddle, dousing his face, muddying his eye. The Dead Knight bucked like a raging bull, but Zarius managed to hold on, lean up, and deliver with his right fist.

Thwack. Thwack. Thock.

Zarius rained down three punches, each harder than the last. The Dead Knight's helmet dented on the second strike and buckled on the third, as if Zarius had iron bones. And perhaps, in that moment, he did. The sight of his enemy so vulnerable brought the power of the Sun coursing out of Zarius, and he distributed it with savage punishment. He just managed to rip the helmet free when the Dead Knight surged and launched him away.

Time sat still as the Dog Knight's tense body tumbled through the frigid air. When Zarius hit the cold, unforgiving ground, it was like a switch flipped. That phantom spirit that had propelled him now fled the husk of his battered body. The impact almost knocked him out, but somehow, through sheer, gritty willpower, he held on. He expected an immediate execution, but when he managed to roll over on his side, he saw the Dead Knight on one knee, huffing and puffing, trying and failing to get up.

And there, the crux of his terror, the specter of inadequacy, was relieved. The Dead Knight's head was desiccated, but even under all that gore, familiar. The big, bald head. The sneering mouth. The first face that ever struck true fear into Zarius's soul so many months ago. Derrick's harvested and mutilated body panted as he snarled and frothed, still trying to stand.

That sparked something deep in Zarius's soul. The sight of that beast, that mutated shell of a man, struggling after the punishment Zarius himself had inflicted, got Zarius up on one knee. Entirely blinded by pain, he pushed his hands through the frigid water and dragged his other leg under him. A shaky foot managed to plant on the ground, and after several seconds, the other joined it. He took a few deep breaths, focused, and pushed on his knees until he was standing upright. The Dog Knight stood, growling in agony.

"*Look at me,*" he snarled. The effort almost robbed him of consciousness. His vision was just barely clear enough to see the Dead Knight gain his feet for a moment before stumbling into a tree, to which he clung like a life preserver.

Derrick—the Dead Knight—fixed his red pupils, glittering with putrid animosity, on the withered form of the Dog Knight.

"I'm still standing," Zarius gasped.

Blood gushed out of both of them. The Dead Knight stooped forward; Zarius thought he was about to fall, but then he reared up, holding Zarius's sword. The Dead Knight looked at DK's motionless body, just a few strides away. Zarius followed his gaze, alarm piercing him like a lance. They were at equal distance. DK still hadn't moved. When the Dead Knight lunged, Zarius lunged with him.

Time dripped through rivulets of molasses, every second stringing out to untenable lengths before finally extricating itself in a panic. Zarius planted his feet, pushing a slain body forward by way of nothing but absolute desperation. One step after another, he ran toward DK, matching the Dead Knight pace for pace. They were on a collision course, but that wasn't enough. Zarius had to be faster. He had to get there first. If a killing blow were to be dealt, he had to be the one receiving it. There was no other choice.

Ruined eye smoldering with Light, face still gushing blood, he sped up, just a fraction. He beat the Dead Knight for one step, then two, and he cut across the shrinking triangle to slam into him. But the Dead Knight was waiting for it. He swept Zarius's sword up, and Zarius barreled into it, throwing up his hands in defense.

Shulk.

Zarius's left arm was shorn off just below the elbow, bone giving way like wet parchment. His disembodied hand twirled through the air, spurting blood, and he threw himself into the Dead Knight anyway. They collided and spilled to the ground in a heap, and Zarius managed to land on top.

In a flash, his right thumb was in Derrick's exposed eye socket, pressing through the flesh, swamped in cold, sludgy black fluid. The Dead Knight shrieked, thrashing, but Zarius clamped himself to his body like a vise, pushing his thumb deeper, gasping as the Dead Knight ripped chunks of his hair free and thrashed his body.

Finally, his thumb sank all the way in, and the Dead Knight set to flopping like a dying fish, fists flailing aimlessly in the night. Tears and blood streamed from Zarius's eye as he choked out sobbing gasps, twisting his finger in the socket. When the Dead Knight ceased to struggle, Zarius collapsed backward, crying. Delirious, he craned his neck until he saw DK sitting there, just a few feet away, as placid as an old cow.

Zarius disentangled himself from the Dead Knight, dragging his shell of a body, his mangled arm and face, trying to reach DK. He just wanted to go home. He wanted DK to wake up. He didn't want to die. One more patrol. One more ale. One more conversation. He wanted it all to go back to normal.

"DK," Zarius groaned. His tongue dragged through the dirt below, hanging out of his face. "DK." Snot and blood bubbled from his shattered nose. He could scarcely draw a fraction of a gravelly breath.

"DK," Zarius whispered. He reached for his brother, his best friend. The life was going out of him.

Finally, his body gave way. He had nothing left, no energy to be found from within, nor from the stars. Utterly spent, the Dog Knight's outstretched hand fell just shy. His fingertips brushed the Day Knight's shin as he lay still. But as soon as those fingers grazed DK's leg, as soon as the moment was final and their fate seemed sealed forever, the Day Knight's eyes flew open. Golden Light poured out of the eyeholes of his helmet.

When those blazing spotlights turned down to Zarius's body, their Light did not fade. DK didn't speak or scream. The only indication of emotion were the tears that trailed down his neck.

DK laid a hand on Zarius's chest, and as Light flowed from DK's palm, a strange peace settled Zarius's thoughts. He felt the Sun in his chest, warming up the frozen depths of his soul. Warmth seeped through every vein, dulling the pain in his untenable wounds. It was like having all that methodical energy that worked Zarius's arm back into shape now injected into him in a single moment. He understood it. Somehow, DK was healing him. Zarius's breathing slowed and deepened, tears and blood still dripping down the sides of his shattered face.

Zarius managed to raise his one trembling hand, and DK took it and squeezed it.

"You did so well, Z." DK let out a strangled sob. "So, so well. I'll always be with you."

Grief overcame Zarius as DK set his sword down and gripped Zarius's hand with both of his own. "I'm gonna do it, Z. I'll find her. I love you, okay? Do good without me. Promise me you will."

Tears streamed from Zarius's intact eye as he shook his head, tattered jaw trembling.

"I'm sorry," DK choked. "I'll always be with you."

Zarius wouldn't let go. He held his brother's hand, afraid to see him leave, afraid to die alone in this wretched, godforsaken place. He wanted them both to go home. Waves of pain wracked his body. Even after the healing gaze of the Sun passed over him through DK, Zarius was on the verge of shock.

DK choked out a couple more sobs and patted Zarius's chest. "You're gonna be okay. I have to go, Z. Before it's too late."

Their grasp broke. Zarius watched his brother go and knew they would never speak again. It wasn't fair. They should be fighting together. DK needed his help. Tears rolled out of Zarius's working eye, and his vile hatred of the bog witch was engraved on his soul forever. His body produced the only version of sobs it could tolerate, and even that robbed him of consciousness. Darkness closed in like a swooping bat, and the Dog Knight lay still.

63

DK afforded himself one single moment to grieve, and then he let it go. There was no other choice. In his mind, though, he put a golden, Sunlit tag on Zarius's body. The Dog Knight would survive. DK made an indelible mark on the Universe that commanded it be so. He would survive.

From there, DK moved into the bog, alone. He feared no darkness, and no visions could reach him. He walked at an even pace, Light pouring from his eyes. The Day Knight locked in on a nefarious pocket of energy, the outermost edges of a whirlpool. The witch was here. Her evil could hide no longer, and he would bring it into the Light.

DK moved without looking, without seeing. Even grief couldn't touch him. He put it out of his mind to tackle the moments at hand. Moment by moment, he owned them, he won them. Pressure began to squeeze him, a fey infection trying to kill his mind and body. But he could not die. He would not falter.

The energy began to pulse around him. He knew he was getting closer, and he was at peace. For him, the Sun was high in the sky. The Sun was all around him, and there were no barriers between it and his spirit. He allowed himself to be the Sun, for the Sun to be him. The distinction faded to the point where it did not exist.

The Sun traveled into the very heart of the bog. Quiet and eternal. A depthless source of peace and power. DK walked through waves of vile hatred, and they broke over him as over an immovable mountain. He could not be harried, and he would not turn back.

Up ahead, he saw it. Sensed it, really. The hole in the ground. The pore through which the bog excreted its purest of evil. Even in his highest form, the Day Knight did struggle for a step. That energy was so malicious, so putrid that it wrinkled his nose. The Light warbled as it came from his eyes, so he stopped and gathered himself, and the beams came back brighter than ever.

No fear. He had no use for fear. He walked forward, not rushing or dragging. He just walked right up to that hole, surrounded by rocks, as black as any darkness he'd ever seen. And he knew she was in there somewhere. Ducking his head, DK entered the cavern. It led into a tunnel so small that he had to crouch to keep moving forward.

Any normal man would have collapsed here, any normal *Knight*. The stench, the malevolence. Utter oppression of the spirit. But DK was beyond his humanity. He was in touch with the Sun, wielding it not as a weapon but a shield. Still, that energy ensconced him, and he was aware of it. He forged through it like a wagon through a rushing, icy river, and he knew there was no going back. As he crouch-walked down this passage in the ground, he knew he was leaving everything he ever knew behind. Except the Sun.

Different passageways broke off in all directions, some straight up or down. The main tunnel forked and forked again until there was no main tunnel. Only one of a dozen identical options snaking all throughout the ground. Disorientation loomed, but DK never stopped to wonder where he should go. He just kept going, kept following a mysterious, invisible line in the soil. He picked directions and stuck to them, never going back. Wherever the Sun guided him would be the right place.

He didn't know how long he was in the tunnel. Time, too, meant so little that it seemed to fall away altogether. All he knew was that each step took him deeper into a well of hate. He stumbled over rocks, had to squeeze or even hack his way through thick screens of roots. But he kept going, and suddenly, the tunnel widened out.

A chamber stood before him, like the hollow pit of a peach buried in the flesh of the bog, oozing rot. The acrid scent of blood tainted the air. Dirty white bones littered the floor, scattered and in piles. Large bones. Human bones.

The walls of dark soil sweated moisture that gathered in silvery pools and soaked his feet. In the center of the small room, on a built-up mound of earth, he could see the contours of what looked like a body. Uncertainty tainted his thoughts, and the Light in his eyes set to flickering. He moved across the room. DK had the sensation of a presence, but he saw nothing else around him. He did feel his stomach drop as he approached the mound, and the Light in his eyes went out for a moment before it sprang back on.

As DK walked up next to the piled dirt, the body began to twitch. He slowed but didn't stop. The Sunlight held in his eyes, pouring from the holes in his helmet, and what he saw cut straight through his peace and repulsed him to the core of his spirit.

The body was small. Strips of tendon clung to bone and held the limbs together under errant patches of blackened skin. Misshapen fingers flexed and trembled, and the makings of a face shuddered as DK peered down.

Bloodshot eyes with shattered pupils appeared to fixate on him. Rotten, bloodless lips cracked as they parted, emitting only a hissing rasp. Chips of white, jagged teeth protruded from a cavernous mouth. But the true horror laid below, in an open chest cavity.

A black, oozing mass pulsed in a gaping hole in the torso. The Light in DK's eyes dimmed. A bunch of mashed hearts and organs, desiccated by death, writhed together in a constant, arrhythmic beat. They began to smoke under the heat pouring out of him. DK turned away. Nausea swelled, and he was forced to pause and stamp it down. The sheer offensiveness of it weighed him down. It slashed at his peace, jostling his placid mind.

The Light went out of his eyes, and he regarded the body anew. What looked like tree roots snaked through and around the lumps of flesh. A dull, blackish color glowed within them, all the way to where they buried themselves in the earth below. And finally, something clicked. DK understood it.

Here was the bog witch. At least, what was once the bog witch. And she was feeding herself to the bog. Herself and whatever other souls she'd managed to steal and bastardize. Because she knew he was coming. She'd known for a long time now, and he sensed that the damage was done. She'd spread her energy throughout the whole bog, where he couldn't root her out. The whole thing was infected. Every rotten inch of soil, every decrepit tree. She knew she couldn't escape him, so she figured out a solution. Her power now resided everywhere. She was everything.

DK looked up. The tunnel he came in through continued through the wall on the opposite side of the room. Something else was here. Goosebumps crawled across his flesh. He went to stand up.

A dagger plunged up under the scrunched hem of DK's chainmail and punched into his lower back. He let out a roar and wheeled around, whipping his sword through the air. His adversary leaped back, grinning, and the sight of it robbed DK of all his energy. Cracked red skin, bleeding eyes, broken-toothed grin. But it was him. No doubt about it. It was Christian.

Blood flooded out of DK's wound. He went down to his knees, and his doppelganger grinned as he lifted the dagger and dragged a black tongue through DK's blood. Here was what she took from him, those years ago. Pieces of his soul she stole and mutilated. But theft was only the beginning. She took what she had and raised it back to life, her and those who served her. He could see the shine of colorful threads beneath the impostor's tattered skin.

DK sat back on his heels and sighed. The wound was bad; he could already feel his strength waning. His mind raced. In a split second, he reached the verge of panic, but as the Thread of himself came toward him, he let it go.

"I'm sorry," DK said. "I had to leave you."

Christian punched the dagger straight through DK's throat and ripped it out. Red, arterial blood spurted onto the dirt, splashing and staining the little puddles. DK didn't move, didn't even raise a hand in defense. His eyes closed, and he let out one long breath as he settled. As his life began to fade, he focused on the Sun. He focused on what mattered. There was no death, only change. He felt no fear; he was at peace. At the same time, though, he knew he had to see this through. Somehow, he had to fix it all, save everything he ever cared about.

The Day Knight connected with the Sun, as strongly and as peacefully as he ever did. As the blood slowed from his wounds, a gentle smile played across his lips under his helmet. Everything was okay, and everything was going to be okay. Tears welled in his eyes. His grin grew. The Sun knew what to do, and he embraced it as he died. Light burst out of the Day Knight's helmet, blindingly bright and instantaneous. DK, his stolen life, the bog witch.

Everything vanished in a lasting flash of Light.

64

Something warm and wet dragged across Zarius's face.

Silence. The long, cold dark. An endless blizzard as he trudged onward, head low.

Warm wetness again. Zarius lurched back, swiping feebly at the air before continuing forward through the void. The snow was up to his waist. His body was so numb that he couldn't tell if he had one at all.

Another swipe of that stinking warmth, right across his lips.

Zarius's one eye struggled open. For a moment, he didn't know where he was—barely even knew *who* he was. Overhead was a black sky, stars in isolated pockets through innumerable tree branches. There was a face over him too. Not red, not menacing, rather long and inquisitive, with big, concerned eyes staring down at him.

A long gray tongue lashed across his face as Louelle licked him.

Zarius grunted in protest, but he couldn't move a muscle. Finally, the agony hit him, and he gasped with the effort of bearing it. Again, Louelle licked him.

You dumb bastard he thought at her. *Stop licking me.*

She licked him again.

Whole body shaking, Zarius managed to lift his head. The bog. A shudder passed through him. He was still in the bog. It was oddly quiet. For a moment, he thought he was deaf. And he was still confused. What happened?

The Dead Knight. Finally, the memories poured in, and Zarius groaned with newfound torment, this of the spirit. DK was gone. DK brought the Sun down to Earth, and he carried it forward alone. Trembling, Zarius managed to lift his shorn arm, and he saw the wound cauterized on the end. He was still alive. DK had promised it would be so. But he never said how Zarius was supposed to get out of here.

Louelle licked his face.

Goddamn you he wanted to snarl. Drool leaked out of the broken floor of his mouth. His throat was as dry as sand. He could see a waterskin hanging on Louelle's side. But that required getting up. How was he supposed to do that?

Louelle stared down at him impatiently. He gazed at her, wondering how she made it here in the first place only to assume that somehow, DK had brought her here. Or perhaps she just knew. Perhaps some of the Day Knight's intuition had rubbed off on his horse.

Zarius grunted at her. Louelle dragged her tongue across his face as if to say *Hurry up, I'm ready to go.*

He could stand up. Right? The Dog Knight would find a way to stand up. He would find a way to climb on Louelle's back and let her take him out of this place. That's what DK would want. That's what Zarius wanted, but when he tried to move, he almost blacked out.

Gritting his teeth, Zarius planted his good hand and thrust himself over onto his stomach. The pain was so intense that he retched, and tears squeezed from his good eye and even filtered from the ruined ducts of his pulverized one. Pain, yes, but he could breathe. He didn't feel so close to death. He was dizzy for almost two minutes, lying with his face and tongue in the dirt, and Louelle licked the back of his head.

Okay, he thought. *Okay. I'll fucking do it. Goddamnit I'll fucking do it bitch fuck.*

The Dog Knight performed a push-up with one hand and collapsed, gasping and writhing for many seconds until his breath returned to him.

Fuck it goddamnit.

He did it again, and he pushed through blinding atrocities of pain, rippling through every fragment of his body, until he was leaning backward on his knees, dangerously close to collapsing again. But he held it. He held himself up. Louelle stepped close to him, close enough for him to reach, and he hooked his hand on a strap of her saddle, panting like a dog.

"Raagghhhh," he spat.

Do it motherfucker. Do it goddamn you. You weak fucking bastard.

He only sighed. Hot tears slid down his cold face. He couldn't do it. He hung his head, ready to collapse again, holding on by a thread. Then, an image of DK flashed into his mind—a memory from the beach.

"You can't?" DK asked. "You *can't? You won't.* Everyone is right there. Everyone you ever knew or loved is ten steps away being raped and murdered, and you won't get up? *You won't save them?* Then you're *shit*. You're *nothing*. You're a coward who won't—"

Zarius stood up, brutalized eye smoldering again, Light buried in the creases of its ruin. He pulled himself up and somehow managed one halfhearted leap onto Louelle's back, laying sideways across her as blood and bile leaked onto her flank. Stars and colors burst and spun in his vision. Gasping, he managed to shimmy and swing his leg around. His ribs were on fire; he checked to make sure he wasn't actually burning. Somehow, the Dog Knight mounted his horse. Little more than a splayed corpse, he passed out from agony as Louelle plodded carefully away, carrying him out of his own grave.

Zarius's eye flew open, mind scrambled for several moments as he found himself traveling across a field. Louelle's hooves crunched over the snow, and little flakes pattered across Zarius's face. He waited for the cataclysm of agony to hit him, and agony did come, but it wasn't as bad as before. He could bear it. In fact, he found the energy to sit up. Whatever DK did to him was working. Even battered as he was, his spirit was invigorated.

Somewhere, DK was still in the fight. DK was *at war*, and Zarius was out here being carried unconsciously to safety. Suddenly, his ears prickled, and he forced himself bolt upright, letting out a grunt of pain. He swung his head to the left and laid eyes on the distant sight of carnage. Slain bodies in a field, the clank and clash of swords coming from beyond.

He went to jerk on Louelle's reins, only to grasp air with his left hand. He looked down and held up a scorched stump, staring at it for several moments. Oh yeah. His fucking hand was gone.

"Come on," he grunted. It sounded more like, "Caugghnn."

Louelle resisted him. Anger flared, and Zarius dug his heels into her side and yanked hard on the reins, muscles thawing. His breath wheezed in and out of him with a horrific rattle. He should've been unconscious—should've been *dead*. Through celestial intervention and sheer, gritty willpower, he held on. Zarius would not be carried lamely back home, not so long as his brother was in the breach.

The energy DK bestowed in Zarius worked in the Dog Knight's chest. Threads of Sunlight pulled his pulled his bones together and stopped the flow of blood from his many lacerations. Even if temporary, the energy swelling out of Zarius told him to go, to *fight*.

Finally, Louelle capitulated, and she hurried to a quick canter. The bodies drew nearer, materializing under the half-moon's lazy illumination. He saw the corpses of knights and armored horses, friend and foe. If his eyes could be believed, there were Thread cavalry strewn among the dead. Long coils of bloody yarn ripped out of rotten bodies. The growing sounds of combat laced aggression into his thoughts. The Dog Knight began to come alive.

The Second Cavalry had come through. Mark had come through. For DK, for Ten-Berry. All was not lost, not yet. Perhaps Mark was still out there, engaged with the enemy. That notion alone injected more adrenaline into Zarius. He sat up on Louelle, drawing his sword as his heart thumped in his chest, riding without so much as a hand to grip his steed. Light grew in the hearth of his ruptured eye.

In the distance, a waning fight still raged. A group of three men rode at breakneck speed away from a dozen pursuers. They were headed away from the bog, back toward Ten-Berry, but the enemies were gaining on them. Zarius dug his heels into Louelle, and she seemed to understand. She built up speed until the wind whipped through his hair and pulled strings of saliva away from his face. Zarius fell into pursuit far behind the cluster ahead.

"Come on," he said, urging Louelle with his heart as much as his heels. "Come on girl. Get me there. Get me there."

Louelle pounded the turf like a racehorse, her legs a blur. They shot across the field, passing bodies. The scream of dying horses filled Zarius's ears and locked his teeth together. Louelle bravely forged on. The group ahead disappeared over a hillside, and Louelle swept up the base of the same hill. Zarius leaned forward to keep his balance, head down, willing her on.

The sight of dead Second Cavalryman struck such a rage into Zarius that his eye was on fire. Smoke billowed out of the left side of his head. His good pupil held a quivering, golden dot. Even Louelle seemed energized. She ran like she was pulling Apollo's chariot, and they came up onto flat ground, drawing closer to the backs of black, shimmering armor ahead.

Fucking Threads, Zarius seethed. The Thread Knight must have made copies of the Second Cavalry. He couldn't see how far ahead the knights were of these wretched monsters, but he promised that he would reach them first. He would slaughter every enemy before the bog witch claimed another life.

Seconds clawed past, and Zarius approached the rearmost horseman. His face and heart were on fire. He raised his sword just as he swept up alongside his enemy. The Thread turned toward him just in time to catch a blade across its neck. It slumped right off its horse and hit the ground with a *whumpf*, disappearing behind them in an instant.

Zarius let out a roar as Louelle galloped up to the next rider. This one looked back at the commotion in time to throw up a block as Zarius swept his sword in again. Wind screamed in his ears, whipping the tattered clothes under what was left of his armor. In the darkness, his head flashed. It looked like a broken, flaming skull. The maw of a beaten dog spitting fire. Such was his intensity that the Thread went to peel off. Others ahead looked back and were struck dumb by Terror, the might of the Dog Knight in his most fearsome form.

Then the whole world exploded.

The battlefield momentarily turned white as a cylinder of blinding Light bored out of the earth and into the sky. One second later, a shockwave threw all the riders from their horses and brought a curtain of snow through, the flakes stinging like hailstones. A big, breathy whoosh of air roared past, as warm as a summer afternoon. Only Louelle and Zarius remained upright. When the enemy swordsmen found their feet, the Dog Knight was there to slay them. In mere moments, through an astonishing display of agility and horsemanship, Zarius slaughtered half a dozen of the enemy. He caught their reddish-black faces and bodies wherever their armor had been blown off, howling all the while. Debris began to rain down. Clods of dirt, pieces of wood from the trees. The survivors of the Second Cavalry curled up on the ground, taking cover, but Zarius didn't falter. Before he could finish mopping up, though, the rest of the Threads began to collapse on their own, writhing on the ground, steam pouring out of their armor.

Shrapnel rained from the sky. The men on the ground cried out and hunkered in divots with no cover nearby. Pebbles and bits of dirt clanked off all the armor wherever it lay. Nearer to the bog, Zarius saw the silhouettes of veritable boulders tumbling out of the sky where they'd been tossed up like children's toys.

Louelle trotted down to a stop. Zarius examined the bog in the distance; the sky bore a greenish-blue tint, like a scar where the Light had drilled through the heavens. Tears streamed down his face, and he broke down into sobs. A great concussion in his spirit told him that his worst fear was confirmed. The Day Knight was gone. But he sensed something else too, a deep and seemingly pointless consolation: Mission accomplished.

The bog witch was dead.

The first messengers of dawn crept over the horizon and brought the faintest tidings of Light.

65

Mark led a ragged, shellshocked squad of men over the low, undu-
lating hills outside of Ten-Berry. His mind and body were numb to
the point where he thought he might just cease to exist. And maybe
that would be a blessing.

A mourning Sun hid behind a thick curtain of clouds as if to
conceal its prostration of grief. It was already past high noon; the
horses were as dead beat as the men. Everything was deathly calm.
No birds, no breeze. Only the cold crunch of snow. As if nature itself hesitated to continue in a world without the Day Knight.

The Dog Knight was unconscious, slumped on Louelle's back.
When Mark checked his pulse, he could only drop his hand and
pray, and the dread already coiled in his heart struck like a viper.
He wanted to fly back to Ten-Berry in a maelstrom, a hurricane.
But he could barely muster the energy to breathe. Tears leaked occasionally out of his bloodshot eyes, and his two surviving men
bobbed dazedly on their horses. Thousand-yard-stares all around.

Even hours past the end of the fight, Mark's mind seemed to be
stuck there. Not only in the faces of the dead and dying, the screams
of men and horses, but in the explosion of Light that seemed to

wipe the bog off the face of the earth. More than that, in the flaming skull he still couldn't convince himself he didn't see. Zarius had appeared out of nowhere at the last moment, borne out of fire and brimstone, and savaged the enemy cavalry just before Mark and his men collapsed. He kept seeing it in his mind. How he glanced over his shoulder, the impossibility of what he saw. And that barrel of Light that vaporized the sky. The Dog Knight. The Day Knight. His head reeled and reeled.

When Mark saw the first couple of bundled peasants streaming toward them, he almost ripped his sword out and attacked them. He was still on a knife's edge, still waiting for another wave of cavalry to come crashing over them. But these were men from Ten-Berry, bearing water and bread, bleating questions so fast that it all mixed up into nonsense.

Mark said nothing, but he accepted the water. Same for his men. The peasants saw Zarius on Louelle and went snow-white, donning the camouflage of the landscape. Without another word, they went sprinting back from whence they came. Minutes later, Mark saw the gunmetal gleam of Second Cavalry armor, and the four of his men he'd left behind rode up on the group. Shock and anguish painted their faces as they examined the ragtag handful of men. They asked after the others.

Gaunt and pale, Mark could only shake his trembling head. "We'll need to retrieve their bodies. I'll, I'll . . ." He looked over his shoulder, back toward a long-vanished battlefield. "I'll take you. But first we need to rest."

Silence gripped the group for the next several minutes, and the squat buildings of Ten-Berry came into view. Black smoke trails wandered into a slate-gray sky. The thought of a fire made Mark dizzy. His stomach was as hard as stone. Latent fear kept his knuckles white around the reins of his horse.

A whole parade of somber faces began to drift past as the Second Cavalry passed through the gates of Ten-Berry. Whispers began to trickle through the crowd. Unfocused, Mark took a moment to acknowledge a freckled face under a mop of curly red hair. Patrick, the head of the guards.

"DK?" Patrick asked again. Anxiety twisted his eyes. He shook Mark's knee, walking alongside Buck. "*DK*?"

Mark bowed his head. He leaned so far forward that it looked like he might tumble to the ground. Patrick kept pace with him for a couple steps, then stopped. He stared after them. Mark glanced back once, saw Patrick staring after him, and hung his head again. Hot tears gathered in his eyes.

The Knights arrived in the town center to find the town hall already made up to receive them. Blankets and bedding from a dozen cold hovels were piled up for the men. A few volunteers stood by, waiting to tend to injuries. Mark dismounted Buck and just stood there for a few moments. Dozens and dozens of people gathered around the cluster of men. Mark couldn't meet their gazes.

Cornelius appeared, as pallid as a corpse. He inquired after the men's health and pried for details, and they all stared at him like he was an alien spewing gibberish. Finally, after much insistence, Mark followed him into the town hall, and all the men came with him. The able-bodied among them picked Zarius up off Louelle's back and carried him into the building. A huge fire roared in the hearth, and the men from the battle sank down in front of it. One passed out immediately. The other ate and ate and ate, like he was retroactively enjoying his last meal. Mark knelt next to where they'd laid Zarius and began to pray.

A hesitant finger tapped the armor on his shoulder. Mark turned, bleary-eyed, and regarded Cornelius anew.

"I'm sorry," Cornelius muttered. "The townsfolk won't let me

rest until I ask . . . Christian?" His eyes shone, maybe with something like hope.

Mark only closed his eyes and turned back to Zarius. Cornelius
let out a long, defeated sigh. He sniffled once and left the building. Broken prayers poured out of Mark. For his men, for DK, for
Zarius. All of them. Regret strangled his spirit. The face of every
man he lost, grinning in a memory, already began to torture him.

One woman was allowed inside—the most learned in herbal
medicine. Silent, she began to tend to Zarius. She examined his
wounds, applied some poultices, and began to spoon feed him
broth. She muttered in shock at the horrific extent of his injuries.
Mark only watched through hazy eyes, as if it was all a dream. He'd
wake up, wouldn't he? Back in Endlin, with Alice and Shailene. No
bog witch, no Day Knight. Not only did he have to contend with the
unthinkable events of the last twenty-four hours, he had to reckon
with the fact that he—the leader of his men, the one they entrusted
with their lives—survived. He survived, and five good men did not.

All through the day and into the evening, peasants filtered into
the room, muttering their thanks to the Second Cavalry, paying
their respects to Zarius. Blotchy, tear-stained faces drifted through
Mark's vision. An auburn-haired girl, clinging to her slight,
black-haired friend, peeked through the door and let out a wail like
a banshee, one that made all the men shudder and huddle closer to
the flames.

The men of the Second Cavalry who stayed behind were already
out near the bog, with Patrick in tow as a guide, and they were
setting about the process of gathering their dead. Details would
reach Mark later about the utter destruction of the bog. It was as
if several square miles of land had been lifted up and turned upside down. What was once a forested wetland was now nothing but
brown, churned-up soil. A bald crater of earth.

Meanwhile, Mark poured his heart out for Zarius. He prayed as ardently as he ever had. He couldn't tolerate another death. The injustice of it made his gut rot. They had already lost so much. Zarius had to survive. And Mark told God it would be so. He *demanded* it. This young man could not perish, *would* not perish. For all his effort, all his sacrifice, he deserved to go on. He deserved to live. Please, God. Just let him live. The Day Knight's torch could not go out. And while Mark would live the rest of his life in reverence to DK's ultimate, selfless sacrifice, he knew it wasn't he who could carry that torch. No. It had to be Zarius.

It had to be the Dog Knight.

EPILOGUE

Mark's beard sported a new dusting of gray as he picked his way through the small, bumpy hills near Ten-Berry. Sweat soaked through his linen shirt and pants as a strong spring Sun beat down from a cloudless sky. The smell of growth and vegetation filled his nostrils with every breath, and the signs of thriving life were all around him. Still, all these months later, a hole remained inside him.

The Battle of the Bog took something that he could not seem to replace, no matter how much time he spent with Alice and Shailene, no matter how long he extended his leave of absence from the Cavalry. It was too hard to train new men; Mark was no longer sure what he should be training them *for*. It was all he could do to join his comrades at the tavern and trade a few memories of their friends or even just stare into space together.

The relatively small scale of the battle prevented true recognition, and none of the veterans spoke out on it. Mark received a tongue-lashing from the King that quickly turned on its head when Mark asked to be decommissioned. When the King pressed for details, demanded an explanation for how the men died, Mark came up short. How could he describe what he'd seen? How could he begin to explain the nature of what occurred? And what did that matter, anyway? He knew no one would believe it. The King, the peasants, anybody. There were too few witnesses, and all of them put together couldn't come up with a believable story. The truth was simply that—unbelievable.

Their brothers were dead. Mark retreated more and more into his home, lost in terrible memories and shaken by the close brush with not just death but evil incarnate. His entire worldview was in question, and he had not yet learned how to navigate these churning waters.

Mark came around the last hill and found Zarius seated with his eyes closed and back straight, perched on the worn patch of grass created by the Day Knight's endless dedication. Gretchen sat next to him, knees tucked up into her arms. When she saw Mark, she managed a weak smile as she stood up and dusted off her light summer dress. Mark mumbled an acknowledgement to her, and she set off toward the badlands, wandering, leaving them to talk. Zarius didn't even stir. From the back, he almost looked normal. He wore a woven black hood over his head but only linen shorts besides that. As Mark came around, though, the real visage of the Dog Knight revealed itself.

The hood covered the left side of Zarius's face. But as the breeze stirred through the little hollow of ground, Mark caught a glimpse beyond it. A big, pink mass of layered flesh compressed together, thickening by the day. The left side of his head bore many small craters and recesses, covered with scar tissue. The sound of footsteps brought the Dog Knight's good eye open, and he managed only a slight grimace of acknowledgement as Mark sat down near him.

Sweat poured off the both of them as birds fluttered overhead, chittering to each other. A couple rabbits hopped over the top of a nearby hill and disappeared down the other side. Mark dragged a shining forearm across his damp forehead and began pulling out clumps of grass.

"How are you?" he asked.

Zarius didn't look at him, only closed his eye again as he held the stump of his left arm in his right hand. The stump was wrapped tightly in rags and dripped with a recently applied poultice.

Nodding, Mark sat in silence for a while. He grabbed a tiny wildflower and spun it, letting the white petals blur. The Sun gazed down upon him, and tears welled in his hardened eyes.

"I still think about him every day. About all of it. What he must have gone through in there. If it was anything like what we went through . . ."

Now Zarius's eye flipped open. He fixed it on Mark and did not tremble. "I'm sure it was much worse." His words were slow and deliberate. He was still learning how to speak with the new shape of his mouth.

Again, Mark nodded solemnly, respectfully. "Probably. And somehow, he succeeded anyway."

"He was always going to."

"Not without you."

Zarius turned away and shut his eye. His face twitched with nascent anger. "I should have been there. In the end."

"*No*," said Mark, harshly enough that Zarius startled and glared at him. That one eye was a dagger, but Mark bore the wound and stared back.

"Enough, Zarius. Once and for all. It's a dark hole that you won't ever have to climb out of if you don't want to. Don't do that to yourself. Don't do that to DK. Would he want you to blame yourself? Would he want you to wallow in it? That's not you. That's not the Dog Knight. The Dog Knight saved his brother's life, and in turn, you protected his chance at success. And he saw it through. You were right where you were supposed to be, and you completed your mission."

"I should have been stronger," Zarius snarled. "He had to face her alone."

The vitriol splashed all over Mark's face like boiling water. "But you weren't. You were as strong as you were, and you did your absolute best. You won."

"I won?" Zarius asked, leaning forward. Water gathered in the bottom of his working eye. "I won? *Look at me*. DK is *dead*. He was better than me. *I'm* the one who should've died. How am I supposed to do this without him?" A sob shook him. It was a thick, wet sound as his tongue jostled in his healing mouth.

"He loved you," Mark choked out, welling with his own emotion. "He'd never want you to blame yourself."

Zarius only cried harder, and Mark crawled over and pulled him into a hug. Zarius sobbed into his shirt and wrapped his arms around him like a drowning man grasping a piece of driftwood.

"It's alright," Mark said, his voice thick. "It's alright, Zarius."

"He was all a-alone," Zarius sobbed. "I-I-I should have been there."

"It's okay," Mark whispered, squeezing him tighter. "It wasn't your fault."

Almost a minute passed as Zarius slowly regained control of himself. He stifled the sobs, then the tears, and finally, he withdrew from Mark's embrace. His face was pitiful, a stark reminder of all the pain he'd suffered and that which continued to haunt him. Mark dried the tears from his own eyes and kept an arm around Zarius's shoulder as they sat next to each other.

"Good men died out there," said Mark. "I'll never forget them, as long as I live. I know that carrying their memory is up to me.

Carrying DK's memory is up to you. Wherever you go, whatever you do, people will know the Day Knight. Either in your words or in your actions. He'd want to see how far you can go."

"I'm going to try my best," said Zarius.

"That's all he'd ask of you."

Together, they stared off into the distance, comforted by their shared company and the bond forged in an experience known only to a miniscule few.

"I just keep wondering," said Zarius. He shuddered where he sat.

"Wondering what?" asked Mark.

Zarius turned to him, grave, almost fearful. "When she died, did they all go with her?"

"It certainly looked like it. I know you don't remember much after the Dead Knight, but they were curling up and dying on their own. When my men retrieved our fallen comrades, they found no trace of the enemy."

"I killed the Dead Knight," Zarius said. "That much I know. You killed the Threads. But I don't know what DK saw, what he fought. And I never saw the Thread Knight."

"It could have been among its cavalry," Mark said.

"Maybe," said Zarius.

A chill skittered down Mark's spine. Thin clouds wrapped around the Sun. "What? What are you saying?"

"I don't know."

Mark paused, gazing into the distance. He closed his eyes and offered a quick prayer. "You think it escaped?"

"I don't know," Zarius repeated. His eye flashed as he bared his broken teeth. "But for its sake, I hope not."

Thank you for reading *Dog Day Knights*. If you enjoyed it, please leave a review; they're a huge boost for the novel, and I would greatly appreciate it. If you hated it, I would recommend a bonfire, preferably with several hundred copies.
That would really show me.

This novel is dedicated to 6 Dogs, Jon Bellion, Ryan Caraveo, Kurt Vonnegut, Cormac McCarthy, Mike Posner, Lil Peep, and countless other artists who inspired me in dark times and in bright ones. I couldn't have made it this far without them. If you're on a journey of your own, keep going.

Find me (occasionally) on social media @jdoll98 on Instagram and TikTok

Made in the USA
Monee, IL
02 November 2024

69181178R00267